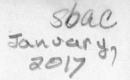
Just as Daryus shut the door behind him, the weasel slipped through into the room.

"No you don't!" He made a swipe for the sinewy creature, but the weasel twisted out of range. It darted to the bench, leapt atop it, then made its way to the table and the waiting wine bottle.

Daryus pursued, only to pull up short as the weasel suddenly turned its one-eyed gaze back at him. The stare was so intense that the renegade crusader almost expected the animal to talk.

Which it did.

"You save Toy's life!" it piped in the voice Daryus immediately recognized as the one that had called for help. "You save Toy's life, but now we must beware! They will seek to obey their master's will! They will come again with more! We must leave this city!"

Daryus reached for his sword. "What are you?"

Toy impatiently shook its head, its single open eye never leaving Daryus. "No time to waste on foolish questions! Must act! Must act before he acts!"

"Who?"

The weasel hissed. It reared, revealing that it was definitely male. "An evil walking on two legs! An evil that will now come looking for both of us, Master . . . unless Toy and Master stop him first!"

And then, without warning, the weasel opened his *other* eye as well—an eye simultaneously of fire and ice, blood red and bone ivory.

A *demon's* eye.

The Pathfinder Tales Library

THE PATHFINDER TALES LIBRARY

REAPER'S EYE

Richard A. Knaak

A TOM DOHERTY ASSOCIATES BOOK
New York

PATHFINDER TALES: REAPER'S EYE

Copyright © 2016 by Paizo Inc.

All rights reserved.

Paizo, Paizo Inc., the Paizo golem logo, Pathfinder, the Pathfinder logo, and Pathfinder Society are registered trademarks of Paizo Inc.; Pathfinder Accessories, Pathfinder Adventure Card Game, Pathfinder Adventure Path, Pathfinder Battles, Pathfinder Campaign Setting, Pathfinder Cards, Pathfinder Flip-Mat, Pathfinder Map Pack, Pathfinder Module, Pathfinder Pawns, Pathfinder Player Companion, Pathfinder Roleplaying Game, and Pathfinder Tales are trademarks of Paizo Inc.

Maps by Crystal Frasier and Rob Lazzaretti

A Tor Book
Published by Tom Doherty Associates, LLC
175 Fifth Avenue
New York, NY 10010

www.tor-forge.com

Tor® is a registered trademark of Tom Doherty Associates, LLC.

The Library of Congress Cataloging-in-Publication Data is available upon request.

ISBN 978-0-7653-8436-2 (trade paperback)
ISBN 978-0-7653-8437-9 (e-book)

Our books may be purchased in bulk for promotional, educational, or business use. Please contact your local bookseller or the Macmillan Corporate and Premium Sales Department at 1-800-221-7945, extension 5442, or by e-mail at MacmillanSpecialMarkets@macmillan.com.

First Edition: December 2016

Printed in the United States of America

0 9 8 7 6 5 4 3 2 1

For my editor, James Sutter, who long ago picked up a novel called *The Crystal Dragon.* The circle is now complete.

Inner Sea Region

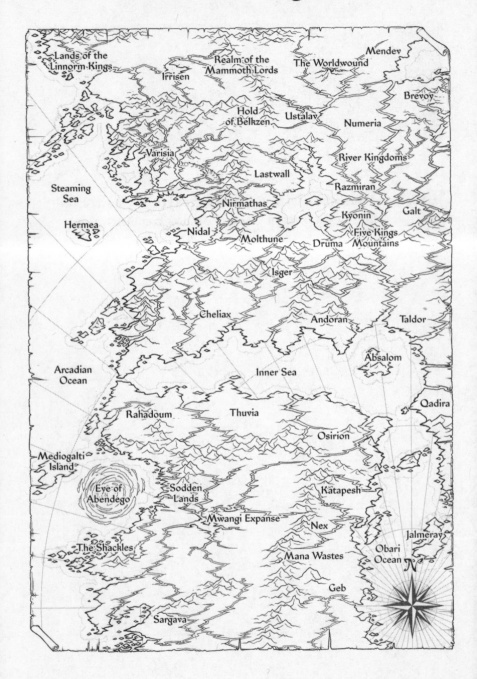

Mendev and the Worldwound

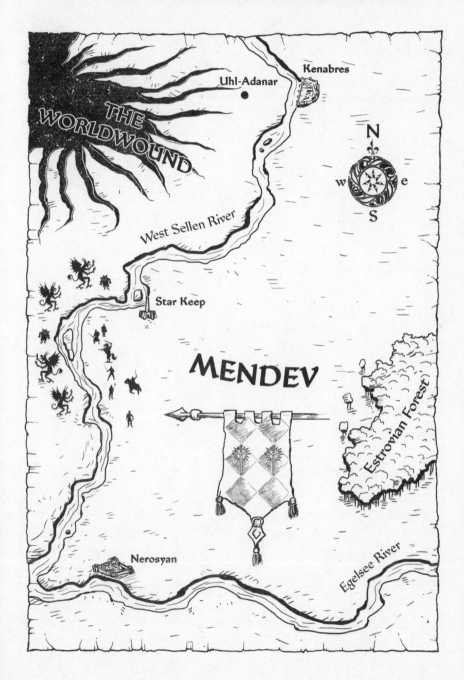

1

THE RESCUE

Daryus Gaunt eyed the two armored figures over the froth-covered rim of his mug, taking in every detail of the pair. Despite his outward disinterest, he remained on edge until the two crusaders took their leave of the tavern.

They had not recognized him—but then, he hardly looked like the earnest warrior he had been when he had worn their same uniform. Scars etched his oddly narrow features, many covered unsuccessfully by the thin, black beard edged with gray. Some of the jagged marks had been earned when he had been a crusader, but the rest—along with the beard—he'd gotten acting as a sword for hire for whoever was willing to pay.

Daryus could have saved himself so much trouble by simply not making Nerosyan his base. Doing so was like poking the proverbial bees' nest. The Order of the Flaming Lance had a significant presence here. If even one of the crusaders recognized him, he risked losing his head.

After all, the order had very little sympathy for traitors.

He set down the empty mug, then rose. Next to him, the two surly thugs muttering to one another about some future robbery immediately eased out of his way. Contrary to his name and his grandfather's supposed elven lineage, Daryus Gaunt was a mountain of a man, just a few inches shy of seven feet. It made his hiding in a stronghold of the order an even more questionable choice to that handful aware of his situation.

Five ales had done nothing to temper Daryus's mood, but he always stopped after five no matter what a part of him desired. The five drinks represented part of his failing, part of his betrayal. Daryus might have so far escaped punishment, but he couldn't escape his own guilt.

The Crimson Hammer Tavern might not have been one of the best-known establishments in Tumbletown—much less the city of Nerosyan itself—but it was a place where those in desperate need of a practiced sword could find such. "Desperate" was the key. Prospective employers had to be willing to wend their way deep northwest into one of the worst parts of the city.

Tonight, Daryus noted two potential contracts. One was a squat, robed figure who tried to keep his face covered with a scarf. The former crusader guessed him to be a merchant attempting to smuggle something either into Nerosyan or out of it. At present, the rotund man conversed with a pale, eye-patched swordsman who Daryus knew would do his best to part the fool from his money without fulfilling the contract.

The other possible client was a thin young man with long blond hair and furtive eyes who gave Daryus a measured glance before heading toward a grizzled ex-pirate from the River Kingdoms by the name of Divalo. Daryus gave the young man some credit. He had picked one of the more trustworthy swords in the tavern. Despite his background, Divalo would live up to his contract and even make certain that any other swords the young man needed would do the same on pain of death.

Seeing no reason to remain, Daryus made for the door. It had been a fortnight since he had returned to the Diamond of the North, as Nerosyan was also known. The name had little to do with any glamorous aspect of the city and more with the base design of the massive fortress initially built here. There was no better forti-fied city than Nerosyan—a good thing, since it was close enough to the Worldwound to attract the attention of demons.

Thinking of the Worldwound, Daryus hesitated just shy of the door. It was not out of any thought of adding a sixth ale to his count, but rather the hope that the rumors he had heard might still prove true. The word was out that some Pathfinders were planning an expedition into the demon-blighted land. What insane reason they had for doing so, the former crusader did not care. All he knew was that Pathfinders paid well. They would need a strong arm out in the Worldwound if they hoped to even survive their first night.

Gripping the swinging door carefully, Daryus slowly opened the way. A slight creak accompanied the door's movement. The tavern's owner liked to keep all the doors creaky, the better to know when someone exited or entered. Daryus appreciated that aspect, save now when he wanted to make certain that no one outside might hear him.

But the two crusaders were nowhere to be seen, even to his skilled eye. If they had recognized him and arranged a trap, they had done a fine job. Daryus doubted it, though.

Some might have wondered at his choices, a renegade at the heart of the crusader city. Even the explanation he gave himself— that they would never expect to find him so close by—was one that Daryus knew he wouldn't have accepted from anyone else.

Shrugging off both the obvious contradictions in his decisions and the reasons behind them, Daryus headed deeper into Tumbletown. For all their power, the crusaders did little to clean out the area. It wasn't due solely to the tremendous effort needed, though. The area around the Crimson Tavern and its like allowed the crusaders to have a particular place to find those tools they would not admit they needed at times. Daryus had seen the supposed clients who he knew were actually servants of the various crusader orders. Even the most pious of the orders' higher-ups occasionally needed those they considered scum.

Only a few dim oil lamps and torches lit the way through the grimy streets and the filthy buildings lining each side. There had been attempts in the past to better illuminate the area in a pretense of making everyone safer, but those had lasted only long enough for someone to steal the lamps. The lesson remained. Only those who could defend themselves could walk these streets at night.

A light some distance to the southwest and high above momentarily caught his attention. While not as large as the city's four main defense towers, Starrise Spire—or, more specifically, the magical beacon floating above it—was a useful landmark when trying to wend through the darkened streets toward where he lived. The only other landmark of any use to Daryus besides the city's towers was the great Cruciform Cathedral, situated dead center in the city. More a fortress than an ordinary cathedral, that massive redoubt housed Queen Galfrey and the rest of Mendev's leadership, those soldiers and bureaucrats charged with organizing all the disparate crusader orders into a solid defense against the Worldwound's demons.

As he moved on, Daryus set one gloved hand on the hilt of the longsword dangling at his side. All it would take was one swift motion to ready the blade for battle. He had been forced to draw it three times since arriving in Nerosyan, but not of late. Most of the regulars knew Daryus Gaunt by reputation now and avoided trouble with him.

Help . . .

He came to an abrupt halt. Cocking his head, he listened.

Silence reigned.

With a grunt, Daryus moved on. Five ales might not be enough to affect his faculties, but exhaustion could. He hadn't slept in three days. As a young warrior, three days awake would have meant little to him, but of late it seemed to Daryus that his strength flagged quicker and quicker. Still, there were few he knew of in Tumbletown with more skill than him, so he wasn't overly worried.

Help!

Again, Daryus hesitated. He listened, only hearing a slight wind struggling through the tightly packed buildings and narrow streets.

Help!

He frowned. It was almost as if he heard the voice in his *head*.

"Help me! Please!"

That cry he heard out loud. Moving with a speed and grace his form belied, Daryus drew his sword. He took one step toward where he believed the faint cry had come.

The clink of metal against metal made every muscle in his body tense. Daryus considered the possibility of a clever crusader trap, but quickly disposed of the notion. The cry seemed too true, too honest.

"Help!"

Daryus got a fix on the direction. With swift but stealthy steps, he headed toward the pleading voice. Whether it was male or female, he couldn't say, but it didn't matter. Every instinct in Daryus pushed him to helping the unseen caller. A renegade he might be, but he couldn't fight his basic nature.

As he entered a side alley, something just ahead of him moved in the shadows. With his left hand, Daryus brought the sword around, but found only empty air.

A second clink warned him just before the point of a narrow sword would have pierced him through the throat. Instead, Daryus managed to bring up his own weapon in time to deflect the attack. The oncoming tip scraped his cheek, adding to collection of scars.

Daryus's fist followed his sword, striking his adversary hard in the chest. The shadowy figure grunted as the force of the blow sent him back a step.

Despite eyes already attuned to the darkness, Daryus had trouble making out the other swordsman's features. No matter how hard he tried, the face remained indiscernible.

The sword did not. Out of the corner of his eye, Daryus spotted the weapon coming at him again. As he shifted his own blade to meet it, he noted another attack coming from the opposite side.

There was no time to reach the small dagger he wore in his belt. Daryus thrust his other arm up, willing to take a shallow slice on his cloth-covered arm rather than have his head skewered.

Deflecting the first sword, Daryus spun to meet the wielder of the second. He had the satisfaction of feeling his blade cut into the other attacker's arm.

Despite the wound, the second figure made no sound. Daryus knew he faced not only seasoned fighters, but determined ones.

The cry for aid had ceased, making the mercenary wonder if he had arrived too late. However, he knew the point no longer mattered; he was now committed to the struggle, whatever and whomever it concerned.

The first attacker tried to take him again. Daryus's left-handed counterassault kept the shadowy fighter off guard, while at the same time, he kicked at the legs of the second figure. He drove his latter attacker down on one knee, buying time to better deal with the first.

"Beware above!" the same voice that had cried for help called.

Rather than thrust at his foe, Daryus had to instead leap back. Even then, he barely missed being crushed under the weight of yet a third figure.

Sword already in play, Daryus lunged at the newcomer. He caught the crouching fighter on the side, but the other managed to roll away before the sword could do more than scrape what Daryus guessed to be a light breastplate.

Daryus sensed the movements of the second assailant. Determined to do something to keep the odds from turning further against him, he threw himself against the kneeling figure. As they collided, Daryus twisted his sword around and shoved as hard as he could.

Although the blade sank deep into the other's throat, his foe's only response before dying was a grunt. Daryus began to wonder whether they could even speak at all.

He hardly had the sword free from the collapsing body before the third of his attackers returned. Despite a hint of illumination from the street beyond, the face continued to be as featureless as those of the original pair. Daryus knew magic when he saw it, and hoped that the obscuring shadows were the extent of their abilities. The trio did not strike him as spellcasters, but rather paid assassins given a trick or two. Still, even one more trick might prove too much for Daryus.

Both attackers converged on Daryus. He fended off their initial attacks, at the same time managing to analyze which of the pair was the more dangerous. As for his foes, they seemed satisfied to harass him, almost as if waiting for something *else* to happen . . .

A clatter arose from his right. Daryus, already suspecting just what the pair had been waiting for, was startled that the *fourth* figure seeking his death could be so clumsy. The murky form stumbled into Daryus's waiting hand.

With all the force he could muster, Daryus threw his latest adversary toward the others. One fighter managed to evade the living missile, but the second wasn't so lucky. The two fell in a heap.

"Beware! One more! One more!" came the voice, this time from what seemed somewhere on the ground to the right.

Daryus couldn't see anyone there, but he responded to the warning. Drawing his dagger, he brandished the smaller blade at the most likely direction from which any additional enemy would attack.

It was all he could do to keep his grip as the sword point thrusting out of the darkness clashed against his dagger. Daryus spun around, forcing the barely visible sword's wielder back while still keeping the foremost of his other adversaries at bay.

Lunging toward his latest foe, he slipped past the sword enough to reach the hand gripping it. He drove the dagger as hard as he could into the wrist.

This time, Daryus was rewarded by a pained cry. The sword slipped free. Daryus grabbed the wounded limb, then pulled his opponent toward him.

So near, he finally caught a glimpse of a face, a peculiarly nondescript face that even Daryus's expert eye could not identify by region. A faint beard covered most of the lower half, but that was perhaps the only detail of any note.

A rough hand shoved Daryus back. The face disappeared into the same sort of odd, darker-than-dark inkiness obscuring the faces of the rest.

Daryus used the force of the push to enable him to roll to the side. As he turned on his back, he brought up his sword.

The point caught the attacker coming up behind him under his armored chest. Before the wounded fighter could stagger back, Daryus shoved the sword deeper.

As he did that, a strange change came over his dying enemy. Not only did the inkiness fade, but the attacker's entire body shimmered. A bland face identical to the other fighter's briefly materialized, then itself faded into something else.

And suddenly a *pitborn* stood before Daryus.

As a crusader, Daryus had come face to face with the demon-tainted creatures before. Generally human in face and form, they bore the curse of some past coupling between a human and one of the foul denizens of the Abyss. Daryus's former order had seen pitborn as little more than demons themselves, though while many were indeed evil, he knew that others could be as pure of heart as the oath-sworn warriors with whom he had served.

The last, it appeared, did not apply to the fanged, thick-browed figure collapsing by Daryus. His dying gaze held only rage, a look that faded a moment later as death took him.

Daryus scrambled back as both the attacker he had knocked over and wounded and the remaining pair regained their footing. He had been fortunate up until now, but even with two dead and possibly two wounded, the odds were still against him, especially if *all* of the three were pitborn. The demon-touched often wielded some level of sorcerous power, which explained their ability to mask themselves in the midst of a crusader stronghold.

Instead of attacking, though, to Daryus's surprise, the two in front of him retreated. Weapons ready, they vanished into the shadows behind them.

Daryus turned to the last, only to find the disguised attacker sprawled in a heap. Suspecting a trap, Daryus approached cautiously. As vicious as the dagger wound had been to the assassin's wrist, it should not have killed him so quickly, if at all.

In death, the pitborn's true countenance lay revealed. Small, sharp horns curled up from his forehead. His gaping mouth revealed sharp teeth. However, it was the pitborn's throat that demanded Daryus's attention.

Something had ripped it out with animalistic tenacity, something evidently capable of moving swiftly and silently.

Not one to question his fortune, Daryus looked around for the caller. He was not surprised to find himself alone. Whoever had been the intended target of these assassins had wisely fled. Unfortunately, that left Daryus alone to deal with the bodies. Bodies were not uncommon in Tumbletown, but three dead pitborn would certainly stir the attention of the city's crusaders. There would be a search of the area, with questions about who in the area would have the skill to kill not one but three.

It would not be long before someone led them to Daryus.

Daryus knew a spot where he could put the bodies, a place where no one would find them for years, if ever, based on the two skeletons he had discovered there the first time he had stumbled into it. He wiped his sword and dagger off on the body with the ruined throat, then sheathed the weapons and hefted the dead pitborn over his shoulder. He could have carried two at once, but that would have made it harder to draw a weapon should someone come upon him. Besides, a single body he could prop against a wall and pretend in the dark was a drunken comrade.

The hiding place in question was a narrow passage between two old, stone buildings farther to the west of his dwelling. Sometime far in the past, the entrance to the passage had been bricked up to make the two structures seem as one. The only way to still reach it was from the roofs above, which was how Daryus had stumbled on it in the first place. He had not expected to have to slide into it, nor had he expected the skeletons with the telltale chips in their ribs indicating death by sword. Now, though, what had been an unfortunate chance discovery was proving to be of use.

For most people, the time needed to dispose of one body, let alone three, would have been measured in hours. Daryus managed to remove the first two in such quick order that he surprised himself. Only then did he realize just how well he had eased into his current life. His earlier existence suddenly seemed farther away than ever.

Gritting his teeth, Daryus returned for the last. Not once had he seen anyone on the street, but he doubted his luck would hold much longer. With growing impatience, Daryus returned to the scene of the struggle . . . and found no trace of the last corpse.

What he did find was a small and curious-looking animal sitting near where he had last seen the body. The long, sinewy mammal licked one of its forepaws, upon which Daryus noted small bits of dark moisture.

The brown-furred creature raised its head to look at him. Daryus had not seen many weasels in this region, but knew what they looked like. This one was average in size and slightly wide in the mouth. There was nothing out of the ordinary about it save that its left eye seemed injured and twisted shut.

Without warning, it scampered over to Daryus and started up his leg. Thrusting the dagger in his belt, the former crusader seized the vermin by the scruff of the neck and brought it to eye level.

The weasel wrinkled its nose, but otherwise didn't react. It seemed perfectly at ease dangling several feet above the ground as it stared with the one eye at Daryus.

A quick survey of the area revealed no sign of either the intended victim or the last body. Daryus knew he had risked himself far too long for what he now felt was no good reason. Indeed, he began to wonder if perhaps he had been set up by someone intending either robbery or vengeance. Perhaps *he* had been the target all along.

Remaining wary, Daryus abandoned the area, taking what precautions he could to keep from being followed. If in fact he had been set up by a rival, or had simply become the object of some thieving gang's attention, he didn't want company joining him at home.

Not certain what else to do with the weasel, Daryus set it down and started off. He didn't get far before realizing that the creature was following close.

Daryus waved it off, but the weasel continued to follow. Its lack of concern for the dead or missing assassins suggested it hadn't been a pet of theirs. Yet if it had belonged to whoever had cried out—assuming there had actually been someone in the first place—Daryus wondered why the animal's owner had left it behind.

Daryus's abode was little more than a shack attached to the back of a warehouse. In the early days of the city, the shack had probably acted as the warehouse guard's quarters. The warehouse had changed hands and functions over the generations, becoming now the front for a merchant of disreputable means. Daryus paid the man's scarecrow of a daughter a month's lodging at a time. He knew that they also saw him as an unpaid guard for their goods, for if something happened to the warehouse, then Daryus would lose his dwelling and the money he had paid out that month.

Other than a creaking oak bed with a blanket to act as mattress, the lone room had only two other pieces of furniture. The well-stained table and accompanying bench were where Daryus spent his time when not sleeping. A half-empty bottle of foul-tasting red wine that reminded Daryus of the swill he had once drank in faraway Sauerton sat atop the table, looking inviting despite his familiarity with its sharply acidic taste.

Just as he shut the door behind him, the weasel slipped through into the room.

"No you don't!" He made a swipe for the sinewy creature, but the weasel twisted out of range. It darted to the bench, leapt atop it, then made its way to the table and the waiting wine bottle.

Daryus pursued, only to pull up short as the weasel suddenly turned its one-eyed gaze back at him. The stare was so intense that the renegade crusader almost expected the animal to talk.

Which it did.

"You save Toy's life!" it piped in the voice Daryus immediately recognized as the one that had called for help. "You save Toy's life, but now we must beware! They will seek to obey their master's will! They will come again with more! We must leave this city!"

Daryus reached for his sword. "What are you?"

Toy impatiently shook its head, its single open eye never leaving Daryus. "No time to waste on foolish questions! Must act! Must act before he acts!"

"Who?"

The weasel hissed. It reared, revealing that it was definitely male. "An evil walking on two legs! An evil that will now come looking for both of us, Master . . . unless Toy and Master stop him first!"

And then, without warning, the weasel opened his *other* eye as well—an eye simultaneously of fire and ice, blood red and bone ivory.

A *demon's* eye.

2

THE ARTIFACT

Shiera burst from the building, her frustration fueling an unreasoning anger. *She* been the one who had climbed through a crevice so narrow no one else had imagined it could be used as an entrance to the ancient shrine. *She* had been the one to find the crystalline artifact. *She* had been the one to dig it out, then scurry back through the crevice with a horde of rats behind her.

But *she* had not been the head of the expedition. *She* had only been a late addition to its ranks, chosen because of her adeptness—even among those of her calling—for puzzling out and translating ancient languages and codes.

And so, the credit for Shiera Tristane's find—along with the lesser finds of other Pathfinders involved in the expedition—had gone instead to Venture-Captain Amadan Gwinn. Gwinn, who had not left his tent save to oversee the cataloging of items as they were brought out.

Running her fingers through her short bangs, Shiera paused in the street to take a breath and calm her nerves. Amadan Gwinn had not earned his status through a lack of effort in his early days. His early expeditions had been what had first inspired the lone child of a court scribe to turn her father's devotion to ancient writings into her chance to enter as an apprentice Pathfinder. Everything Shiera had learned from her father she had built upon with a natural aptitude that had seen her rising rapidly in the Pathfinder Society.

Then, Shiera had been given what at the time she had believed to be her most fortuitous break as a Pathfinder. One of Amadan Gwinn's trusted assistants had had the misfortune of falling ill just before Gwinn's latest expedition had been ready to depart for the Worldwound. Venture-Captain Gwinn had needed someone with her expertise to take his place. The first two weeks of the expedition had been all that she imagined, save for her realization that the famed Pathfinder no longer did any of his own work, but relied on younger, more able hands like hers. Even that, though, had not bothered her so much since she had finally been able to follow through on research that had—or so she believed at the time—coincided with Gwinn's own.

Now too late she realized that the senior Pathfinder's greatest talent these days was ferreting out those new to the calling whose abilities would most benefit his reputation.

"Unf!"

Caught up in her fury, Shiera had failed to notice the oncoming figure until they collided. Despite being small and slim, it was she who nearly bowled over the much taller, albeit lanky man. Only a quick grab by Shiera prevented the well-dressed blond man from toppling backward. Even then, the silken shirt under the crested blue jacket proved almost impossible to keep hooked in her clutching fingers.

Finally managing to right himself, the stranger glared down at her. He was not much older than Shiera—which was to say, he wasn't very old at all—but his strong-jawed face held that expression that so many of the higher castes wore around all but their own. Shiera knew he wouldn't be impressed with what he saw. With her short, nearly cropped red hair and leather pants, she hardly looked like one of the glamorous ladies of his station. Shiera didn't consider herself ugly, but neither did she see herself as beautiful. She was who she was, and had no time to care what this jackanapes thought of her.

Releasing her grip, Shiera gave him curt nod. "Didn't see you. Sorry about that."

A sneer was his only response. He started past her, only to abruptly pause and turn back. "I know you . . . I saw you when the expedition returned. You're a Pathfinder, yes?"

"I am, sir." Shiera tried hard to keep a civil tone as she uttered the last word. "Is there something I can help you with?"

He snorted. "Not you. Just tell me where I can find the abode of Venture-Captain Amadan Gwinn. *He's* the one I need."

Despite his arrogance, there was a hint of something else in his tone—an innate nervousness. Shiera briefly—and very *seriously*—considered sending him in the wrong direction, then relented. "You go that way, then to the right, *sir*. The building with the eagle statue out front. I'm sure you can't possibly miss it."

For her utter kindness, she received but a curt nod. The well-dressed young man turned from her as if she no longer existed.

Shiera glared at his back, then moved on herself. The interruption had caused some of her initial fury at how she had been wronged to subside. She was still angry, but knew that letting it get the best of her would change nothing. She had to concentrate on moving ahead.

She was grateful she had never had the opportunity to bring to Amadan Gwinn's attention a fragment she had found on a previous expedition. Shiera had spent the better part of two years puzzling over it, but had been unable to locate any written records concerning it even in the vast archives of the Pathfinder Society. Scholars she had carefully questioned had shown no knowledge of what it represented. Shiera had been hoping that Venture-Captain Gwinn would have some answers, but fortunately for her, circumstances had prevented her from revealing it to him.

Shiera had barely left the area of her brief encounter before a disturbance arose from one of the main streets. With others, she paused to watch as a squadron of heavily armored crusaders from

the Order of the Flaming Lance marched double-time past the
onlookers. Their grim casts indicated that this was no exercise. She
glanced the direction in which the crusaders headed, noting its
close proximity to the seedier quarter of the city. Shiera's interest
waned at that point. Likely a fight had broken out among the
darker elements in Tumbletown, a fairly common occurrence.

It took her only a few more minutes to return to her modest
dwelling in Bitterwind, a staunchly middle-class neighborhood
northwest of the city center. While not very large, her quarters
were clean, comfortable, and in the midst of the district most
frequented by artisans, professionals—and, of course, Pathfinders.

Shiera had few living relatives, all of them distant. Her mother
had died when she was young, and her father had passed away
shortly after Shiera had joined the Pathfinders. Family rumor had
it that she had a much older half-brother by her father, but neither
of her parents had ever spoken on that subject. Still, whether Shiera
had had no siblings or a hundred, it wouldn't have mattered to her.
The Pathfinder Society was her family now.

A small shelf on the wall across from her cot displayed a few
particular treasures from her career thus far, including an ivory
vase emblazoned with the profile of an eagle from the Five Kings
Mountains to the south and a fragment of bronze plate from a
ruined citadel located in the midst of the barren regions near
Brevoy to the east. However, it was to neither of these, nor any of
the other prominent pieces she had gathered that Shiera now cast
her attention. Instead, she headed to a large, oak travel case set in
the far corner of the room. Kneeling, she pulled a key from the
pouch at her waist and unlocked the case.

The tiny copper box she removed from the case was itself
unremarkable, save that it had no discernible keyhole. Shiera
shifted the box around, then touched two spots on opposing sides.

The lid flipped open. Her eyes fixed on the small fragment of
parchment contained within. To Shiera, the parchment was more

valuable than gold or diamonds. It represented all she lived for, all her role as a Pathfinder meant to her.

With great care, Shiera removed the parchment and brought it to her table. From a small wooden tray on the corner of the table, she removed a circle of glass two inches wide. Placing it near her right eye, she peered at the well-worn script.

It had taken her all the time since discovering it by chance near the edge of the Worldwound for Shiera to even translate the first few "words." While she was well aware that her translation might be off, she couldn't help but believe that she had begun to understand the gist of what the writer had been trying to convey. The script was close to that of ancient Hallit—the nation of Sarkoris, lost in the Worldwound's creation, had been one of the few places where the barbarian tongue had evolved a written form—but with significant variation that suggested it might precede most documents from that fabled kingdom.

"Uhl . . ." Shiera muttered. "Uhl-Adru. Uhl-Adrys. Uhl—" She paused to stare at the torn edge, where the rest of the word had fallen off into eternity. She considered every language and dialect with which she was familiar. Studying the curve of the script, Shiera tried to imagine how it extended to the missing piece.

Perhaps fueled by her recent experience with Amadan Gwinn, Shiera finally noticed the slight extra curving just disappearing in the rip. Suddenly, it matched with something Master Gwinn had shown her.

"*Adanar!*" Shiera blurted happily. "Adanar!" Her brow wrinkled. "Adanar?"

Her pleasure at translating the second part of the name was not at all muted by the fact that she had never heard of any location called Uhl-Adanar. Indeed, that only excited her more. She had uncovered mention of a lost settlement, likely a temple-city from what little else she had gleaned.

That thought brought her back to the other bit of the fragment that she had thus far translated. Here, her final choice remained even more questionable. The second part, as best as she could guess, meant *eye,* as in when one cried.

As for the first portion, of one thing she was certain: that it was meant to be a name. A very *peculiar* name, but still a name. She assumed it to be of some minor deity, perhaps the one for whom Uhl-Adanar was built. In that regard, the choice she had made for her final translation made as much sense as any. *Tzadn.*

Tzadn's Eye. It had, she admitted to herself, a bit of a poetic touch to it, but that figured. Priests were always trying to romanticize elements of their religions. It was, in her mind, the only way some of the sects could survive. Certainly, it was not due to their seemingly endless sermons . . .

Shiera set the parchment and magnifying glass down, then leaned back. Exhaling, she chuckled at her earlier anger. Gwinn's glory-hogging seemed a small thing now. If Uhl-Adanar was indeed a lost temple-city, she held the potential key to a discovery that overshadowed anything she might have gained from that expedition or her previous work.

"Uhl-Adanar," Shiera murmured with pleasure. She leaned forward to inspect the script one more time . . . and then paused.

In setting down the parchment, she had left it slightly askew. To her surprise, at that angle, the name Tzadn became a word. Shiera mouthed it slowly in order to make certain she read it correctly.

Reaper.

Shiera shook her head to clear it. She plucked up the parchment and glass and studied the writing again. No matter how she tried, she couldn't find the angle that made it spell out the odd word again.

After a few more futile attempts, Shiera gave up. She was certain she had only imagined the word. Shiera had heard stories of other Pathfinders following false trails they thought they had found in their research. She had no doubt as to the name of the artifact and the place where it was located. Those were facts. Those were what she needed to concentrate on.

Looking over the rest of the scrap, Shiera noted a couple of symbols she thought represented landmarks. If so, then she had a fair idea of where to look for this lost temple-city. It would be an arduous journey deep into the Worldwound, but well worth it if her deductions held true.

Fingers tapping on the table, Shiera pondered what to do next. If she had been a senior Pathfinder like Amadan Gwinn, all she would have had to do was contact the Grand Lodge in Absalom and have the Society's accountants pen a promissory note, or else strike a bargain with some noble relic hunter for any valuable but historically insignificant artifacts the expedition might run across. Gold would have poured in, more gold than Venture-Captain Gwinn needed, but less than he was always willing to accept.

The accepted routine for most younger Pathfinders such as herself when seeking to head an expedition was to approach a Pathfinder venture-captain and make a case for requisitioning Society funds set aside for that purpose. If that didn't work, those with wealth or connections could always finance it themselves or try to find a patron. Shiera had neither, and the idea of begging Gwinn was far from appealing.

Somehow, she would have to find another method of financing at least a small party. Shiera considered herself clever and adaptable, but for the moment she had no idea where to start.

Her stomach growled. Caught up in her earlier anger, she had not bothered with dinner. Setting the parchment and glass aside, she rose to deal with her hunger. Food and rest would give her some perspective. Tomorrow, she would have a better idea of what to do.

Someone pounded on Shiera's door.

She jerked to her feet, not at all able to recall how she had ended up fully clothed atop her bed. On the table still lay half a loaf bread and some meat and cheese. A partial bottle of wine stood on the smaller table next to her bed.

There was something in her left hand. The parchment. Fortunately, despite evidently having fallen asleep with it in her grip, Shiera had done it no apparent harm.

The pounding continued. Shiera set the parchment down and brushed herself off.

Swinging open the door, she discovered perhaps the last person she would have expected to see. Still clad in the same garments in which she had last seen him, and clearly looking as if he had not slept, the man with whom she had collided peered pensively at her.

"You're the Pathfinder Shiera Tristane?"

"I still am," she managed, growing defensive. "If you think I did anything—"

He quickly raised a hand. "No! My apologies! I was remiss!"

While Shiera appreciated his change in demeanor, she still couldn't fathom why he would seek her out to apologize. "Master . . ."

"Raffan. My name is Raffan. I am no master. I serve . . . I serve an elderly—and if I may be frank, *eccentric*—man of noble means. He has set me on a quest I thought I would never manage to even start, but with you at last I can—"

Shiera's world swirled around her. She blinked, then interjected, "Please, Master—Raffan—step in."

He eagerly obeyed. His new demeanor continued to confuse her. She gestured him toward a chair near the table, then hurried to put away the remains of her last meal.

When Shiera returned her attention to Raffan, it was to find him nervously fiddling with a silken handkerchief. At first she thought he took offense with his surroundings, but then she saw there was some tiny object wrapped in the handkerchief.

"I thought you had business with Venture-Captain Gwinn," she commented, trying to surreptitiously see the piece.

"That was my hope. My master, who always dreamed of becoming a Pathfinder but because of the family name did not, has long admired Amadan Gwinn. Each time there was a local expedition, my master purchased all records published of it for his private collection."

"Who is your master?"

Raffan gave her a look akin to the one from the other day. Shiera understood then that the one thing he would not discuss was his master's identity. That was not entirely a surprise; many patrons preferred anonymity unless the expedition proved wildly successful. Others kept quiet due to their reputations in other fields. Not everyone respected the Society the way she did.

Raffan fiddled with the handkerchief's contents. "My lord gave me authority to determine if Amadan Gwinn would indeed be the best recourse. Sad to say, I found that not to be the case."

"He wasn't interested?"

The man made a face. "I never let it get that far. I made inquiries with others around him and observed the festivities around his return from his latest journey. Far too much public interaction for my lord and master. Too much of a—of a—"

"Circus?"

"Exactly."

Shiera did the polite thing and offered him some of her wine. He wrinkled his nose, which she took for a refusal. "And you come to me for what reason?"

More fiddling with the handkerchief. "In my inquiries, I learned that one of the reasons for Master Gwinn's recent success was the hard work of one of his assistants, a full Pathfinder herself. One Shiera Tristane. You actually performed much of the work."

"I *discovered* the damn thing, just to be clear," she could not help blurting.

For the first time, Raffan responded with a smile. "That is exactly what I wanted to hear from you. Mistress Tristane—"

"Call me Shiera."

"*Mistress Tristane*," Raffan repeated with much emphasis. "From what I gather, you are an expert in script, in cartography, in—in intuitive thinking. You are also someone, I believe, who would be willing to keep your profile low as you set out on a search. Do I read you well?"

"Well enough, but I hope you're going to get to the point about all this and what it has to do with whatever you have there."

The smile briefly returned. "My master has for years had this dream. Ever since he came across this piece in a bazaar. He has so much knowledge at his disposal, yet none of it made mention of his discovery. That made him only more determined to find out the truth."

You can talk and talk, can't you? Shiera would have already shown Raffan the door, but her curiosity over what he held continued to grow.

"I am empowered to finance an expedition of moderate means in return for you or your team presenting any and all findings to my master upon your return and before you make any public announcement concerning those finds."

All Shiera heard was "finance an expedition." Raffan—or rather his unnamed employer—was offering Shiera her *own* expedition. She could finally go in search of whatever this eye was, finally be given the due she was meant for—

Calm yourself! Shiera reminded herself that Raffan's employer had a specific focus for the expedition. If she tried to subvert the expedition for her own interests, she might soon find herself in chains. It had happened before.

Still, perhaps this expedition will provide a chance to go after Uhl-Adanar and the Eye.

"Of course," Raffan went on, "that is assuming you can make something of this."

He pulled back the handkerchief to expose a small coin. A ceremonial coin, Shiera saw. A token passed out as a blessing or a symbol marking members of a crusader order.

But as she took the coin from Raffan, the exact purpose for it became moot. Instead, all she could see were the marks on the one face.

The marks she had translated as *Tzadn's Eye*.

3

THE WITCH

From under the deep hood of his cloak, the witch peered down at his workers. The diggers coughed as dust filled their lungs. For four months, the pitborn had obediently broken through rock and baked earth in search of the tomb his studies insisted lay here. Three other shafts in the vicinity marked earlier aborted attempts. This time, though, he was certain he had found the location.

The only question remaining was whether what he wanted would be in the tomb. Time was precious. Too precious.

Without meaning to, Grigor touched his cheek with one white-gloved hand. Even through the glove he could feel the incredible dryness of his skin. Yes, for Grigor Dolch, time was definitely too precious.

With swiftly growing impatience, the mustached figure stepped to the very edge of the dig. Deep in the hole, a dozen pitborn of various forms toiled without pause.

Find it. They will find it. They must find it. Eyes glistening, Grigor focused on the most exhausted of the workers.

"Too slow." He held out his right hand. A black, wooden staff covered in runes formed in his grip. Its head was that of a hungry rat whose mouth gripped a dark red crystal.

Grigor pointed the staff at the pitborn in question. Behind him, the expedition's mounts stirred nervously as they sensed the magic stirring.

Before he could finish, both his target and the other pitborn flanking him leapt back as if about to be eaten by something. Grigor had chosen among the hardiest and most vicious of the tainted for his workers, well aware that the faint of heart would not last on this quest. He had already lost a handful to the ancient traps and poisons left behind in some of the previous ruins he had investigated. Grigor cared not a whit how many of the demonspawn perished, though, only that enough survived until he was able to achieve his goal.

Somewhere in the back of his mind, he heard the damned familiar laughing at his efforts.

Growling at the thought, the witch dared pull his hood back a bit in order to better see what had struck such fear into the pitborn. What passed for the light of day in the Worldwound illuminated his face, revealing his smooth but oddly sallow complexion and magnifying the glassy glint in his eyes. Small, odd lines crisscrossed his entire face, as if someone had mapped out every inch. Not scars or wrinkles—*lines*.

"What have you got there?" he demanded in a voice much older than his youthful appearance. "Stand aside!"

The nearest pitborn were all too ready to acquiesce. Grigor immediately saw the reason for their fear. A demonic face carved in stone lay half unveiled by the axes and shovels. The face alone was not reason enough for his servants' displays of fear; that had to do with what the face symbolized. The face marked this tomb as that of a cursed being. It was not the first time Grigor and his servants had come across such images, and the memories of just what had happened to two of their fellow pitborn clearly remained with them.

"Never mind that!" the witch commanded. "You know the rewards awaiting you. Crack the seal. Hurry!"

"Master Grigor—" the pitborn in the center began.

Grigor Dolch tapped the bottom of the staff against the ground. The stone atop flared threateningly.

"Crack the seal," Grigor repeated in a cold voice.

Although still obviously fearful of the tomb's curse, the pitborn quickly went back to work. Raising pickaxes high, two of them attacked the partially seen entrance. Grigor's servants were not without their own abilities, but the witch wanted no magic but his own involved. The more magic loosely thrown about, the more chance for disaster.

The clatter of metal against rock resounded in the otherwise empty region. Still, despite the apparent desolation, Grigor remained alert. Not only was the Worldwound full of threats; it also housed its share of potential rivals interested in taking what the witch found. Grigor did not fear his power against most foes, but he didn't want to waste what magic was left to him.

But soon I will no longer have to ration it. Soon, I will have all the power I desire. He will surely grant me that.

That reminded him of the past he still needed to eliminate. He had heard nothing from the band he had sent to the city. They were all skilled killers, and all protected by masking spells so that they could infiltrate the crusader stronghold. Grigor had expected the leader to contact him through a small crystal Grigor had supplied. He wanted to know the moment that the foul beast was dead.

A sound like thunder erupted from the excavation. Despite the witch's threats, the pitborn scrambled from the entrance as if a thousand witches threatened them.

A darkness escaped from the crack one of the pitborn had created. It shot forth, falling upon the nearest two servants with ease as they fought to climb out. Neither even had time to cry out. The darkness swallowed them, leaving no trace.

Grigor did nothing at first, instead watching as the last of the pitborn fled the excavation. He did not hold back out of any concern for them, but rather because he knew that this assault was only the beginning. His true target remained hidden within the darkness. Grigor had more than just the staff and his knowledge of witchcraft at his command. His journey into magic had begun in another calling. The witch wanted to conserve his power until the last moment.

The darkness shifted toward him as if it somehow knew that he was the true adversary. Grigor let the darkness draw near him, then tapped the staff on the ground again.

The stone flared. Its crimson light burned away the darkness, revealing something else hidden within.

The floating corpse had a desiccated appearance to it. A few wisps of long gray hair decorated the back of the skull. Worms and small insects crawled in and out of the mouth and eye sockets. Grigor recognized the fragments of garment still clinging to the bones as belonging to a priest of some sort.

Raising a shriveled hand, the corpse pointed at him. Already expecting such an attack, Grigor held his ground and cast his own spell.

A wall of fire formed atop the moving corpse before it could finish whatever foul spell it planned. The priest flung itself aside, but not before everything below its ribcage shriveled to ash.

As the creature struggled ineffectually to pull itself farther away from the flames with its bony hands, Grigor approached. "So, let us see what you might know." He placed one boot on the creature's chest, pinning it to the ground.

The fleshless jaw clacked open and closed in what Grigor thought was perhaps protest. The empty eye sockets somehow still managed to glare at the corpse's captor.

"You *know* why I'm here!" Grigor Dolch shouted at the creature. "You know what I want from you!"

This only made the corpse struggle harder. Grigor thrust his staff's tip into one of the skull's empty orbits, and those struggles ceased—not dead, but waiting.

"The temple-city!" Grigor demanded. "You know where it lies! Speak!"

The jaw dropped open. A single word echoed in the witch's head. *Tzadn.*

"Yes, I know to whom it is dedicated, thank you very much."

The corpse briefly stirred again. The jaw shut.

The reaction only served to encourage the witch. "Ah! You thought that bit of knowledge beyond me, did you? I surprised you, didn't I?"

Tzadn, the undead finally repeated.

"Yes . . . Tzadn. I think we've already established that much. Now, show me *the way* to the tomb. Show me the *path* to him."

The jaw opened and closed. The spirit within still fought back, but now Grigor was confident of his victory. The corpse would tell him all he needed to know.

Tzadn, the ghoul rasped again. *Hajak di . . . Hajak di . . .*

Hajak di. The witch's mind raced as he tried to translate the ancient phrase.

At that moment, the corpse crooked one hand in an arcane gesture, shrieking a magical command. Grigor leapt back, preparing a protective shield.

But the attack wasn't aimed at him. The corpse's already blackened jawbone broke off. The ghoul's bones crackled, then crumbled to ash that spilled out onto the ground before Grigor. The skull was the last to go, perched atop the scorched robes until both collapsed into dust.

Exhaling, the witch nodded. The tomb would be open to him now, not that he suspected he truly needed the contents anymore. The priest may have managed to end itself, yet with those last two words, it had still told Grigor something worth knowing.

The staff had once again served him well. It had already been strong with spells when he had appropriated it from a colleague. Overconfidence was a common trait among spellcasters, one that Grigor had played upon when both stealing the staff and slaughtering the witch. Fortunately, unlike his former mentors, he had more control over himself. He would not fall victim to overconfidence, not—

Grigor felt an irritation on his left cheek. Shoving aside his long, ebony hair, he touched the spot.

"The amber solution!" he snapped. "Now!"

A pitborn rushed to the horses, returning a moment later with an emerald jar. The horned servant gingerly opened the jar.

Dismissing the staff, Grigor removed one glove. A hand with the same sallow, lined skin dipped into the jar. As he did that, the anxious pitborn held up the lid so that the underside faced the witch.

Glittering silver-blue eyes that seemed more artifice than flesh stared into the mirrored bottom of the lid at the angular features. Grigor studied the spot on his cheek. There, his dry, patterned skin had begun to peel away, as if from a dead body as desiccated as that of the creature Grigor had just destroyed. Visible beneath the skin was rotted yellow flesh.

He quickly applied the amber solution. The alchemical mixture seeped into his skin, making it supple and helping it to adhere to the flesh beneath. The yellowish tone grew more pronounced.

Too soon, the witch thought bitterly as he wiped his fingers and replaced his glove. *Too soon. I will have to make more of the solution before long, and use some more of the staff's stored power to do it. Curse that Toy!*

Waving away the pitborn, Grigor pictured the weasel. If he had been able to seize his treacherous familiar and drain the demon's magic from the beast, then there would have been much more power in the staff from which to draw. Grigor also would have severed the last dangerous link between himself and his former patron. So long as Toy lived, the witch remained in danger.

You cannot do much yourself, Toy, but what will you do? Find another dupe like the fool who thought his sword through my heart would end me? Grigor Dolch still kept the eyes of the would-be assassin for possible later use. The witch had an affinity—some would have said *obsession*—for eyes and their potential magical uses.

Of course, that overwhelming affinity for power had been what had finally caused all of Grigor's earlier plans for power to go awry. First with his former master, when he had been a promising apprentice in the field of wizardry—and murdered that same master in the process of stealing his secrets. And then as a witch, when seeking to *amend* his deal with the demon to whom he had sworn himself.

Before Grigor could delve further into his past excesses, a cry from above turned the witch's attention to the sky. There, a raven cawed three more times.

The pitborn assigned to Grigor's messengers quickly held up his arm. The raven dropped down, then alighted. The fiery-eyed demonspawn removed a small parchment from a tiny leather pouch strapped to the creature's leg. The servant ran over to Grigor and knelt, then cautiously handed the witch the parchment.

Grigor snatched up the note and read it eagerly.

Trap failed. Experienced sword. Two dead. One dying. Orders?

Rage filled Grigor Dolch, a blinding rage.

"Toy . . ." he growled. "Toy . . ."

Without thinking, he summoned the staff once more. His baleful gaze washed over the pitborn who had brought him the message.

Quicker of wit than the demonspawn, the raven fled to the air. That finally warned the pitborn of the imminent danger.

"Master!" the horned servant rumbled. "I did noth—"

The stone glowed. The rat's eyes narrowed.

It was not out of any sympathy that Grigor finally held back, only the knowledge that he needed to conserve power. The spells he had used against the undead had taken enough toll on his body. If things took longer than he intended, he'd need the staff's power to preserve him until he achieved his goals.

Fighting down his anger, Grigor glared at the missive. Only then did he see there was more written below.

The bait is taken.

The witch grinned. It was a sight that left the nearest pitborn even more anxious, an expression as grotesque in its own way as the fleshless grin of the tomb's animated protector.

The bait was taken.

"At last . . ." Soon, so very soon, he would not have to concern himself with either Toy or the demon the familiar still served. Soon, Grigor would have more power than any other witch or wizard.

The bait was taken.

4

THE CLIENT

Daryus sensed the tension in the air as he returned to his quarters after purchasing food. He knew that no one could have found the bodies. Indeed, the overall aroma of the quarter guaranteed that even after the corpses began to decay, no passerby would take note of the smell.

No, something else was going on. Daryus saw that others sensed the same. He was glad to return to his so very humble residence, even if that meant facing Toy.

The weasel lay curled around the wine bottle on the table. He opened his normal eye upon Daryus's entrance.

"You better not have been drinking the wine again," Daryus warned. "I warned you last night . . ."

The familiar immediately uncurled, then scrambled off the table. "No, Master Daryus! I only kept guard should some diabolical and thirsty thief break in!"

"You mean *another* thirsty thief, don't you?" Daryus set down the new bottle that he had brought with him. As far as he was concerned, the weasel could keep the one on the table. Daryus had no desire to share a drink with the creature. He had already witnessed a couple of examples of the familiar's taste in food. True, it meant a cleaner room, but the thought of that mouth then touching the bottle was too much for even the veteran soldier.

Digging into the small leather bag he also carried, Daryus tossed a small, wrapped piece of goat meat. "This what you wanted?"

The familiar quickly tore through the wrapping and began digging into the meat. Daryus's nose wrinkled. The meat was well past selling for human consumption, but apparently that meant nothing to the weasel.

"At least take that somewhere other than the table. I'd like to be able to eat, too."

Toy wasted only enough time to nod to Daryus before returning to his respite and utterly ignoring what the human had just asked of him. Daryus raised a hand to swat the familiar from the table, then gave in. Moving over to the bed, he sat down and concentrated on his own meal. As he ate, he pondered what to do next. All the activity outside unsettled Daryus. He didn't want to be accidentally swept up in whatever was happening. He decided that it would be best to leave Nerosyan for now, but to do that he needed to find immediate employment.

Once finished with his food, Daryus readied to depart again. As he headed for the door, Toy, still in the process of swallowing the last bit of goat, suddenly bounded after him.

"Must not go alone again!" the familiar insisted. "I will go with you! Toy will go with you!"

"You'd be better off staying here—"

"No! He has eyes everywhere! He always has eyes! The witch has *my* eye!"

The renegade crusader frowned. "What do you mean by that?"

"He sees me with my eye! He follows me with my eye!"

Daryus frowned. If he understood the creature correctly, Toy's former master could keep track of the familiar through the orb that the witch had removed. That should not have been any concern to Daryus; after all, he had no true argument with the witch. He had simply become caught up in the attack due to his decision to intercede.

Of course, from his past experiences with practitioners of the magical arts, such logic was not enough to keep them from seeing someone like Daryus as a potential threat. That was why Daryus hadn't just thrown Toy out once the familiar had revealed himself. Even if the weasel had run off, Daryus knew that the witch might still seek to eliminate anyone with even the most minute knowledge of his sinister activities, whatever they were. Witches just did that.

And not just witches. Everyone with power was the same in the regard.

"All right," he finally responded. "Climb atop my shoulder . . . but try not to breathe on me. Not after that goat."

Toy scrambled up Daryus's body, finally taking a place to the right of the fighter's head. Toy let his tail wrap loosely along the back of Daryus's neck.

"Don't speak," he warned the familiar.

Toy nodded.

With the weasel secured, the former crusader headed out to the Crimson Hammer. It was late enough in the day that some of those needing a hired sword would already be lurking around the tavern. Not only would Daryus have to make himself more noticeable to any potential clients, but he would also have to make certain they did not reject him for someone else. Daryus knew that he would also have to possibly accept a contract with a client he might otherwise have shunned.

Does it matter? he asked himself. *The oaths of honor you swore don't matter anymore, do they?*

Do they?

Halfway to the tavern, Daryus paused. He felt Toy stiffen, although perhaps not for the same reason as the human. Daryus quickly slipped into the shadows of an alleyway.

Mere moments later, six armored figures marched past the hidden pair. Daryus watched with a combination of regret and frustration. He made an estimation of their likely destination and exhaled when he realized that they were not headed toward where he lived.

Slipping back out into the open, he continued on at a quicker pace. The sooner he reached the tavern, the better.

Turning a corner, Daryus all but collided with a *second* patrol.

The lead crusader was half a head shorter than Daryus but broader of shoulder. Daryus instinctively surveyed the officer, wondering if the crusader might be one of those who would still recognize him.

"Name!" snapped the officer.

"Rogan Rolfsson," Daryus answered without hesitation. It was not the first time he had used the false name.

The crusader eyed him with open contempt. "Mercenary."

Daryus merely nodded. He was used to being greeted with such disdain for his profession.

"You look like you can handle a sword well enough. Keep it ready, mercenary. There's assassins—*pitborn* assassins—about. We found a dead one in the middle of the city. Tied him to an earlier slaying of a merchant."

Although Daryus managed to keep from showing any surprise, he felt Toy dig in his claws as the familiar digested the news. "Assassins *here*? Your men at the gates not getting paid enough?"

He would not have been surprised if he had been punched for suggesting that some crusaders at the gates had taken gold in return for entrance into the supposedly impregnable citadel. Still, it was a necessary comment, keeping in character with the role Daryus played.

Instead, the officer simply growled and shoved him aside. Most men would have been thrown to the ground by the crusader's strength, but Daryus only stumbled back a few steps. Still, it was enough to satisfy the officer. "Just watch yourself, scum, and report anyone unusual immediately. There's a reward for good information, if that's what you wonder."

Daryus gave him an avaricious grin. "You should've said so in the first place!"

With a sneer, the officer led his men on. Daryus waited where he was until the patrol vanished from view.

"So one died of his wounds," Daryus mused. "But that still leaves at least two."

"Strong is Master Daryus!" Toy cooed in the renegade's ear, at the same time bathing Daryus's face in scent of half-digested goat. "Swift of limb and skilled of sword is Master Daryus!"

"Quiet." More than ever, Daryus wanted to find a client, especially one needing to leave quickly. He pushed on toward the tavern . . . only to pause when a familiar figure flanked by two insignificant-looking ceremonial guards passed by.

Daryus had seen the merchant in the Crimson Hammer seeking to hire protection his two overdressed servants clearly could not provide. That no one from the tavern followed the merchant meant that no deal had been made.

Although the rotund figure was well dressed, Daryus could read enough of the man's personality from the face to know that here was a client he would have generally not have accepted. Despite his fall from grace, Daryus still prided himself on choosing patrons who were for the most part honest.

Now, though, he could not afford that luxury. That in mind, Daryus followed his potential client to what he quickly recognized would be the main market. The destination suited Daryus fine. In the crowds, he could approach the merchant and offer his services. It would no doubt mean accepting a lower pay—the man would surely understand that Daryus either needed money or needed to escape—but the former crusader could not help that. Once he had taken the merchant to wherever he needed to go, Daryus would sever all ties.

The market was a huge place filled with items from all over the known world. While on the surface the wares the various sellers displayed were of a harmless nature, even here in Nerosyan one could locate illicit items banned by the crusaders. Daryus suspected that the man he followed dealt in the delivery of some of those very pieces.

The merchant paused to speak with a scrawny, bearded man whose name Daryus did know, but whose reputation among those like Daryus was very well known. It did not surprise him to see that the pair knew one another well.

"You'd better stay here," he muttered to Toy. When the weasel gave no response, Daryus brought one hand up to where the familiar perched.

Toy leapt off.

Daryus turned as casually as he could, but by then the weasel was already out of view. Why Toy would abandon him now, Daryus could not say, but it only encouraged the mercenary to find a patron and find one immediately.

One of the two men with the merchant noticed the tall figure approaching. The guard immediately reached for his sword, only to have the merchant place a warning hand over the guard's.

Peering over his shoulder, the heavy man smiled slightly and nodded. Daryus had to assume the merchant recognized him from the tavern.

"You're still looking for someone to make up for this pair," Daryus commented under his breath. In his profession, he had to not care what he said about men such as the pair flanking his potential employer. They might be useful in some chest-puffing display with one of the merchant's counterparts, but not in a pitched battle against bandits.

"You have a sharp eye, my friend," the man said in nasal tones. "I remember you from the tavern. Someone said you had already been hired, but I see they were mistaken."

Daryus held his annoyance in check. There were those among the mercenaries who lacked anything remotely resembling his sense of honor. They were willing to lie about the free status of one fighter in order to gain a few coins from another for pointing them out to a mark.

"I'm available, for the right price. Where are you heading?"

"Toward the River Kingdoms."

The River Kingdoms. Daryus exhaled ever so slightly in relief. *Not Kenabres. Not Kenabres.*

Eyeing Daryus up and down, the merchant remarked, "You're not the usual sellsword. You had, if I am not mistaken, a good place, a strong position." When Daryus revealed nothing, the man chuckled. "Got yourself in wrong with the powers that be? Some blood on your sword, perhaps? Or some dalliance with the master's wife, hmm?"

This was not the first time Daryus had faced such questions. He was *not* like so many of the others found in the tavern. Even after five years, he could shake neither his training nor his own self. Some clients rightly saw him as a valuable addition and paid him accordingly. Others—and Daryus read in the merchant's eyes that the man was part of this second group—saw it as a way to force Daryus to take less money for more work.

A horse's annoyed snort briefly caught Daryus's attention. The animal, one of two at the head of a heavy supply wagon, shook its head and seemed to be looking for something near its front hooves.

"I can pay you . . . a modest sum. I think you'll take it, too. How about we—"

At that moment, the horse whinnied loudly, then abruptly reared. The other reacted. The wagon shook and almost tipped over.

The horses started running. Some of the onlookers nearest to the wagon panicked. Fear spread through the area as the frightened horses charged, the wagon bouncing behind them.

Unfortunately, they chose to charge at Daryus.

He shoved the merchant away from him as the horses neared. Even despite the heavy wagon, the horse came at a swift pace. Daryus had two choices: he could try to jump out of the way or try to take the horses head-on.

Most men would have attempted the former, and had even odds of surviving. The horses would also have continued on, crashing into tents and likely injuring or killing several innocents.

Instead, Daryus leapt between the two horses, using them to push himself up. Flipping into a sitting position on one, he grabbed at the loose reins for both and started pulling back as hard as he could.

Daryus was a strong man, but even he had to strain to pull the reins tight enough to force the horses' heads up. The beasts slowed.

Tugging hard on the reins of the horse to his left, Daryus forced the pair away from the nearest bystanders. At the same time, he used his body weight to add more pressure against the reins.

The animals finally slowed. Daryus brought them to a stop.

Before he could dismount, a squadron of crusaders arrived nearby. Silently cursing, Daryus slid off the opposite side. He looked for the merchant, but the man and his two bodyguards had disappeared. Daryus could only assume the merchant had seen the crusaders approaching and decided he did not want to be seen.

That still left Daryus needing a path out himself. He quickly studied his surroundings.

"Master Daryus!" Toy called from beneath him. "This way! Come this way!"

Not certain how much he could trust the familiar, Daryus nevertheless followed. However, barely had he begun to do that than the weasel paused to look back at him. "To the east! To the east!"

Although ordering Daryus to go east, Toy headed in the opposite direction. Still caught up in the incident with the runaway wagon, the crowd paid no attention to the small creature as he wended between their legs.

Hesitating only a moment, Daryus did as Toy suggested. Yet, as he headed away from the vicinity, a shout made him glance back. There, two of the crusaders stood in the process of helping their squad leader rise to his feet. The lead crusader glared at something down near his feet, something that Daryus immediately assumed to be Toy.

As if by magic—and Daryus could not help but wonder if perhaps some magic *was* involved—the weasel darted back to him.

"Hurry! Hurry! They will not see you if you hurry!"

Seeing no reason to argue, Daryus pressed on. In moments, they left sight of the patrol.

Pausing, Daryus looked back. A curse escaped him. He could still make out no sign of his potential employer.

"They were asking about pitborn," the familiar suddenly said. "They were asking about pitborn who were near your dwelling, Master Daryus! It had to be done!"

"What do you—" Daryus frowned. "Toy, did you do something to frighten the horses?"

Toy's ears flattened. "For good reason! It was done for—"

"You could have gotten someone killed! And you also cost me the client we need!"

"But I have another! I have another! A better one! You could not trust that other one! Look! See? There she comes now!"

Stifling his anger, Daryus looked to where the weasel indicated. He saw a small woman in coat and breeches impatiently pushing through the crowds. Despite her stature, she somehow managed to make men nearly as massive as Daryus move out of her way.

"Who is she?"

"Better is the question—why have you not yet followed her?"

Daryus started to say something, then realized he now had no real choice but to do as Toy suggested. Gritting his teeth, he spun from the familiar and hurried after the short woman.

Unlike her, Daryus had trouble wending his way through the crowds. It was not that they tried to be in his way, just that she seemed to have the ability to make a path for herself that he couldn't imitate. All he could do was try to keep her in sight, a difficult enough task considering that many of those between them were taller than the woman.

Then, to his surprise, they left the market and headed into the very quarter from which he had come. Daryus considered Toy's suggestion and wondered if the woman planned to find a sword for hire in one of the taverns he frequented.

The crowds quickly thinned out here. Worse, the remaining figures they passed grew of a more and more unsavory nature. The woman seemed not care, though. She passed the first tavern without even pausing.

Shadows created by the nearby buildings began to offer several places where an unsuspecting visitor could find her throat cut. Once again, though, the woman continued on without evident fear. Daryus saw she wore a short sword and some other weapon on her belt. He had no doubt she could use them, but still, in height, weight, and reach, she was at a great disadvantage.

When she passed the second tavern on their trek, Daryus grimaced. If he had to make a calculated guess, she was heading for none other than the Crimson Hammer. Daryus realized that he might have been better off simply waiting there for an employer.

However, when the tavern came into sight, Daryus's quarry surprised him by not only ignoring the establishment . . . but also taking a turn that would lead her past his *home*.

His grimace widening, Daryus cut the gap between them by half. He now had no idea just where she intended to go. There was one more tavern in the vicinity, but only the most wary went there.

And then, the young woman surprised him one last time, turning to a different street, a street Daryus knew very well. He was no longer surprised when, a few yards later, she turned to the lone door.

His door.

5

A PACT MADE

Shiera had known for some time that she was being followed. She had actually expected it in this part of the city. Taking such a risk had been necessary to find someone who could fulfill her needs for the expedition.

Her original plan had been to go to one of the inns and taverns known among fellow Pathfinders as a ready source of bodyguards willing to do anything and keep silent about it so long as they were paid. Venture-Captain Gwinn had utilized such establishments for his own expeditions.

She had posed the suggestion to Raffan, who had surprised her by making a suggestion of his own.

"My patron . . . he's considered this for some time, and had me investigate some possibilities. There is one in particular he thinks would be a viable choice."

Shiera had only shrugged. So long as she remained in charge of the expedition, she had been willing to take the ever-anxious Raffan's suggestion. Of course, Shiera had every intention of being the final judge when it came to whether or not this hire, one Daryus Gaunt, would become part of her work.

As she neared the single door, Shiera kept her hand near her short sword. She had trained long and hard to use the blade, as well as the more complicated weapon at her side.

Still focusing her attention on her nearing stalker, Shiera knocked twice on the weathered door. There was no answer.

Raffan had suggested this time of day to better locate Daryus Gaunt without having to enter one of the taverns. Raffan didn't want to draw extra attention to their efforts, and since his master was footing the expedition, Shiera chose to humor him.

She tried once more, acting nonchalant so that her would-be attacker remained ignorant of the fact that she was prepared for him. When Daryus Gaunt still did not come to the door, Shiera gave the stalker three more steps . . . then spun and drew her sword with one smooth movement.

Despite her initial confidence, she had to admit that she could not have predicted the tall, scarred, and lightly bearded figure standing just out of range. Shiera guessed that he could lift her up with one hand, though she was probably faster.

"One step closer and I'll gut you," she warned.

"What do you want with me?"

At first, his question made no sense. Then understanding dawned. "You—you're Daryus Gaunt?"

"I am."

She lowered the sword, but did not sheathe it. "You're for hire as a bodyguard?"

The hint of some expression appeared and disappeared. Despite its brevity, Shiera recognized it. The burly man had looked *relieved*, almost as if he'd thought she had come here for a different reason.

"I am for hire, yes."

"You were recommended by someone as honest and skilled," she went on. "They say if I make a pact with you, you'll fulfill it to the letter."

"'They' say a quite a lot. I should speak with them sometime about that—who they are and why they know so much about me."

Shiera ignored him. "I'm a Pathfinder. I need a strong, trusted arm to ride with me into the Worldwound. Just him and me. Knowing that, are you still for hire?"

Daryus shrugged. "I've journeyed the Worldwound more than once and survived. If you insist on going in there, pay my price and I'll do my best to help you do the same."

"How kind of you." Something moved by man's boots. At first, Shiera took it for some huge, pale rat. "What is that?"

The creature took up a position just in front of Daryus. Only then did Shiera see that it was a weasel with one eye shut tight.

"That is Toy," Daryus finally answered with some sudden frustration. "If he bothers you, feel free to use that weapon on him—"

"No. No, he doesn't bother me at all." Although she had no time for pets, Shiera did like animals—something Daryus's tone indicated that he did not share with her. That made it odd that he would have any sort of pet in the first place.

The mercenary tapped his shoulder. Toy immediately scurried up the man's leg and torso. The weasel curled around Daryus's neck. Curiously, Shiera noted again that Daryus did not appear pleased with the arrangement.

Daryus gestured at the door. "Inside."

From anyone else, even a guard she was hiring, Shiera would have taken such a curtly spoken offer with caution. Still, Raffan had told her a few more things about Daryus that made her feel safe joining him.

He led her to the lone chair in his tiny quarters. At a glance, Shiera noted there was nothing permanent about Daryus's abode, no real sign the man actually lived here. There were no personal effect, no clutter. There were a few bits of food and a couple of bottles of cheap wine, but they only added to the sense that the man before her only slept here while he waited to be somewhere else.

"Sit," he ordered.

She realized she'd been hesitating about sitting. Obeying, Shiera noted each dangerous creak. The table and the chair were so old that anywhere else they would have been thrown in a fire or a trash pit. She marveled that a man as large as Daryus could use them without them breaking apart.

He leaned on the wall behind the table. "How much are you offering?"

"Don't you want to hear exactly where we're going?"

"You're going into the Worldwound. That's all that matters where the price is concerned. You plan to leave soon?"

"In two days, if possible. This will be a small expedition. I want to move fast and lightly. I'm searching for—"

He cut her off with the wave of his hand. "Some great artifact. All of you Pathfinders are always looking for some great artifact. How much?"

Biting back a retort, Shiera named a low price.

He grunted. "Food provided?" When she nodded, he grunted again. "Done."

He needs to get out of the city, Shiera finally understood. *Badly.*

At some point, Toy had slipped from his master's shoulder. Now, Shiera discovered the weasel nestled near her feet. He peered up at her with his one open eye. She wondered what had happened to the poor animal's other eye.

"He's fine," Daryus said, as if reading her thoughts. "Am I to pick out our gear? Where do we meet?"

Somewhat defiantly, Shiera leaned down and patted Toy on the head. The weasel nestled his head in her palm until she withdrew it. "Everything else will be handled. I just need you to be there when we need to leave. Do you have a horse?"

"I did. I don't."

Shiera had a hard time trying to figure out if Daryus had some strange sense of humor or just answered things very bluntly. "Find one. It'll belong to the expedition, but I want you to have an animal you trust. I've learned that works best."

He nodded. "I'll need half now, then."

Without hesitation, she pulled free the pouch in which she kept the money Raffan had already paid her and pulled out the necessary amount. Shiera offered it to Daryus, but he nodded for her to just set it on the table. As she set the coins down, Shiera surreptitiously studied her new bodyguard. His eyes were not on her, but rather the coins. Unlike any other sword for hire, Daryus peered at the payment as if it were some foul thing. Daryus did not want to accept the gold, but had to do so.

That brought to mind the most intriguing thing that Raffan had told her about the mercenary. Well . . . that and the fact that he supposedly had elven blood going back a couple of generations. Shiera imagined that she saw the latter in his eyes and a bit in the shape of his face.

"You look to be a man worthy of his oath," Shiera began as she sealed the money pouch. She decided to broach what Raffan hinted might be a delicate subject. "Someone who keeps it as strongly as a *crusader* might."

He rewarded her with a severe narrowing of his eyes. "I keep my oath, yes."

"The crusaders—"

Without warning, he turned to the door. "Do you need me before our departure?"

"No, but—"

Gaze turned from her, Daryus opened the door. "I'll meet you by the Woundward gate at sunrise in two days. The money you left. I'm going to spend it on the supplies and pack animals we need for the expedition. It'll be better that way. There are some things even you as a Pathfinder might not realize we'll need. You can pay me back when we see each other. Agreed?"

Seeing that she had overstepped where his past was concerned, Shiera rose and simply replied, "Yes. Thank you. That would make things simpler on my end."

"I'll have everything ready. You have my . . . *oath.*"

He stood silent after that. Shiera moved past him and stepped through the open way. She was not surprised when the door shut right behind her.

Well, that was interesting, Shiera thought as she moved through the quarter. Curiously, she felt no uncertainty about Daryus. Whatever his troubles, Shiera believed he would indeed stand by his word.

She had nearly left the seedy area when she felt she was again being followed. Yet this time, there was something odd about whoever tracked her. They had such a light touch to their walk that only by the sheerest chance had she heard the movement. Even then, Shiera had not been certain at first.

She casually let her hand slip near her sword. This time, she had no intention of hesitating. Whoever was following her now had to be doing so for nefarious reasons. Certainly, Daryus Gaunt would not be trailing her again.

Shiera turned a corner. As she did, she drew the short sword and spun to face her foe.

Her sword met air.

For a moment, Shiera was baffled. Then, she realized there *was* someone on her trail . . . someone much tinier than she had been expecting.

Daryus's pet weasel twitched his nose at her. Toy trotted back and forth, acting more like an eager puppy than what Shiera would have expected of one of his kind.

"Go home!" she ordered quietly. "Go!"

Toy scampered in a circle, returning to his original spot. His one open eye seemed to twinkle.

"Go back to your master! He'll be missing you."

Toy remained where he was.

Feeling somewhat foolish, Shiera sheathed her sword. She waved her hand toward the weasel, but he simply scampered back and forth a bit.

Exasperated, Shiera turned and continued on. Not at all to her surprise, she heard the light steps behind her.

Shiera paused. Looking over her shoulder, she muttered, "I said *go home*."

This time, Toy blinked, then, with some hesitation, started back. Shiera watched the weasel, making certain he continued on. Only when Toy finally vanished into the darkness did she at last renew her journey.

However, even then, Shiera stopped a short distance later to check again. This time, there was no sign of the weasel.

Chuckling, Shiera left. Her mind began racing. Her expedition was coming together so quickly. It was almost as if the gods favored her decision.

Peering out of the darkness at the Pathfinder's retreating back, Toy quietly chuckled, then pursued.

For Shiera, the two days passed quickly and yet much too slowly at the same time. There was so much to do that she had not considered. Even so, it was all Shiera could do to keep from rushing to the Woundward gate and waiting impatiently for Daryus to arrive with the supplies and the mounts.

But as the time finally neared and an anxious Shiera neared the gate astride her favored gray gelding, she encountered a surprise. There, seated on a horse and looking around with exasperation, was none other than Raffan. The moment he saw her, a sense of relief spread over his youthful face.

"Praise be! When you sent the note saying you were planning to depart two days hence, I expected you to be here well before dawn!"

"I intended that, too, but got delayed by a few things . . . but what are you doing here?"

"In his wisdom," Raffan began, the last word said with a touch of uncertainty, "my master has decided that for the sake of his interests, I should go along with you."

It was not an idea that appealed to Shiera, nor did it seem that Raffan liked it any better. He was clearly not someone who had labored hard physically. Still, Shiera decided that if the man wanted to simply sit somewhere and let her work, she could live with that.

"Ah! Praise be!" Raffan repeated, this time glancing beyond her. He looked even more relieved.

Shiera looked behind her. She expected Daryus, but instead beheld four rather unsavory men clad in brown and black. The lead rider had a long, narrow beard and a brow so thick his eyes were barely visible until he raised his head slightly to look at the pair.

"Captain Galifar," he rumbled to her. The other three men did not speak.

"Shiera Tristane," she responded, hiding her concern.

"I decided that the three of us alone can hardly journey into the Worldwound," Raffan informed her. "Fortunately, I was able to quickly retain the services of the good captain here. It was like a miracle. He came across me as we both sought to enter the tavern where I hoped to find sellswords. The captain had just finished another contract. Isn't that timely?"

Returning her gaze to Raffan, Shiera carefully answered, "When moving through the Worldwound, a small party is the safest bet. Larger parties get noticed easily. We don't want that. With too many of us—"

"Of course," Raffan interrupted, indicating the captain. "That's why I'm relying on the expert skills of Galifar and his men. They are well qualified and should prove sufficient. I did consider hiring an *entire* squadron, and still *could*—"

"Captain Galifar and his men will do *just* fine." As she said that, Shiera heard the officer—if indeed Galifar was one—snigger. She started to glare at him . . . only to find the reason for his amusement perched behind her.

Toy wrinkled his nose at Shiera. She tried to be annoyed, failed, and instead searched for the weasel's master. To her puzzlement, Daryus was nowhere to be seen.

Raffan picked up on her action. "Where's this man *you* hired? Does he need to sleep off a drunk, or will he be here soon?"

"He'll be here."

"You wrote that you let him handle the supplies. Are you certain he just didn't run off?"

Before she could say anything, Daryus rode into view. Never had Shiera been so grateful for someone's arrival. Not only did he clearly have the necessary supplies, as evinced by two fully loaded mules following Daryus's mount, but he also guided an extra horse. If he had done all that with the money she had given him, then he was a shrewd negotiator.

As he approached, Shiera noted how his gaze took in Raffan, the captain, and the other mercenaries. Although she doubted any of them could see it, Shiera was fairly certain Daryus was no more pleased with the additions to their expedition than she was.

"Sorry for being late," he rumbled. "Took a little longer to get the extra horse. Always good to have a spare."

"Well, glad we're all here now." Raffan sniffed. "Captain, if you'll lead the way."

Shiera started. "Raffan, it would make more sense if I, or even Daryus, who's familiar with the Worldwound, took the lead—"

"Oh, assuredly. Once we're *in* the Worldwound. Until then, I think it's best if the captain heads the party."

"Seems reasonable," Daryus murmured, much to Shiera's surprise. "I'll take the rear."

For some reason, this choice did not sit well with Captain Galifar's men. The captain himself kept his expression neutral, but Shiera suspected he was no more happy. Clearly none of the four trusted Daryus.

Raffan, meanwhile, looked oblivious to the situation. He sniffed again, then commented, "Well, that's settled, then. Shall we begin, Captain?"

Galifar nodded. With a wave, he gestured his men forward. One joined the captain, while the other pair flanked Raffan protectively.

Daryus rode up beside her. "Your word is the final one as far as I'm concerned."

"It was his master's money. That makes him in charge."

"It was you who convinced me to come. If he'd been the one seeking me out, I'd have found another way."

He did not clarify, instead slowing his mount so as to take his position at the rear. Even though she could no longer see him, Shiera discovered she felt much more secure now that he was there. It was an odd feeling—being glad there was someone else literally at her back—but Shiera chalked it up to the trek ahead. The Pathfinder thought herself a good enough judge to believe that Daryus was more than equal to the four men Raffan had hired.

Captain Galifar led them through the Woundward gate. A shiver ran through the Pathfinder—not of fear, but of anticipation.

From the Worldwound, the lost temple-city—and the mysterious Eye—beckoned her like a lover.

6

WHIRLWIND JOURNEY

Although he gave no sign of it, Daryus did not relax until he was well past the heavy wooden gate and the crusaders guarding it. Each moment, he had expected someone to recognize him, but no one did.

Yet, with his own situation of less significance now, Daryus's guilt concerning Shiera Tristane grew. He hoped he had not involved her in more than she expected.

His gaze fixed on Toy, who sat atop the back of the Pathfinder's saddle as if he had been her pet all his life. Despite the familiar's earlier entreaties, Daryus did not completely trust the weasel. Toy tried too hard to ingratiate himself. The creature was up to something, but exactly what, Daryus could not say.

However, what he did trust was that whoever had sent the pitborn assassins into a crusader stronghold was someone with ill intent for more than merely an escaped familiar. The witch—Grigor Dolch, if Daryus remembered the name correctly from Toy's rambling explanations—was likely everything Toy had portrayed him as. After revealing his monstrous eye, Toy had gone on to describe the tortures Dolch had inflicted upon him, tortures culminating in the demonic orb.

Now that he was safe from discovery by his old order, Daryus considered carefully the options open to him. Toy had insisted that Dolch would see the mercenary as an enemy since Daryus had interfered with the familiar's slaughter. According to the weasel, the assassins would have already marked Daryus. Indeed, they probably even believed that he had been in some alliance with the familiar even before the incident.

Again, Daryus could not deny Toy's suggestion. Witches—*most* spellcasters, in fact, at least in his experience—had a tendency to remove anything they thought remotely an obstacle to their goals. Moreover, the same traits that had made Daryus a good crusader now demanded that he perform his duty and remove the threat of the witch. The witch was evil. Evil had to be crushed—

Trying to push such thoughts to the far recesses of his mind, Daryus shifted his attention to the other bodyguards. It was clear that the only one who would receive their protection was Raffan, but Daryus wasn't concerned about that. He had seen the likes of Captain Galifar and his followers. They might be skilled, but they were the type willing to change allegiances immediately if the money was worth it.

The sky was mercifully clear, the weather cool but quiet. The party made good headway as it headed to the river crossing to the north, moving well ahead of the pace Daryus had expected. If the weather remained on their side over the next few days, he estimated it would not take long to reach the point where they'd enter the Worldwound.

The Worldwound. Daryus had tried not to think much about the demon-blighted land, but now, without warning, memories suddenly stirred. A terrified family. Several dour crusaders. Swords coming down. *Daryus's* sword coming down.

He shook his head to clear it. At the same time, Toy sat up as if sensing something.

Peering around, Daryus saw nothing out of the ordinary. Once more, his thoughts returned to Toy and Grigor Dolch. Exactly how he might deal with the witch, he still could not say. He wasn't even sure that—

The wind shifted. The change was so abrupt—at least to Daryus—that he immediately turned to see to protecting Shiera. As he did, he also noticed something amiss.

The weasel had vanished from his perch on the saddle.

Certain that Toy's vanishing could not be taken as a good sign, Daryus put one hand on the hilt of his sword. What he could do with it against the wind, he did not know. Still, doing so made him feel a little more secure . . . at least until the wind more than doubled.

Now everyone noticed it. Raffan struggled with his suddenly wary mount. Captain Galifar grunted something to his men, but it was lost in the abrupt howling of the violent gale. Shiera did the wise thing and planted herself against the back of her horse's neck.

A burst of wind caught Raffan's long cloak, winding it around him as if it were a constrictor. The young man gasped, then fell from his horse.

Dust erupted from the party's left. It spilled into the eyes of Galifar's men, blinding them.

Keeping his head low and his eyes slits, Daryus covered the rest of his face as he urged his hesitant mount toward the Pathfinder. Cutting the gap proved troublesome; his horse did not want to move about in the hellish wind that Daryus felt certain was an effect of the nearby Worldwound. Still, with much coaxing to his mount, he slowly fought his way to Shiera.

She, meanwhile, had not remained idle. Shiera had wrapped her own travel cloak around her as best she could, like Daryus, avoiding being blinded in the process. As Daryus came up behind her, she started to slide off her animal.

"Stay on!" Daryus ordered. He understood that she had planned to walk her horse to somewhere both could hunker down, but Daryus expected he could guide the animals better. Already under his steady control, the mules and extra mount followed obediently.

Shiera's horse calmed as Daryus reached the Pathfinder. Dismounting, Daryus reached to Shiera. "Hand me the reins! I know the best place—

A gust at least three times stronger than any previous buffeted both of them. Instead of handing over the reins as both intended, Shiera fell from her horse.

Daryus barely caught her, now half-blind from dust despite his best attempts. He quickly set her on her feet.

"Where did this wind come from?" she shouted.

"We're near the Worldwound! The land itself is drenched in demonic magic, and sometimes it spills over!" Still, despite that obvious explanation, a part of Daryus could not help briefly wondering if the witch were responsible, if only due to Toy's seeming prescience. Of course, the Worldwound was dangerous enough—it needed no help from any spellcaster.

Shiera nodded agreement. "Where do we go?"

"There's a rise just ahead! We'll guide the animals over there!"

"What about Raffan and the others?"

Daryus wanted to say that they could fend for themselves, but, in truth, he could no more leave them than he could her. "We'll move past Raffan and help him follow! Galifar should be able to handle his men!"

Yet no sooner had he said that than the wind increased again. The abruptness of it nearly threw him off his feet. Shiera just managed to grab her horse's bit. Even then, her feet briefly left the ground.

Struggling back to his own mount, Daryus regained control of the anxious animal, then started to lead it and the other animals alongside Shiera and her horse. Shiera positioned herself to make the best of the protection of both her steed and Daryus.

Shielding his gaze, Daryus searched the path ahead for the best route to the rise. Out of the corner of his eye, he thought he could make out movement that might have been Toy. Daring to glance that way, the former crusader saw nothing but vague hints of the wind-wracked terrain.

"It's gotten worse! I can't see more than a couple of yards!" Shiera shouted.

"We need to get to the rise quickly!" Daryus roared back. "Do you see your friend anywhere?"

She pointed to their left. "I think—yes! There's Raffan!"

So much dust and refuse now flew about that Daryus himself could only see the other man's general shape. However, after a few more steps, he made out Raffan, his cloak still wrapped around him, now clinging to the side of his horse.

Daryus spat out dirt. "Can you take the reins of my horse?"

She did not hesitate. "Yes!"

Handing them to her, Daryus pushed toward Raffan. The other man remained still, enabling Daryus to reach him faster.

Raffan tried to speak, but could only cough. Indeed, all he seemed to do was cough, over and over. Daryus pointed at the rise, then took the reins of the man's steed. Keeping Raffan close to him, Daryus headed on a path that would lead them to both the rise and Shiera.

Shiera nodded as they joined her. Daryus left Raffan in her hands, then reluctantly paused to look for Captain Galifar and the others.

Instead, a pair of dark eyes stared back at him from the storm—a pair of dark eyes with nothing else around them.

He stiffened as the eyes snared him. A voice cultured but cold, muttered one word.

Toy . . .

Immediately, every memory that Daryus had of the familiar coursed through his mind, even up to the last time he had seen the weasel in the storm. Try as he might, Daryus could not keep the images from repeating over and over.

There was no doubt at all in him that these were the eyes of the witch, Grigor Dolch.

"Daryus!" Shiera shook him violently. The eyes in the storm vanished. The memories sank back into the recesses of his mind.

As he recovered, Daryus focused on the fact that the Pathfinder was with him. "What're you doing here? You should be with Raffan and the animals!"

"Captain Galifar joined us! I let him lead Raffan and the beasts to safety! I saw you standing in the windstorm, staring at nothing!"

Nothing? Daryus took one last glance at the spot where the eyes had been. He could see no trace, but clearly the storm indicated that Dolch remained a presence in the area.

Shiera slipped her arm around his waist and pulled him toward the rise. Daryus embraced her as well, pressing tight together to cut resistance to the storm. The faint shape of the rise beckoned. Ahead of them, the silhouettes of horses, mules, and men revealed that Captain Galifar and Raffan had nearly reached their destination.

"This storm is not natural!" Shiera managed. "I saw no wind in the distance!"

Daryus only grunted. He wasn't certain just how much he should tell her.

With effort, they finally managed to reach the others. To Daryus's surprise, it was Captain Galifar who came to help them the last few feet.

"Get behind the middle of the rise!" the mercenary growled. "Safest spot!"

They joined the others where Galifar suggested. The wind continued to race. It strength was such that branches and other large bits of debris went flying by with deadly potential. Daryus had every suspicion that if Toy had been anywhere visible, one or more of those larger pieces would have struck the familiar hard enough to kill.

Something tangled Daryus's legs. Only Shiera kept him from falling. As he looked down, Toy innocently met his gaze.

Daryus had some choice words for the weasel, but kept them buried inside. The one-eyed creature scrambled up the back of Shiera's horse, once more settling down on the rear of the saddle.

Galifar returned to his men and Raffan. Daryus and Shiera planted themselves close to the horses and waited.

The wind died. It simply ceased to exist. Debris already in the air spilled over the hapless party.

The sky cleared. For a moment, the group stood frozen, the former crusader especially wary about the wind's possible return. However, after a long hesitation, Daryus and the rest finally began moving about.

"What was that?" Raffan muttered. "Where did that come from?"

"Just a bit of freak weather," Galifar offered as he joined them. "Seen it before." He chuckled. "A touch of the Worldwound, that's all."

"'Freak weather.'" Raffan hmmphed. "'Freak weather,' he says."

Daryus eyed Toy, who rested on the saddle as if nothing had happened. To the others, Daryus suggested, "There's not much light left. We should set up camp here."

"Ridiculous!" Raffan blurted. "Anything that gets us closer to our goal in the least time possible is welcome! We can't afford to lose time due to this."

"With all due respect, Master Raffan," Galifar interrupted. "We should stay here. Safer ground than what we'll have anywhere we can reach by nightfall."

The well-dressed young man looked peeved, but finally nodded. Galifar's men immediately went to work setting things up. Daryus did the same. Raffan seemed inclined to let others do the tasks, but to Daryus's surprise, Shiera joined in with the efforts.

"This isn't your work," he commented.

"I always set up my own site."

"The last Pathfinder I worked for had a different manner. Very different."

Shiera chuckled. "I'd probably know the name if I heard it."

Daryus shook his head. "He paid me. I owe him that much loyalty."

"You have a *really* strong sense of loyalty, then. That's not that common, even among the crusaders, I'd say."

Without thinking, Daryus brought a finger to one of the scars on his face. A particular scar. He pulled the finger away almost as soon as he touched the ruined skin.

Shiera's good humor faded. Daryus knew she had seen his reaction, but had chosen not to comment on it. Instead, she concentrated harder on her own work.

Daryus bit back a curse. In the city, he had been able to drink just that right amount to keep the memories at bay. When hired, he was usually too busy staying alert to think of them, either. Now, though, despite the threat of Toy's former master, the memories had returned for a second time. Daryus had hoped that the brief surge he had experienced just prior to the windstorm had been a one-time event. Now, he worried they might *keep* coming back.

At that moment, Toy inserted himself into their work. The weasel did not go to Daryus, but rather Shiera. She smiled as she paused to pet the animal, clearly unaware of its true identity.

"He's a clever fellow, isn't he?" she commented as she scratched Toy's head. "Glad he returned to you after he tried to follow me home."

Daryus managed to keep from visually stiffening upon hearing this. "When was that?"

"When I hired you, naturally. He followed me for some distance. I should've kept him with me until the next day and brought him back, but for some reason I was certain he would have no trouble surviving the run back to your home."

"No . . . no trouble at all. He's quite the survivor, Toy is."
Daryus threw himself into his work. The less opportunity he had
to speak, the less opportunity he had of saying too much.

Shiera suddenly frowned. "I've just thought of something I
need to discuss with Raffan. I won't be long."

"Do as you need. This is your expedition."

She rose and headed off. Toy started after her, but Daryus,
waiting for this moment, grabbed the weasel by the tail. With a
squeak, the familiar looked back.

"You have explaining to do," the fighter whispered. "If you
want to keep on 'surviving.'"

"Master Daryus is swift, so very swift—"

"Spare me the compliments! You knew what was about to
happen! You gave no warning!"

"No, Master Daryus, no! Toy made a mistake! Opened the eye
for just a moment, just to see something! Sensed the witch seeking
me out and shut it again!"

"So Dolch found us because you—"

"No!" The familiar insisted. "It's you! He searched through
you!"

"How could he do that? And did he create this storm?"

"Nay! The witch, he is powerful, but not so! He sensed my
mistake, but it's you he found! The assassins, they surely found
a way to mark you, and now Master Grigor, he knows you! He
knows you and hunts you as I warned—"

The familiar's voice grew too loud for Daryus's tastes. He
shook the tail hard. "Quiet!"

He heard Shiera speak. Instinct made him glance her way.
As Daryus did that, his grip loosened just the slightest . . . but it
was enough for Toy. The weasel wriggled free, scampered a short
distance away, then turned to look at him again.

"We must beware . . ." the creature said, just barely audible.
"Master Grigor will try again. Very soon."

With that, Toy trotted off toward Shiera.

Scowling, Daryus returned to the task of finishing shelter. A part of him cursed himself for answering the call for help and then listening to the familiar's warning that the witch would be after Daryus as well. Yet, another part of him realized that, in truth, he had been looking for an excuse for more than just an escape from the city. Daryus knew that he had been searching for more purpose than merely being a hired sword, a purpose closer to his former calling, one that might give him some measure of redemption.

Yet now . . . As Daryus glanced at Toy near Shiera, he wondered if, for the second time, he had made a decision that would have dire repercussions not only for himself, but for everyone around him. Worse, if he understood the weasel, at some point in the struggle with the assassins, one of them had marked him, and now, with effort, the witch could track them wherever they went because of *Daryus*.

Trying not to think what that might mean, Daryus threw himself into his work. He had just completed things when Shiera—watched from a distance by Toy—returned. Her troubled expression immediately set him on edge. "What is it?"

"Raffan's lost some valuable equipment, and some of our own supplies are missing from the mules. They must have slipped off in the storm."

Standing, the former crusader peered back in the direction they had come. There was no sign of any of the articles nearby. Daryus considered hunting for them, but knew the odds of finding much. He berated himself for not having noticed the losses during the storm.

"Let me retrace out trail. I won't be long."

She exhaled in relief. "Do you want me to come with?"

"No, I know where we went. I'll be right back."

Daryus mounted his horse and rode back. His expert eyes scoured the trail, seeking any of the missing supplies.

Curiously, though, other than one small pack half-buried in dust and dirt, the only other evidence of their lost supplies was a water sack whose contents had spilled into the soil. Daryus dismounted, then inspected the area around the water sack.

A few prints and a brief furrow in the ground was all he needed to verify his suspicions. This near the Worldwound, there were all sorts of scavengers eager for whatever meals they could find. Many had very sharp senses of smell. It hardly mattered that they had also dragged off the other articles in the process.

Exasperated, he rode back. Shiera met him at the edge of camp.

"You didn't find anything?"

"Scavengers already had just about everything. Probably a pack. Had that happen once, but these must've been nearby. They were very thorough."

She swore, using epithets that made him flush. "Can we follow them?"

"I tried. I suspect they've dragged things to a burrow. The ground's too hard to leave tracks in some places and the wind covered most of the rest."

"Do we go back to Nerosyan?" Daryus asked.

"No . . . no. This only makes my decision easier, I suppose. While we were riding earlier, I remembered the libraries in Kenabres. There were some scrolls I looked over the last time I was there that I now realize had some potential links to the artifact Raffan showed me. This should actually help shorten our quest . . . I hope."

A sense of unease filled Daryus at mention of the other city. He had surveyed a map after agreeing to the contract with Shiera and knew that choices were limited from here. He also knew which choice he preferred, no matter how it might sound to Shiera. "We can cut straight into a secondary route that'll take us to—"

She cut him off with a shake of her head. "No, the more I think about this, the more it might be a blessing in disguise. I'll get the map and show you—"

"No need. I know where we're heading."

"Yes. You would, I guess." She paused, as if waiting for him to say something. When he did not, the Pathfinder continued, "Captain Galifar is starting food, such as it is. It doesn't look like much, but it should fill our bellies."

After a moment's hesitation, he answered, "I'll be along soon."

With a nod, she left.

Absently rubbing the one scar, Daryus grimaced. He caught a glimpse of Toy now observing *him*. Daryus immediately lowered his hand, but the memories had already begun to stir. The swords coming down. The frightened, not quite human faces. The grim aspects of several helmed crusaders.

Daryus considered stealing a horse in the middle of night, but knew he would not abandon Shiera. She had paid him to protect her while she searched, and he would do that.

No, despite his misgivings, he would ride with the party to Kenabres. He knew if he returned there, discovery by those he had betrayed was all but certain.

A city that was the heart and soul of the Order of the Flaming Lance, the order to which he had once belonged and which he had betrayed.

The order that still sought to hunt Daryus down for his transgressions.

7

THE WOLF

It was all Grigor could do to keep on his feet after the spellwork. Drained beyond the limits of normal men, he leaned heavily on the staff. He thrust the dried eye into the pouch from which he had drawn it.

The assassin had indeed marked the human who had aided Toy, but it had been Toy's mistake of opening his demon eye that had drawn Grigor's attention. When that trace had vanished again, the witch had used the prize from his pouch to locate the man, a fool of a mercenary Grigor now knew was named Daryus Gaunt. Grigor had nearly insinuated himself in the man's mind, but then something had broken the link. Still, the witch had some idea now just who and what had allied itself with the familiar.

Panting, Grigor forced himself straight. It would not do for the pitborn to see him so weak. They were kept in order through a combination of gold, fear, and the promises of what they would share in once he found the tomb. However, if they thought him too weak to achieve that goal, they might abandon him for better prospects. That would just not do. The witch still needed them, at least for the time being.

The windstorm had not been his creation—such grand power spread over so great a distance was beyond him—but rather just one example of the Worldwound's unpredictability. However, it had provided him with enough chaos and distraction to nearly enable his efforts to break through the mercenary's primitive mental barriers. Next time, Grigor swore, the man would have no reprieve. Whatever he knew, the witch would know.

After that, Toy's fool of a puppet would be disposable.

Grigor frowned as a sudden fear overtook him, interrupting his thoughts concerning the mercenary. Removing his glove, he gingerly touched his cheek. The flesh felt dry, but still pliable. Thus far, his latest spellwork had not taken any toll.

Reassured, Grigor briefly considered the weasel's puppet again. The man who had rescued Toy—the *fool* who had rescued the familiar—had proven of relatively strong will, but there had been no hint of any magical abilities. He was as he appeared, a simple sword hand. No concern at all for the witch.

Grigor stalked over to where the tomb was being looted. The pitborn currently at work had set up quite a pile of ancient artifacts for the witch to study. As he had expected, most of them had no use save as possibly a source of magical energy. It was doubtful he could gain much, but anything to keep him going until he corrected matters was welcome.

"Rubbish. Nothing but rubbish," he declared to the cowering pitborn near the pile. "But tell your comrades that if one of them touches anything before I say otherwise, they'll be a cinder."

"Yes, Master!"

Some of the items had gold and jewels in them, but although Grigor could have used those to help keep the pitborn pliable, the witch intended to destroy most of them. Things taken from a tomb, even a tomb whose guardian Grigor had already destroyed, might still have residues of whatever curses the ancients might have put on the place. The witch wanted to take no chance that—

Grigor Dolch suddenly faced Grigor Dolch.

Barely stifling a cry, he stumbled back as his sallow face gaped back. There before him, he beheld the features of a handsome young exile of noble—if unacknowledged—blood. Young, if one did not look too close and see the crisscrossing lines. Handsome, if one did not notice the parchmentlike quality of the flesh and unliving glitter of the eyes.

The witch struck out with the staff, sending the reflection flying to the side with a loud clang. The two pitborn carrying the old ceremonial shield fell back in abject terror.

Still filled with both rage and fear, Grigor swung the staff hard at the nearest servant. The rat's-head top proved far stronger than the pitborn's skull. With a crack, the staff sent the unfortunate servant tumbling in a bloody heap.

Grigor shook the blood angrily from the staff. He glared at the second pitborn, who was already on his knees. The servant's scaled face was devoid of hope. Grigor eyed the pathetic thing for a moment, then, snarling, continued on into the tomb.

The silence of the ancient edifice enabled him to come to grips with his emotions again. The pitborn had long-standing orders to obscure, hide, or cover any large reflective surface they came across. The witch swore he would slay every one of his servants if it took them that long to remember one simple, clear rule.

He came across another pitborn, this one immediately prostrating himself before the witch. Any of Grigor's servants in the tomb had surely heard the latest scream. They would realize their master would be in a foul mood. It bespoke of their great eagerness to share in his future glory that they risked his deadly ire. Grigor had promised them much. Very much.

And with the power he knew he would obtain, he could give them all he had promised and more . . . if only they learned to obey to the letter.

"Get out of here!" Grigor ordered.

The horned and tailed creature leapt to his feet and scurried past.

It did not take long for Grigor to reach the main chamber. The tomb was a compact one, as had been common among the people the witch researched. Some civilizations built great structures that were promptly robbed or razed to the ground. Others, the more clever ones, made smaller, more cunning tombs that became part of the landscape, thus escaping notice for not just centuries, but millennia.

The sepulcher was also a simple one, a stone sarcophagus with little ornamentation the focal point. Grigor walked up to the now-empty coffin and peered inside. With the tomb's occupant gone, little about the actual resting place interested him. The priest or witch—given the builders of this tomb, the occupant's actual calling was a bit questionable—was not the ultimate reason for which this structure had been built, but rather merely a component of it. Indeed, if Grigor's readings of the old texts were correct, it could not technically even be called a tomb, the man within having actually been sacrificed on this spot so he could guard whatever secret the ancient edifice held.

Grigor wiped away dust from the back wall. He grinned. *There* was the symbol for which he had been looking. The great wolf head peered to the left, the one eye visible narrowed as if the beast were in the midst of a hunt. Grigor Dolch followed the wolf's gaze to the wall on the left. There, he saw nothing but more dust.

He wiped away the dust there. Markings lining up with the wolf's eye caught Grigor's attention. Unfortunately, they were of a different script than that which he had studied. Try as he might, Grigor could make no sense of them.

He swore, then raised the staff. Fortunately, sense returned to him before he could waste valuable power. Instead of a spell, he dismissed the staff and produced parchment and charcoal from a pouch at his belt. The ancient builders had been good enough to carve the arching words into the wall, which made his task easier. Rubbing the charcoal over the parchment, he reproduced the script.

Taking one last glance at the ancient writing, Grigor rolled up the small parchment and replaced it in the pouch.

Something at the edge of his vision caught his attention. He turned back to the image of the wolf.

The eye glistened.

Grigor strode over to the wolf, then leaned close to better study the eye. With the utmost caution, he gently touched it.

The click that followed was barely audible. Still, it was all the warning Grigor Dolch either needed or knew he would receive.

Spinning around, the witch darted through the tomb. As he ran, he summoned the staff.

The walls creaked. They began to close together. In touching the area, Grigor had set off a mechanism designed to trap treasure hunters. The witch paid no mind to the threat of the walls, though. He knew that the true danger would come in an unexpected form.

Sure enough, the corridor ahead of him filled with an impenetrable mist. Grigor Dolch stumbled to a halt just before reaching it. Had he been one of the pitborn, he likely would have run through the mist without thinking.

Run through it . . . and probably been left a mass of liquefied flesh and bone. This was not the first such tomb the witch had ransacked. He had lost two pitborn to just such an acidic mist, an alchemical concoction apparently popular with the civilization that had built these structures.

With the walls closing on him, Grigor spun the staff in a circle. This time, a wind *he* summoned through the staff blew open a path for him. The witch quickly let it expand, then plunged forward.

He felt the sting of acid on his face. Aware what too lengthy an exposure would mean, Grigor threw himself forward.

Landing on the other side of the mist, he wasted no time in retreating down the remainder of the corridor. He stepped out just as a great moan arose from the structure. As Grigor had expected, the tomb began collapsing in on itself. With a loud cracking of stone and hard earth, the outer structure of the tomb gave way.

The witch watched as a huge cloud of dust rose over the devastated edifice. Grigor was not bothered in the least by the loss. He had seen what he wanted to see.

A tiny, yellowed fragment of what looked like parchment drifted past his gaze. Stiffening, Grigor thrust the staff under one arm, then removed his glove. With care, he ran his fingertips across the cheek nearest to the direction from which the fragment—or rather, *flake*—had drifted.

His fingers came away with several minute pieces of dried flesh. Grigor swore at his hubris. His efforts in the tomb had had more consequence than he'd imagined.

He had but to turn to the watching pitborn to send the one assigned to guarding the amber solution scurrying. The witch took a deep, calming breath and focused on his triumphs. He had taken another vital step in his quest.

The nervous pitborn held up the container, then raised the lid so that the underside was visible to Grigor Dolch. A sharp intake of breath escaped the witch. There was now a gap in his right cheek, a gap through which hints of his cheekbone could be seen.

"Hold it steady, you fool!" Grigor liberally applied the solution to the area, working it into the crumbling skin. The dryness gave way to a pliability of which Grigor immediately made use. Reaching into the cavity created by the loss of skin, he retrieved flakes of flesh from deep inside. With deft skill, he began applying them so that they covered the hole.

The amber solution allowed the inner flesh to blend with that from the face. By the time Grigor finished, there was barely any hint of the damage.

Still, he was not satisfied. He had let overconfidence rule him. That had been what had gotten him into trouble in the first place . . . that and Toy's subsequent betrayal.

"We are done here," he informed those pitborn near enough to hear as he finished with his face. "I want the animals packed up and ready to leave within two hours."

"As you command, Master," one of the largest growled. He was Grigor's current second-in-command. The witch did not even know the demonspawn's name, and had no intention of learning it. Grigor had already executed the creature's three predecessors. If this one failed to act exactly as the witch desired, he would join them. There were many others eager to take the creature's place, however risky the station. Those who served Grigor best would reap the greatest rewards.

Such a swift departure would mean leaving some of the tomb's other treasures behind, but that was the pitborn's concern, not his. They would take what they could easily carry, nothing more. As for Grigor himself, he had no interest in riches, only the answer to his troubles and the power those answers would bring in the process.

That . . . and Toy preferably skinned alive.

His interest again on his former familiar, Grigor turned to stare in the direction he and his band would travel. The trek would be arduous—at least for the pitborn—but time was of the essence. Time . . . and the manipulation of his unsuspecting puppet.

"Anyone not ready when it is time to leave will suffer the consequences," he needlessly reminded the others. "I will see us within sight of our destination in three days. Is that understood?"

The demonspawn bowed their misshapen heads and rushed to obey. From there on, Grigor Dolch paid them no mind, his gaze focused on the path ahead.

On the path, and on the one stop on the way to his eventual glory. *Kenabres.*

8

KENABRES

Shiera exhaled as they neared the walls of Kenabres. The detour to the other city had gone without incident, but, unfortunately, at only half the pace for which she had been hoping. That, at times, had pushed her patience to the edge.

Once through the massive and aptly named Southgate entrance, the party moved quickly past the temples dedicated to patient Abadar and the more stoic Torag—two of Kenabres's patron deities—and into the Southgate Market. The clang of metal surrounded them, and the tinge of smoke and searing iron floated heavy in the air.

Yet, while Shiera was relieved to finally enter Kenabres, she noticed that Daryus was anything but pleased. The fighter had been fairly calm and steady throughout the trek, but now that he had reached the great city, he seemed even more eager to leave than he had been in Nerosyan.

The reason why became obvious the first time Shiera caught sight of a contingent of crusaders from the Flaming Lance crossing their path. Somehow, Daryus managed to maneuver behind Captain Galifar and stay clear of the marching figures until they were long gone, but it was clear that he and they had a bad history.

What did he do? Shiera's knowledge of the order—of *all* the crusader orders, really—was peripheral at best. Staunch believers—some would even say "fanatical"—willing to give their lives to achieve the world their leaders preached. In main, a force for good, but Shiera had heard rumors about overzealous members of the Flaming Lance committing troublesome acts in the name of "justice." Could Daryus have done something so awful that he'd had to escape the order?

It seemed at odds with the sort of man she had come to know on the journey thus far, but Shiera also recalled her former admiration for Amadan Gwinn. Still, she didn't care what Daryus had done so long as he kept his word as per the contract. In the end, whatever Shiera might think of Daryus, what mattered most was locating the lost temple-city.

Captain Galifar and his men spent most of their time eyeing the nearby taverns as the party rode through the thick crowds. Shiera couldn't blame them; she needed a strong drink herself after the trek. If left to her choice, she would have given them permission to go, but since Raffan had hired the band, it was his responsibility.

Raffan was his usual anxious self, the somewhat rumpled young man peering at a small notebook he had pulled from his pack. Whatever he read had his rapt attention.

She urged her mount next to Daryus. His expression shifted as he noticed her, all emotion disappearing.

"How familiar are you with Kenabres?" Shiera asked nonchalantly.

"I've been here before."

She wrinkled her nose in frustration. "Yes, that I've already gathered from your reaction to your friends who passed us by." When he stiffened at the comment, Shiera quickly shook her head. "I don't care about that. Do you know where we can find a place to hole up until we're ready to depart?"

His eyes narrowed slightly. "Aren't we leaving first thing in the morning?"

"I'd like to," she replied, shrugging. "The information I need, I should be able to gather today, but at the moment I think our actual departure depends on Raffan."

He glanced at the other man, who continued to peruse the small notebook. "He's got business here?"

"I wouldn't have thought so, but I overheard him talking to Galifar, and—"

Before Shiera could finish, Daryus urged his horse toward Raffan. The younger man looked up from his reading as Daryus neared. Raffan quickly shut the notebook and returned it to the pack.

"Is there something you wanted?" he asked Daryus with clear disdain.

"Begging your pardon, sir," Daryus responded far too respectfully for Shiera. He bowed his head. "Will we need to stay more than one night? I need to know how to house the animals."

His deferential treatment assuaged Raffan. With a nod to the fighter's "appropriate" attitude, Raffan answered, "We will need to stay for three days. My master has some contacts here I think I should locate."

"Three days? Begging your pardon again, sir, but each day we remain might risk the ultimate goal—"

"I am very aware of all aspects of this venture, my good man! Since we are here, it behooves me to make the best of the visit, and I will require two days to accomplish what I want. That includes garnering some information from these contacts that might impact our expedition in the long run. Now, that should be a sufficient answer even for you, should it not?"

Even from where she sat, Shiera could hear the utter dismissal in Raffan's tone. She watched as Daryus bowed his head, then still very respectfully turned from the younger man. However, the look on the man's scarred face as he returned to her was hardly one of satisfaction. If anything, Daryus appeared more disturbed than ever.

That look vanished when he noticed her eyeing him. Daryus took up a place beside Shiera, then whispered, "You heard?"

"How could I not? I doubt Raffan has the ability to talk below a pompous bellow. Don't think you're the only one displeased with this. If he intended this once we changed direction, why didn't he say anything until we got here?"

"It does pose an interesting question, doesn't it? I would recommend leaving tomorrow, if we can. That looks to be your desire, too. I have no say, but you might be able to convince him."

Shiera considered the matter. Raffan was relying on her knowledge and skills to find the secrets that had evaded his lord for so long. All she had to do was come up with a reason why time was of the essence.

"I think I have some notions," Shiera finally answered. "Leave it to me."

His gaze suddenly shifted to something behind her, and his mouth became a tight line.

Shiera instinctively twisted around to see what would make the stolid man react so violently.

The four cloaked and hooded forms were not merely passersby, but rather a group of crusaders clearly on a mission. Two were dour men who by comparison made Daryus seem a cheerful sort. Another was a sturdy woman with just as dark a cast as the men.

Yet, most of all, it was the apparent leader who seized Shiera's attention. Slimmer and more lithe than the other woman, she moved through the crowd with eyes constantly sweeping over each individual she passed. Shiera estimated her to be a decade or even two older than the others, but clearly fitter than most fighters half her age. A hint of pale blond hair peaked out of her hood.

The steely gray gaze took in Shiera, and the lead crusader slowed her pace long enough to study the Pathfinder. Without meaning to, Shiera swallowed anxiously, as if guilty.

The gray eyes moved on. The quartet continued through the throng, gradually fading in the distance.

Recovering, Shiera turned back to Daryus. "Who is—"

She was alone.

Swearing under her breath with a talent worthy of any of Captain Galifar's men, Shiera found no trace of her hired sword. Grunting, she chose to forgo concerning herself with Daryus and instead focus on the suggestion that he had made. Whatever her frustrations with the man, his idea still held merit.

She started after Raffan, only to have Galifar confront her before she could cover half the gap. The mercenary captain grinned. "Master Raffan has a task for you."

Shiera bristled. Raffan's employer might be paying for this expedition, but that didn't mean that Raffan could order her around like one of the mercenaries, or even Daryus. She *was* the key to the expedition's success, after all. "You must be mistaken. I don't jump at the command of anyone. I—"

Still grinning, Galifar held up a small parchment. Shiera recognized it as identical in make to the pages in Raffan's small book. "Maybe he said 'request.' Maybe."

Shiera no longer listened to him. Instead, she fixated on the symbol that someone had drawn in the center of the page. The hand had evidently been shaking, perhaps from great age, but had still retained the skill to make a very good image.

A one-eyed wolf peering to the left. That in itself would have been enough to catch the Pathfinder's interest, but there was also a set of small symbols beneath the head, some of which Shiera recognized.

She snatched the sheet from Galifar's fingers. The mercenary laughed at her eagerness. "So you'll do it, then. Glad that's settled."

Shiera hadn't even paid attention to the rest of the page. Belatedly she saw that Raffan had written a note above the image.

Found in dig west of Kenabres. Symbol recognized by elder worker as seen somewhere in city. Located one instance near city center, but spot later destroyed. Believe other matching symbols exist. Should be investigated by you since we're here, don't you think?

The comments sent several conflicting thoughts rushing through the Pathfinder's head, not the least of which that according to what Raffan had written, hers was apparently not the first expedition sponsored by Raffan's mysterious benefactor. It bothered her, but hints of what secrets the city still held quickly assuaged her.

"You'll not be seeing Master Raffan until we're supposed to depart," Galifar went on, his sarcastic smile still strong. "Doubt that'll be a problem for you after all, though, eh?"

It took a moment to catch just what he meant by the last. Clearly, Raffan had expected that she would attempt to back up Daryus's hope of departing Kenabres tomorrow. With some guilt, she shook her head. "No, it won't be."

"That's a good girl." The captain winked at Shiera, then headed off.

Her anger at the mercenary's condescending attitude quickly faded as she peered again at the page. Despite Daryus's hopes, Shiera knew she would need every minute of the three days Raffan had given her to research these new clues. She cursed both Raffan and herself, but not for a moment considered rejecting Raffan's suggestion. Shiera had not pushed this far to miss a chance of finding more evidence that could lead her to her goal. Daryus was a capable man; she was certain that he could fend for himself for three days, even here.

Looking around, Shiera once more saw no sign of him. She also saw no sign of her horse, which she realized he had taken along with his own and the pack animals. The Pathfinder surveyed the buildings beyond and tried to guess exactly where Daryus taken the beasts.

Instead of the fighter, something else caught her attention: a tiny figure she knew so very well by now. Toy scurried along the top of a wagon, the weasel peeking over the other side as if following a trail.

Daryus. He must be following Daryus. Before she started her research, Shiera needed to find out where he planned on arranging rooms. Of course, she also needed to tell him that they *would* be staying for all three days.

Feeling somewhat better about her decision, Shiera hurried after the weasel. At first she feared the animal would disappear down into the throng, but fortunately, Toy seemed inclined to stay high and in sight. When the wagon ended, the weasel leapt to a passing merchant. The hefty man had just time to start reacting before Toy jumped to the saddle of a crusader. From there, the weasel jumped to another wagon. All the while, though, Toy kept in view.

Curiously, Daryus's pet scurried far beyond the establishments that Shiera would have expected the fighter to choose. She could only assume that the first inns had left some indication that they were full. Daryus would have to keep moving along until he found some place for the party, even if that meant going far afield from where Raffan might desire.

Toy jumped atop another horse, this one that of a grimy figure Shiera judged to be a mercenary she likely could have hired for less than half what Raffan had paid Galifar's men. Shiera's hand immediately went to her sword. She doubted the rider had as much training as she did, and he likely depended on brute strength to succeed.

The mercenary turned his mount to a shadowy side street. Toy looked unperturbed, the weasel actually settling down. His gaze continued ahead, though, presumably in order to keep Daryus in view. A good thing, too, since thus far Shiera had not gotten one glimpse of her quarry.

The rider continued into an older, less maintained section of the city. Shiera wondered how long she would have to follow the mercenary, only to stumble to an abrupt halt when Toy abandoned his place and leapt to the ground. The weasel veered off into another side passage, vanishing from sight.

Growing uncertain as to whether the animal actually followed Daryus after all, Shiera nevertheless continued to follow. She had committed herself, and if Daryus had not gone this way, then she had no idea why Toy would be rushing along so intently.

Yet her uncertainty only multiplied when, instead of turning toward three slightly rundown but serviceable inns, the weasel headed toward what appeared to be a shuttered temple.

Shiera paused. She saw no hint of the horses in front of any of the inns. It was possible Daryus had stabled them already, but she doubted that was the case.

A chittering noise brought her attention back to Toy. The weasel sniffed at the boarded-up entrance, turned from the temple to a gap near one of the city sewer openings.

Toy slipped into the large gap, disappearing below the street.

Something urged the Pathfinder to head to where the weasel had gone. The discarded temple stirred her interests. She recalled Raffan's request and wondered if perhaps the wandering Toy had inadvertently given her a place to start.

Telling herself that Daryus would certainly have everything well in hand where lodging for the party was concerned, Shiera gave in to her desire and began intently studying the temple exterior. It was not uncommon in great cities such as Kenabres to find such abandoned structures. She had explored two such places herself. One had been nothing but masonry and dust, but the other had still held valuable texts.

Shiera peeked into the hole where Toy had gone. At first glance, she saw nothing. Curious, Shiera made a slight whistling sound in the hopes of attracting Toy back to her. When the weasel did not appear, she tried again.

Something landed on her back.

Shiera lost her balance and fell into the hole. That might have meant her death, save for the fact that just below the entrance and out of sight from her angle, a sloping wall she guessed was designed to let rain water spill in easier now acted like a slide. She rolled all the way to the bottom, but ended up with only a few bruises and sense of foolishness.

The moment she regained her senses, Shiera looked up. There was no sign of whatever it was that had collided with her. She wondered if she had somehow disturbed a feral cat.

A faint blue glow greeted her from another passage at the far end of the chamber. Shiera started toward it, but after stumbling over something in the nearby dark, paused again. It would not do to go any farther unless she could see the ground. The glow was not strong enough to illuminate her surroundings.

Like most Pathfinders, Shiera kept the necessary components to light a fire. Drawing her tinderbox, she located the driest piece of wood she could find. A few strikes and she had herself a fair torch.

She almost doused it again after taking in the generations of trash, small decaying shapes, crawling vermin, and piles of refuse that had accumulated down here. She had already *smelled* how awful it all was, but seeing it proved even worse. Swearing, she tried to focus on something—*anything*—that would take her mind off of the stench.

The path proved precarious, with a dark, slippery slime over everything. Twice, Shiera almost fell, the second time too close to the nearly clogged river of refuse. She also noticed that the slime lined the walls almost to the ceiling, a sign that at times this chamber filled high.

With great relief, the Pathfinder finally reached the other side. There, she noticed the glow had somehow retreated deep into the other passage. Where originally Shiera had believed she would be able to see into the new area once she reached it, now the glow lay some distance ahead.

Something about the arching entrance caught her attention. Upon examination, she noted that whoever had built it had done so long before the chamber she had just crossed. Here was part of some more ancient section of the city waterworks, one built even more securely. She found an area devoid of the slime and ran one finger over where two of the stone blocks touched one another. She felt no trace of any mortar or other material sealing the blocks together, and suspected there had never been any. Some of the most amazing constructions she had studied had been built without mortar.

She pulled back from her examination to stare into the darkness preceding the faint blue glow. Gone were all thoughts of Toy, Daryus, Raffan, or even her own expedition. Here was something solid, something real. Taking a deep breath—and instantly regretting it—Shiera held the torch before her and stepped forward.

The walls abruptly glowed.

It was the same pale illumination she had noticed before, but now the source of that illumination revealed itself. Embedded in both walls—walls that were no longer carved blocks but now part of some *natural* cavern—were rows of small, triangular stones from which emanated the blue light. Thanks to both the stones and her torch, Shiera could see more of the former lining the walls. Simultaneously, she noted the glow in the distance fading farther away.

As she continued on, those stones nearest to her glowed brightest, while those just ahead and behind glowed only faintly, trailing off into darkness after a short distance in either direction. So the stones guided one's walk, then conserved whatever magical power they contained by returning to a dormant state.

That, of course, begged the question . . . who made the stones far ahead stir to life?

She had to assume that it was Toy, but, if so, she wondered why the weasel continued down this ancient path. It also seemed odd that the ancients would have designed the illuminated path so that a creature as small as Toy would cause it to function. That would mean that every rat that raced down the corridor would cause it to light.

Pushing on, she watched the glow shrink. If it was Toy, he had to be running at a breakneck pace. Indeed, barely a breath later, the last vestiges of the distant illumination faded away.

You'd better turn back, came a voice in her head, one that oddly enough sounded a lot like Daryus's. Shiera pushed aside the warning. It made no sense to turn back; she would end up with nothing. This ancient passage promised so much more.

Shiera picked up her pace. She still did not see any end to the corridor, but assumed that it could not go on much longer. To her relief, the stench had either faded much or her nose had simply gotten used to it; whichever the case, it enabled her to breathe easier and thus push harder.

Shiera's father and teachers—and pretty much everyone she had been supposed to listen to throughout her life—had always warned her of her tendency to charge into situations without enough consideration of the perils. Shiera generally thought of that as a positive trait in her calling, but as she continued on into the darkness, she began to wonder if maybe they had a point.

And then she beheld the ancient chamber at the end of the corridor.

The same stones that illuminated the corridor attempted to do so for what Shiera guessed to be an old altar room. As with the corridor, the walls were part of another natural chamber. Many of the light stones set into them were missing or had been pried off. Judging from the shattered debris on the floor, someone had clearly ransacked this chamber long ago.

Small wonder this place has been forgotten, she thought with some regret. *Nothing but a bunch of rocks and broken—*

Shiera stopped in her tracks as her last step caused a few stones to reveal the far wall. All her frustration faded away as she beheld what was now becoming a familiar symbol.

The one-eyed wolf peered to the side, where Shiera saw a combination of symbols she could already half read. With growing anticipation, Shiera stumbled over the ruins to the wall. The carvings had all been set at eye level, which enabled her not only to study them closely, but even to touch them. Shiera did so very gently. She did not want to add to nature's—and humanity's—relentless attack on the ancient display, but long ago Shiera had discovered that some artifacts did not give up all their secrets unless one came in contact with them.

Yet, even up close, the full message the ancients had set here escaped her. Shiera thought she understood what they intended to convey, but the most important part remained agonizingly absent from her understanding. The symbols didn't match up. They should have been turned differently. The meaning they currently presented made no sense.

She touched the most offending symbol, wondering if perhaps part of it had been broken off by either time or vandals. Instead, to her horror, the piece tumbled out of the wall. She let the torch drop as she grabbed for it.

But horror changed to astonishment, which then changed to triumph. Shiera eyed both the piece and the wall, where in the gap another symbol had been carved—a symbol that, read together with both the wall *and* the fallen part, revealed the full meaning. It was a unique manner of writing, and one she doubted most would be able to translate without having a physical representation.

More important than that, though, was just *what* she was now able to read. The entire wall made sense. Even the artifacts made more sense.

Shiera knew just where to find Uhl-Adanar.

Toy peered back at the underground chamber where Shiera stood. He had no doubt that she stood mesmerized before the carvings. He also had no doubt that she would decipher them even faster than his former master had when they had visited this place long ago. Back then, Toy had not yet suffered the agony of having one eye magically wrenched from its socket and replaced. Back then, Toy believed he had been aiding a master whom their benefactor could trust.

The weasel's nose twitched. He smelled other creatures down here, creatures Grigor had wisely avoided. Toy assumed the Pathfinder was competent enough to do the same. If she did, then she would use the knowledge here to help him find the witch. If she did not . . . then Toy had other avenues by which to hunt down his treacherous master.

Sniggering, the familiar ran off to deal with the next step in his plans.

9

HARRICKA MORN

Daryus exhaled with some relief. He had managed to evade the notice of the crusaders, especially the one who would certainly recognize him. It had meant leaving Shiera to her own devices, but the flight had been necessary.

You were a fool to come here! he chided himself. *But then, you have always been a fool . . .*

His fingers went to the one scar. Unbidden came the images, this time in a more cohesive arrangement. The marching crusaders, Daryus among them. The slaughter of the pitborn foes, a great victory. The purging of the demonspawn.

The frightened faces. The swords coming down.

"Somethin' else you want?"

He stirred. The moment Daryus had been certain he had avoided the patrol, he had quickly found a place for his party. The same establishment was already taking care of the animals as well. It had not been Daryus's first choice, but it had been the most convenient one he felt could be trusted with their supplies and animals.

Shaking his head, he paid the man and quickly stepped back outside. It had only been a short time since he had left Shiera, which meant he should be able to find her quickly. For all he knew, she would still be where he had left her.

However, it didn't take long for Daryus to see that he had assumed wrong. There was no hint of Shiera, nor even the direction she might have gone. Raffan and the mercenaries were also nowhere to be found.

Where Raffan and Captain Galifar were, Daryus didn't care. It would be up to them to find him. Only Shiera was of any concern, since she was the one who had hired him.

Daryus circled the Southgate Market, looking for someone who might have been in the area a few minutes ago and seen where she'd gone. He spotted a bearded old man sweeping in front of one of the better inns.

Daryus headed toward the sweeper—

Strong hands seized Daryus's arms from behind. He was brought down to his knees before he could react.

That, however, did not mean they had actually captured him. He let their momentum push him beyond his knees. Daryus knew they would expect him to resist, and his sudden cooperation sent them leaning forward and off balance.

Twisting around, Daryus tore his arms free. He locked a foot around the leg of each man and continued twisting.

Both men fell backward. Daryus pulled his feet free before he could become too entangled, then spun to the side and rolled to a crouching position.

A noose fell over his neck. It instantly pulled tight, cutting off his air.

Choking, Daryus grabbed for the rope.

More hands seized his wrists.

The tip of a sword touched his throat. "That'll be enough of that, Gaunt!"

The sharp, female voice cut through his thoughts. He knew that voice well. Much too well.

With the noose still tight, his captors dragged him to his feet. Around him, the area cleared as the rest of the crowd drank in the sight.

The two brawny crusaders held his wrists behind his back while the unseen third pulled back on the noose. Yet, at that moment, Daryus cared not a whit for their efforts. All that mattered was the ponytailed figure wielding the sword, the same handsome woman he'd seen earlier. Her icy-blue eyes warned Daryus that she would be perfectly happy to run the sword through his throat.

"Harricka," he said calmly. "You're looking well."

"That's *Captain Harricka Morn* to you." To emphasize her point, she let the sword leave a slight red trail across his throat. "And you've got either a lot of nerve or a tremendous death wish. Maybe both, considering it's you. What would ever make you think it was safe to return to here of all places?"

Daryus did not respond.

Harricka shrugged. "Doesn't really matter, does it, Daryus? All that does is that you'll finally face judgment for your treachery. Bind his arms tight! You've no idea just how dangerous he is."

They heeded her words well, tightening the bonds enough to make them painful. Daryus did not utter a sound, but merely kept his gaze on Harricka's. Of the four crusaders, only she truly knew him. They had served together for many years, including during the very incident for which Daryus had committed a crime against the order.

"I'd thought you dead for a time," she went on, once she was certain that he was secure. "For the sake of both your honor and ours, you should've followed through on that."

"I almost did," Daryus said. "Instead, I prayed for us—not that it appears to have done any good."

"How very noble." To his other captors, she asked, "You're certain you have him? That was the mistake last time. I will *not* have a repeat!"

"He won't get free."

"If he does, it'll be on your heads." Harricka withdrew the sword, then sheathed it. "Let's get him back to headquarters. The sooner this one is delivered to them, the better."

"I did what had to be done," Daryus suddenly found himself blurting.

"Not your decision or mine. Especially not then." With that, Harricka signaled for the other crusaders to drag Daryus on. It mattered not that they made a spectacle of the prisoner; the crowd naturally assumed anyone taken into custody by the crusaders had committed some heinous crime.

And as far as Daryus was concerned, they were correct.

He did not resist as they led him off. If there was a chance of escape, it would not be here, not now. A part of Daryus had always wondered what he would do if captured—or if he would do anything at all—but at least he knew that to attempt anything at this juncture would only end in failure and possible innocent blood being shed.

Captain Morn marched ahead, her gaze enough to separate the crowds. She was everything a crusader was meant to be— everything he had once thought he was as well. Harricka would not have done as he had, would not have shown the weakness that he had. She would never have betrayed the order.

"It was supposed to be a dull day," the captain went on with a shake of her head. "A routine patrol. Then I see a dead man, just riding around the city!"

Daryus wisely kept silent now. When last he had seen Harricka, she had been lying on the ground, stunned by his unexpected punch. She no doubt still seethed about that punch after all these years.

"But then, the Daryus Gaunt I remember abandoned all sense, all honor! Small wonder he would also be mad enough to return to mock those he had betrayed." She leaned close. "Nothing to say? Perhaps planning your confession? Some elegant last words?"

She grew quiet then, but each movement, each breath, continued to hint at her pent-up emotions. Daryus understood that after his flight she had likely taken the blame for his failure.

When last he had been here, the Order of the Flaming Lance had utilized an old inn to the northeast, near the legendary Librarium of the Broken Black Wing for their headquarters. However, now Harricka led them directly north, toward the wall leading to the New Kenabres District.

"The order gets tired of being so near Orlun's collection of demon bits?" Daryus finally quipped, referring to the old wizard who had created and still oversaw the macabre collection of the librarium.

"We now utilize the former guard barracks near the New Kenabres wall. It serves us well for training, for living, and, not coincidentally, for execution of criminals and heretics."

Hearing that, Daryus gave silent thanks that he had already begun testing his bonds. He had managed to retain a hint of looseness that the crusader who had tied him up had failed to notice. Daryus had already managed to loosen it a bit more, but still not enough. Not nearly enough.

And now I know. All this time wanting in part to be caught . . . only to find out I really don't.

Halfway to the barracks, Harricka suddenly stopped them, dropping back to study him. "Hold up his hands a bit."

Daryus gritted his teeth. He might fool the others, but Harricka would know just what he had done with the ropes. He held his breath as she tugged at the area near the wrists.

"Just as I thought. Not enough honor left in you to even accept your captivity. Look here, you fools! He managed to keep his forearms tensed enough while you were tying them that when he relaxes, there's slack. I'll hold the sword on him while you do it *right* this time."

The captain stepped back and drew her weapon as one of the men began to untie Daryus's hands. If not for Harricka's sword, Daryus knew that now would have been the best opportunity for him to escape—

"You there!" snapped a familiar voice. "What the blazes are you doing? What trouble have you gotten yourself into?"

The speaker was none other than Raffan, who glared down at Daryus from his horse. He looked from Daryus to Harricka. "What's he done? Gotten himself drunk already?"

The captain turned ever so slightly to the young man, her sword shifting at the same time.

Daryus moved.

He threw himself back into one man, then shoved the other pair into Harricka. He then spun around, seized the third man, and tossed him at the tangle of bodies.

Fortunately for Daryus, Raffan's mount panicked and reared, forcing the crusaders to move or be trampled. The uncontrolled horse darted in front of the furious captain, who grabbed for the bit.

By that time, Daryus had slipped deep into the moving throngs. He darted around startled onlookers, seeking a side street leading not toward the southern gate, but rather deeper into Kenabres. He hoped that Harricka and the others would assume he would try for the nearest exit from the city—which meant he'd head for the farthest. Once free, he'd hide just outside the walls and keep an eye on Shiera and Raffan's most likely route north, and hopefully meet up with them again.

Thinking of Raffan, the former crusader silently thanked the young fool for his timely appearance. Raffan was still probably trying to make sense of what had happened. Harricka would give him trouble for a few moments, but her major concern would be Daryus.

As he moved, Daryus gradually slowed his pace. He let his breathing become more relaxed. Fewer and fewer people took note of him. Soon, he was just one among many.

Or maybe not. Daryus stepped inside a cloth merchant's stall as a pair of riders shot past—both part of Harricka's patrol.

Daryus cursed. He had underestimated his former comrade. But then, she had known him better than most.

Shifting course again, Daryus made his way northwest, into the Waller slum near the western walls, just above the river.

The dank area was a contrast to the bright bustle of other districts. Daryus slipped into the nearest shadowy alley, praying he'd at last given Harricka the slip.

The alley went on much farther than Daryus desired, but he had no choice. Each step took him farther and farther from both his intended goal and any convenient exit from the city. He could feel the time slipping away. How long would it take for Harricka to alert the rest of the Flaming Lance and get his description to all the gate guards? Once that happened, leaving the city would become significantly harder.

A sudden sense of foreboding overtook him. Someone was still following him, but not directly down the alley. Still moving, Daryus glanced up, but saw nothing. Yet, he could not shake the feeling that whoever gave chase did so from the roofs above.

Finally reaching the end of the alley, Daryus paused. The street beyond was sparsely populated. Another alley beckoned ahead. Daryus took a step forward—

He had his sword out even as he turned. A fortunate thing, too, for the blade coming at him nearly skewered his skull. Even though Daryus managed to push the tip to the side, it still nicked his ear.

At first, all he could see behind the other sword was the darkness of the alley. A darkness that moved with the sword.

Pitborn.

He had no doubt this was one of the pair left from Nerosyan. That raised the question of whether Daryus's foe had followed him here or had merely come to the great city for other reasons. Certainly, the fact that the demonspawn had immediately begun to hunt him down made the first suggestion more probable. Whichever the case, Daryus knew he had to deal with this adversary swiftly if he hoped to evade capture.

The pitborn moved with much more craftiness than the other had shown during the previous encounter. Three times Daryus sought to break through the shadowed figure's defenses, only to have his attack deflected. Once, his failure nearly ended with him being skewered in turn. Daryus gritted his teeth in growing frustration as he imagined Harricka and her men closing in on him.

From nearby, a warning horn blared. Although Daryus had no idea whether the warning concerned him, he had to assume that it did. There was no more time for this duel.

He lunged. As expected, the pitborn shifted to counter that maneuver.

Daryus released his grip on the sword, letting the force of his lunge send the weapon flying at his foe. Naturally, the pitborn instinctively reacted by bringing his own weapon up, just as Daryus had hoped.

He let his full body weight help him take down the demonspawn. Daryus and his adversary crashed to the ground.

Before the shadowy figure could react, Daryus located the throat and squeezed. The pitborn grabbed for Daryus's face, trying to push him away.

The demonspawn's strength surprised Daryus. It was all he could do to maintain his grip. His fingers fumbled around the throat, two from his left hand finally snagging something invisible.

The pitborn shoved hard. Daryus fell back. His fingers, still tangled, pulled hard on the invisible item.

As it came free, both it and the pitborn took form. The object proved to be a chain on which hung a small silver object with what looked like jewels dotting every side. The pitborn, meanwhile, did not need the murderous expression spread across his face to make him one of the ugliest demonspawn Daryus had ever seen. There was very little humanity, and the former crusader had to wonder how the pitborn had survived to adulthood.

Daryus's adversary snarled, his sharp, yellowed teeth like those of a hungry cat. Despite his precarious condition, he did not seem at all that concerned, just angry.

That was all the warning Daryus had. Trying to keep his foe pinned with one hand, he turned—

Too late. The long, curved dagger pressed tight against his throat.

The voice of the other surviving pitborn filled his ear. "Where is he? Where is the foul little creature called *Toy*?"

10

THE TRAIL BENEATH

How long Shiera stared at the display, she could not say. Even though she had already divined enough to have a good idea where the lost temple-city lay, she had begun to realize that the script had more than one meaning. *Several* meanings, perhaps.

It had begun with the discovery that the ancients utilized a form of writing with a three-dimensional aspect. That had led her back to that moment in her room when she had read the name Tzadn as something even more ominous. That second name—or title, as it was—now burned in her thoughts. *Reaper.*

The name Tzadn appeared nowhere on the wall, but that wasn't the point. Now that Shiera saw how the ancient script worked, she used her chance reading of the name and title to see if other words formed if she looked at them the same way.

The first attempt revealed nothing. No matter how she peered at it, only the one angle proved to be anything. Somewhat disappointed, Shiera decided to try the next . . . and to her surprise, quickly discovered the beginning of a new sentence.

The translation was not always word for word. The new reading of the first symbol brought instead a phrase. *Let he sleep . . .* Shiera grabbed her notebook and scribbled down both the old and new reading and their relationship. Then she went to the third symbol.

To her puzzlement, Shiera once again found no meaning. She tried variations, but every angle proved as useless as with the first symbol.

After several minutes, she pushed on to the fourth. Barely had she begun than the fourth symbol revealed a second meaning. This time, it was a single word. A word as ominous in its way as the title given to the lost deity, Tzadn. Shiera read over it several times, just to make certain.

Nightmare . . .

Shiera wasn't concerned. Ancient tombs and lost temples always had sinister warnings. Most meant little, especially after so long. Shiera was confident that whatever traps remained functional after all this time would be ones she could easily outwit.

It did not surprise her when the fifth symbol did not reveal a second meaning. Now she understood. Only the even-numbered symbols made up this additional message. She grinned, thinking of Amadan Gwinn. Despite his reputation, she doubted he could have discovered so quickly the process by which the ancients' written language worked. Despite being a venture-captain, Gwinn was a man of linear thinking. He might have been able to translate the initial line, but from there he would have remained stumped.

Grinning, Shiera moved on to the sixth, the eighth, and, finally, the tenth. By the time she was finished, she had a rolling, peculiar message whose meaning she could only partially understand.

Let he sleep . . . Nightmare to come . . . let he sleep . . . until the wolf sees both . . .

Stones rattled in the shadows far to her right. Shiera glanced that way, but saw nothing. A moment later, from another direction came a squeaking sound very familiar to her. A rat.

She chuckled, then dismissed both noises from her thoughts as she mulled over her translation of the second message. Shiera was not at all certain what it meant. The Pathfinder ran her fingers over the bottom edge—

Something thudded hard in the corridor from which she had arrived.

Shiera paused to listen.

Again came the thudding, like two ponderous footsteps.

Two ponderous *footsteps*.

Only then did it occur to her that she was far, *far* under Kenabres. There were legends—no, *histories*—about the deep caverns and tunnels beneath the cliff city, where creatures descended from the unfortunate survivors of the First Crusade were said to dwell.

Shiera stood there for a moment, torn between trying to decipher more and doing the sensible thing.

A third thud echoed through the chamber.

Shiera retreated, away from the entrance and the footsteps. There was no sign of another passage, but she was certain there had to be some second exit. Priests always had escape routes.

Running her hand along the wall, she eyed the main entrance. She heard an intake of breath that could not have originated from anything remotely human. That encouraged her to search harder.

Then, despite the oncoming danger, Shiera suddenly backtracked. Something her hand had grazed finally registered with her. She tried to carefully but quickly retrace her steps.

Her index finger sank into an indentation that was not part of the natural rock face. She bit her lip. Even though she heard the slight click she'd hoped for, no secret passage swung open. She could only assume the door no longer worked properly—not a surprise after so many centuries, but certainly a bad omen for her.

She pressed harder.

There was another click.

Part of the wall to her right opened inward slightly. The gap was only inches wide, but it was all Shiera needed. She shoved herself against the partially open doorway just as a shadowy form entered the chamber.

Shiera wasted no time trying to make out exactly what it was. With one more powerful effort, she opened the way just enough for her to slip inside.

Dust-laden cobwebs draped over her, but she paid them little mind as she jammed her shoulder against the other side of the door. Despite her best efforts, she could not close it completely. Inhaling, she abandoned the door and stumbled down the dark passage.

Unlike the other chambers, no stones illuminated this area. Shiera tripped more than once over unseen articles that she had no doubt included bones.

Behind her, a hard thump warned that whatever pursued was attempting to follow her into the darkness. She suspected the creature would probably have more acute senses than her.

Shiera continued down the passage, hoping that it would not end in some wall. She located a corner and turned, then paused to listen. Despite hearing nothing, she picked up her pace.

Her right foot came down on air.

In desperation, Shiera reached out with her free hand for anything to grab. She briefly managed to snag some carving on the wall, but not enough to prevent her from landing hard on what she now knew were crude steps.

She rolled several steps before managing to stop herself. As she sat on the steps trying to catch her breath and get over her pain, she heard the crush of rock and bone that warned her that whatever followed was getting closer again.

Shiera stumbled to her feet and continued down the steps. More than three dozen steps later, she was still continuing down, something that began to disturb her. Yes, Kenabres was on a cliff, yet even if there was a river exit at the bottom, going down just meant she'd have come up again.

It took another three dozen steps before Shiera reached the bottom. There, to her relief, a few stones lit the immediate path ahead. While it was true that the lights might also alert the creature of her location, she was grateful to have *any* illumination.

She reached into the pouch at her side and withdrew her other weapon. Although it was dark, practiced hands enabled her to set it up quickly. She cocked the bow and set into it one of the small bolts.

The hand crossbow was a weapon her father had first taught her to use, although he had soon admitted that she had a far better eye than he did. The same acute senses that enabled Shiera to puzzle out the intricacies of ancient script also made her an excellent shot.

The walls and floor were of a gray stone she assumed was granite. Here and there, a hint of fungus marked the vicinity, but for the most part this ancient passage was neat and tidy. Shiera wondered if it was still used. That made her tighten her grip even more on the crossbow. She could not imagine that anyone down here would be friendly, especially if they kept some sort of monstrous guard around. Shiera entered the hallway . . . then stopped.

Illuminated by the stones was another line of script.

This was different than her previous discovery. This script had been scrawled on the wall in clear haste. Leaning close, she tried to make out the first few markings. "'City lost,'" she murmured, translating. "'Word of One wrong.'" She moved to her right, causing the next stone to illuminate. "'The Reaper watching fear—'"

Shiera stepped back in confusion. She understood nothing. *City lost? Word of One wrong? The Reaper watching fear?*

Why can't people ever just leave clear notes? Why is the past always be so damned vague? Shiera considered how the note had been written. Someone familiar with the lost language, likely a native speaker, but from toward the end of the mysterious civilization. Someone who had come here in search of a truth, if she read the line as it was intended. Someone—

There was movement in the darkness behind her.

She spun about, firing. The bolt struck something not made of stone. There was an angry—not *pained*—grunt and increased movement toward her. At the same time, the passage darkened.

As Shiera reached for another bolt, she leaned back against the wall. There was another click. Suddenly, she was falling backward and down again. At the last moment, she caught sight of a long, twisted hand with talons reaching for her. There was a hint of a face at the edge of the darkness, a face that was a macabre, almost canine parody of a human's.

Then the door shut. Shiera continued to drop, falling through what felt like a tingling membrane, light filling her vision..

She landed on soft grass. Natural light shone through from somewhere, revealing the wall through which she had slipped now shutting again.

Quickly rising, Shiera reloaded as she surveyed where the path had now led her. She was indeed outside, but not just of the old passages. Somehow, she had ended up beyond the city walls.

Looking back and forth, she estimated that she if she headed to her right then she was a good half hour from Southgate. Grimacing, Shiera started off.

However, she had only gone a few steps when the distant sound of hoofbeats made her pause. She crouched in the shadows of the wall just as three riders came into sight.

It was all Shiera could do to stifle a call as she recognized the trio. Galifar's men. The three appeared intent on the landscape, as if they were searching for something in particular.

Or *somebody*.

Shiera could think of no possible way the three would know she was nearby, nor why she should hide from Raffan's hirelings, and yet still she kept quiet and in the shadows.

The foremost of the trio reined his horse to a halt. As the others pulled up next to him, he dismounted. The others followed suit.

Shiera decided to move on. She crept along the towering wall.

Nearby, a branch snapped. She looked back at the trio to discover one of the three peering at her.

The choice taken from her, Shiera straightened, then waved at the trio. The lead rider said something to the others, then mounted. He urged his horse to a gallop and quickly reached her.

"The dandy was lookin' for you," the mercenary, a hawk-faced man, remarked more companionably than Shiera liked. "Captain *thought* you might be outside the city. Guess he was right. 'Course, he chose the wrong direction, which means I win the bet on who'd find you first."

"I was following some of Master Raffan's research," Shiera quickly responded as she put away the crossbow. The weapon implied fear, and she needed to project confidence. "It led me outside."

He offered a mailed hand. "We'll bring you back."

"I can make my way—"

He shook the hand once, signaling that Shiera had no choice but to take it. With reluctance, she did so.

The mercenary pulled her up as if she weighed nothing. He helped her sit behind him, then returned with her to the other pair. At her companion's signal, they fell in behind.

The ride back toward the gate was a silent one. Shiera wondered what Raffan wanted of her now. He had only just sent her off on this hunt. She wondered if he had discovered some other clue to his master's research. Otherwise, Shiera had no interest in dealing with Raffan at this moment, even if he was the one footing the bill for—

Her companion suddenly raised his hand. Peeking around him, Shiera saw another rider coming from the direction of the city. Captain Galifar.

As Galifar rode up, he caught sight of Shiera. "Where'd you come from?"

"She was by the wall," her rider replied before she could. "That way. I win."

Ignoring the last comment, Galifar looked the way he pointed. "That so?" He looked back at Shiera. "Following Raffan's work?"

"Yes," she replied cautiously.

"Find anything?"

Shiera's mind raced as she tried to decide what would be the best answer. Galifar had no need to know, not just yet. "I didn't have a chance. I followed a trail and it led me outside instead of where I thought."

Captain Galifar squinted at her, then shrugged. "Too bad."

Shiera allowed herself the slightest exhalation of relief.

Galifar shifted his horse, only halting the animal when it blocked her view of the gate . . . and vice versa.

"Raffan's getting suspicious," he said. "We've no choice. Bind her."

Shiera gaped, yet instinct immediately took over. She shoved herself to the right, away from Galifar and the man with whom she rode.

Unfortunately, one of the other mercenaries grabbed her arm just as she leapt. Shiera ended up dangling halfway off the horse.

"Let's not have that happen again," snarled Galifar, nodding to the man who had caught Shiera's arm.

An armored fist came down on her jaw.

11

WITCH IN THE
WORLDWOUND

T*he solution is no longer sufficient.* Grigor touched his cheek, where the flesh had already dried to the point of crumbling. Even though he had applied the unguent again only scant hours ago, it was as if he had never used it. *I must take stronger action.*

The mounts needed a rest, and certainly the pitborn did, too. Those concerns were minor to Grigor, of course, and if not for this terrible discovery, he would have pushed both animals and servants until they fell. Now, though, his own existence was at stake.

A full moon hung low over the desolate landscape. Something howled in the distance. For the Worldwound—or at least this part of it—the night had proven relatively quiet. The landscape had not unexpectedly shifted. No army of demons came scuttling their direction. Twice today, he had been forced to use power to fend off creatures who saw the column as food. True, the amount needed had not been much, but it still left him with an ever-decreasing reserve from which to draw. Now, he not only required that energy for his quest, but also to sustain himself.

The lowering of his hand was accompanied by a slight cracking sound. Grigor did not have to roll up his sleeve to know the flesh and bone there was also drying out. His entire body was growing more and more desiccated with each passing minute.

It must be done here. Done immediately.

Raising the staff, he brought the column to a halt. One of the pitborn rushed to aid him, but the witch waved him off.

Dismounting, Grigor sought out the highest point in the vicinity, a squat hill on which the remnants of some ancient well still stood. With long strides, the witch reached the top.

A glance down the well revealed no hiding beast, nor even a trace of the water for which it had been built. Holding the staff over the well, Grigor muttered under his breath.

The runes along the staff flared as he spoke. A soft light emanated from them.

The ground at the bottom of the well stirred, as did a handful of spots surrounding the vicinity. Still muttering, the witch tapped the edge of the ancient well with the bottom of the staff.

The ground stirred more. Something began to bubble up from the bottom of the well. A thick, brown substance.

Grigor Dolch ceased his incantation. Brow furrowed in impatience, he tapped the staff against the well again.

The well filled to the brim, then overflowed. Now at last it became clear to the watching pitborn that what poured forth was not water, but rather molten clay. The thick, bubbling mass spilled out on all sides, but immediately began to converge on the witch.

Grigor spread his arms and looked up to the sky. As he did, the edge of the flow touched his boots. However, rather than flow around, the molten clay *crawled* up over the edge of the boots. In seconds, the feet were encased. Yet, the clay, its speed increasing with each passing second, continued up past the ankles and kept going.

The witch remained still throughout it all, welcoming the clay that engulfed him. Within a minute, he stood covered up to his shoulders. Even then, the clay persisted, crawling up his neck, pouring over his chin and sealing first his mouth and then his nostrils.

Only when all of Grigor stood enveloped in clay did the flow cease. The remaining molten earth simply melted away, leaving the living statue.

Then, just as some of the pitborn shifted nervously, the layer of clay encasing the witch thinned. Slowly but surely, it faded, almost as if absorbed from within.

Before the eyes of the pitborn, the molten clay vanished into Grigor's skin in the manner of a tiny puddle of water dwindling in the sun.

When it was done, Grigor opened his eyes and smiled. He did not have to see himself to know the difference. His dry, jaundiced skin was no more; now he had the fresh, supple skin of the age he appeared. The witch touched his cheek and felt it give and rebound as healthy flesh should.

I'm me again! Grigor allowed himself a chuckle. *I am as I once was and will be again!*

Grigor laughed louder, then faced the pitborn. Arms still spread wide, he displayed himself for his servants. The pitborn, well aware of the witch's moods, quickly dropped to their knees and dipped their heads forward.

"Yes, bow to me," Grigor mocked under his breath. "Bow . . ."

Suddenly, all humor left him as he noticed a change on the staff. All of the runes had taken on a dark blue hue. To one unversed in the magical arts, the change might have seemed like nothing more than what it appeared—a simple alteration in the staff's appearance.

They could not have been more wrong.

This was not the first time Grigor had utilized the staff as he had. Twice prior, he had been forced to summon from the bowels of the world the rich, healing clay, a perversion of the natural renewal of life. With the staff's assistance, Grigor's body had devoured the clay as he might a plate of meat. For a time, he would once more be the Grigor of more than a hundred years past, the young, vital witch just into his power.

The young vital witch who, nearly nine decades past, had made his pact with a demonic patron—one he had eventually betrayed.

Twice more. I can only attempt this twice more before it destroys the staff. I cannot let that happen before I find the temple-city . . . and him . . .

Kenabres still lay a few days ahead. Although now fully restored to his great self, Grigor knew he could not wait until then to follow one of his other leads. If he could verify one more thing, it would not only help guide him to his goal, but guarantee he would at last be able to rid himself of the accursed weasel, the last but most dangerous link to the patron Grigor had betrayed.

"Bring me one of the fliers," he ordered.

It took but moments for a pitborn to bring him one of the four cages. When he had embarked on this quest, there had been eight. Grigor had been forced to use the creatures judiciously, well aware that he could not replace them if something went wrong. They had one flight in each of them. Only one.

The cage had a cloth cover over it designed to keep the creature more at ease, but as the pitborn approached, the hissing from within warned Grigor that this flier was already in a foul mood.

The witch opened the cage and reached in without looking. A set of claws immediately sank into his arm near the wrist. Grigor ignored the pain, not to mention the sensation of blood flowing, and pulled his arm out.

The bat, its eyes shut, clung tight as he removed it from the cage. In all ways, it appeared to be one of the long-snouted variety the size of a very large rat that ate both insects and fruit. Indeed, when Grigor had obtained both it and its brethren, that had been exactly the case.

Naturally, the witch could not leave what nature had wrought alone.

Rubbing the bat under its jaw, Grigor whistled a note. The bat's eyes opened.

Two large crystalline orbs stared back at the witch. The bat's long, forked tongue darted out, another adaptation on Grigor's part. All from the days when he had been powerful, when he had been given his desires by his patron.

Almost all his desires. Grigor grimaced. All he had done was ask for a few more things, experiment with the arts in a few ways that his former patron deemed insubordinate.

"It's your turn now," the witch commanded. "Fly deep. Fly fast."

He lightly shook his arm. The bat spread its wings and released its hold. It dropped only a few inches before gaining enough momentum to rise up into the air.

Grigor watched the bat dart high into the sky. The witch quickly surveyed the rest of the heavens. *All clear. Safe to begin.*

Holding the staff over his eyes, Grigor focused.

His view shifted. Suddenly, he saw the land from high above, through the bat's eyes. Yet that view was not simply as the bat would have ordinarily seen the world. Rather, thanks to Grigor's adjustments, the view expanded in every direction, giving the witch more than twice what should have been possible.

Grigor surveyed the inner depths of the Worldwound.

The blighted land lay covered in sulfurous mist and volcanic ash. Unsettling flashes of multicolored light emanated from an area far to the west. The rumble of either a stirring crater or an earth tremor warned the witch that his party could not linger for much longer, yet Grigor continued his study of the land. Ravines and crevices crisscrossed much of the ground within sight. Things shambled, crawled, ran, or scurried along the areas below. Here and there, ancient ruins rose above the murk, ruins these days acting as dwellings for some of the Worldwound's more monstrous denizens.

A scaled creature lumbering on six legs and possibly descended from something like a deer before generations of raw, dark magic had mutated it into its current state scurried toward a tangle of dead trees. By its movements, it apparently fled from some other creature. Only when it reached the first of the trees did it slow, as if losing its fear. The trees would hide it. The trees would—

Several of the leafless branches lunged down. The sharp points of the branches pinned the beast with such swiftness that all the victim could do was squeal briefly before growing still.

The branches drew the corpse up. As they did, individual branches pulled away, tearing off bits of flesh at the same time. Those bits quickly began seeping into the bark of each sinister limb.

Grigor watched a moment more, just to learn the limits of the carnivorous plants, then urged his servant on. He knew that what he sought lay not in those directions. The bat continued to fly at a breakneck pace, seeking the signs Grigor needed to verify his intended steps beyond Kenabres. If he found them, then that would make the Pathfinder's work all the easier . . . and enable Grigor to dispatch her all the sooner.

A small rise to the northeast snared his attention. At his command, the bat dove down for a better look.

Sure enough, just as Grigor had thought, the cracked foundation of a rectangular building came into view. One partial column thrust up on the left side, but otherwise nothing remained of what had surely been a proud edifice.

The bat alighted on the marble stump, then turned its head in nearly a complete circle. Grigor saw bits of marble here and there that marked what was left of the roof and verified his suspicions. This *was* a temple.

It was not by mere chance that the bat had located it. Yet, finding it where the old charts had indicated still pleased the witch. The fates were on his side.

The bat crawled around the ruins, seeking further signs favorable to Grigor's quest. It burrowed in the rubble, looking for markings, bits of script, even some partial carving that would prove this had been constructed by the same people who had built Uhl-Adanar.

Something moved in the rubble nearby.

Instinct made the bat turn toward the sound. The huge eyes took in everything—the stones, the weeds, the bones of some long dead lizard—but not the source of the shifting material.

The long tongue darted out. Through the bat's enhanced senses, Grigor tasted the air.

He knew what hid from his servant. The bat's tongue flickered again as it reinforced the fact that somewhere near was a rat.

Rodents in the Worldwound were hardly the same as those elsewhere. While they would prove no threat to Grigor himself, it would be imprudent not to investigate. That in mind, the witch had his pet bend one wing at an awkward angle and hop around.

The image of a wounded animal did exactly as the witch wished. Out of the rubble to the bat's right, a huge, furred form leapt. The rodent was at least five times larger than any Grigor had seen before. It had teeth that stuck out far past the lower jaw, giving it a vampiric appearance that put the bat's own to shame.

The vermin sought to pounce on the supposedly injured bat, but the bat fluttered above the predator at the last moment, then immediately descended, becoming the hunter instead of the prey.

Sharp talons sank into the rodent's flesh. The rat attempted to shake off the winged threat, but to no avail.

The bat's mouth twisted into as much of an approximation of Grigor's as was possible. Teeth enhanced by the witch bit into the back of the rodent's neck.

With ease, Grigor's pet ripped out a chunk of flesh. The rat shrieked in pain and tried again to free itself. Grigor had the bat sink its talons deeper. Caught up in the bat's bloodlust, the witch had the creature spit out the gobbet so that it could take a second bite.

The rodent's next cry was much weaker than the first. It tried once more to free itself, but instead ended up collapsing.

With growing gusto, Grigor—or rather, the *bat*—finished off its prey.

The witch let out a gasp of dark pleasure. The temptation to continue dwelling in the bat's savagery was strong, but Grigor managed to remind himself there were greater pleasures awaiting him.

The bat wanted to continue its attack, but Grigor forced it to return to its search. The ruins called to the witch. He felt certain they held another clue.

The bat hopped over a small pile of cracked marble. As it did, Grigor noticed something at the edge of his view. He guided the bat to the spot and had the creature shove aside some of the rubble.

The profile of a wolf revealed itself.

Grigor blinked. The profile in itself as a good sign, a true sign, but there was something, some minute change, that he couldn't put his finger on. He had the bat clear away more of the rubble, revealing a further portion of the image. Tongue continually darting, the creature then backed up so that the witch could study his findings.

Even with the full gaze of the bat fixed on the relief, Grigor could not fathom just what it was that was different. The wolf faced the same direction. The etchings around it were identical to those he recalled. The symbols to the side—

The symbols.

The witch had his servant focus on those farthest to the left. Grigor eyed each one in turn. The difference was *there*. It was minute, but he was certain that—

Through the bat's tongue, Grigor suddenly tasted a worrying scent.

The bat took to the air—or rather, tried to.

All Grigor heard was a brief growl. Then, pain wracked him as something ripped apart his winged servant.

With a gasp, Grigor quickly lowered the staff. His link to the bat severed, the witch no longer felt its death throes.

His mind was awhirl with conflicting thoughts. Part of him continued to try to define the difference he had seen in the relief, the memory already slipping away despite his best efforts.

The rest of him concentrated on the scent he had noticed just before the bat's grisly demise. Had it been that of another rat, the witch would have paid it no mind, save for the magical cost of losing yet another valuable tool.

Unfortunately, he had detected the one scent he most wished he had not. A scent he had noted twice before, both times revolving around his quest.

A demon . . . yet with a very *lupine* scent . . .

12

FUGITIVE

Water splashed Daryus in the face. He swallowed what he could of it, then opened his eyes and glanced up at the pitborn who had thrown it at him.

"Thanks. I got thirsty waiting for you." As he spoke, Daryus shifted as best he could on the chair to which he had been tied. The old wood remained as sturdy—as unbreakable—as before.

"Should have killed you," his captor replied, displaying sharp teeth. "Still no sign of the accursed thing."

"I told you what I know of him. If you can find Toy, you're very welcome to him." Since being taken in the alley, Daryus had spent most of his time trying to figure out his captors. By rights, they *should* have killed him, but instinct had made him go along rather than fight what was likely to have been a futile—and fatal—battle.

The remaining two pitborn had quickly bound him so that he could be no threat to them. Even then, there had been a few tricks Daryus could have used to possibly escape. However, he had deemed his chances much better by cooperating until the duo made some mistake.

They had brought him to this unused building in the slums as if they knew it very well. From the signs he had seen, the building had gone through plenty of use by others. Daryus had wondered what Harricka would think if she knew that pitborn and others used her fair city for refuge as they passed from the Worldwound to the outside realms and back.

The pitborn grunted in response. From a distance and with his mouth closed, he could pass for human, something his companion could not have done. Curiously, despite that, it was the latter now out among the populace on some mission that had thus far meant the former crusader's life continuing to be spared.

Despite appearances, Daryus had not been inactive. The pitborn had bound him tight enough to deal with his strength, but did not know about some of the tricks he had learned since having left the order. Given a little more time, Daryus knew he could have the ropes loose enough for him to escape. His weapons lay nearby, prizes the pitborn had yet to decide what to do with.

"You were a fool to trust the weasel," his captor muttered.

"And you're a bigger fool if you think ever I did. What do you want with him?"

If the pitborn intended to reply—which would have been a change from previous conversations—his opportunity passed quickly, for they were at that moment joined by the other survivor.

"Too late," the uglier pitborn growled. "He's gone."

"The witch won't like this," the first returned. "Betrayed twice . . ."

"The mercenaries—"

"Have their task. This was ours."

"Maybe we can still find the familiar." He jerked a thumb at Daryus. "Maybe we should cut his throat and see if it shows up. It seems to need him."

Daryus worked harder on the ropes.

The first mulled the suggestion over, then shook his head. "Not yet. Toy picked him for a reason. The witch may want to know that reason."

Daryus paused. Toy had *picked* him?

"I don't care if he does," the uglier pitborn retorted. "If the human won't draw the weasel to us, he's no use! Let's slit his throat!"

"If I slit any throats, it'll be yours!" argued his companion. "He's our only chance to find the weasel! I'll see that tube-rat skinned—the others are dead because of him!"

"And because of this one, too!"

As the pair argued, the former crusader suddenly felt activity by his wrists. Barely a breath later, his bonds loosened completely.

Daryus hid his surprise. Instead, he focused on the distance between his weapons and himself. That done, he looked from one pitborn to another, judging the odds there as well.

"There's something I just remembered about Toy," he announced.

His second captor took a step toward him. "You know nothing! You just want to keep your life!" He drew a dagger. "I should—"

Daryus lunged.

He crossed the distance in half the time most men would have needed, catching the nearer pitborn while the latter was still adjusting his grip on the dagger. Daryus threw himself at an angle, sending both of them colliding with the other captor.

As they all went down, he twisted the dagger from the one pitborn's grip. Taking a risk, he grabbed for the fallen weapon even as the duo tried to recover.

His fingers closed around the hilt, and he thrust at the closest of his foes. The dagger sank deep into the uglier pitborn's shoulder. The demonspawn cried out.

The force of Daryus's blow worked against him. Driven into the pitborn's shoulder to the hilt, the dagger refused to be removed. Swearing, Daryus kicked his wounded adversary to the side as he went for his own weapons.

The first of the pitborn snagged his leg just before he could reach his sword. Daryus kicked the horned assassin in his blunt features, forcing him to release his hold.

Daryus seized his sword and faced the pair. By this time, the second pitborn had managed to pull the dagger from his shoulder.

Looking more furious than wounded, he threw the blade expertly at Daryus.

Waiting for just that particular attack, Daryus deflected the missile. However, as he did, the wounded assassin drew his own sword and charged.

The pair exchanged blows. Despite the bloody gap in the pitborn's shoulder, he showed no sign of slowing. Indeed, very likely urged on by the injury Daryus had caused him, he pressed the human hard. Daryus found himself backing into a corner—not a place he wanted to be.

Behind Daryus's attacker, the other assassin rubbed his ruined nose, then drew his own sword. Daryus knew he had to finish off the nearer pitborn quickly if he wanted a chance to survive.

Then, something caused the assassin with the broken nose to stumble and fall. The pitborn cursed as he fell, then spouted something in a language Daryus didn't understand.

Whatever he said made Daryus's foe turn. Daryus didn't question his luck. Too close to use his blade effectively, he satisfied himself with punching the distracted assassin with his sword's pommel.

The stunned pitborn tumbled back. Daryus readied his sword, only to hear a new voice.

"Run!"

He recognized Toy immediately, although exactly where the familiar was, he could not say. Still gripping his weapon, he shoved past the wounded pitborn, then leapt over the other.

As he reached the door, something seized his shoulder.

"Faster!" urged Toy near his ear.

Daryus burst through the door and out into the dank slums. He was not at all surprised to find no one in the immediate vicinity. The pitborn would have hardly chosen a place too near where people tended to congregate.

It was not like him to run from a fight, especially against only two. The assassins had gotten the better of him in the alley through subterfuge. Daryus was now certain he could have taken both in the building, but Toy's urging had made him fear that some other danger lurked.

This far from his foes, Daryus turned his concern to Shiera and her patron. While Raffan was not of much interest to Daryus, Shiera was tied to the man.

"Back to the market, back to the market!" hissed Toy.

"Is that where they are?"

"No questions!"

That answer made Daryus come to an abrupt halt. "Tell me straight or I'll save those demonspawn the trouble and skin you myself! Where's Shiera?"

"She has been kidnapped, kidnapped!"

"By who?"

"The four who rode with us!"

"Galifar and his men?" Whatever his mistrust of Toy at times, Daryus didn't find the weasel's declaration particularly hard to accept. He had seen Galifar's ilk enough to believe the weasel about the duplicitous nature of the mercenary captain and his small band.

"Yes!" the familiar insisted. "Toy followed them! Saw them take her outside the city!"

Daryus held back a wider frown. He was certain that Toy was not exactly telling the entire truth, but that could wait until Daryus located Shiera. While some hired swords would have considered their contracts ended by such events, he couldn't find it in himself to abandon Shiera to her fate. The Flaming Lance might have cast him out, but Daryus still inherently believed in the most basic of their tenets: that the crusaders protected the good from evil.

"Why would they do that? Slave traders?"

"No! No! The witch's men they are! Grigor's men! We need to follow! Yes, follow!"

Daryus had no intention of leaving Shiera to either the mercenaries or the witch. Of course, that meant getting out of Kenabres without Harricka or some other veteran who knew Daryus spotting him.

Barely had he thought that than Toy jumped off his shoulder. After a pause to look behind them, the familiar pointed his nose to the right. "There! We go there!"

"Why there?"

"You must have a mount, Master Daryus . . . and the pitborn have good mounts . . ."

The pitborn's mounts? "They're that direction?"

"Yes, both!"

Daryus nodded. "Show me the way."

Toy scurried off, and Daryus followed.

The familiar led him down an alley, then onto a narrow, deserted street even deeper into the slums. The area was such that it did not look at all odd for Daryus to be keeping his weapon handy. The pitborn clearly trusted their disguises only so far.

Toy finally led him to a decrepit set of stables watched over by a hefty, balding figure who had likely once been a soldier and now clearly acted as a guard for the seedy establishment. The burly sentry nodded lazily at Daryus, who walked into the stables as if keeping an animal of his own there.

Toy had vanished the moment they neared the stables, but reappeared just inside the stables. "This way! This way!"

"Keep it down!" Continuing to follow the weasel, Daryus inspected one dirty stall after another. Most were empty, but at last Toy stopped before one where a brooding dark mare eyed the intruders with distrust.

"This one of them?"

"Yes, yes!"

Daryus grunted. "You know a lot, don't you? You seem to have been busy. Much too busy."

Toy gave him a one-eyed look of puzzlement. "I am a familiar. It is my task to know as much as possible."

The weasel moved on as if he had explained everything. Still not satisfied but aware he had no time to question Toy further, Daryus entered the stall.

The mare snorted uneasily. Daryus made soothing noises as he inspected the animal. She was covered in small scars, most of them, Daryus decided, being the work of the mount's rider. Still talking calmly to the mare, Daryus began preparing the creature for the journey.

The saddle was a standard one he was easily able to secure. Daryus tried to work quickly, aware that at any moment the pitborn might come for their horses. If they trapped him in the stall, he would stand no chance.

He mounted the moment the animal was ready. The mare snorted again, then moved around as best as the stall allowed. Daryus leaned forward and gently tried to shush the horse—

Voices arose from near the entrance, voices that did not sound much like the pitborn.

Daryus urged the mare out of the stall.

Three crusaders stood blocking the way out. They did not seem prepared for Daryus, but immediately compensated.

He urged the mare to as full a gallop as she could manage despite the cramped surroundings.

The crusaders already had their weapons drawn before Daryus managed to get the mare halfway down the central corridor. He gently kicked the beast in the sides, trying to get it to move faster.

The youngest-looking crusaders broke away as the mare neared. Daryus maneuvered the horse toward the sudden gap.

A sword came at him from his right. Daryus twisted to his left, just managing to evade the attack.

Leaving the trio in his wake, he steered the horse out the entrance. The guard made a grab for him, but much too late.

"Faster! Faster!" Toy shouted from behind him.

Daryus had no idea just how the crusaders had known he would be here. Only as he rode out into the street did Daryus consider that perhaps they had not been after him at all, but rather the assassins. Even still, he wondered at that timing as well.

Suspicious as he was about his tiny companion, Daryus chose to say nothing to Toy until they were far from the stables and into the Ring District, which engulfed not only the Waller slums, but also Old Kenabres.

With crowds finally around him, Daryus finally dared to speak, albeit under his breath. "Which gate? The south one?"

"Yes, yes!"

"Any idea where they want to go after that?

Toy climbed up onto his shoulder again. "The Worldwound, of course, Master Daryus! The Worldwound!"

"Well, that narrows it down." Daryus held his tongue as he noticed a mounted party moving through the crowds from the other direction. He squinted, scarcely believing his bad luck.

Sure enough, at their head was Harricka.

The dark look on her face matched his thoughts. In her mind, once more, Daryus had played her for the fool. She would not be as kind to him as she had been last meeting.

He steered the mare to the right. The crowd made the going slow. Daryus bowed his head and tried to look like any of a hundred other people riding through Kenabres. The turn he desired beckoned, but the way continued to be clogged with people who seemed not to understand that a horse outweighed them.

A shout cut through the noise of the throng. A shout Daryus recognized without looking as coming from Harricka.

He had no doubt he was the reason for that shout. Scowling, Daryus forced his mount through the confused crowd and down the side street. Moments later, he raced past a startled guard at a gate and reentered the southern part of New Kenabres. There, the way opened up better. However, Daryus did not breathe any easier. Harricka was not one to give up so easily.

He pushed the mare as hard as he could, at the same time shouting a warning to anyone who threatened to be in his path. Despite his urgency, Daryus did everything he could to avoid endangering those around him. All he wanted was to get out of Kenabres quickly enough to lose any pursuit.

Toy seemed less inclined to worry about those on foot. "Faster! Faster!" the weasel cried in his ear. "Faster!"

They charged through a stunned throng at the next wall, entering the Gate District's southern arm. The final district became a blur as Daryus fought for a safe route through the citizenry of Kenabres.

The southern gate at last beckoned. Daryus dared not slow the mare. That forced him to shout more, which in turn caused some of the guards to notice him sooner than he had hoped.

One of those atop the gate ran to the rail and called down. Daryus could not see the reaction from below, but had to assume someone would begin trying to shut the way very soon. Fortunately for him, the gates were massive and the guards focused outward, better suited to repelling a demonic siege than stopping a single rider from trying to escape.

From somewhere far back, Harricka's voice cut through again. Daryus dared peer over his shoulder.

The captain and four of her crusaders fought to get their horses through the crowd. Unlike with Daryus, they, as crusaders, were having better fortune.

As he returned his attention to the path before him, he saw that there were now also four sentries gathered ahead. Daryus swore, then bent low over the mare. Despite his wish not to hurt anyone, he charged the four.

The guards stood their ground until the very last moment. Two threw themselves to the left, while another dodged to the right.

The remaining guard attempted a feat of daring. His weapon sheathed, he jumped up as the horse closed on him. Strong arms sought to snag the mare by the neck in what Daryus supposed must have been an effort to steer the animal to a gradual stop.

Daryus tugged at the nearest fingers, which proved enough to make the sentry lose the rest of his grip. The guard tumbled to the side. Daryus prayed that his would-be foe would not be trampled, but could not look back to see.

Unfortunately, the delay enabled two of the other crusaders from the gate to reach him. One seized Daryus's leg, then tried to bring up a sword.

Using his other leg to kick at the second attacker, Daryus threw his weight into a punch against his first foe's jaw. The guard stumbled, but did not fall. Daryus brought his sword into play, forcing the crusader back.

By that time, the guard he had kicked at had closed again. She slashed at his side, cutting into his clothing but only barely scraping his skin. Daryus was forced to bring his sword around to fend her off, then tugged on the reins to make his mount turn toward her.

Once more, the guard retreated. As she did, a grinding sound alerted Daryus to another danger. Other guards were attempting to shut the gate.

Daryus planted his head in the horse's mane and spurred the animal forward.

A whistling sound near his ear warned him that at least one archer had gotten a shot off. Fortunately for Daryus, the risk of hitting the wrong target evidently remained a very real danger, for no second shot came.

He burst through the gate. Even then, Daryus did not breathe easy. There were still people trying to enter, which slowed him slightly, but at the same time prevented another volley from above. Unfortunately, there were more guards outside, including a mounted officer who immediately steered his horse toward Daryus. Daryus attempted to ride around the man, but failed.

They traded blows, swords clanging loud and sending the crowds scattering. Daryus cursed under his breath. If the way cleared much more, not only would the guards on the ground be able to better reach him, but a sharp-eyed archer might get off a fatal shot.

The officer was a younger man, which gave Daryus hope; he'd learned a few tricks since his own youth.

Daryus started a lunge. The crusader moved to counter, only to find Daryus suddenly twisting around in mid-attack, seeming to open himself up to his foe.

The officer couldn't help but take the bait. The sword veered toward Daryus's open chest.

Daryus twisted down, letting the blade nick his shoulder. Coming up from where he bent, he seized the officer by his wrist, pulling the younger man off his horse.

As the crusader fell toward him, Daryus used his fist and the hilt of his weapon to soundly strike the officer. He then shoved the stunned crusader in the path of the guards charging toward them.

A whistling sound was Daryus's only warning. His horse let out a pained cry and shook.

Daryus threw himself at the newly riderless mount, another mare. He felt Toy's claws dig into his flesh as the weasel sought to maintain a hold. Scrambling as best he could onto the saddle, Daryus urged the crusader horse on.

One guard slashed at Daryus's new mount, but missed. Two more arrows flew past man and horse.

The way cleared. The mare started to slow, but Daryus slapped her sides, refusing to let her. The animal picked up her pace again. Horns blared, but Daryus ignored both those and the dwindling shouts.

Daryus did not simply let the horse run wild. As soon as the road curved behind a rise, out of view of the city walls, he turned off it and rode overland through the trees.

He knew most of the paths into the Worldwound, including the ones that Shiera's captors were most likely to choose. Any of the paths were dangerous, but the latter were truly so. Daryus was not so concerned with the mercenaries as he was what they might encounter. He had not thought Galifar that big of a fool, but if the man believed that he and his three companions were enough to counter any situation, he was sorely mistaken. They did not have Daryus's knowledge of the benighted land, one of the main reasons for which Daryus had been hired, he suspected.

Only after some time cantering up a muddy stream to throw off any trackers did Daryus finally dare rein the mare to a halt. Immediately, Toy expressed his displeasure with the decision.

"Night comes! We cannot stop! Must go on!"

The human eyed the failing light. "We'll go on a little more, but there needs to be a short stop. I know a place to settle in, but she'll never get us there if we keep on like this."

With a hiss of frustration, Toy leapt off of his shoulder and onto the ground. The weasel scurried into the brush.

Daryus found himself happy to be rid of the creature for the moment. His distrust of the familiar had only grown, but for now he needed Toy. Once they managed to find the Pathfinder, Daryus would divest himself of the weasel, witch or not.

While the mare chewed on some grass, Daryus went in search of the spring he knew lay hidden nearby. Not even many of the crusaders would be aware of its location. Daryus himself had only discovered it by accident many years ago after fleeing his former comrades—a situation much like this one, honestly. If the spring was untouched, he would bring the mare there for water. Then, it would be easier for the three of them to move on to shelter.

He had only gone a few steps when he saw the tracks.

Crouching down, Daryus studied the fragmented hoofprints. One horse, possibly more. He exhaled in disappointment. There was no way of telling just who it was who had ridden past here, only that they had done so very recently.

But if not her and Galifar . . . then who else would be out here? Daryus wondered.

Just in case, he drew his sword, then closed on the location of the spring.

A horse snorted.

Daryus paused. He heard the trickle of water.

He heard someone *drinking* from the water.

In the dimming light, he made out a figure clad in a travel cloak bent over the spring. Daryus's gaze went from the cloaked form to the horse, where a small blade hung in a scabbard. The weapon was entirely unsuited for anyone so near to the Worldwound, which to Daryus meant that either the stranger was a fool or had some hidden manner of defense.

And then, with unsteady movements, the figure stood, turned, and gasped.

Before Daryus stood Raffan.

Who promptly collapsed.

13

Savage Salvation

S hiera woke to find her world rocking.

She belatedly realized that the rocking was due to the motion of the horse upon which she sat. Darkness surrounded her—the darkness of a shrouded night, not the hood she had at first thought covered her head.

Shiera was just able to see the rider in front of her. She recognized him as one of Captain Galifar's men, and with that knowledge came the rest of her memories, especially her chase through the city. More and more, she wished that she had stayed and tried to deal with whatever had pursued her instead of fleeing.

Her attempts to struggle free only resulted in pained wrists. Not only were her hands bound tightly behind her, but her mouth was covered so that she could barely make a sound. After a few minutes of squirming, Shiera earned the attention of one of the mercenaries. The bearded man checked her bonds, then returned to his place.

They rode on for what she estimated as two more hours. Although her eyes adapted somewhat to the dark, Shiera still had no idea just where she was. She had her suspicions, but not until a strange howl in the distance made all of her captors ready their weapons was she sure.

They were within the Worldwound.

While Shiera had been more than eager to reach the blighted land, she had not wanted to do so in such straits. She wasn't so overconfident as to think she was safe from outside dangers simply because she was surrounded by four heavily armed men. Indeed, with their clinking and clanking, Shiera was concerned that Captain Galifar and his men would only *draw* danger to them.

Galifar signaled for a halt near a squat hill. In silence, he and the others made camp while Shiera sat waiting impatiently on her horse. Only when everything was done to the captain's satisfaction did he come over and lift her off.

"You're a sturdy one for so tiny," the mercenary noted as he set her on her feet. "Not some weak court lady. I like that."

Shiera hid her disgust, instead very politely indicating as best she could for him to remove the gag.

He laughed harshly. "Only when it's time to eat. Too many of you Pathfinders have magic, or at least silver tongues."

The mercenary captain led her to a place near the small fire one of the others had built, then forced her into a sitting position. A few minutes later, he brought her a bowl of some foul-smelling broth. With care, he removed the gag just enough to enable her to eat.

"Just remember, I won't hesitate to cut you if you try to say anything else besides 'more,'" he warned.

The pungent scent of the broth already assailing her nostrils, Shiera wondered if this last declaration was meant as some sort of bad jest. She wondered that again once she actually tasted the disgusting mess. There was meat, yes, but what its animal origins were, Shiera couldn't say.

Midway through the meal, she dared try to speak. "May I ask a question?"

"Let me guess: Where are we going? Is that it?"

She nodded.

He leaned back. "Why, we're going to take you where you want. How does that sound?"

Shiera raised an eyebrow.

Galifar chuckled. "You ain't going to want to be there when you see it, or so I'm told."

She opened her mouth to ask more, but the captain shook his head. "Enough talk. You know all you need to know for now. Eat, then we'll see about your other matters."

After dinner and said necessities, during which Galifar tied her to a tree and stood guard a polite distance away, he tied her wrists again, then led her back to the fire. One of the other men took an interested glance at Shiera, but the captain grunted his direction and the mercenary immediately shifted his gaze away. The others feared Galifar.

"You'll sleep well here," he told Shiera as he pushed her to a sitting position near the fire. "So long as you don't make trouble."

At first, Shiera thought he might actually leave her legs free, but Galifar continued to prove himself a thorough man. He bound her at the ankles, then finally left her to her own devices.

Shiera tried her ropes and found them as snug as expected. She had absolutely no chance of freeing herself.

One by one, her captors settled down for the night. Galifar took first watch himself, marching back and forth through the camp. Despite everything, Shiera found his precision comforting enough that she finally fell asleep.

When she woke later, Galifar had been replaced by the same beady-eyed mercenary who had studied her upon her return from the edge. Unlike the captain, he did not march around, but rather squatted near the fire.

Somehow, despite her situation, sleep again claimed her. Fragmented dreams swirled through her subconscious, some slowly becoming longer, more coherent. Most had to do with her expedition and generally ended with her standing triumphant before some place she could not see.

Then Shiera began dreaming about her captivity. Only, in the dream, she was no longer tied hand and foot. Instead, she stood in the center of the camp, almost exactly on the spot where she vaguely recalled the fire being. There was no fire, though, but rather a glow that emanated from the area around her feet and rose up to encompass her entire body.

Looking around, Shiera saw that the guard had fallen asleep. Yet despite this opportunity to flee, she did not move, almost as if something still held her in place.

Thunder rumbled. The sound came so sudden and so loud that it shook her. A wind picked up and lightning crackled. Yet, despite this storm materializing from nowhere, none of her captors had so much as stirred.

Then Shiera discovered herself still unbound, but farther back. The glow where the campfire had been remained, but now in its midst formed a monstrous, winged thing with a long, gray head ending in two high horns and only one eye. It stretched out a narrow arm that ended in a hand with four long claws.

Lightning flashed. The demon—for it could be no other creature—opened a wide, lipless mouth filled with teeth and grinned at the gathering storm.

Shiera wanted to recoil, but her body would not move. She would have shouted out warning to her captors, if her mouth only worked.

Moving along on thin, bent legs ending in two narrow toes, the winged creature stalked toward the unmoving forms. The talons closed on the first of the mercenaries.

Shiera's mouth finally opened, but in slow motion. Worse, no sound issued forth. She attempted to wave a warning, but even moving her hand proved ponderous.

Yet almost as if he heard her, Captain Galifar finally awoke. He looked up, saw the creature, and shouted. Despite his voice not carrying to her, evidently it did at least reach his comrades

Well-seasoned in combat, they all had weapons ready. Unfortunately, that was still not good enough for the errant guard, the one toward which the thing had headed. As the mercenary started to rise, the creature raked him with its talons.

The man shrieked—silently, like everything else—as his body opened up like a piece of cut fruit and blood and organs spilled forth. He contorted, then tumbled to the ground, where he continued to writhe as the last of his life fluids pooled around him.

Galifar and the others had not simply stood around during that time. Even as the demon lunged for their comrade, the captain and his companions charged.

The first of the mercenaries immediately thrust. Despite his aim being true, his blade somehow slid past his target.

The demon's mouth opened wider than Shiera would have thought possible, revealing yet even more sharp teeth.

With speed akin to the lightning itself, the demon leapt forward and bit out not only the hapless fighter's throat, but nearly *all* of his neck.

Eyes still wide in shock, the mercenary's head collapsed onto his shoulders. The man, already dead, teetered for a moment before falling back.

Galifar and the last man came at the demon from opposing sides. The captain wore a determined look, his underling one of fear.

As Galifar feinted, the younger man thrust, his form perfect—only to have his sword point slide off the demon's hide without a scratch.

That was too much for the younger mercenary. With a cry, he turned and ran for the horses.

His flight only served to draw the demon's attention. Wings fluttering, it rose just enough to catch up to the fleeing man, then raised both sets of talons and ripped apart the mercenary's back. The man staggered forward, then dropped with one hand still outstretched toward the horses, who struggled hard to free their reins from where they were tied.

Galifar used the moment to strike. He aimed not for the torso, but rather for where the head met the thick neck.

The sword point pierced the scaled flesh at the base of the skull. The demon's entire body shook.

The fiendish creature turned as if not even noticing the gaping wound it had received. With one savage swing, the demon forced Captain Galifar back. Baring his teeth, the mercenary slashed again, only to miss.

The demon lunged. Despite Galifar's defensive position, the talons still managed to reach through and grab his throat.

Nails digging deep into the captain's neck, the demon dragged Galifar's face within inches of its own. The hand flexed, cutting off the human's air and forcing his mouth open.

Galifar tried to get his sword around, but failed.

The demon opened its mouth wide, then wider and wider yet . . . and bit off Galifar's entire face.

The captain shook. Unable to help, Shiera watched in horror as Galifar, still clearly alive, tried to overcome his terrifying injury. Somehow, he yet managed to bring up the sword, but there he lost his last bit of strength.

Still holding its prey, the demon tore into the captain's chest with its other talons. Armor, flesh, bone . . . nothing withstood the force of the attack.

At last, the demon released its victim.

Dropping his sword, Galifar fell to one knee, then sprawled before the demon.

The winged fury turned its attention to Shiera.

Try as she might, Shiera could *still* not move from the spot, could not even call for help, not that any would come. She stared in horror as the fiendish being drifted toward her, its single eye filled with obvious ill intent—

A howl broke through the silence of her dream.

And just like that, Shiera's nightmare ended.

She awoke still bound. Darkness surrounded her. Remembering the nightmare, Shiera fought hard to push herself up enough to see Galifar and the others. However, before she could, a tremendous exhaustion filled her, and she collapsed onto her back.

A moment later, she was asleep again.

Day came, such as it was in the Worldwound, and with it consciousness. Shiera moaned. Her entire body ached. She stretched her arms and legs, then took a deep breath.

Only then did she realize that she was, as in her nightmare, unbound.

With growing dread, she stared at her freed hands. Someone or something had cleanly severed—or bitten off—the ropes.

Despite her stiffness, Shiera found the strength to rise to her feet.

Around her lay the slaughter she had been hoping she had only dreamed. Galifar and his men lay in the same awful conditions.

Shiera stumbled forward, then stopped as she was once again reminded that she was free. None of this made sense. If, as she believed, she had actually witnessed the slaughter, she saw no reason why the demon would have left her alive. Yet here she was.

A sound from her side made her jump . . . then added further to the mystery. As with her, the horses remained untouched. Indeed, they now stood calmly waiting, as if no longer aware of the horror that had transpired.

Why was I spared? It makes no sense! With those thoughts continuing over and over in her head, Shiera took a step back. Only then did she notice something on the ground next to the nearby body.

The drawing was crude, just lines scratched in the dust, yet its shape was unmistakable.

A one-eyed wolf.

14

HUNTED

It was an hour before Raffan regained consciousness. Daryus had considered throwing the young man over his horse and dragging him along, but had decided against it. If they came across danger, Daryus thought that Raffan at least deserved the chance to defend himself, however meager that defense might be.

Raffan was clearly out of his element so near the Worldwound, which made it all the more curious why he would be here alone. Daryus could only assume that either Raffan had followed Galifar and the others or that he had decided to pursue some trail of his own, perhaps in order to gain more favor with his unnamed patron.

As Raffan stirred, Daryus readied a piece of the rabbit he had caught. The rest he had already prepared as best as possible for the journey ahead. Unfortunately, most of the supplies were still back in Kenabres and there was no hope of returning there. Whatever Daryus and Raffan had with them was all they would be carrying into the Worldwound.

The young man rubbed his head. "You. I thought I remembered seeing you . . ."

Daryus brought the piece to Raffan. "You look like you need food. Eat this."

Raffan looked as if he would have preferred to cut his throat rather than eat the seared meat before him, but finally accepted the offering. After the first bite, he began eating with more gusto. Hunger could change even the most delicate sensibilities.

"How did you end up out here?" Daryus asked after a moment.

"I finished up with the first of my master's associates here, then went in search of Captain Galifar to coordinate some details," Raffan answered after swallowing. "Only to find that the captain was not where he was supposed to be. In fact, when I did a little more searching, I discovered that he and his men had been seen leaving the city . . . and that a woman resembling the Pathfinder was seen with them beyond the city walls."

Daryus saw many holes in Raffan's story thus far, but only asked, "What did you do?"

"The master has several friends in the upper echelons of Kenabres society. I made use of the master's name to gain what I needed in terms of some quick supplies and a fresh horse." The other man frowned. "I never thought to run into you again, either, not after what happened with those crusaders. You left me in a devil of a situation, trying to explain how I only knew you as a hired sword!"

"So sorry to inconvenience you. Next time, I'll let myself be carted off without a struggle."

Raffan glared. "I know you used to be one of them and committed some offense, Daryus Gaunt. I'm willing to overlook that so long as it doesn't interfere with the expedition."

"How kind of you. So you pursued? You knew to follow them here?"

"Not here . . . not exactly." Daryus's companion flushed. "I got lost even though I was following a path Galifar himself had pointed out on a map. Finally, I became so exhausted that I accidentally let the horse lead instead of the other way around. The damned beast must have smelled water. I suppose I should be grateful to it for that, at least."

"No doubt." Daryus continued to let the story remain unquestioned. He would divine the reasons for Raffan's inconsistencies soon enough.

However, as he finished speaking, Raffan suddenly clutched his head. Daryus leaned close, studying the other's face.

"Let me see your eyes. Make them wide."

Raffan obeyed. After a moment's study, Daryus nodded. "You've ingested something. Either by accident or by design." Daryus rubbed his chin. "Did the good captain give you anything?"

The younger man looked perplexed. "He provided the emergency food kit in my saddlebags. I transferred everything to the fresh horse before setting off. Had some then and more on the trail. Dried meat and such. Awful stuff. This is better, by the way."

"I'm honored. Which bag?"

"The one on the right side as you sit in the saddle."

Leaving Raffan to finish his food, Daryus hurried to the saddle. Digging into the bag in question, he found what remained of the food kit. Raffan had not left much, but there was one piece of meat large enough to test.

Daryus tasted a tiny bit. Under the heavy salt layer, he noted a slightly peculiar seasoning. It reminded him of something . . .

Returning to Raffan, Daryus asked, "Did this meat taste at all odd?"

"Of course! It's salty, leathered beef."

"More than that. There's something else on it. I can't recall what, but I think it's the reason you lost your senses and your way."

Raffan stared open-mouthed.

"Captain Galifar apparently intended something dishonest once we were deep in the Worldwound. This was how he planned to put you out of the situation." Daryus straightened. "Hurry up with that. We'll be on our way as soon as you're ready."

"We're continuing the expedition?"

"If you mean, 'Are we going to rescue Shiera?' then yes. You did mean that, didn't you, Master Raffan?"

Daryus's companion blinked. "Yes, yes, of course that's what I meant."

Nodding, Daryus left Raffan to his remaining food. After dealing with the campfire and other small necessities, he glanced back. Not at all to his surprise, Raffan had somehow managed to finish the tiny bit of rabbit just as Daryus finished all the work.

"Are we ready, then?" asked the well-clad young man.

In reply, Daryus silently mounted. Raffan rushed over to his own horse and followed suit. He grunted in exasperation as, without a look back, Daryus rode on.

Daryus did not wait for Toy, either, but it still did not surprise him when, just a few minutes into the journey, he felt the weasel's claws on his shoulder and heard the voice from right behind him.

"We should leave him!" whispered the creature. "We should find her ourselves!"

A side glimpse at Raffan revealed the young man to be focused entirely on the rough ride. He would hear no part of any conversation. "Not going to leave an innocent out in the middle of nowhere. He would've tried to continue after us and likely gotten killed. I'd be happy to leave *you* behind, if you like."

"He will slow us."

"Shut up or you'll follow the rabbit next stop we make."

That was enough to silence Toy for a time, but eventually the weasel regained his voice. "There *is* a better path."

"I know all the trustworthy paths in this region. This is the one they would've taken."

Raffan finally stirred. "What did you say?"

Daryus felt the familiar scurry down to the saddle. "There's another small spring a little ahead. We'd best top out our water sacks there."

"Mine's still at least two-thirds full—"

"There won't be much water for some time after that. I know."

Their route first led them up a hill, then down the other side. They rounded part of another hill, finally ending near the spring.

The two men went about filling the sacks. Leaving Raffan for a moment, Daryus climbed back up part of the hill to get his bearings. Although he had indicated to Toy that he knew just which path was best, it had been many years since he had taken it. A glance from above would help verify that nothing major had changed.

The weasel scampered alongside him. Daryus ignored his four-footed companion as he reached the lookout point and began studying the land ahead. The dark skies over the Worldwound beckoned a short distance ahead.

"Master Daryus . . ." came the whisper from behind him.

Something in Toy's tone eradicated any annoyance Daryus had with the familiar and made Daryus quickly look down. However, Toy did not look back at him, instead appearing more interested in something behind them.

A slight dust cloud.

Even had it not been rising along the same general path that he and his companions had traveled, Daryus would have recognized it immediately. A group of riders were heading the same direction as the trio, something that could not be a coincidence. Indeed, Daryus knew exactly who they had to be.

Harricka Morn was on his trail.

Quickly descending, Daryus returned to Raffan, who was already mounted. Swinging up into the saddle, the former crusader said, "From here, we pick up the pace. There's somewhere I want to be by the time darkness arrives."

Raffan silently shrugged. Glad that the other man did not realize why they were going to ride faster, Daryus urged his mount on. Toy jumped up behind him even as the mare picked up speed.

They rode on . . . and Harricka followed.

Daryus kept them going at as fast a pace as possible. Once, Raffan called for a stop, but Daryus pretended not to hear and rode on. That forced Raffan to do the same.

Three times, Daryus dared peer over his shoulder. Three times, he saw the dust. He judged it to be no nearer and, in fact, slightly reduced in size, as if the crusaders had fallen farther behind.

That was not enough for Daryus, though. Despite his original intentions, he finally veered off the expected trail. Daryus hoped to lead Harricka and her party in a different direction, then double back.

That left the going tougher. The terrain turned uneven and in some places soft to the point where Raffan's mount nearly tumbled forward as its hoof sank deeper than expected. After that, Daryus was forced to slow their pace, even if it meant further risk of the crusaders catching up.

To his relief, though, when he looked back just before nightfall, it was to discover no hint of the crusaders' party. It was still too soon for them to have stopped for the night, which to Daryus meant he had managed to shake them off.

Even then, Daryus pushed the trio as long as there was light. He had lied about having a particular spot in mind, but knew the area well enough to believe he would find *some* location safe enough.

He finally settled on a flat area surrounded by low hills that gave them a view of the path behind while protecting them from any eyes farther ahead. Setting up the camp naturally fell to Daryus. Raffan spent his time constantly perusing his notebook as if it were some sort of religious text. He only looked up when Daryus began taking what was left of the rabbit to prepare for a simple meal.

"We're eating that again?"

"Do you see anything else?"

Raffan wrinkled his nose. "I thought you would go hunting."

"Not a good place to do it, although you're welcome to try, if you disagree." Daryus made no mention of the pursuit. "We've enough. There will be a better place tomorrow."

The other man wrinkled his nose again, then returned his attention to the notebook.

From near Daryus's feet, Toy snickered. Daryus kicked at the weasel, who deftly evaded the foot despite it coming from his blind side.

Thinking of that eye, the former crusader determined that when Raffan slept, Daryus and the familiar would have a long, thorough conversation. There was too much that Daryus believed Toy held from him.

He handed Raffan his share of the meat, then, carrying the remainder, started up toward the tallest point. As he neared the top, he crouched. After first peering in the direction of the Worldwound and seeing nothing, he focused on the trail behind them.

A cloud of dust in the distance warned him immediately that he had not lost Harricka's patrol after all. They were not following the same path, but one close enough that there was still a chance Harricka might actually figure out where Daryus was.

We'll have to move on if they start veering to their right within the next hour. He started back down . . . then paused as something farther toward the Worldwound caught his attention.

It was another party. The dust was unmistakable, as was the fact that this second group had to be larger, based on how the dust rose.

Daryus could think of very few groups that would come from the Worldwound save another crusader patrol heading back after some hunt in the demon-benighted land. That did not bode well for Daryus; he had no doubt that if they ran across one another, Harricka would convince the second officer to combine the two patrols.

Gravely concerned, he remained where he was and watched. True to his luck thus far, Harricka's band turned to their right just where he feared, setting them on a course for where Daryus hid.

That settled it. Daryus rose, mind already running over potential locations ahead. However, barely had he started down than something about the second group of riders made him hesitate. They were now near enough to Harricka's party to see some trace of them and yet they did not either move to meet Daryus's pursuers or keep on toward Kenabres. Instead, they were taking a path that would bring them just behind Harricka.

For some reason, that made the hair on the back of Daryus's neck stiffen. Common sense demanded that he shut down the campsite and drag Raffan on, but still Daryus lingered. His gaze went back and forth between the two oncoming groups, his wariness growing with each passing second.

"Master Daryus!" Toy whispered. "Master Daryus, I think you must come—"

"Not now, Toy!"

"But Master Daryus—"

Frustrated, Daryus swung a heavy hand at where he heard the weasel. Toy deftly evaded it.

Trying his best to ignore the creature, Daryus continued to study the new group. Its choice of trails seemed designed to evade notice by Harricka's party.

"Master Daryus . . ."

Gritting his teeth, the human finally responded. "What is it now, Toy?"

"Your Master Raffan appears to be wandering off. He may be seen by the riders following us before the last light fades enough."

Swearing an oath that would have had a new Flaming Lance recruit scrubbing latrines for a week, Daryus rushed down to the campsite. Sure enough, Raffan was nowhere to be seen. It did not take Daryus long to find his footprints, though. As Toy had indicated, they led back along the way the trio had come.

Is he mad? Then Daryus recalled that the younger man had no idea about the crusaders nipping at their heels.

Hoping to catch Raffan before it was too late, Daryus raced after.

Raffan proved to be quick on his feet. Daryus wondered if his companion had started off the moment the fighter had left. That was about the only way Daryus could see Raffan making such distance.

As he feared, Raffan stood in the open, his attention on something Daryus could not yet make out but that he suspected was Harricka's band. Cursing again, Daryus closed on Raffan.

The younger man turned as he neared. "I think someone's heading our way."

"You have a talent for noticing the obvious. We need to get to our horses and go."

Raffan pointed. "Look! Something's happening!"

There was more than merely "something" happening. Daryus's earlier suspicions now proved too true. Harricka's band was being attacked from behind by what he had to assume was the second, larger party.

It should have been a relief to Daryus, but instead all he could think about was that fellow crusaders were in terrible trouble. Never mind that he was no longer one of their ranks, or that they'd be all too happy to execute him; all that Daryus saw was comrades-in-arms perishing before his eyes.

"Get back to the camp and stay there," he ordered Raffan. "Stay near your horse. If I don't come back in an hour, ride like hell to the south, then turn west again. Take whatever path you have to from there to get back to Nerosyan."

"Wait! What are you—"

"Do it!" Even as he gave the command, Daryus hurried back to the horses himself. He wasted no time, leaping atop his mount and turning it. Kicking hard, he rode past a running Raffan, then out into the open.

A pitched battle filled his gaze as he raced toward Harricka's band. Harricka and three other crusaders struggled against their attackers while also trying to keep astride their mounts. Two more crusaders lay sprawled on the rough landscape.

Even as he took this all in, another of Harricka's men fell from the saddle with an axe in his skull. Not at all to Daryus's surprise, the wielder of that axe proved to be a brawny pitborn with two long horns and a hook of a nose. He laughed as he gave the bloody axe one wipe on the side of the dead crusader's horse before pushing to reach Harricka.

A part of Daryus screamed at him for risking himself like this. The pitborn were actually doing him a favor removing the captain and her men. Yet Daryus could not let the crusaders be slaughtered. It wasn't in him, even after several years as a hired sword.

The choice, though, turned out not to be his. Despite killing one pitborn, another of Harricka's patrol perished when two foes skewered him.

Pushing the mare as hard as he could, Daryus finally reached the struggle. He brought down the nearest pitborn—a lanky rider with a mouthful of sharp teeth and a thick brow—with one swing, then immediately turned to face a second foe.

Yet even as Daryus gained that victory, another crusader fell victim. Growling, Daryus dispatched the killer, then the pitborn next to him as well.

He caught a glimpse of Harricka fending off two more adversaries, both among the ugliest and nastiest pitborn that Daryus had ever come across. They were also among the most imposing, which was why Harricka remained hard pressed. Daryus had seen her fight two opponents more than once, each time dealing with her foes with ease.

However, before he could reach her, one of her foes suddenly threw himself at her. Harricka and the pitborn fell from sight between the horses.

Despite his best efforts, Daryus could not reach her. Instead, he had to fend off the two pitborn who turned to face him. Daryus deflected the axe wielded by one, then traded sword blows with the second.

The axe came at him again. Daryus managed to evade it, only to see the second pitborn lunging.

Something hopped over Daryus and onto the oncoming sword. The abrupt weight forced the sword down, giving Daryus an opening.

He caught his foe in the throat. The pitborn glared, then toppled backward. Curiously, Daryus realized that the glare had not been for him, but for the cause of the sword being pressed earthward.

Toy.

The familiar had not waited. Once the sword was no longer a threat, the weasel had leapt to the other pitborn. Now, Toy crawled over the creature's back, harassing the pitborn and biting at any open flesh.

It was all Daryus needed. The pitborn tried to compensate for both attacks, but moved too slowly. Daryus gutted him.

He looked around for his next foe, only to discover he was the only one still mounted. Harricka's troops had been outnumbered from the start—

Harricka! He quickly steered his mount around to where she and her adversary had fallen. A tangle of legs was his first sighting of the two. He jumped off his mount, then pushed past the other riderless horses to the bodies.

The pitborn lay atop Harricka, the point of a dagger sticking out of the back of his neck. Daryus shoved the corpse aside, then bent to investigate the captain.

Harricka's eyes opened. Gritting her teeth, she grabbed Daryus by the throat.

There was no strength to the attack. Daryus easily removed her fingers. Coughing, the captain closed her eyes again and fell still.

Leaning close, Daryus could hear her breathing. It was steady, for which he gave thanks. He checked her for wounds and found only superficial ones, save for a severe bump on the back of her head that she must have gotten when she fell.

Daryus looked around. They were too far from Kenabres for him to dare send her unconscious astride her horse in the direction of the city. Likewise, he could not simply drag her from the other bodies and leave her here. There were too many carrion eaters about that were also willing to partake of helpless fresh flesh when the opportunity presented itself.

That left but one choice. A part of him wished that he had not been so determined to help, but another part knew that, given the choice over again, he would have done the same thing. Hefting the captain carefully over his shoulder, Daryus brought her to her mount. With effort, he managed to set her upright in the saddle. Cutting the reins from another horse, Daryus tied her in place.

As he did this, he noticed Toy scurrying from one pitborn corpse to another. Daryus frowned. "What are you doing?"

Toy looked up. For only the second time, the familiar had his other eye open. The demon eye balefully studied the human in a way Toy's normal orb could never match.

"Had to take the chance to see! These are the witch's! They have his stench!" As he spoke, Toy quickly shut the demon eye again.

"What were they doing out here?" Daryus suspected he knew the answer.

"Hunting us. They knew we were near."

There had been some hint by Toy in the past that assassins had been in touch with the witch through some magical method that enabled them to speak across great distances. The pair that

Daryus had left behind in Kenabres had probably reached out to their comrades, who had come seeking Daryus and the weasel but found Harricka's party instead.

"Let's get out of here. We need to get Raffan and get far from here." He left unspoken that there might be other pitborn in the area.

Toy peered at Harricka. "Leave this one."

"No."

The familiar flickered his demon eye open and shut, then trotted toward Daryus's horse.

Bringing the captain's horse alongside his, Daryus mounted. He studied Harricka again, wondering exactly what he would do once she awoke. He could not have her pursuing, but he knew she would not give up so easily, even after the rest of her party had been wiped out.

Then Daryus considered just where he was heading, and knew that Captain Harricka Morn was the least of his problems.

15

PLANS GONE AWRY

Toy was getting nearer.

That fact should not have disturbed Grigor so much, for the familiar had no great powers of his own. He was a talking animal, little more.

But still the weasel's continued progress bothered the witch greatly.

It had as much to do with what had happened to his flying scout as it did the familiar itself. This was not the first time Grigor had come across hints of some lupine—for lack of a better description—interference with his plans. Each time, Grigor could not help but consider the fact that much of his quest revolved around one of the key symbols of the focus of his hunt . . . the wolf, a member of the same family. The paw prints didn't not quite look like those of one of the desert animals, but that didn't mean there wasn't a connection. Grigor didn't believe in coincidence.

Ahead lay the weathered remains of a structure he knew had once been an outpost from a civilization that had existed after those who had built the lost temple-city. Grigor was not here to search for lost artifacts or clues. He was here to see about dealing with the weasel once and for all . . . and the fool of a man who had fallen prey to the familiar's lies.

The ruins provided him with a shadowed, private place to do his casting. Kneeling, Grigor placed the staff over his eyes just as he had when seeing through the bat's enhanced orbs. This time, though, he focused on another servant far, far away. A servant in Kenabres.

Master . . .

Grigor's view changed. Before him bent one of the pitborn who had briefly held Daryus hostage, the one the former crusader had wounded in the shoulder. The witch stared at him through the eyes of his companion.

Something's happened . . .

The pitborn looked nervous. *The familiar and the man escaped. We warned the others to watch for them beyond the city. Now, we hear nothing from them . . .*

Grigor had paid one group of pitborn to remain on hand near Kenabres at all times. They had been his backup plan in case Toy reached this far. What he heard now did not please him at all.

How long ago?

Two days.

You have attempted more than once?

Many times, Master, the pitborn responded, now more nervous than ever.

Grigor let the ugly creature sweat while he thought. The answers from the pitborn did not encourage the witch. Grigor considered a moment more, then, without warning, cut the link. Now he reached out to the leader of the other pitborn party.

No response. Even though Grigor had paid the pitborn well and made certain they all knew just how much they would be rewarded for their efforts when he triumphed, he had also made certain to instill in them a proper sense of fear. If they didn't earn their way, they stood a good chance of not surviving Grigor's wrath.

Unfortunately for the witch, these pitborn were beyond his reach. The blankness his mind met indicated only one thing: not one of the band still lived.

One man and that damned Toy could not do this! They could not! And yet, something or someone had slaughtered the small but capable group. Suddenly, Grigor's paths to success had shrunk again.

He had to have the Pathfinder. With her, locating the temple-city would become so much easier.

Once more, Grigor held the staff over his eyes. He had earlier that day sent out another of the bats in the direction he knew the woman would lie. By now, the beast had to be near its destination.

The mercenaries had long been in his employ, a secondary precaution should Toy intrude in his plans. Sure enough, that had happened. Once aware of Toy's presence near the Pathfinder, Grigor had ordered the mercenaries to separate her from the dandy and continue on with her alone. Grigor had wanted her to believe she was doing all this of her free will, but the kidnapping had been necessary now that time was of the essence. Either way, she would do as he desired. She had the skill, the natural aptitude, that he needed.

The transition to the bat's view was instantaneous. The winged spy soared over the Worldwound, seeking out Galifar's group. The captain knew where he had to be. The man's greed would make certain that he and his men would have the Pathfinder with them at the appointed place and time.

The bat flew low, but not so low that Grigor Dolch risked yet another creature. The memories of the other's violent destruction remained fresh.

The flier's presence stirred up a number of small, dark creatures that quickly darted for the nearest burrows. Grigor knew them for carrion eaters. The Worldwound was full of carrion eaters, of course. A place where death was common attracted every kind of vermin and, even in this place, created more.

Ahead, the landmarks Grigor had relayed to the mercenaries finally came into view. There was no sign of the campsite, but

Galifar would be clever enough not to make their presence known to the denizens of the Worldwound.

A horse suddenly came into view. The animal looked nervous, as would any sensible beast here. It wandered in the general direction of the border, but Grigor doubted it would reach it. The local predators probably already smelled its fear.

Then, it occurred to him to wonder why this horse would run loose so near where the mercenaries should have been. Gritting his teeth, the witch had his pet pick up the pace—

And came across the first body only seconds later.

The carrion eaters had already begun their work on the dead man. In fact, he looked to have been dragged some distance. Diving lower, the bat revealed to Grigor that most of the face had already been eaten away, as had any other flesh not protected by armor. What had killed the man was not readily obvious, and not of great import to Grigor. What did matter was that the witch was almost certain this was one of Captain Galifar's followers.

Seconds later, the bat flew over what remained of the campsite. There, Grigor beheld a second body, then two more.

A closer inspection of the last revealed what was left of Captain Galifar, face eaten away, identifiable only by his armor.

This cannot be! It cannot! It seemed to Grigor that at almost every turn some force appeared to intervene. Something attempted to keep him from his destiny—he was certain of that now. Not Toy or their former patron—they would take a more direct route, want Grigor to know who was responsible.

But if not them, who? Some guardian left behind by Uhl-Adanar's builders, determined to stop anyone who might release its prisoner?

Chewing over that disturbing thought, Grigor continued his search for the only thing that truly mattered here: the Pathfinder.

A quick but thorough flight over the camp revealed no other body. While it was possible that the Pathfinder's lighter body might have been dragged off to feed young vermin in some underground nursery, Grigor preferred to think she was still alive. She *had* to be. She was key. She—

"Ah!" The exclamation escaping Grigor did not in any way reflect the true depth of his relief. The partial footprints near the edge of the campsite led directly to where several sets of hoofprints had mercilessly pummeled the ground.

At his whim, the bat circled the spot. Sure enough, while most of the hoofprints headed either toward the border or along it, *two* sets followed a route deeper into the Worldwound.

She lives. Grigor smiled. Fortune was with him. The woman had an admirable survival streak.

He ordered the bat to follow the tracks, then broke contact. When the creature drew near the woman, Grigor would know.

Exhaling, the witch straightened—

Poor, poor Grigor! Does he miss Toy? Toy misses Grigor . . .

Grigor froze. It had been a long, long time since he and the familiar had touched thoughts, the last such moment just after Grigor had broken his oath to his patron and dared find yet another way by which to augment his power. The eye cut from the tortured demon had fit Toy's socket perfectly, almost as if the success of the witch's experiment had been preordained.

But there Grigor's luck had ended . . . and with it, almost his life. Of course, he knew he might have been a little responsible for all that, too, his patron having forbidden any delving into stealing actual demon magic, even from one of the patron's lowliest servants. Setting the eye in his familiar should have given Grigor a new avenue of power, theoretically drawing from the creature's innate magic. It was something the witch had always wanted to test, but had not, due to his awareness of the potential consequences.

Yet, in the end, Grigor just could not resist the temptation . . . and so things were where they were now. The most frustrating part had been that the experiment had proven a failure. Grigor had gained no access to demon magic.

Toy . . . devious little Toy . . . His moment of surprise over, the witch took command of the situation. He was the one with the power. Toy had only his cunning, which was a reflection of Grigor's, nothing more. *You really should not play games with me . . .*

As he responded, Grigor reached into one of the pouches on his belt. It took him no more than a breath to find what he wanted. He pulled the soft, oval object out.

With Toy's mummified eye in his hand, Grigor continued, *I would have given you a swift death . . .*

How magnanimous is Grigor! Toy mocked in turn. *Would that every familiar had a master so magnanimous . . . but not so treacherous . . .*

The witch smiled grimly. *You should never have betrayed me.*

We were sworn to the great one, Master Grigor! You weren't satisfied even with all he gave, especially life when life was over.

Grigor fought down the temptation to reach up and assure himself that his flesh remained pliant. *There were limitations. There were always limitations . . .*

Not a thousand patrons could ever satisfy Grigor Dolch. That was the problem.

Are you seeking something, Toy? the witch countered. *Are you seeking that which you need to be whole again? I have it with me.* He imagined the mummified eye, aware that by doing so, the weasel would see it, also.

The fury he expected to hear from his former familiar did not materialize. Instead, Toy's vile chuckle echoed in the witch's head. *Thank you. I wanted to make certain that you had it. I know you will now no matter what.*

The familiar's voice vanished from Grigor's thoughts.

The witch acted, but it was already too late. The simple spell for which he had in part saved the eye would have made it so very easy for him to end Toy's existence once and for all. Unfortunately, Toy had obviously calculated well just how much time his former master would have needed and had given him slightly less.

Grigor stood quietly waiting for a moment, but the weasel had no plan to risk himself again. He had discovered what he needed to know, that Grigor would never have destroyed the eye.

For a moment, the witch seethed. Then, slowly, sense returned. Grigor needed the eye, but then, so, too, did Toy. Indeed, Toy needed it more.

Toy needed it *more.*

Very well, my little monster, Grigor thought with growing satisfaction. *Now I know how to make certain that you will be where I want you when I want you . . .*

He replaced the eye in the pouch. For the time being, the wisest thing he could do was continue on. Kenabres was no longer his destination. The Pathfinder had entered the Worldwound. That actually placed her nearer to Grigor. What mattered now was reaching her before anyone or anything else did.

You will *lead me to my glory,* the witch promised. *And then you and Toy will be my first sacrifices to it . . .*

16

HUNTED AND HERDED

She should have turned back. Every sensible thought said turn back. One did not journey into the Worldwound alone unless one had a desire for an agonizing death. With Daryus at her side, matters would have been different. He had braved this place's horrors many times and lived to tell about it. He would have seen them to their destination, of that Shiera was certain.

Yet still Shiera rode deeper into the foul land. That she did so had much to do with what had happened back at the camp. A terrifying force had slaughtered Captain Galifar and his men, but left her untouched. Indeed, she had even been freed from her bonds.

Of course, having been fortunate enough to survive one demon encounter should have sent her running from the Worldwound. The odds of surviving a second—and this being the Worldwound, a second encounter was inevitable—were astronomical.

Impossible, actually. The Worldwound was more than just a demon-blighted realm. It had manifested on Golarion shortly after the death of the man-god Aroden. It was said that his dying caused a planar shift—a very slight alteration in Golarion's existence tilting it closer to the Abyss. The nation of Sarkoris had been engulfed and destroyed as demonic energies and creatures poured into the region. The former had meant the continual reshaping and distorting of everything, including any surviving inhabitants.

Since that time, a constant war had raged. Demonic forces sought to encroach on the rest of the world while human crusades arose seeking to eradicate them.

At best, the result was a tenuous stalemate. However, the lure of ancient treasure—and in the case of a Pathfinder, *knowledge*—meant there were always those willing to enter the Worldwound . . . and perhaps somehow make things worse in the process.

She tried not to think about that last part. She had reasons for being here. *Good* ones.

Not for the first time, Shiera's horse slowed. The animal had more sense than her. It wanted to follow the ones she had sent off toward Kenabres.

The horse trailing behind them snorted warily. Laden with what supplies Shiera could quickly pack onto it from the rest, it made for a prime target for any predator. Shiera felt guilty about forcing the animal into such a role, but ever the hunt for Uhl-Adanar beckoned her.

Your ambition is admirable . . . in moderation. So Amadan Gwinn had told her when first she had posed the question of just who deserved the recognition for the expedition's discoveries. *It needs more seasoning before it can be allowed to flourish, though.*

She wondered what he would make of her now. Perhaps when he had been much younger, Amadan Gwinn might have taken the same risks she had. Now, though, Shiera was certain that he would have been the first to recommend turning back. Daryus Gaunt would not have represented much of a defense to the senior Pathfinder. Amadan Gwinn would have had fifty soldiers armed to the teeth around him . . . which had been near the truth on his last expedition.

But right at this moment, Shiera Tristane would have been very happy with just the former crusader at her side.

She left herself scant thought concerning Raffan. She had agreed to him traveling with her because he had been the controller of his master's purse strings. Now that Shiera was well into the Worldwound and had enough supplies for a lone person, Raffan was not important. When she returned—*when* she kept telling herself, not *if*—she would present her findings to the overdressed man. That would certainly assuage Raffan and his master.

Thunder rolled. Shiera peered up at the sky, but didn't worry overmuch. The sky here was overcast, but not in the way she thought it had been prior to the demon's storm. Of course, this being the Worldwound, she remained well aware that natural conditions did not exist. For all she knew, a storm was imminent. However, she dared not think in those terms, lest she never reach the lost temple-city.

Thus far, she had chosen her route based on the general area where she believed she would find Uhl-Adanar. Prior to departing Nerosyan, Shiera had poured over every reasonable map of the Worldwound that she could lay her hands on. Now, those maps remained a part of her memory, every detail there to be summoned when she needed it.

Twilight was nearly upon her, but she hoped to still squeeze out an hour of riding. If she was correct, then just around the low hill she was currently skirting she would find—

Shiera pulled hard on the reins as she stared at the landscape ahead. Instead of the rocky plain her memories of the maps insisted had to be there, a long, narrow valley stretched as far as the eye could see.

Either the maps are all wrong . . . or the Worldwound has changed itself . . . She glared at the valley as if that would transform it back into the missing plain—something that was not altogether out of the question.

Seeing the landscape's mutability for the first time on such a scale proved daunting even to her. Suddenly all her cartographic knowledge was suspect. If such a huge landmark could exist despite what all the maps said, then even her carefully crafted route might be worthless.

Unwilling to admit to such a devastating blow, Shiera immediately set about locating another landmark—any landmark—that would give her some notion as to where she was.

She had nearly given up when she caught sight of a ridge far to the south shaped like a hawk's beak. Pleased to find that at least one of her landmarks existed, she immediately began reassessing her current position. With some urging, Shiera convinced her horse to ride toward the ridge. If all went well, she believed the ridge would lead her to specific clues regarding—

A dark form raced between the mounts. The other horse shied, then pulled free. Try as she might, Shiera cold not focus on the scurrying creature in time to make out what it was. She only knew it had to be larger than a cat, almost as large as a moderately sized hound.

Shiera dismounted. She gave a short whistle that brought the second horse to a halt. With both nervous animals under her control again, she glanced left and right in search of whatever had been stalking the horses, but found nothing. Still, she could not shake off the feeling that the thing remained nearby.

Mounting again, she forced herself to keep the horses at a slower, more deliberate pace. The stronger control proved beneficial to the animals, who moved along more calmly.

As she rode, Shiera summoned up in her thoughts the landmarks that would follow after the ridge. If even one or two of them were still recognizable, then she would have no trouble keeping on her quest.

Despite her best efforts, she did not make as much distance as she hoped. Darkness descended, and with it the knowledge that not even a fool would continue through the Worldwound at night.

A gnarled, decaying tree overlooked the most likely spot for her to use as a campsite. She dismounted, took care of the horses, then tried to settle down. Although she had the makings of a campfire in the dry, scattered branches from the dead tree, Shiera decided against building one. A fire here would be like a beacon to whatever else lurked in the vicinity.

That did not mean she intended to simply sit there and take her chances. She pulled out the small crossbow and set one of the bolts into it. The other bolts she kept within easy reach. Then she sat against the tree, weapon cocked. As a Pathfinder, she had learned to put herself into a mental state between waking and actual sleep. It was not the best way of resting, but it would serve her here. If the maps retained enough accuracy, tomorrow she would find a safer place to sleep.

From another pouch, Shiera drew a few pieces of dried meat. While it wasn't the most appetizing of meals, she had long ago grown used to the taste. What mattered was that it would keep her strong. She thanked the late Captain Galifar for providing her with enough to last quite some time—long enough, so she hoped, for her to get the lay of the land and start hunting.

This is insane! Amadan Gwinn's voice in her head again. Shiera knew these were not words the veteran Pathfinder had uttered, but rather her own mind using his voice in yet another attempt to convince her to turn from this foolishness.

Yet no matter how many times the voice repeated the declaration, Shiera knew she would go on.

The horses huddled together and shifted as close to her as they could. Shiera was grateful for their nearness. Thus far, aside from the small matter of the mercenaries, the Worldwound had been very quiet, but she knew that could be the lull before the storm.

The horses suddenly snorted. Shiera tensed. There was a brief pattering of feet in the darkness.

Tiny gibbering voices rose around her, but especially from one direction.

She fired.

A harsh squeal erupted from the darkness. A flurry of movement followed, growing more distant with each second. The mad gibbering faded with the movement.

The crossbow reloaded, Shiera leapt up and took a few steps toward where the creature had been. Something glistened faintly on the ground. Blood, she decided, but of a yellow-green color and thicker than hers would have been. She had hit squarely whatever had been lurking in the dark. Shiera doubted it would live out the night. Either the loss of blood would kill it . . . or the smell of blood would bring other predators seeking an easy meal.

Returning to the tree, Shiera settled down once more. While she had taken some satisfaction in finally being able to strike back at some enemy—even if but an unseen beast—she knew that the incident was just a hint of what might come.

Dawn—or rather a fiery gray facsimile of it—came at last. Shiera had heard a few other noises hinting that she and the horses were not alone, but nothing had repeated the overconfidence of the gibbering creature.

She wasted no time in moving on. Somewhere nearby she knew there had to be a water source. That and food were her only priorities other than moving on in search of the temple-city.

Once more Amadan Gwinn's pompous voice reminded her of the odds of surviving the Worldwound, and once more she ignored it. More and more, Shiera truly believed that she was on the right trail, that Uhl-Adanar would soon be in her sights.

Her confident thoughts were interrupted by an anxious snort from her mount. Crossbow at the ready, Shiera looked for whatever threat the animal had sensed.

Instead, she spotted the splatter-covered fragments of what looked like bits of a giant wasp or some similar creature. The splatter was the same bloody goo she had seen last night.

Whatever the creature had been, it had been had been the size of a small dog.

And whatever it had been still had her bolt buried in the remnants of its carcass.

The utter destruction of her wounded night visitor did not bother her so much as how *near* to the campsite it had been brought down. Whatever had slaughtered the beast had not been all that far from where Shiera had slept.

Double-checking the bolt in her crossbow, Shiera urged her mount on. Even when the ruined corpse was far behind her, she did not relax.

The narrow valley beckoned to her. Shiera paused as three different routes offered themselves. The one in the center looked the best, but that alone made her suspicious. Shiera eyed the one to her left, which seemed to wind into the rockier part of the valley in a very uninviting way. The third revealed no outright objections, yet did not give her enough to be certain that it did not go wandering off the wrong way later on.

Grimacing, Shiera decided to stick with the center. However, no sooner had she done so than she felt a coldness at her side.

Reaching down, she sought the source of the peculiar chill. To her surprise, it was the ancient coin that Raffan had given her in her chambers. Shiera had kept the coin on her in order to study it from time to time, but hadn't paid it any mind under the circumstances of the past few days.

Now it not only radiated the strange coldness, but also glowed a faint blue. Shiera eyed the artifact, both marveling at what it did and wondering what it meant.

When nothing else happened, she impatiently gripped the cold coin and shook the reins. The horse started down the center path.

"Aaa!" The coin was now so cold it threatened to give her frostbite. Pulling tight on the reins, Shiera opened her palm and glared at the offending artifact.

Then, on a hunch, she eyed the other two paths. After a moment's consideration, she steered her mount toward the path on the right.

The coin grew colder.

She immediately forced her horse to the remaining trail. As she expected, the chill faded.

Shiera pondered her discovery. Some ancient force in the coin reacted either to the paths or to some other artifact along the correct trail. Either way, her heart pounded with excitement at this new clue. Finding Uhl-Adanar and the tomb of the supposed god Tzadn seemed not only imminent, but truly her destiny.

With growing eagerness, she rode into the valley. In contrast, the horses remained reluctant, but Shiera overrode their concerns. She was aware they smelled the foulness of the Worldwound. However, other than turning around and riding from the region, she could do nothing to assuage their fears. The Worldwound was, after all, the Worldwound.

The path was not an easy one. Much of it was steep, with loose rock all along the way. That made for much slower going and also caused Shiera to wonder if she had been misled concerning just which way to take.

As the hours passed and her progress continued to be far less than she hoped, Shiera tried to decide where best to pause. The area was quiet, which on the surface seemed a good thing, but she could not help feeling she was missing something.

She suddenly looked over her shoulder. For just a moment, Shiera had felt as if she were being watched, yet there was no hint of anyone or anything.

The trail leveled out. She spotted a trickle of water and guided the horses toward it—

This time, the sense that she was being observed was so strong that she had to swivel in her saddle to make certain she looked in every direction. Even after that, the feeling persisted, to the point that Shiera finally looked skyward.

Something darted out of sight.

Shiera brought up the crossbow. It had only been a brief glimpse, but the wings hadn't been like those of a bird, but rather leathery like a bat's.

After more than a minute of futilely watching, Shiera lowered her weapon. With more caution, she brought the horses to the water and, after checking the stream for anything suspicious, let them drink.

The brush nearby rustled. Shiera spun and shot.

The bolt hit the brush, but apparently nothing else. However, a second later, a small fringed lizard scurried from the area.

Grimacing, Shiera went and retrieved the bolt. She returned to the horses, mounted, and started back on the trail.

From the brush arose more rustling, this time with a violence and intensity no tiny lizard could have created.

Shiera did not hesitate. She brought the crossbow around and fired.

As the bolt hit the brush, an angry chittering arose. A winged form burst from the branches.

A horrific winged form with a body akin to some macabre melding of a locust and a wasp the size of a small dog rose to eye level. The creature had no discernible eyes, no other features at all save a wide humanoid mouth full of teeth. A mouth that, if anything, managed to open twice as wide when the monstrosity began the unsettling chittering she had heard earlier.

And from the brush all around her rose *more* . . . each of them seemingly larger and hungrier-looking than the previous.

Vescavors. Shiera had read about these when researching the Worldwound's myriad dangers. Not true demons, but vermin that prowled the steaming crevices and jungles of the Abyss. While she might normally be proud of such a quick identification, in this case the knowledge brought Shiera little comfort, as did the fact that somewhere in the vicinity might be their queen, an even deadlier threat.

She reloaded quickly and fired again. This time, she caught one dead center. Yellow-green goo flying everywhere, the chittering monster plummeted.

With a manic increase in their chittering, several of the others turned to the free meal. Shiera breathed a sigh of relief, then cursed as out of other parts of the surrounding brush burst more of the vermin. Unlike the others, these focused solely on Shiera and her animals.

Shiera urged her horse on . . . and three more of the hideous creatures jumped out in front of her. Her horse reared, causing Shiera to lose her grip on the pack animal.

Bereft of Shiera's control, the second horse panicked and ran off. Immediately, most of the swarm scattered after it. While that aided Shiera some, there were still more than enough of the horrific vermin to be a danger.

Using the gap opened by the other horse's flight, Shiera pushed her mount. The horse galloped down the uneven trail, stumbling here and there and at times threatening to toss Shiera off. The vescavors soared after, proving that they were capable of astounding speed and grace.

She managed another shot, which missed but at least sent one of the lead creatures darting away for a moment. That bought Shiera precious seconds, but little more.

The horse stumbled again. Suddenly, the desperate animal began sliding down the valley. Shiera gripped the reins tighter and tried to guide the horse to safer ground, but the beast was no longer paying her commands any mind.

The trail finally leveled out some. The horse succeeded in regaining some balance. That in turn enabled it to pick up its own pace. The gap started to grow.

Some of the swarm fell away. However, half a dozen determined fiends continued after, their blood-red eyes eager.

The trail converged ahead. Shiera had to make a swift decision. The horse already leaned to the left, so she chose that direction.

Barely had she committed them than the chill touched her side again.

"No, damn it!" Despite the discovery that she had chosen wrong, Shiera could do nothing but keep riding. She hoped that somewhere along the way, she would be able to adjust.

The trail dropped steeply.

This time, the frightened horse could not keep itself righted. Its hooves scraping for some sort of hold, it slid several yards down . . . and then toppled forward.

Tossing the crossbow ahead of her, Shiera managed to jump just in time. As she dropped to the side of the path, the horse flipped over once, then rolled farther down.

Shiera struck hard, but forced herself to roll into a crouching position despite her pain. She quickly drew her sword, then searched for the crossbow. She plucked up the weapon and hung it at her side. For now, the sword would do better.

But when she turned to face the pack, she found herself alone. Only when she heard the horse's terrified cries did she realize that the vermin had continued on after the biggest and easiest meal available. Shiera could not imagine the horse having gone through such a fall without breaking at least one leg. That would be all it took for the fiends to finish it.

The cold radiating from the coin continued to irritate her side. Keeping a wary eye on the trail she had abandoned, Shiera attempted to reach the correct route on foot.

The cold eased slightly as she moved on, a potential sign that she had chosen wisely. With no hint of the pack behind her, she sheathed the sword and reloaded her crossbow. She could draw the blade at a moment's notice, but the crossbow would now give her the advantage of distance.

Farther back, the horse shrieked over and over. Each successive cry grew weaker. Shiera swallowed hard. She had demanded much from the horses, and now both had paid the price for her stubbornness.

Silence overtook the canyon, that dread silence following an awful death. Shiera kept the crossbow ready, certain that some of the monstrous hunters would decide fighting over the carcass wasn't worth the trouble with other meat afoot. She cautiously wended her way along the treacherous landscape as best she could, aware that the swarm could be right behind her at any second.

When Shiera was far enough away, she pulled free the coin. It glowed faintly. The chill had reduced to a slight coolness. She took comfort in knowing she was heading the right direction, although what she would do when darkness—now imminent—came was a question for which she had no answer. True, her skills as a Pathfinder would help her in creating shelter and even locating some sort of food and water, but there remained the threat of the swarm, and other horrors of the Worldwound. Shiera still remained on the periphery of the accursed realm; things would only grow more dangerous as she continued deeper.

Hours passed. She had to move cautiously, not only because of the potential threat of predators but also the increasingly unstable nature of her route. The rough, stony trail caused her to slip more than once. Only the fact that the coin continued to show she was heading the right direction kept her from simply stopping out of frustration.

Even Daryus would have likely told her she was mad to keep going in the dark. If one was at all intelligent, one did not wander about the Worldwound at any time, much less the middle of the night. Yet, thus far, she had been fortunate—

The rattle of stone as something wended its way toward Shiera from the direction of the wrong trail made her spin about and nearly fire the crossbow. She held back at the last moment, a good thing since there was no target in view. Still, she doubted what she had heard was another tiny lizard.

More movement . . . but this time it came from ahead of her. Quietly cursing, Shiera turned around—

And nearly dropped the crossbow.

The wolf stood nearly as tall as her at the shoulder. Shiera had seen more than a few hounds and mastiffs, but even those sturdy canines could not compare in muscle and powerful jaws to the animal before her.

The hound stood watching her intently. Shiera knew she should fire, but something inside made her hold back.

Then, something made her glance to the unsettling wolf's left. There, she beheld a second wolf identical to the first.

Fire! Fire! a part of her mind insisted. *Fire before they rip you to shreds!*

Yet, still she held back. As strong and deadly as this pair looked, Shiera felt no threat. Instead, she stood almost mesmerized by their staring eyes.

Their great, *cyclopean* eyes.

17

DEATH IN THE DARK

Not for the first time, Raffan peeked back at Harricka, who still sat unconscious and bound astride her mount.

"Must she be with us? Can't you just send her horse in the direction of Kenabres? I've heard the horses of the crusaders can bring their wounded masters great distances to where they can get aid."

"Those are just stories." That wasn't *entirely* true, but Daryus didn't want to encourage such thoughts.

"She's going to die, anyway."

"No, she won't." Indeed, after checking on the captain during a previous pause, Daryus was relieved to see that Harricka had improved. He had been careful to bind her wounds well and his effort had paid off.

Of course, that just meant he was helping her recover enough to go after him again.

"We can't continue dragging her around the Worldwound . . ."

That was perhaps the only thing upon which they both agreed. Daryus had no intention of dragging Harricka through the accursed land, but neither would it have been wise to leave the captain where he had found her. Daryus knew a couple of fairly safe spots where Harricka would likely be found by other crusaders or, more likely, use her skill to quickly free herself.

Naturally, he did not plan on trusting to the whims of fate as to whether she was discovered by her comrades before some animal or pitborn came across her. Well aware from his own experience as to Harricka's skills, Daryus was certain that if he left the captain a dagger, that would be more than sufficient for her to take care of herself.

"You're only making this worse on yourself."

Daryus blinked, then looked at his former comrade. Harricka eyed him like a hawk. He wondered just how long she had been awake.

"You would do best to save your strength," he replied quietly.

"I'll have enough strength with which to deal with you, Daryus Gaunt. I promise you that."

Daryus grunted. Harricka had never been one for idle threats. When she swore she would follow through on something, she did.

"This isn't my doing," Raffan piped up. "I know nothing about all this. I just hired this man for a job that he's already complicated."

"You are inconsequential in this matter. Your crimes are meager compared to this villain's offenses."

Daryus could not hold back. "I did what was right. I would do it again."

"Your lack of remorse only magnifies your crimes. You'll either hang or lose your head. Which it will be is the only remaining question."

"Better to lose my life for good reasons than fail to be what the order once preached."

The captain spat. "They were *pitborn*."

"They were innocents. What we swore to protect. Other crusaders, even other members of our order, don't see them as you do—"

"Pitborn, Daryus. Pitborn. Hiding from the law, infiltrating human lands."

Raffan gave the duo a confused look, but wisely kept quiet this time. Harricka continued to glare at Daryus, who finally gave up trying to convince her and turned his thoughts back to how to safely rid himself of his former comrade. He would have to make certain she was bound well enough, but still able to escape after a suitable time. If the captain freed herself too soon, she would be right on his trail.

Realizing that his thoughts were coming full circle without any progress made, Daryus focused on getting the party moving. His trained eye caught telltale glimpses of recent activity heading in the same direction as the trio, which to Daryus could only mean he was still following the route taken by Shiera and her captors.

He still doubted that Galifar and his thugs were aware just how dangerous the Worldwound could be. Often there were stories of travelers crossing the edge of the ominous realm without any trouble whatsoever. What those stories didn't mention was that many of those supposed close calls had actually taken place far from the true border of the Worldwound—many civilians did not know exactly where the benighted land truly started, thinking themselves bold explorers while still well within the crusader-maintained buffer zone. And then of course there was the fact that such stories naturally skewed toward success—for the unsuccessful rarely survived to tell about it.

Making a calculation, Daryus said to Raffan, "We ride for another hour, then halt for the night."

"But there will still be more than another hour of light! Almost two!"

"Any deeper tonight and we risk ourselves. If we stay where I say, we'll make good time the next day and reach another potentially safe area."

The younger man looked unconvinced. Daryus would have dearly loved to continue on himself, if only to catch up to Shiera. Still, he knew better than to give in to such considerations. The Worldwound would not allow for mistakes in judgment.

"Listen to him, young fool," Harricka muttered. "He knows the Worldwound better than most. He might as well be a pitborn himself. He loves them enough."

"Harricka—"

She stopped talking, but only because she had said what she had wanted to say.

Raffan frowned, then nodded. "As you say, then."

His acquiescence did nothing to make Daryus feel more comfortable. The trio rode on without speaking for quite some time. While Daryus had to take the lead, he made certain that Harricka was always near enough to keep an eye on. He had done his best to make certain that even she would not be able to free herself, but knew she might yet have some trick up her sleeve.

It was for that reason that when Harricka first signaled him with a low, brief cough, Daryus at first ignored her. Only when she persisted did he slow his mount enough so that they were side by side.

"I say this because it is my duty to bring you to justice, not let some other fate befall you," she whispered. "We are followed."

"You're just now noticing? They've been after us for more than an hour. You're getting old, Harricka."

Her brow arched. "I see. I don't think they're crusaders."

"No. I imagine that they're pitborn."

"Former friends of yours?"

"Assassins, unless I miss my guess. You probably found traces of them in Kenabres." Daryus had expected the two surviving pitborn to follow his trail, but was surprised at how efficient they had been.

"Them?" For the first time, Harricka's eyes radiated a disdain for someone other than Daryus. "A disgrace to discover they infiltrated the city! I will see that heads roll . . . after theirs do."

"They may have a different notion in mind. These are no ordinary saboteurs."

"Give me my sword and I'll deal with them."

Daryus allowed himself a slight humorless smile. "Before or after you use it on me?"

"That would depend on circumstances."

She meant that, he knew. Even though there might have been some minute chance that he would have considered her request, Harricka had stayed true to herself and told Daryus exactly what she would do. Daryus admired her single-mindedness, even if it made his troubles greater.

A glance passed between them, silent agreement that Raffan need not know what was going on. The man would only tip their hand.

The assassins stayed far behind and out of sight. Daryus called for a halt just as planned, but now did so with one eye ever behind them. He caught no hint of either pitborn, but knew that the pair were wending their way closer with every second.

A blithely ignorant Raffan settled down while Daryus set up camp. Harricka watched with some amusement as the former crusader did the work. Daryus had no doubt she was sizing him up, ready to exploit any weakness he showed.

The preparation of food also fell to Daryus, but, in this case, Harricka, her unfortunate comrades, and even the dead pitborn provided the fare. Daryus had gathered everything he could from all the saddlebags. They had food for at least four days—five if he managed to leave Harricka behind soon.

"They're near," she whispered as he finished feeding her.

Daryus did not doubt her. While his own senses were highly attuned—and generally better than that of most men—his need to also pay attention to his captive meant he could not entirely focus on the surrounding terrain.

"I'll take care of it."

"Give me my sword."

"Will you use it only against the assassins?"

She said nothing.

After a moment's hesitation, Daryus reached to his belt and drew his dagger. Making certain that Raffan was not looking, he tossed the dagger near—but not too near—Harricka.

The captain gave a brief grimace. Daryus ignored her, instead concentrating on searching for the relatively invisible fourth member of their party.

Of Toy, there was no sight. He had ridden quietly behind Daryus for most of the journey, not willing to risk discovery by the crusader officer. If Harricka recognized the weasel for what he actually was—the former tool of an evil witch—that would make Toy as big a target to her as Daryus was.

A few brief footprints in the dusty soil revealed the direction the weasel had gone. Toy hunted his own food and hunted it well. Daryus gave up on the creature. He would have to finish with the assassins himself.

Darkness came. He checked on the captain, found the dagger untouched, and returned to the fire.

Where would I be? Daryus asked himself the question as he pretended to settle down for the evening. *Where would I be if I were an assassin here?*

The area did not allow for anything larger than a small snake to sneak up on the group. Yet Daryus remained aware that the assassins had access to magic thanks to the witch.

Thinking of that, he rose. Raffan already slept, but Harricka's eyes remained open. In fact, they had never left Daryus's once.

He bent over as if to test her bonds. They still felt quite snug.

As he straightened again, Daryus made certain to kick the dagger closer.

Something shot out of the darkness.

Had it not been for his half-elven eyesight, Daryus would have never even seen the dart. The wicked missile shot past his ear and continued on beyond the campsite.

Daryus drew his sword.

Three more darts came at him, two from his left, the other from the original direction.

He deflected two with his sword, then twisted out of the path of the third. As he expected, four more darts closed on him, two from each direction.

He flung himself to the side, avoiding two of the darts. The sword deflected another.

The fourth hit his shoulder.

Cursing, Daryus grabbed at the dart. To his relief, it had not penetrated his leather.

Rolling over, he turned to Harricka with the intention of freeing her after all.

A pile of severed ropes was the only sign left of her.

Now aware that he had three potential threats with which to deal, Daryus twisted around into a crouching position. No more darts came his direction, but Daryus did not see that as any positive note. The darts had been more of a test by the assassins, a way of seeing just what limits their target had out here. The real attack would be swifter, more sure.

He quickly looked over his shoulder at where Raffan still slept, the young man oblivious to the danger around him. Daryus would have liked to have left Raffan slumbering, but dared not trust that the assassins sought him alone.

Keeping alert, Daryus headed for the other man. He did not call out, not even quietly, preferring that Raffan remain still. Daryus was fairly certain that if he woke the younger man before he reached him, Raffan would jump up and make himself an easier target.

Silence reigned over the campsite as he moved. Daryus listened for any sound, the slightest hint of movement that would be the only thing presaging the assassins' work.

To his surprise and growing concern, he made it all the way to Raffan without any trouble. Keeping his eye on the area surrounding them, Daryus gently shook Raffan by the shoulder.

The other man did not wake.

Daryus quickly looked down.

A small dart stuck out of Raffan's neck.

The whirling blade nearly took off Daryus's head. He managed to evade death only by falling atop Raffan, who still breathed regularly. Even then, Daryus felt a trickle of blood slipping down his neck toward his shoulder.

Without looking, he swung his sword up. The clang of metal against metal echoed through the darkness as Daryus just barely managed to keep the sword above him from doing what the flying blade had not. The pitborn looming over him—the one with the broken nose—said nothing, instead drawing a smaller dagger with his other hand.

Grabbing Raffan with his free hand, Daryus rolled both of them away from the assassin. Ending the tumble atop the drugged man, the former crusader slashed at his attacker.

The pitborn countered his attack, then jabbed with the dagger. Daryus noticed his foe favored the small blade more than would have made sense, which meant it probably had some drug or poison on the end.

As he dueled with the pitborn, several things disturbed Daryus. First and foremost was where the other assassin might be at this moment. Beyond that was what Harricka was up to while this was going on. Not for a moment did he think she had abandoned the area, but neither did he expect the captain to aid him. Harricka was just as likely to let the assassins come within an inch of killing Daryus before she intervened.

The pitborn smiled grimly as he thrust. Something else about the horned figure bothered Daryus, but it took him a few precious moments to realize what it was. Unlike his initial encounter with the pitborn, this time the assassin made no use of the masking artifact. Daryus wondered why, since in the unpredictable illumination of the campfire, it could have given the demonspawn a very distinct advantage.

Too late, Daryus understood why. The assassin was only another distraction.

He tried to bring his sword behind him, but it was too late. The powerful arm of the second assassin wrapped around his throat, cutting off his air.

"Where is the damned creature? Speak!" grated the second pitborn.

Daryus wondered how he was supposed to answer without any air. He eyed the first assassin, now approaching. The only reason the second one had not immediately slain Daryus had been because they still needed to find Toy. The moment they had the weasel, Daryus would be a dead man.

That was, of course, assuming he intended to simply stand still.

However, before he could act, a missile struck the first assassin in the shoulder. The pitborn cried out as he reached up for Daryus's own dagger.

The arm cutting off Daryus's breath suddenly pulled away. The act was accompanied by a choking sound.

Harricka Morn had finally entered the fray.

The dagger her only weapon, the captain now fought to maintain her own chokehold on the taller pitborn. Daryus would have helped her, but despite the dagger to the collarbone, the first assassin seemed hardly slowed. Sheathing the dagger, he pulled Daryus's smaller blade free, then tossed it aside.

But even that brief action gave Daryus the opening he finally needed. Daryus lunged, cutting past the pitborn's blade and catching the assassin in the side. While not a deep cut, it acted with the other wound to finally slow the pitborn. Glaring, the horned demonspawn started to retreat—and promptly fell back over something Daryus did not see.

Daryus took a step toward his foe, but before he could do anything, the assassin suddenly contorted. He opened his mouth in a silent scream . . . then slumped.

Daryus had no chance to see what had caused the assassin's death, for the sounds of struggle behind him grew louder and more desperate. Despite her expertise, Harricka was having trouble keeping her chokehold on the larger pitborn, who pulled at her arm with one hand while drawing his sword with the other. Given time, Daryus knew there was a good chance the assassin would break free.

He brought the tip of his own sword to the pitborn's face. The assassin's gaze narrowed. He lowered his weapon . . . then brought it up again in a desperate thrust at Daryus.

Daryus ran him through. He would not get any useful information from the pitborn, and taking him prisoner would just make things more complex, especially when it came to tracking Shiera and the mercenaries.

Harricka eyed him with mild surprise as the dead pitborn slipped from her grip. That allowed Daryus to grab at the assassin's side for something he had seen there earlier.

Before Harricka realized what he was doing, Daryus stuck her in the arm with one of the assassin's sleep darts. She had a moment to try to reach for him, then slumped forward.

Dropping the dart, he seized her before she could fall.

"Sorry, Captain." Daryus brought her back to the campfire, where he bound her. He then turned his attention back to Raffan, whom he had left unconscious nearby.

The body was gone.

Frowning, Daryus looked to the horses. One of them was missing.

"Toy! Where are you?"

Somewhat to his surprise, the weasel actually popped out from the stones nearest to Harricka. "Bravo, Master Daryus! They are dead! They are dead!"

"Where's Raffan, Toy?"

The familiar blinked. "How would I know?"

"Where is he? He didn't just ride off, did he?"

"Master Daryus! I swear!"

Daryus hesitated. He studied Harricka. He had purposely only pricked her lightly. With grim determination, Daryus took water to the unconscious crusader. Propping her up, he splashed some of it in her face.

The moment she woke, the captain struggled. After a few seconds of futility, Harricka realized what was going on around her.

"Such gratitude," the captain growled.

"Gratitude? I would've been next, wouldn't I?"

"Of course."

Daryus had to admire her bluntness, at least. "The young man. Did you do something with him?"

"This will not end here, Daryus Gaunt. You will either have to surrender or kill me."

Daryus wondered if he had been so single-minded when he had been of the order. "Let me repeat myself. The young *man*, Harricka. Did you do anything with him?"

"I freed myself and slipped to the horses. I took one and brought it around. You were just beginning to face the first assassin when I got to the one you mean. I thought it best to put him on the animal and then guide both off. I assumed you could take on the assassins long enough for me to get him to safety."

"You were trying to protect him. How suddenly magnanimous of you."

"He was an innocent."

Feeling a bit better about Raffan's safety, Daryus asked, "Where'd you guide the horse? Which direction?"

After a moment, Harricka replied, "Over to the east. Just beyond the camp. I tied the horse loosely to a small, gnarled tree in case I needed to get him farther away. You should see him there. That dart the assassin used should be wearing off about now, at least if what you did to me is anything to judge by."

It did not surprise Daryus to know that the captain had seen the darts before. Glad to hear that Raffan would be all right, Daryus quickly went in the direction Harricka had indicated.

But when he reached where Raffan should have been, it was to only find a few hoofprints stretched far apart and heading, of all places, deeper into the Worldwound.

Crouching, Daryus tried to follow the trail farther, but the darkness hid it. Still, he had some idea where the horse would have to go.

As he turned, he noticed something else. He took a short but careful look to verify what it was, then hurried back to the campsite.

Harricka Morn remained where he had left her. "Where is he?"

"Gone. The horse ran off." Daryus went to the other animals. Mounting his own, he took the reins of the one with the most supplies alongside him.

"You're going to leave me like this?"

"You did well enough before."

The captain scowled. "You have done a better job of tying me up this time."

Daryus pointed at the weapons of the dead. "They should be useful enough. By the time you're free, I'll be far enough away. Would your superiors really want you riding alone out here?"

Urging his horse on, Daryus left without another word. As he reached the far end of the camp, he felt Toy leap up behind him.

"She will escape?" the familiar whispered.

"Eventually." Daryus focused ahead. "Very soon, actually, but not soon enough to follow, if she has any sense."

"You will track the other human?"

"You know I will."

Toy said nothing. Daryus was not certain whether that had to do with the familiar's driving desire to push on farther into the Worldwound or because he recognized in Daryus's answer that the human knew the truth about Raffan's disappearance.

The prints had been slight, yet even in the dim light of the far-off campfire, Daryus had recognized the two marks matching Toy's paws. The weasel had undone the reins. The weasel had sent off Raffan's already-spooked horse, not caring at all where Raffan went so long as it meant Daryus would proceed deeper into the Worldwound and not think of turning back.

The weasel had a plan . . . and everyone, including Daryus, was expendable.

18

THE WOLVES

Shiera stood there in awe, unable to take her gaze from those of the two single-eyed wolves. Then, she began to notice just how still they stood, even when she finally took a step to the side.

Only as Shiera dared move a bit closer did she realize that these were *statues*.

"This can't be a coincidence," she muttered. She removed the coin from the pouch. Not at all to her surprise, it had no touch of cold.

"You *are* tied to this," she murmured to the statues. "Now if you could only talk . . . but that would be too easy, wouldn't it?"

Shiera smiled grimly. These statues must be meant to guard something, but what? And why did it seem that some mysterious force wanted her to find the tomb?

To her horror, from not that far away, she heard the now-familiar chittering.

Shiera quickly put away the coin and readied her crossbow.

The sounds grew nearer. She whirled around just as the brush behind her suddenly rustled madly.

Four vescavors fluttered up from brush, gaping mouths snapping hungrily at her. Behind them, the brush stirred more. This swarm had apparently learned to keep to the ground until near their prey. Their gibbering only arose when they thought they were near enough that the prey could not escape—a fact not lost on Shiera.

Shiera stared at the swarm, realizing that with each encounter—and two healthy horses—she had been constantly drawing the vermin to her from all around the area. Such a feast as she had unintentionally offered could not be ignored by the monsters, who probably subsisted on their own kind as much as other victims.

She fired, bringing down the first. The nearest monsters turned on their wounded comrade, tearing it to shreds.

Unfortunately, the reprieve lasted only seconds. More of the bizarre beasts swooped in out of the darkness. One buzzed her head, teeth nicking her scalp and tearing hair as she ducked.

Stepping back, Shiera quickly reloaded. She had no idea what to do except keep firing and hope for a miracle. Without a horse, she could not outrun the swarm.

Shiera managed a second shot, but to her frustration, her target veered aside. She stumbled into one of the statues as she sought for another bolt. Shiera cursed, the collision costing her precious seconds. Slipping around the stone wolf, she continued her efforts. The statue wasn't much defense, but it was something.

To her surprise, the swarm didn't follow, instead buzzing back and forth just beyond the statues. Shiera raised her crossbow, but paused. She was not certain if firing on them would start the swarm attacking again.

Shiera rested a hand on the nearby statue, only to pull back out of surprise. The statue had a soft texture to it, almost as if it were fur instead of stone.

At the same time, she noticed the *eye* was glowing faintly. A swift glance at the other statue revealed that its eye also glowed.

The swarm's numbers increased, yet all paused before the cyclopean wolves. Was it her imagination, or did they seem mesmerized by the eyes?

"Good boy," Shiera breathed, patting the first statue as she tried to figure out what to do. The coin—or whatever power controlled it—had guided her this far. It could be no coincidence that she had come upon these statues. This place had meaning. Shiera did not think the tomb was here . . . but it was somehow connected to these statues.

With one wary eye on the swarm, she studied the area behind the statues. For the first time, she noted beneath her feet a marbled floor half-hidden by dust. Crouching, she found two odd indentations shaped like feet that, if she stood in them, would enable her to just reach the back of the head of each wolf.

Despite common sense screaming at her to keep a weapon in hand, she removed the bolt and slung the crossbow at her side. Then, with caution, she stretched her fingers to the first statue.

She again felt what seemed like fur . . . but also something else. A round mark that grew warm to the touch. She probed at it and found her finger sinking in.

The swarm started chittering.

Shiera felt a moment of displacement and pulled her hand back. The sensation passed, as did the gibbering. Once more, the swarm hovered, eerily silent.

She looked around. The vague outline of a wall caught her attention. Once, the wolves had stood inside a small temple or other structure, of which only the wolves and the floor remained. She bent and ran her fingers over a part of the floor, noting that it had been sealed well. The builders had been determined that the statues and the floor would last, no matter what happened to the rest of the building.

As Shiera rose, she saw with much consternation that the swarm had increased in numbers again. She wondered if there were limits to the wolves' power, which she imagined had to be some defensive measure against any invader of the temple.

Once again, she set her feet in the indentations. Gritting her teeth, she checked the second statue. Sure enough, there was an identical mark there.

She made a decision. Placing a finger on each mark, she took a deep breath.

A shape vastly larger than any of the creatures thus far arose from the brush. Although it was only a silhouette, Shiera realized that the swarm's *queen* had finally arrived.

As if the queen's coming had removed the wolves' spell, the other fiends started to move toward Shiera.

Praying that she had judged correctly, Shiera pressed the marks simultaneously.

The peculiar silence engulfed her once more. Shiera again felt a sense of displacement, but now far more intense than previously.

For a brief moment, it was as if the world ceased to exist. Then, suddenly, there was wind and ground and the dark of night.

But no more stone wolves . . . and certainly no more savage swarm. As Shiera had suspected, the sense of displacement was due to the wolves and the floor opening a doorway to another place. She had heard of such things from other Pathfinders, but had until now never confronted such a discovery herself.

She looked around, trying to get her bearings. A marble framework met her gaze, the cracked stone still managing to bear enough weight to enable at least a partial opening to remain, tunneling into the stony hillside.

An entrance, but to where? Uhl-Adanar itself, or somewhere else?

The structure looked as if it had been ancient even before the coming of the Worldwound. Shiera knew that from many angles it would have gone unseen. On a hunch, she pulled out the coin. It was cool to the touch in a surprisingly comfortable way.

Putting the coin away again, she drew her sword and carefully approached the entrance. With her free hand, she ran over what was left of the frame. She felt vague impressions, a series of carved symbols sanded it obscurity by centuries of weathering. Despite her skills, she could not make out anything. Shiera peered close, but doubted she could have read anything even if it had been the height of day with a shining sun behind her. Still, the entrance's very existence, and the magic leading to it, hinted at much.

All that remained of the passage through was a narrow slit that at first Shiera feared might be too small for her to fit through. Forced to momentarily sheathe the sword, Shiera squeezed into it. Even then, midway through, she found herself stuck. Exhaling as far as she could, Shiera managed to push on the last few inches.

She entered complete darkness.

Shiera located her tinderbox and one of two small candles she carried. A few seconds later, she had at least some dim light to help guide her.

Her first glimpse of her surroundings included generations of webs. Spiders ranging from the very minute to nearly the size of her palm skittered away. Other bugs and crawling creatures rushed off in every direction. Unperturbed by her newfound companions, Shiera drew her sword once more and took a few steps deeper into the ruined structure.

A gaping skull stared back at her.

Shiera grimaced. The skull was attached to what remained of a robed figure seemingly floating before her. The cause of death was readily evident; the savage iron spike impaling the man from behind had left him forever a macabre sentry.

Using her sword, Shiera tapped the tip of the spike. Part of the point crumbled off, a sign of just how long ago the man had perished

Shiera felt both warier and more excited. No one set traps who did not have something worth protecting. She began studying the walls with more interest, not only searching for other carvings, but also for any hints of traps that might lie hidden behind them.

She found what she could be one of the latter first: a small hole drilled in the rock. She looked around at the floor and saw one piece of the rocky surface that seemed slightly askew. Leaning back, she slid one foot to the spot in question.

There was a hiss and something popped out of the wall. It fell short, dropping a few inches from her foot.

Chuckling, Shiera nudged it aside. As originally constructed, the trap should have shot a dart filled with a long-lasting but quick-reacting poison. Pathfinders had been killed by such in more than one excavation. The hole, set at what was generally shoulder height, should have sent the missile flying into the victim's neck. However, so much time had passed that the springs or other mechanisms used had begun to decay.

Despite that heartening sign, Shiera moved carefully as she wended her way through the narrow passage. While the one trap had failed, other types must have survived the ages better.

However, it was not some timeworn trap that finally bested her, but rather the much more mundane thing she had most feared. The passage ended abruptly in a collapse. Tons of rock filled the rest of the passage ahead, thoroughly halting her.

A short epithet escaped her. She had not come this far to simply give up. Shiera held the candle close to the rockfall, studying the position of the fallen stones. After a long moment, she shifted a few strategic pieces of rubble, revealing a gap through which she might fit. Candle and sword held tight, she wiggled through.

The passage she came out in was cleaner, less touched by time or spiders. The air was stale, but breathable, which to Shiera meant there was some sort of flow, just not very strong. That encouraged her to continue her trek through the ancient edifice.

However, after several more minutes of walking and seeing nothing of import—not even an old trap—Shiera started to grow frustrated. The ancient structure had to have had a purpose other than to drive her mad. She had to be on the right trail—

And there it suddenly hung before her, larger than any previous incarnation and outlined in gold and silver ornamentation: a huge profile of the one-eyed wolf, positioned to face the etched script that Shiera Tristane already recognized so easily as a name . . . or a title.

Tzadn.

The Reaper.

19

SPAWN

Daryus raced through the night, now forced to delay his pursuit of Shiera and her kidnappers in order to catch Raffan before he rode into some monstrous danger in the Worldwound. He considered abandoning the young man and continuing on after Shiera, but, to his relief, Raffan's mount appeared to be heading along the same trail Daryus believed Galifar and his men would have chosen.

Still, hours passed before he saw any actual hint of Raffan. The first trace came near dawn, when a wrinkled white object in the dirt proved to be a fairly fresh handkerchief. Another few miles on, Daryus discovered one of Raffan's gloves.

And finally, at just about what was laughingly called sunrise—a sunrise draped in a sulfuric fog that Daryus did his best to circumvent—he spotted the other man's horse.

Daryus felt some initial concern when he saw no one near the animal. He pondered places behind him where Raffan might have fallen off and rolled out of view. Then, just as he was about to turn back, he heard a retching sound.

Daryus urged his mount forward to find Raffan on his knees, apparently trying in vain to throw up. The reason for his attempt was very clear.

They had found Shiera's kidnappers . . . or what remained of them.

A pale Raffan looked up as Daryus dismounted. "Thank the gods it's you!" He leapt to his feet. "I woke—I woke to find myself in the saddle. I nearly fell off. There—there was some water nearby. I rode toward it, dismounted . . . and then found them."

Daryus paid little attention to Raffan's words, instead quickly searching the camp. Three of the mercenaries, including Galifar himself, lay in various postures of painful death. Of Shiera Tristane, there was little sign, save an odd pile of ropes that would have been perfect for binding a prisoner.

Then, just a bit beyond the camp, Daryus found the fourth mercenary.

Some larger animal had clearly dragged the body off and begun feasting, only to be interrupted. However, that was not what interested Daryus most. What did was the middle of the torso, just under the ribs, where it almost looked as if something had burst *out* of the body.

Kneeling near it, Daryus gritted his teeth. Horror came in many forms in the Worldwound, and while the former crusader had never seen any creature responsible for this, he *had* come across a body in such shape. One of the older crusaders with him at the time had identified the culprit for him.

Raffan came up next to him. "Gods! What happened here?"

"This looks like the work of a grimslake," Daryus muttered. "Planted eggs in this one, one of which hatched. Ate the innards until it was big enough to go hunting for fresher food."

"They breed in corpses?" Raffan asked with dismay.

"If you're lucky . . . but even though they develop swiftly, they shouldn't be spawning this fast. Not unless something else disturbed them."

"Grimslake . . ." murmured Raffan, heading back to the camp. "Is there nothing normal in this—"

Raffan let out a gasp.

Weapon drawn, Daryus rushed to the younger man. However, as he approached, he wondered just what had so disturbed Raffan. Other than the corpses, Daryus could see nothing.

"What's the matter?"

"He— It—" Still walking, Raffan pointed at the ruined corpse of Captain Galifar. "He moved!"

"He did what?" Daryus considered himself a fairly good judge of death, and Galifar had clearly been dead for many hours. Yet he doubted that Raffan, as jumpy a character as he seemed to be, could already be imagining—

Galifar's body shook.

"It's those things!" Raffan suddenly blurted. He drew a dagger and rushed to the body. Before Daryus could realize what he intended, Raffan began stabbing at the stomach.

"You fool! You're not going to stop them like that!" Daryus roared. He grabbed at Raffan and pulled the man back, but it was already too late.

The ruined area just below the ribs tore open, but this time from within. The mercenary's intestines began spilling out.

No . . . not his intestines, but rather an increasing number of serpentine maggots that quickly spread around the body in search of prey. Each was already nearly a foot long, with an armored back, barbed tail, and round mouth full of sharp, hooked teeth.

Daryus dragged Raffan farther back. "Stay behind me!"

They were grimslakes, of course . . . grimslakes hatching too soon. However, that did not make them any less dangerous. Unchecked, grimslakes could multiply like flies. The only thing preventing it was that, without an immediate new source of food, the young always turned on one another. Generally, only one or two survived to adulthood, or so Daryus's old commander had sworn.

But now this batch, though born prematurely, both saw and smelled the freshness of the two men and their horses.

"Don't let them touch you!" Daryus warned. "They'll burrow inside you in seconds!"

"Well, do something, then!"

Biting back a retort, Daryus slashed at the nearest young. He managed to sever the head of one . . . only to find the body still trying to crawl toward him. At the same time, the other grimslakes spread out, making them much harder targets.

"Gods! Do they burrow inside and then lay the eggs?"

"No, I'm told the young just eat you! It's the older ones you have to watch out for if you don't want to become a host . . ."

As he spoke, Daryus chopped apart the rest of the first parasite. This time, the bits stayed dead.

"They're everywhere!"

Daryus glanced to the side. Sure enough, several of the young were circling Raffan.

"Keep behind me! We'll move toward the horses!"

But even as he finished speaking, Daryus heard the sound of retreating footsteps as Raffan chose instead to flee for their mounts immediately.

His rash action did exactly as Daryus feared. The swarm instantly focused on the moving object and raced after Raffan. Daryus had heard that young grimslakes could be especially fast, and this was borne out as several of them quickly cut the distance between Raffan and themselves.

Despite it being the younger man's own fault, Daryus couldn't let the grimslakes have Raffan. Butchering the last few near him, he charged after the man.

To his surprise, though, Raffan abruptly shifted direction. In doing so, he caused the grimslakes to not only pause, but even in some cases turn toward Daryus. Daryus, already running, had to struggle to keep from stumbling right into the vicious parasites. He only managed to not do so by thrusting the sword into the ground among the grimslakes, then using it to push himself back.

Even then, it took quickly plucking the sword free and sweeping the tip across the oncoming beasts to keep even one of them from reaching him.

He had no idea why Raffan had nearly created a new calamity, and couldn't waste time worrying about it. He was now surrounded by the small but deadly grimslakes seeking him as a meal. Daryus dared not pay any more attention to his companion. He hoped that Raffan had at least finally had the presence of mind to get on his horse and ride off, preferably for Kenabres.

The grimslakes moved with astounding fluidity, darting around Daryus's sword with eagerness. The gaping, toothy mouths snapped at his legs. Daryus was aware that those teeth could tear through his leather boots without any trouble.

He cut off the head of one, and then another. He succeeded in spearing one through the head, then tossed the wriggling corpse at another. While that one was distracted, Daryus beheaded it.

Gasping from effort, he killed the last.

A horse shrieked.

Cursing, Daryus turned to see just what now threatened them.

It was another grimslake.

Another, much *larger* grimslake.

The monster stood as tall as Daryus himself. Its rounded mouth snapped hungrily at Raffan's horse, which in turn reared and kicked at the danger before it. Raffan, meanwhile, hung on for dear life, his grip on the reins the only thing keeping him from falling backward.

Clearly sensing Daryus to be a threat to the bounty Raffan and the horse presented, the grimslake slithered toward him, then lunged.

Letting out a fierce roar, Daryus dropped beneath the attack, throwing himself underneath the gaping maw. As he did, he thrust up with the sword.

His blade made a deep cut in the pale flesh. With a shrill sound, the grimslake twisted away from the blade.

Daryus started to roll away, only to be struck by the tail end of the beast. Stunned, he tumbled the opposite direction, in the process losing his sword. He glanced at his hand and wrist, both cut by the grimslake's incredibly sharp scales.

He instinctively threw himself as far as he could from where he thought the grimslake was. As his head cleared, he looked back just in time to see the horrific mouth closing in on him. Still straining, Daryus grabbed for whatever was available nearby . . . which proved to be the arm of one of the corpses.

He shoved the dead body in front of him. The grimslake snatched the corpse up. It shook the mercenary twice, then tossed the limp form aside.

However, by that time, Daryus was already racing for his sword. Out of the corner of his eye, he saw Raffan *dismounting.*

"Get out of here!" Daryus shouted. "Get out!"

That was all the aid he could offer the foolish man at the moment. If Raffan didn't listen to reason this time, Daryus planned to wash his hands of his companion. Assuming he still had hands when this was over.

He seized up the sword. Feeling a little safer, he spun to face his monstrous foe.

Keeping its head high, the grimslake slithered toward him. Daryus studied the creature, especially where he had wounded it. Even though the cut had been deep, it had clearly not affected the grimslake as much as he had hoped. In fact, the wound looked as if it had sealed over already. Daryus was not familiar with the healing properties of such beasts, but hoped he was not facing a horror that sealed its wounds faster than he could inflict them.

The grimslake's fetid breath kept threatening to overwhelm Daryus. He slashed at the monster, keeping it at bay while he sought some weakness. Unfortunately, nothing presented itself.

Daryus could only try to consider what he knew about the beast from both his long-ago commander and the young grimslakes he had already destroyed.

Much to his regret, that meant only one possible course of action. Shouting at the top of his voice and waving the sword like a madman, Daryus charged.

His audacity, along with all his noise caused the monstrosity to rear back in uncertainty, and Daryus used that moment to come under the grimslake.

The moment he had the reach, Daryus cut into his grisly foe. This time, he did not simply plunge the blade in. Instead, he used every second given him to cut a long, savage ravine in the grimslake's torso.

The creature reared higher. Daryus forced the blade's edge another half foot along, then finally retreated.

He did so just in time, the grimslake seeking in its agony to crush its enemy beneath it. The heavy body struck the ground just a breath after Daryus fled.

Unwilling to give the beast any chance to recuperate, Daryus charged a second time. He leapt onto the grimslake's back, then began hacking across the back behind the head. What passed for the grimslake's blood and other life fluids splattered him as he went to work. Sharp scales sliced through the protective leather like cheesecloth, but Daryus gritted his teeth and ignored the wounds. He had suffered worse. Giving in to the pain would only risk the grimslake still managing to kill him.

The monster shook and shivered, more than once almost throwing Daryus from it. Yet still Daryus cut.

When he finally had the wound open wide enough, Daryus gritted his teeth and plunged the sword into the head. He wasn't certain just exactly where what the grimslake called a brain could be found, but hoped that thrusting into the center would have the effect he desired.

The grimslake's hissing grew ragged. The head rose, nearly ripping the sword from Daryus. Teeth bared, he held on as he twisted the blade around.

The wild movements of the head slowed. The head shivered one more time . . . then ceased to move.

The same could not be said for the rest of the grimslake. It convulsed violently, at last managing to unseat its tormentor. Daryus barely held on to the sword as he fell off.

The body trembled, then finally went limp.

Panting, Daryus pulled his sword free. The weapon and his arm were covered in foulness, the rest of his body not much better. He had cuts over his arms, legs, and torso—anywhere not covered by protective metal—but fortunately all proved to be shallow. Daryus wiped his brow, hoping this was the end of the Worldwound's surprises for at least a little while.

Thought of Raffan's safety stirred him to action again. Despite having decided he would no longer concern himself with the other man, Daryus now worried that perhaps Raffan had fallen prey to some other danger while the fighter had been dealing with the grimslake.

"Raffan!" As he called, Daryus turned to where he had last seen his companion. "Are you all—"

He stopped short. There, near the horse, a slightly disheveled Raffan argued—with *Toy*.

"Well, I've had enough!" Raffan snarled. "Enough! I nearly got killed because of you!"

Toy said nothing, but the weasel's body bespoke a great tension.

Raffan looked over at Daryus. "And I've had *more* than enough of you."

The well-dressed man had a small mechanical device akin to a tiny hand crossbow pointed Daryus's way.

Daryus lunged.

Raffan fired.

The needle struck Daryus in the neck.

The world faded away.

20

What Lies Beneath

She's found something!

Grigor forced down his anticipation. There was so much that could go wrong at this point, especially revolving around just exactly how the Pathfinder had located the vital clue to the witch's quest. Grigor had also pushed the pitborn to their limits, which meant their assistance would be questionable at best when the time came.

"Spread out," Grigor ordered the pitborn. The twenty or so demonspawn did as commanded, albeit at a far slower pace than the witch desired. While they moved, Grigor considered his own next step. He did not want to sacrifice another bat even this close. There was still a chance this was only another step in what had already been a very long search. Besides, Grigor did not appreciate the pain he felt each time such a creature died.

"Damned wolf . . ." The witch had long known that some force sought to prevent the discovery of Uhl-Adanar, some magical force he believed those who had buried the temple-city in the first place had long ago set into motion. They did not want anyone finding the tomb of Tzadn for the simple reason that it was *not* a tomb by normal definition. From every indication, Tzadn was not dead— not surprising, given that what the ancient people had called a deity, Grigor was certain was actually a *demon* of tremendous power.

Grigor's entire life had been a thirst for power. The seventh son of a seventh son in a noble house, he had been given a small inheritance and promptly forgotten by his family, especially the patriarch, his grandfather. However, Grigor had never managed to forget them, nor the resentment he had felt toward his grandfather for literally dictating with the wave of his hand that Grigor was of no value, despite that tiny bit of blood tying them together.

The witch smiled grimly. His grandfather's blood had not looked any better than Grigor's once the younger man had spilled it over the elegant carpet of the patriarch's study.

It had turned out that several of those with no more blood ties to the old man had actually cared more for him—or perhaps his money—than Grigor had. For twenty years and more, Grigor had been hunted by his kin. He had killed three and maimed a few more, but they had finally had their justice.

Grigor still remembered the pyre vividly. The death by flame his distant cousins had condemned him to for his crimes. He remembered the pain, the screams . . . but most of all he remembered feeling his body turning to dry kindling as the heat first sucked all moisture from him before letting the flames devour his body.

Of course, he had not died then. His new patron had kept that promise at least.

Damn you! Grigor knew that when one dealt with demons, one had to beware of their promises. He had already been seeking out new avenues of power when it had been clear that his choices in the family had been few. Magic had proven the most intriguing, but most of the wizardry he first studied had been slow to learn, nowhere near the level of power he desired. Only when he had turned to the calling of witchcraft had he discovered methods by which he could gain tremendous power quickly.

And only once Grigor had made his pact with an actual demonic patron had he truly understood what gaining such power involved.

With the pitborn spread out, Grigor strode toward the nearly buried structure. He kept the staff ready, aware of the impediments still before him.

A savage growl erupted from behind him. A pitborn screamed.

Whirling, the witch beheld a winged demon ripping out the throat of one of his followers. Other pitborn charged the cyclopean creature, although clearly there was already no hope for their comrade.

One of the pitborn attempted a spell, but suddenly the demon shimmered. It became a huge, wolflike beast that cut the distance between it and the pitborn with remarkable swiftness. The "wolf" lunged at the would-be spellcaster and brought one powerful paw across the pitborn's chest.

Grigor concentrated.

The staff shimmered. Grigor vanished, materializing right behind the creature just as it reverted to its demon shape. To his pleasure, he saw that there was already a wound in the back of the demon's head. A minor one, but sufficient to help.

He thrust the tip of the staff at the wound and released the spell.

The demon howled in agony as missiles of pure energy burned into its head. The missile spell was one of the earlier ones that Grigor had learned, yet he had twisted it, made it stronger.

Writhing, the demon tried to turn. Grigor shoved hard on the staff.

With another pained howl, the demon staggered, then tumbled to the ground. It shimmered briefly, hints of the lupine form appearing and disappearing in the blink of an eye. Grinning, the witch held the staff tight.

"I owe you a bit more for my winged pet," the pale man added.

He shifted the staff and rammed it into the struggling demon's gaping mouth.

The demon's head exploded. The mixed stench of burning demon and wolf filled the air.

He watched for a moment as it burned. That the demon had a lupine shape, too, did not surprise him. This was no doubt a guardian, bound to the tomb by the powers of the same ancients who had built it. They had melded it with the spirit that to them represented Tzadn most on this plane—a wolf. It had made for a very capable servant, albeit a frustrating impediment to Grigor until now.

And with its destruction, he thought that surely now his destiny was assured.

Turning from the carcass, Grigor shouted, "Resume your places! Follow as previously commanded!"

He approached the narrow exit. Through one of the bats, he had seen this part. Unperturbed by the slit's width, Grigor shoved the staff into the frame, then turned it.

Stone and frame spread apart, creating enough room for him to pass.

Instead of entering, the witch gestured to the two nearest pitborn. "You first."

With obvious trepidation, the horned warriors entered. When Grigor did not hear screams, he followed. Four more of the pitborn trailed, while the rest waited where ordered.

Once inside, the witch surveyed his surroundings. He briefly admired the corpse, the robes of which marked the dead figure as a spellcaster.

"Not patient enough, were you? Tsk." He moved on to the rockfall. "This will not do."

The pitborn started forward with the obvious intention of trying to remove the rocks, but Grigor shook his head. Instead, he turned to one of the walls.

"Even a Pathfinder, as astute as she is, can miss a few tricks." He ran his hand along the wall farthest from the corpse. "Of course, no one knows those of Uhl-Adanar as I do."

The witch paused at a tiny crack. He removed his glove and dug one nail into it.

With a harsh grating noise, the wall separated.

Grigor put the glove back on. "Come."

They entered another empty passage that ran perpendicular to the one they had left. Grigor allowed a bit of light ahead of them, which revealed only more dust.

The passage arced to the left as they journeyed. After a few moments, Grigor estimated that they were now underneath the rest of his band. The path continued on for a bit longer, then turned right.

At that point, he silently raised the staff to call a halt. *She is near. Very near.*

A bat would have been too obvious down here, which forced Grigor to use another spell. He eyed the staff before doing so, aware that he had grown reckless. If it turned out he was wrong as to her progress, then he risked more than a simple loss of power.

Thinking of that, the witch touched his cheek. Even through the glove, he could feel the skin stiffening, as if all the moisture in his flesh was rapidly evaporating.

It had taken more than just blood to reach the demon he had sought. It had taken additional costs to garner the bargain he desired. For that price, he had gained himself a patron who had granted him the power for which he had hoped.

But with demons, there was always a catch. Once bound to his patron, Grigor Dolch had to be willing to pay more and more to keep what he had. Each time, the price grew greater. Grigor had resisted for a time, and because of that resistance, he had been easy to capture by his kin. His patron had naturally kept him alive, but barely. At that point, Grigor had been willing to give anything to not only survive, but get his revenge. Over the years that followed, however, he began to resent his pact, the idea that his patron could control him. He began looking for alternatives.

Unfortunately, he had not counted on *Toy* betraying him to their patron. He had assumed that his familiar would remain loyal to him.

Shaking off both the memories and his worries about his flesh, Grigor raised the staff over his eyes. He concentrated, focusing on the Pathfinder. His view suddenly shot forward, racing through the long passage, down another, and into a final corridor . . . where he at last found Shiera Tristane.

She stood before a vast carving so familiar to Grigor. To his frustration, the Pathfinder just stood there staring. Grigor waited a minute, then finally decided to investigate the image himself through the staff. He probed the wolf, inspected every mark for some hint of just what the symbol meant, yet, after a short but exhausting study, the witch could find nothing. To him, this was merely a large carving.

What am I missing? What?

His failure went against everything he knew about the builders of Uhl-Adanar. They had had the habit of meshing the magical and the mundane together to achieve their goals, most of which concerned keeping secret the location of the temple-city.

While he was caught up in his thoughts, Shiera Tristane reached up to the wolf's eye. The size of the carving meant the woman had to actually crawl up a small part of the way using a narrow gap carved in the wall that Grigor had somehow not seen before.

The Pathfinder ran her index finger along the right side of the orb. She seemed to be searching for something in particular, something that, despite magnifying his view, the witch could not make out.

The eye shifted . . . then swung open, floating free from the wall as if on invisible strings.

Grigor let out a gasp he was glad distance kept the woman from hearing. Understanding began to dawn. As he watched the

Pathfinder continue probing the now-open orb, the witch noticed he was still unable to sense anything in and around her discovery.

I am blind to what they did to hide this key—but it can't just be mechanical! It must be hidden from wielders of magic. How cunning . . .

He had never come across such a thing before—neither magic nor mundane. Most assumed that one was the opposite of the other, but in his studies, Grigor had come to believe differently. The opposite of magic was an *emptiness* of magic, an antithesis of magic.

Somehow, the builders of Uhl-Adanar had learned how to harness the power of that antithesis, that un-magic. Perhaps only someone with no magical abilities, no magical tendencies, would be able to see or detect it.

With fascination, Grigor watched her efforts. Now his earlier respect for the woman and her knowledge of the ancients returned. *It appears I have chosen well after all. I'll see to it that your death is swift and painless . . . once you find me the tomb.*

Shiera could not shake the feeling that she was being watched. More than once, she peered over her shoulder to see if someone was back there. It was such a strong sensation that the Pathfinder actually felt chills down her spine.

It's this place, Shiera finally decided. *It must be this place.*

She tried to focus on the eye. Although she had discovered much about it, managed to make the crystalline top of it float free to display the mechanism inside, she was still missing the final key to how to reach the temple-city.

Shiera wished that she had better light, but there were other ways to see. She had learned one of those ways from her second teacher, Yosen. Yosen had been born blind, but he had learned not only the raised script his people had developed, but also how to do the reverse . . . read what was carved *into* stone.

The skill was a difficult one, but Shiera had persevered. Shutting her eyes, she moved her index finger along the left side. At last, she felt the markings. Her mind raced as she matched what her finger ran along with what she already knew of the ancients' written language.

And what she read startled her so much she nearly lost her footing.

"Thank you, Yosen," she murmured. Too many of her counterparts—Amadan Gwinn included—did not appreciate the intricate learning techniques needed by the blind or the deaf. Shiera had chosen her teachers with care . . . and now those choices were paying off.

Then, running her finger over the last part in a slightly different direction, she suddenly saw another meaning. Once again, it amazed her how the builders could write so much with so little—

Another chill went through her. She *was* being watched. She was certain of it.

Glancing back, the Pathfinder called, "Who's out there? Show yourself?"

There was no answer. Still, someone *was* there.

And then . . .

"Please. Don't let me stop your work. Do continue."

A shape formed in the dim illumination, a robed figure Shiera pegged as younger than her but with oddly colored skin. He carried a four-foot-long staff that she recognized as no mere wooden stick.

Behind him arose the patter of booted feet and the clink of armor. The spellcaster—Shiera could not yet determine his calling—paid those sounds no mind, which meant that whoever rushed toward them served him.

As he approached her, Shiera suddenly realized he was much older than she had first thought. Indeed, there was something unreal about his countenance, as if it were more a mask than living flesh.

"Do continue," he repeated. "You've more than impressed me thus far. You've been worth all the effort it took to get you here."

She did not care for the way he said that.

"You've done more with that coin than the last three fools who dared called themselves Pathfinders." He tapped one end of the staff on the ground. "I can assure you that they will never disgrace your calling again."

As she faced him, Shiera continued to run her finger over the side of the orb. Based on what she had read thus far, there had to be one more find to make, one she had been looking for before the spellcaster's appearance, and one she needed to find even quicker now.

"Who are you?"

He bowed. "Grigor Dolch—a simple witch, on a quest for knowledge. Not unlike your own, Shiera Tristane. Now, please remove your hand from the orb. I would hate to have to inflict pain on you when we have been working together so well thus far."

As he spoke, a small party of pitborn entered behind him. Weapons bristling, the horned demonspawn spread around the chamber.

The witch smiled. "Please. I mean you no harm."

Shiera didn't believe that for a second. Once he gained what he desired, Shiera would be a burden.

Her finger finally grazed what she had been looking for. Shiera swallowed, hoping she had read everything correctly.

"All right," she answered. "I'm going."

Shiera pressed the stone under her finger.

The chamber shook violently. Shiera smiled. As she'd expected, the builders had been very protective of their city.

"'Going?'" Grigor's false smile turned into a scowl as he realized what she had done. "No, you don't—"

The staff glowed—

Shiera's surroundings faded away.

The pitborn waiting above had no chance. The ground beneath their feet sank with such swiftness that most perished immediately as they fell into the great gaps yawning open.

Two of those still alive tried in vain to reach the horses. The animals, farther from the destruction, wasted no time in breaking their tethers and running.

One of the pitborn slipped. The ground cracked open beneath him. He fell into the gap, which almost instantly closed.

The other pitborn took one more step, and then what remained of the ground crumbled, swallowing up the last of Grigor's followers.

Grigor used the staff to protect himself as soon as the shaking began. The very reason he had chosen Shiera Tristane in the first place had now brought him to this precarious moment. Still, the witch was not as perturbed as his followers, who tried to run for the passage as the complex began to sink and collapse.

"Stay with me, you fools!" Grigor commanded. A pair of the pitborn had sense enough to listen, but the rest sought escape.

What they received instead was death. The ceiling near the passage broke apart, sending tons of rock and earth spilling down. The four pitborn vanished in an instant, bodies crushed to a pulp.

Grigor led the remaining pair to the wall where the huge image remained untouched. The ancients would have given themselves a safety area just in case some accidental touch caused everything to collapse while they were still working on things. Indeed, as he suspected, once the trio got within half a dozen feet from the wall, they ceased being threatened by the devastation.

"Against the wall!" the witch ordered. He and the two pitborn planted themselves against the wolf image. Once there, Grigor waited. At some point soon, the quake would cease. Then, the witch would turn his attention to the wolf's eye. He had been watching the Pathfinder's hand very carefully. Despite all the ancients' plans, Grigor suspected that if he found the very same spot Shiera Tristane had touched, he and his servants would be transported to wherever she had been sent.

The quake began to subside.

Grigor Dolch smiled.

Shiera fell forward, striking the ground hard. The force of the collision left her stunned, every bone vibrating. She moaned, all the while hoping that Grigor Dolch was not at her heels.

Silence surrounded her. Slowly, Shiera's head cleared. Her bones ceased screaming.

She tried to rise, but discovered it was too soon. Her arms and legs refused to support her. Shiera slipped to the ground again, only just managing to keep her face from hitting.

Although her eyes would still not focus, she once more used her sensitive touch to study the ground. Not at all to her surprise, it proved to be of artificial make, and not merely the granite floor of the chamber she'd just fled. Indeed, as she ran her fingers along, she guessed it to be a polished marble, like that of the wolf temple, but untouched by the elements.

"Come on!" she growled at herself. "Come on!"

Shiera shook her head to clear the last haze. Her gaze started to normalize. Strength returned to her limbs.

She managed to push herself up to a sitting position. A dim illumination that reminded her of that in the ruined building in Kenabres gradually allowed her to see what lay around her . . . or at least for as *far* as the light permitted.

Shiera had hoped—no, *expected*—to find herself in a temple, or perhaps directly in the tomb of Tzadn himself.

What Shiera had not expected was to find herself sitting in the midst of a marble courtyard extending to a tall, arched structure, beyond which lay six more similar buildings, all in pristine condition. Around her, tall statues of solemn-looking men and women in robes peered down on her, statues so lifelike she could see every detail in the craggy faces.

When she stood, it was to have verified for her by a sudden flood of illumination the fact that she had not merely found the remains of Uhl-Adanar, but the *entire* temple-city.

A temple-city that not only stretched far beyond even the seven structures looming ahead, but also spread wide to left and right. Uhl-Adanar in all its glory lay around her for as far as the eye could see . . . as did the carefully carved ceiling running above the entire thing.

Like the ruined outpost temple she had just escaped, Uhl-Adanar was underground . . . and had apparently been *built* that way.

21

THE TRAITOR

Y ou made a deal, you little vermin, and if you don't abide by it,
I'll feed you to him."

"There is no lie! I have not lied!"

As Daryus slowly stirred, the two voices echoed in his head like
a pair of bronze drums playing the Order of the Flaming Lance's
long, tedious hymns. He knew he had heard both voices before,
although it did take him a moment to recall just who they were.

The second he identified first. Toy. Cunning, untrustworthy
little Toy. Daryus imagined squeezing the weasel's throat, a notion
contrary to his usual manner, but quite pleasing at the moment.
Toy appeared to bring out the worst in people. Such as the other
speaker.

Raffan. The name finally came to him. Raffan, the constantly
anxious agent of the unnamed noble. Raffan, who had shot Daryus
with some sort of dart akin to what the assassins had used.

What the assassins had used.

Daryus tried to stretch his arms and legs to get rid of the
burning sensation in them, only to realize he was bound tight.
Moreover, it gradually dawned on him that he was sitting on a
surface that kept shifting. With further consideration, Daryus
determined that he was on horseback.

At about that time, he grew conscious enough to finally force
his eyes open.

Not at all to Daryus's surprise, he rode behind two other horses, the lead of which belonged to Raffan. In contrast to how the younger man had always presented himself, now Raffan rode with a visible arrogance in his bearing. Daryus could not decide whether his captor had been that good an actor or had simply grown more confident now that he had the upper hand against someone.

Then, the odd contraption strapped to the back of the third horse—a third horse that Daryus could only guess had followed his own—caught his attention. It was a *cage*.

In it, scurrying back and forth in clear frustration, was Toy.

The sight was enough to make Daryus chuckle. That made Raffan pull hard on the reins and twist around to view his prisoner. At the same time, Toy also turned to face Daryus.

"You're a strong one," Raffan muttered. "You should still be out for a few hours."

"Sorry to disappoint you. I'll try to do better next time."

"You would be wise to remember your place, renegade. I could've left you for your former comrades."

Daryus grunted. "But instead you've got something much more pleasant in mind for me, I suppose."

Raffan frowned. "If we weren't behind, I would slap that smirk off your face. You're still important to the weasel here, and until I get what I want from him, you're going to tag along."

Brow arching, Daryus looked at Toy. He didn't trust the familiar any more than he trusted Raffan. Toy hadn't done anything to save Daryus for Daryus's sake, but because, as Raffan indicated, the fighter was still of some use.

Toy said nothing, but the one eye narrowed. What the weasel tried to relay with that narrowed gaze, Daryus didn't care. He was only concerned with escaping and then continuing on after Shiera.

Daryus shut his eyes as if seeking rest again. Instead, though, he thought about Shiera.

There was a very good chance that she was dead, the victim of some Worldwound monstrosity. If she was alive, it was likely she was the captive of the witch. Either way, it was doubtful that Daryus had any true hope of saving her . . . and yet he still hoped to do so.

Harricka would laugh at him, Daryus knew. She considered him an honorless creature. Daryus disagreed with that description, though he knew now that his idea of right and wrong differed from what he had first believed upon becoming a crusader. Then, he had seen things as the captain and his instructors had, in simple black and white. Unlike Harricka and the rest, however, Daryus had been changed by what he'd seen, and the way the acts of those who were supposed to be good and those who were supposed to be evil sometimes seemed reversed.

Memories rushed back. The sword falling. The screams. The pitborn children. The horrified pitborn mother. The pitborn father, trying to shield them all with his body.

The demonspawn who had not been nearly so demonic, only tried to be as human as they could be.

But that had not been enough for the crusaders of the Flaming Lance. Pitborn were products of the Worldwound, were the blood of monsters and looked the part. Unless thoroughly vetted by the church, they were suspected of serving the dark powers. Never mind that these pitborn had been *farming*. They, with some others, had built a tiny community in a hidden part of the Worldwound just close enough to the border so that the most human-looking of them could occasionally slip into the lands beyond and buy, sell, or trade for what they needed.

But they had *still* been pitborn sneaking across the border. In the eyes of Captain Harricka Morn and the other crusaders of the order, that made them insurgents. Who knew what sabotage they might have carried out, what information they might have sold to demonic masters? Unlike some holy orders, whose servants were often priests and paladins, Daryus's unit had consisted solely of ordinary soldiers, those who did not make distinctions between good and evil where demonspawn were concerned. Pitborn were tainted by the legacy of their births. And they had broken the law. That was all those like Harricka Morn cared about.

As he carefully worked on the ropes, Daryus noted Raffan's certainty where his route was concerned. Either the other man had ridden this way before—which seemed unlikely considering what Daryus knew of Raffan—or he had access to knowledge he had not given to the fighter earlier.

Raffan appeared unperturbed by the fact that they were heading deeper and deeper into the Worldwound with hardly any protection. Toy had no power save his cunning brain, while for the moment Daryus could not even protect himself. Raffan had his darts, but against so many of the threats of the Worldwound, they were all but useless.

Toy continued to pace his cage. Daryus caught the familiar's attention.

Leaning forward as best he could, Daryus whispered, "He knows where he's going?"

"He does now," muttered the familiar.

"You told him."

"Had to! Had to!"

"I heard him talking with you before he shot me. You knew him before this, didn't you, Toy? Did you bring him into this?"

The weasel looked cowed. "Yes. It was another plan. The patron, he removed the witch's gifts, but Master Grigor is cunning. Toy knew he must attack him from more than one direction."

"Gifts—you mean magic?"

"Yes, too clever is my former master, so clever. He found a way to survive without those gifts—at least for a time. Time is the one thing truly against him!"

"Why? How much time does he have left?"

Tulsa City-County Library
South Broken Arrow Library

Customer ID: ************9081**

Items that you checked out

Title: Reaper's eye / Richard A. Knaak.
ID: 32345077923275
Due: 3/5/2020

Total items: 1
Account balance: $0.00
2/20/2020 5:18 PM
Checked out: 1

To renew:
www.tulsalibrary.org
918-549-7323

We value your feedback.
Please take our online survey.
www.tulsalibrary.org/Z45

"Enough. Enough still. So long as he has the staff."

Glancing back at Raffan, the familiar explained as quickly as he could. Early on, Grigor had begun experimenting with how to create reservoirs of power. He had constantly sought new and better methods, as if by doing so he prepared for some cataclysm in the making.

And then the witch had committed his betrayal.

Daryus didn't need to hear more on the point. He knew those like Grigor Dolch. From the moment they swore allegiance to one master, they were already looking to defect, to trade up and find a better offer. Apparently that applied even to demonic patrons. There was always a more powerful master to seek.

But breaking a pact with a demon that was the major source of one's power had repercussions, apparently. Dolch had probably thought himself well prepared for his betrayal, but from the way Toy acted, it hadn't all gone well. It sounded as if what the weasel had said earlier was true: Grigor was living on borrowed time, albeit more time than Daryus would have preferred.

Which to Daryus still meant that the more desperate the witch became, the more dangerous he would be to face.

They rode on at a consistent but not overly swift pace. That confused Daryus, who would have thought that Raffan would be in a hurry.

That Shiera was not only likely alive but perhaps even relatively well brought some relief to Daryus. However, it also made him wonder how he could get Raffan to increase his pace. Surely the traitor did not think he had all the time in the world to reach his goal.

And yet, Raffan continued to be satisfied with things the way they were . . . save for Toy. It seemed that Toy irritated the young man more than anything else.

It was that which finally caused the trio to come to a halt. Raffan turned his mount toward the one on which he kept the weasel caged.

"You've got little time left to tell me what I want to know," Raffan snarled. "I didn't cut the old man's throat and ransack his vault to end up with nothing! You know what Dolch is looking for, and you know that *it's* just as likely to give everything to me . . . if Dolch is dead."

"Gladly would I see that last part finally accomplished," Toy returned. "But what you ask of me, I am not permitted. I exist at the sufferance of he who was betrayed by the witch . . ."

"I can wield that power just as well, if you let me have control of it. I'll give you Dolch." With a sneer, Raffan indicated Daryus. "That's more than you renegade crusader has been able to do."

"We will need Master Daryus," the familiar insisted. "You will want Master Daryus at your side if the witch confronts us before—"

The three of them froze as a menacing hum arose from ahead. Daryus immediately began working harder on his bonds.

Toy began pacing his cage. Raffan turned his nervous mount around to face the direction of the noise. He fumbled in a pouch at his side, anxiously seeking something.

A glistening winged form swooped up before the trio. It had a long, narrow body that ended in a rounded end with a foot-long sting.

In his time as a crusader guarding against the Worldwound, Daryus had seen warmonger wasps. Once found only in the Abyss, they now inhabited many parts of the Worldwound. They were not that different in general design from the small insects they resembled, but as with all in the tainted land, they had been perverted. A golden metallic layer covered their skin. They were creatures of the foulest tempers, very territorial and to be avoided at all costs.

The warmonger buzzed back and forth as it studied the intruders.

"You told me this path would be clear!" Raffan shouted back.

"You deal with Grigor Dolch at your own peril!" Toy countered, cowering at the bottom of his cage.

Not for a moment did Daryus believe the weasel's show of fear. He suspected Toy of trying to make certain that Raffan and Raffan alone became the warmonger's focus.

The humming came from the wasp's wings, which beat faster and faster. Daryus, aware what that meant, struggled harder.

"Damn it! Where is it?" growled Raffan as he continued to fumble in the pouch. "Where is it?"

Daryus could wait no longer. "Move your mount, Raffan!"

To Daryus's surprise, his captor actually listened. Raffan steered his mount to the side just as the humming reached a crescendo.

A charge of electricity struck the ground just where Raffan's horse had been but a moment before.

"It'll take time for it to build up its strength again!" Daryus added. "We should pull back and—"

More humming arose from their right . . . and then from their left as well.

Two more warmongers buzzed into view.

"Untie me!" Daryus demanded.

Raffan ignored him, his attention still on the contents of the pouch. Daryus fought hard and finally felt the bonds slip a little more.

Suddenly, a voice whispered in his ear. "No . . . not now."

Toy's voice.

Daryus looked to the cage, the origin of which was still a mystery to him. The door was not only shut, but locked from the outside. Despite that, Toy was nowhere to be seen.

"No . . ." repeated the weasel's voice. "Let it play out, Master Daryus."

That was an easy thing for the tiny familiar to say, but Daryus couldn't hide behind a saddle. He magnified his efforts.

Unfortunately, that served to bring him to the wasps' attention.

The foremost wasp floated closer, wings quickly building up a static rage. Daryus slapped the sides of his mount with his feet in hopes that the animal would run, but instead the frightened horse just stood where it was and shivered.

Daryus gritted his teeth as the wings beat their loudest.

"Ah! Here's the damned thing!"

The wasp suddenly shook as if buffeted by a powerful wind. The charge it unleashed flew wide, hitting the ground some distance to Daryus's right.

"Away with you damned bugs!" Raffan cried out. "Get away! I command you!"

The young man held up a round object that Daryus could not otherwise make out. He waved it back and forth in whatever direction there hovered a wasp. Each time, the nearest warmonger spun about as if caught up in a whirlwind.

"Go on! Get out of here!" Raffan continued.

Daryus could only guess that whatever his captor carried was a talisman of tremendous power. The warmongers were not simple creatures easily rebuffed. Any one of them could kill both men with ease.

Yet, all Raffan had to do was continue waving the talisman around. The second wasp retreated from sight, followed quickly by the third. That left only the original, a beast Daryus estimated was larger than the other duo by at least a third.

It struggled to reach Raffan, but his device again threw it back. Grinning, Raffan urged his mount toward the last warmonger. He laughed as the wasp fought.

The long, sharp stinger darted out. The huge warmonger slipped under Raffan's aim with the talisman.

With a yelp, the younger man leapt off his horse. A second later, the sting drove deep into the luckless horse's side. The animal shrieked, then tipped over.

Pulling its bloody stinger from the carcass, the warmonger searched for Raffan. As it did, the overdressed young man came up from behind it and held the talisman for all to see.

"Begone with you, I said! Begone!"

The wasp fluttered close to him, the wings building up for another discharge.

Raffan took another step.

The warmonger's wings slowed. The static charge dissipated.

With a last buzz toward the young man, the huge wasp followed after the others.

"Ha!" Raffan whirled on Daryus. "What do you say to that?"

Daryus gave him a slight nod, nothing more.

"Hmmph. You should be more grateful." Raffan bent down to look at his horse, then started for the mount atop which sat Toy's cage.

Daryus eyed the cage, wondering what would happen when Raffan discovered that the familiar had escaped.

But to his surprise, from the bottom of the cage popped the weasel's head. Toy pushed himself up as if having been cringing in the cage all this time.

"You're fortunate you didn't lie about the talisman," Raffan told the weasel.

"I have not lied at all."

In response, Raffan shifted the cage. Daryus saw that the bottom had a hook mechanism that allowed it to be attached by the base in a number of ways.

The other man glanced at him. "The weasel here provided me with a few magical tricks, including a way to hide large objects in a tiny space. He never thought I might include something to keep him in."

Daryus remained silent. He continued to work at his bonds, which were almost loose enough. Once he was free, he would teach Raffan the price of overconfidence and betrayal.

But as Raffan mounted the other horse, Toy turned back to Daryus. He made certain the former crusader saw him, then shook his head.

Daryus paused in his efforts and frowned at the weasel.

Toy used his good eye to wink . . . and then ever so briefly opened and closed his demonic one. The weasel then spun around to face Raffan's back.

Daryus sat motionless as his captor reached back and grabbed the last horse's reins. Pulling hard, Raffan guided the mount up next to his.

"Keep in line and you'll have a chance at survival," the traitorous young man remarked as he took the lead. "Otherwise, I'll dart you and leave you for those bugs."

Daryus kept silent. As he slowly renewed his work, he thought not about Raffan, but rather what he had seen when Toy had opened the monstrous eye.

Whatever had stared back at him, it had certainly not been Toy.

22

IN UHL-ADANAR

Shiera wandered through the temple-city in awe, all other concerns briefly forgotten as she drank in the greatest discovery of her lifetime. Venture-Captain Amadan Gwinn could have his small glories; this would prove Shiera's abilities to the rest once and for all.

It was as if the builders had just stepped away moments ago. There was hardly any dust, hardly any sign that so much time had passed since Uhl-Adanar's construction.

The trek to reach here had been an odd, dangerous one, but to Shiera it now seemed all worth it. She wandered from structure to structure, touching a wall, peering as best she could through windows made of an odd, black glaze. That the glaze prevented her from seeing inside only made her excitement greater. Uhl-Adanar clearly had many wonders to bring to light. All she needed was time.

The illumination spread as she moved, ever providing her with sufficient light. Now and then, Shiera made out the wolf symbol high above a doorway. Unfortunately, thus far, those doors had refused her efforts. Still, with so much else to look at, her frustration remained low.

At the end of the lengthy courtyard, she found a fountain. There was water in the base and a spiral tower in the center that Shiera suspected had once shot a stream of water through the top.

Shiera suddenly felt her thirst. She bent down and studied the water. It looked clear and had no odd smell. A slight ripple revealed the water still flowed, albeit at a slow pace.

Believing it to be fresh enough, Shiera cupped her hands and brought some water to her mouth. It was cool and tasted as if it had just come from a woodland spring. Grateful, she took another handful—

In the water's reflective surface, a mummified face stared at her from behind her shoulder.

Gasping, Shiera rolled away. As she came up, she pulled free her sword.

There was no one behind her.

Shiera surveyed her surroundings from floor to distant ceiling, but saw nothing. Still, she returned to the fountain with caution and used only one hand to gather water while the other gripped the sword tightly.

By the time she finished drinking, her worry had faded. More and more she became certain that the image had just been a side effect of her incredible thirst. Shiera had not known just how much in need of fluid she had been until she had started drinking. In fact, she could not recall the last time she had drank anything.

Feeling calmer, she studied Uhl-Adanar anew. Although she still stood in awe of it, she now considered her choices. Somewhere in here was the tomb, the reason for all this. She had been meant to find it. That much was clear.

Sheathing the sword and removing the crossbow, she went to the nearest door. As before, it refused her attempt to open it, even when she shoved her shoulder hard against it. Stepping back, she eyed the small window next to the door. The material *looked* like glass, but when she tried to batter it with the butt of the crossbow, she did not even leave a scratch.

Shiera went to a second and then a third building with much the same results. Awe began to give way to frustration as she found herself prevented from locating any of the great secrets of the city, especially the tomb.

She eyed the edifice on the other side of the fountain. Mouth set tight, she strode up to the door. In contrast to the previous buildings, which had single, iron doors, this one had a double set that only up close did she see also had the wolf symbol embossed in each. Hopes rising slightly, she reached a hand to the doors.

The two swung open just enough to admit her.

"Oh, of course," she commented wryly to the doors. "I'll just walk in, shall I? Nothing to fear, is there?"

She waited for a moment, then, shifting her stance slightly, kicked the right door. The door swung back hard, finally slamming against the inner wall.

Keeping the crossbow ready in one hand, Shiera drew her sword with the other, then cautiously slipped into the building.

The interior proved to be a vast chamber lined with pews leading to a dais upon which nothing stood. The wall beyond bore the one-eyed wolf symbol, with phrases in the ancient script carved on each side.

"'The silence of Tzadn must be maintained,'" she read on the left. Then, cocking her head, she studied the phrase again at a slightly different angle. "'Let not the Reaper's Eye fall upon you . . .'" Shiera rubbed her chin. "How curious . . ."

She attempted a translation using both angles and again came up with the same answers. Focusing on the phrase on the right, she worked out the first variation.

"'For darkness comes in varying and greater shades.'" More perplexed than ever, Shiera tried the second angle. "'For his reward to you will be service forever.'"

Shiera read the right part over, then, exasperated, dropped down on one of the pews. After taking a breath, she looked to the left, then read all the way to the right. Both sets of phrases seemed linked, but what they meant was beyond her. She could not help thinking there was more substance to them than just words to worshipers of the obscure deity.

As she sat pondering the inscriptions, she noticed for the first time that the wolf pattern also graced the floor of the dais. However, in contrast to the image carved in the wall, the one in the floor looked the opposite direction.

Approaching the pattern, Shiera saw that it was nearly a perfect match to the one that had brought her here. That made her wonder if, like the previous, it had a special purpose. She cautiously circled the design, seeking clues as to its function.

Sure enough, on the side next to the end of the wolf's muzzle, she made out a tiny blue crystal embedded in the stone. Looming over it, she studied it a moment more, then sheathed her sword and slowly waved her hand over the area.

What sounded like stone clattering nearby made her quickly glance around. Despite seeing nothing, Shiera wished that Daryus were here to watch her back.

At that moment, a cloud of dust rose up from the pattern. Even as Shiera stepped back, the small dust cloud expanded to eye level. Slowly, the cloud turned in on itself, creating an odd spinning motion that at first made it hard for Shiera to keep her eyes on it.

Without warning, the dust in the middle separated. In the gap left in the wake, murky forms took shape. Shiera leaned near, trying to make them out.

The nearest one began to coalesce . . . and revealed itself to be none other than Daryus Gaunt. Seeing the renegade crusader caused a wave of guilt to wash over her, even more so when the rest of the vision revealed he was a bound captive on the back of a horse. In front of him rode a scowling Raffan, who did not look at all like the perpetually nervous figure Shiera knew. It did not take her long to also realize that the two traveled deep in the Worldwound.

Daryus. Without thinking, she reached out her hand to him, the fingertips actually touching where the image floated.

Thoughts and images raced through her mind with such force that she shook. She saw the world through Daryus's eyes, saw him as he fought pitborn in Kenabres, fled from former allies in his crusader order, and journeyed into the Worldwound.

She also saw that, all the while, his greatest concern had been finding her.

Shiera pulled her hand free. Shaking, she tried to digest what had just happened. Somehow, she had been able to reach into the man's thoughts and memories, if only for a moment. Yet it had been enough to let her see more about Daryus than she could have learned in a year of traveling with him.

And what she saw renewed her guilt. Shiera swallowed. While she had been concerned about Daryus, in a vague way, her desire to find the lost temple-city and the mysterious tomb had far overshadowed it. True, a part of her had suspected he was capable of taking care of himself—she *had* hired him to protect her, after all—but . . .

Admit it. You saw him like the rest of them, like Galifar and his mercenaries. You thought he'd just mark you as lost and head back to find another client. And so you treated him the same way.

She watched for a moment more as Raffan led his prisoner on. Behind the betrayer and locked in a cage was Daryus's curious pet.

As she watched, Shiera grew more and more frustrated to see Daryus helpless. She angrily slapped the image in the dust cloud.

Some of the dust separated, then became a series of floating symbols.

Shiera forgot all else. She quickly studied the symbols—seven in all—and tried to match them with what she knew of the ancient script. Four or them made no sense whatsoever, but three hinted at other markings she had seen for the concepts of time, place, and movement.

She touched the one she denoted as time, but nothing happened. Attempts at the other two met with the same lack of results. Biting her lip in thought, Shiera tried touching the four mysterious symbols.

Not until the fourth one—the one in the center—did anything happen. Then, all seven symbols turned a bright silver.

On a hunch, Shiera touched the marking denoting time once more. Now, it flared red.

The dust altered course, spinning in the opposite direction. The image swelled in size and seemed to sharpen.

Not at all certain what she was doing, but fascinated by the results thus far, Shiera touched the symbol for movement. When she did, two smaller symbols separated from it, one in front and one behind.

"Let's try this one," she muttered, tapping the smaller marking closer to her. It turned bright green, which she took as a good sign.

Simultaneously, the symbol she read as "place" shifted to an orange glow. Shiera knew that something was imminent, but knew not what. She suspected that if she touched the orange mark, there would be no changing her mind afterward.

Shiera touched it.

The dust cloud swelled, taking on an iridescent shimmer. She had to quickly step back or be engulfed.

The vision of Daryus and Raffan grew with the cloud. The image became more detailed, almost lifelike, as if what she saw now took place just before her and not miles away.

Then she heard the snort of the horse.

Stunned, Shiera stared, unable to believe what she had just done.

Daryus, Raffan, and Toy had just been transported to Uhl-Adanar.

It struck Daryus first in the form of a strange nausea and sense of displacement. Next, he became aware of Toy leaping up and down in the cage in clear glee. Daryus had no idea what was happening, but if the familiar was pleased by it, it boded no good.

Daryus struggled with what was left of his bonds just as Raffan, too, became aware of the change coming over all of them. The younger man twisted in the saddle, his ire aimed not at Daryus, but at the weasel.

"What have you done?"

Toy snickered. "I have done nothing! Fate is with me and neither with you nor Master Grigor!"

Daryus freed his hands. In doing so, he attracted Raffan's attention. The other man's eyes widened and he reached into his pouch.

Daryus's horse snorted—and the Worldwound gave way to the vast interior of some sort of church.

Both mounts were understandably upset. Daryus had to fight to keep his under control. Raffan also struggled, an effort hindered by Toy, who made monstrous hissing sounds clearly designed to add to the horses' fear.

"Daryus?"

The voice cut through everything else. Gripping the reins as tight as he could, he peered in the direction of the call.

A startled Shiera stared back at him. Daryus's relief at finding her was tempered by Raffan's angry shout and Toy's renewed hissing.

He turned back to find Raffan rubbing his hand where a set of red marks indicated a small animal had bitten him hard. Toy was no longer in his cage, the weasel clambering around their shared horse.

Raffan spurred his horse forward, sending it stumbling down the dais and dislodging Toy, who tumbled onto the floor.

Raffan urged his horse down the narrow corridor between two sets of pews. Daryus glanced at Shiera, who seemed safe enough, then gave chase.

Daryus did not want to leave Raffan loose wherever they were. He followed the other man through the chamber and out the two large doors. The temple-city beyond startled him only briefly, confirming what he had thought the moment he had seen Shiera in the chamber. Despite everything, she had *found* Uhl-Adanar.

Raffan raced across the vast courtyard stretching beyond the building. The combined clatter of both horses' hooves resounded through the otherwise silent temple-city. Both mounts struggled on the hard, somewhat slick surface. Raffan's animal slipped twice, but Daryus could not gain ground, his own horse sliding to the side as the two riders reached the curved end of a pathway.

Then, Daryus's mount stumbled for no reason that the former crusader could at first fathom. A moment later, the horse slowed. Its breathing grew ragged.

"Come on, damn you!" Daryus did all he could to urge the animal forward, but instead it started to wobble to the left. Seeing that, Daryus quickly leapt off.

Barely had he done that than the horse fell to its knees. It let out a snort, then rolled onto its side.

Scurrying over to the stricken beast, Daryus put a hand on its chest. The horse breathed normally. When Daryus checked closer, he spotted the small dart at the base of the neck.

Whether the dart had been intended for the animal or Daryus didn't matter. What did was that Raffan had made good his escape, at least for now. Daryus had every expectation that the other man would not go far. It was dangerous enough that he had to worry about the witch and Toy—now he had this third threat looming over Shiera and him.

Shiera. Daryus had left her behind on the assumption that she would be safer where she was, but now he wondered if he had made a mistake.

He had left Shiera with Toy.

The scene that had so rapidly unfolded before Shiera had left her breathless. Through the ancient artifact, she had actually transported two men on horseback from far away to right in front of her.

The symbols had faded away once Daryus and Raffan had appeared. The dust now settled back in and around the wolf pattern. As a test, Shiera repeated what she had done the first time, once more creating the cloud and then summoning the symbols. The ease with which she was able to recreate her earlier success made her confident enough to experiment.

It could not have been by accident that she had summoned up an image of Daryus. Shiera was certain that her desires had something to do with what vision revealed itself, but when she concentrated on Daryus, what she got instead was another view of the Worldwound.

Frowning, she adjusted the symbols, then tried a second time. The vision shifted from the Worldwound to the temple-city, but just before Shiera could congratulate herself, it shifted back.

"It has to be due to my thoughts," Shiera muttered to herself. "How else could I have done it before?"

She took a deep breath and tried one more combination of markings, then pictured Daryus as best she could. The Worldwound faded away, replaced by the temple-city. Gritting her teeth, Shiera peered into the vision, demanding that it remain as she desired.

Even so, once more it returned to the Worldwound. Frustrated, Shiera struggled with the symbols, trying to summon up some more mundane, distant things, such as her home in Nerosyan or the site of Amadan Gwinn's last dig.

Each time, the Worldwound took prominence again. At last, Shiera stepped away from the cloud, which continued to swirl and mock her with the image she did not want.

"Be that way about it, then," she snapped. "I have more important things to do."

Shiera stepped from the dais. While she had not seen much of Uhl-Adanar, she believed from the glimpses she'd had that the temple-city was large, but not too large. She doubted that a man on horse would need more than a quarter hour to ride from one end to the other, if even that much. If there was another entrance or exit, it would probably be hard to locate, which meant that Daryus would probably end up turning back quickly, Raffan or no Raffan.

"He'll be fine," Shiera told herself. "He won't mind if I go on."

"Rest assured, he will come back in his own time," a smooth voice quietly remarked from her right.

Whirling, Shiera looked for the speaker. However, all she saw was row upon row of pews.

A small head popped up near one set of pews. Toy gave her that one-eyed stare, nose twitching.

"But you do not truly need him, now that you have me."

The voice was Toy's.

"I can help you find all you seek, Shiera Tristane." The weasel jumped up onto the back of one pew. He cocked his head,. "You are clever, otherwise I would never have told that fool Raffan to seek you out. Now, you and I will find the tomb."

Shiera swore as she eyed the creature. "You . . . you're a *familiar*, aren't you?"

"Oh, bravo! Long did I search among those of your calling for one with your cunning, your *adaptability*."

"Where's your mistress . . . or master? Daryus is no wizard, and you have to have one . . . don't you? Don't—" She shook her head as the answer came to her. "No . . . you're *his* familiar? That damned witch's?"

Toy chuckled. It was so human a sound that Shiera had to blink.

"Ah . . . now that is a tale I should really tell you . . ." The weasel opened his other eye.

Shiera stepped back as the demon orb burned bright.

"For I think that soon he will find us . . . and then the fun will begin . . ."

23

SEARCH FOR THE TOMB

Grigor smiled as he located the Pathfinder's find. With the two pitborn anxiously waiting behind him, the witch touched the mechanism.

The world shifted. The ruined chamber vanished.

Grigor stood in the midst of a vast courtyard in what he knew instantly could be nothing but Uhl-Adanar.

He drank in his surroundings, heart pounding as it had not since he had slaughtered the last of his treacherous kin. Only one more step remained. Grigor knew better than anyone what would be found in the tomb. The Pathfinder likely only knew a hint of the truth, or else she would have turned and put as much distance as possible between herself and Uhl-Adanar.

He turned to give orders to the pitborn . . . only to have the pair stare fearfully at him. Grigor touched his face, felt a familiar texture, then pulled back his gloved fingers to inspect them.

Large flakes of dry—almost mummified—skin covered much of his glove.

Swearing, the witch looked around for a reflective surface. The nearest one proved to be the water in a large fountain. Striding over to the fountain, Grigor quickly leaned over and studied his face.

His skin was crumbling to dust. Already, he had sunken cheeks and a crisscross pattern of lines over the rest of his visible face. The area he had touched now had a dark gap in it where a hint of his cheekbone could be seen.

The transportation spell has affected my own work!
Straightening, the witch looked around. Immediately he spotted
the building he suspected was his best choice for locating the
tomb.

"Follow!" With the pitborn trailing behind, Grigor headed for
the edifice. As he walked, he reached into one pouch and pulled
out the dried eye belonging to Toy.

*I know you are near, my treacherous little pet! Show me where
you are . . .*

He held the eye before him. As he did, he saw through it a
towering chamber and in it, a female figure. Shiera Tristane.

"So . . . there we are." Replacing the eye in the pouch, Grigor
readied his staff. "Be prepared."

"What are you talking about?" Shiera tried not to stare at the
weasel's tainted eye. "Your master is here? You *are* talking about
that witch with the staff, right? Grigor?" She kept her weapon
pointed at Toy. "I'm no puppet for you and your master—"

"Not my master anymore, not after his betrayal to our patron!"
The familiar leapt from pew to pew until he perched right in front
of her. He shut the foul orb, then continued, "But, yes, that is Grigor
Dolch, and he is near and coming nearer! He would have what you
would find in the tomb, have it to make him not only whole again,
but stronger than ever! He would have the Reaper's Eye!"

The Reaper's Eye . . . "You mean the Eye of Tzadn?"

Toy chuckled. "Tzadn or the Reaper, they are the same, but
the Eye is all that matters! With it, it is said, the Reaper gives his
favor . . . and that is what Master Grigor needs! He needs a new
patron before his past sins catch up!"

Shiera only understood a fraction of what the weasel said, but
what was important was that the witch who had surprised her in
the other ruin was still after her—or rather, the tomb. She recalled
Grigor's words, that Shiera had essentially done his bidding in

getting this far. "He said he was responsible for me finding the temple-city. What did he mean?"

"Ah, Grigor cannot take all the credit! You would have followed a few false trails—not by your own fault—if not for my efforts!"

She grimaced. "Is that so? This story should be a very interesting tale."

The weasel looked back and forth, which caused Shiera to instinctively do the same. "Grigor sought out a clever Pathfinder . . . well, more than one, but others, they foolishly lost their lives. You proved more worthy, though, with my help . . ."

"Your help? How magnanimous of you! I've done this *all* on my own—"

"Oh, yes! Oh, yes! All on your own!" the familiar agreed quickly. "I sought only to balance things out against the forces working to distract you from your desires!"

Shiera had just about had enough of the familiar. "What forces? What do you mean?"

The weasel's nose twitched. "Have you never noticed how whenever you found a clue to your quest, something else would come along to steer you from your course?"

Shiera thought about the various directions her search had turned. "The path to knowledge and discovery is often a meandering one."

"Yes, so the others said. But those impediments were not always by chance, Shiera Tristane! Think about it! Think how no one has ever even *heard* of the god Tzadn or found this temple-city before!"

"The Worldwound created a great upheaval. Much knowledge of the past was lost."

Toy snickered. "Yes, there is that . . . but there is also that the priests of Uhl-Adanar worked hard to keep him hidden! Grigor sought Uhl-Adanar long before you were even born, before he had even betrayed out patron, yet with all at his command, the temple-city and the Reaper's Eye remained hidden! This was not by chance. This was by intent!"

"You're saying that the ancient priests here put together some great spell to protect the location?"

"So it would seem. Yet you, despite everything—and with my good assistance—triumphed in the end! Triumphed in great part because you did not use magic to seek it, but rather your mind alone. That was the ancients' trick. They knew spellcasters would come for the tomb, and so made the tomb forever invisible to the works of magic. How clever is that? To find the tomb of a magic thing, you could not use magic yourself!"

Her mind raced. "You seem to forget that I've not actually found the tomb yet. You could be completely wrong . . . not that I want you to be, at least in that regard."

"But you will find it, you will—" The weasel abruptly paused. He quickly looked to the entrance. "No! He was swifter than calculated! Hurry! Flee from here! Flee! It is—"

Breaking off, Toy slipped from his perch. Shiera readied her crossbow just as the doors flung open seemingly of their own accord.

Grigor, the staff held before him, smiled as he sighted her. "Ah! There you are! You have my sincerest admiration, but circumstances demand that you locate the tomb of Tzadn immediately or I will be forced to treat you to tortures learned from a demon lord."

In response, Shiera fired.

The bolt should have struck true, but it stopped only inches from the witch. Grigor Dolch, his smile reminding Shiera of nothing less than the eternal smile of a corpse, watched as the bolt dropped harmlessly to the floor.

"Take her with the utmost expediency."

Two pitborn stepped from behind the witch. Weapons drawn, they separated, coming at her from opposing sides.

Shiera reloaded, then fired. The pitborn at whom she aimed easily dodged the bolt.

"Where is the damned weasel?" the witch called as his servants converged on her. "I know he's in here somewhere. I can feel his vile little presence!"

Out of the corner of her eye, Shiera caught a glimpse of fur vanishing amid the pews. While she hardly trusted Toy, at the moment the familiar seemed hardly as much a threat as his former master.

"I have no idea what you're talking about. Why don't we instead have a conversation about our goals? You want to find the tomb. I want to find the tomb. I can direct the way just as I—"

Grigor spun the staff around once, then tapped the floor with one end. A brief flash of azure energy accompanied the tap. "There's no time for this. Take her now!"

The pitborn charged.

Shiera threw aside the crossbow and drew her sword. The first pitborn to reach her found to his surprise that a student of letters could also be a student of the blade. Even Venture-Captain Gwinn had his skills with the sword, although Shiera knew he had not practiced them for a long time. She, on the other hand, had continued her own practice until just before embarking on the expedition.

The pitborn retreated under the unexpected onslaught. Shiera doubted that her skills were enough to take on two opponents for very long, but that was not her intention. She knew there had to be another exit somewhere behind her. All she needed was a moment away from her attackers and she would be able to slip away. While Grigor did appear to be fairly powerful, he seemed to keep most of his power ready to protect himself. That seemed to match with what Toy had said and worked now with what Shiera planned.

She lunged at the second pitborn, then retreated. Shiera counted on the fact that the witch still wanted her alive. The pitborn mercenaries would have to overcome their own instinct to slay, causing them to hesitate. That multiplied her chances of escape.

Then, without warning, she stumbled over something just behind her feet. She landed hard on her back.

One of the pitborn fell upon her immediately, twisting the sword from her grasp. Shiera struggled in vain against his armored weight. The horned mercenary grinned wide, displaying a set of very sharp teeth. She spat in his face.

Before anything else could happen, strong hands pulled the pitborn from her. The other demonspawn growled at his eager comrade, then both cowed as a shadow spread over them.

"If you've injured her . . ." the witch muttered.

"No, Master! No, I've not!" whined the pitborn who had fallen on her. "I swear!"

"Pull her to her feet."

The two demonspawn obeyed. Using the moment, Shiera kicked one of them hard in the shin. The pitborn swore.

Grigor chuckled. "Strong of spirit! Excellent!"

She turned to him with the intention of spitting in his face, too, then froze as she beheld the witch's countenance close up.

Grigor was decaying.

What had appeared a youthful, bearded man with unsettling skin was instead clearly a being much older than Shiera had first imagined. Worse, as she looked the witch in the eyes, she saw that even those were not what they seemed, but instead looked like stones or some clever constructs that could actually turn as Grigor desired.

"Yes, I have had some . . . difficulties," Grigor remarked casually. "You are going to help me overcome those difficulties once and for all. If you do, I will let you live. Do you understand?"

Without meaning to, her gaze drifted to the gaps in his skin.

The witch pushed her chin up, forcing her to once more meet the false eyes. "I said, do you understand?"

"Yes . . . yes."

"Better. You would do best not to make me repeat myself." The witch turned from her. "Now, where do you imagine the tomb would be located? Take your time, really."

Aware that he meant just the opposite, Shiera thought hard. She knew Daryus was outside somewhere, which meant that at the very least she had to stall. At some point, he was certain to come looking for her . . . or so she hoped.

"The other end of the temple-city," Shiera finally answered.

His back still to her, Grigor asked, "And what brings you to that conclusion? I'm intrigued."

Shiera improvised. "This is surely the main temple. If you take into account that the wolf image generally looks to the left for a reason, then I think this is the point where the image is indicating it wants us to look for the tomb. However, that makes me think the tomb is the opposite direction. It fits with what I've seen of the builders' thinking. They often show things as the reverse of what they mean." The last was not true, but Shiera hoped she sounded believable.

Grigor raised an eyebrow. "And why not the other way, here in the heart of their temple-city? Why wouldn't the tomb be to the left, just as it shows? Perhaps behind this building, in an underground chamber."

That was what Shiera actually suspected, but she stuck to her story. "That would make sense, if not for the fact that they seem to have been doing their best to confuse searchers. You of all people should appreciate that."

The witch turned back to her. His eyes glittered. "I see . . . you may have something there."

"It'll take us a bit to reach the other end. If you want to search here first—"

In response, Grigor snapped his fingers. Despite the gloves, the sound echoed in the ancient temple.

One pitborn secured her arms. Grigor, the staff tucked under his arm, strode toward the entrance. Without a word, his servants dragged Shiera along.

As they headed through the pews, she tried to spy Toy. Although she did not see the weasel, she knew he had to be near.

The small head popped up briefly. Shiera's guards, focused on their master, did not see the familiar. Only Shiera did.

Toy winked at her. She suspected that the wink was to reassure her, to give her hope that somehow Toy would effect her escape. Perhaps the wink might have had that result at one point, but not since her capture and subsequent realization.

For it had been *Toy* over whom she had tripped.

Not for a second did Grigor grow complacent merely because he finally had the Pathfinder guiding him to the tomb. Toy was near, so very near. The witch thought about retrieving the eye again, but knew that now the familiar would be on guard. That suited him just fine, anyway. If Toy followed now, he would be doing just as Grigor desired.

Once they were outside of the temple, Grigor had Shiera brought up in front next to him. As the pitborn released her, the witch touched the upper tip of the staff against the hollow of her throat.

The tip flared bright. With a grunt, Shiera grabbed at her throat. The pitborn reacted to the sudden movement, but Grigor waved them off.

"Consider your next moves very carefully, Pathfinder. Disobeying me will now have . . . consequences." The witch did not bother to explain what those consequences were—but that was the point. He assumed Shiera had the imagination to come up with an appropriate punishment. In truth, Grigor hadn't even cast anything, only awakened the magic in the staff. A simple ruse, yet a clever one.

"There was no need to do that," she responded without fear.

"We shall see. Get on with it."

Shiera nodded slightly, then moved on. Grigor followed, the two pitborn anxiously bringing up the rear.

Grigor glanced left and right as they journeyed along. He did not do so out of any admiration for what the builders had left, as glorious as most would have found Uhl-Adanar. The only thing that Grigor studied with interest was the sign of the wolf, which marked certain areas along their path. Grigor's avarice grew as the trek stretched on. He suspected that each of the buildings marked by the symbol held something of magical value, and made a note of the ones that looked most intriguing.

"There's no need to concern yourself with those places," Shiera remarked unexpectedly.

"Why? Did you search one? What did you find?"

"I *tried* to get inside. I failed. I tried to see through those black windows and failed there, too. Whatever they hid in there, they protected it well."

"Wait." Grigor knew she might be trying to distract him from his goal, but still . . . "Watch her."

The pitborn flanked the woman. Grigor stalked up to the nearest building. He glanced up at the wolf symbol, then at the door.

Turning the staff horizontal, he touched the door with the tip. The wood glowed bright red.

A sharp, cracking sound shook the area. Next to him, Shiera belatedly covered her ears. As the noise echoed through the ancient temple-city, the door shimmered.

Nothing else happened.

"Hmmph." The witch tried again, with the same lack of results.

"I did warn you," Shiera called, once the second echo subsided. "Please don't try that again."

Grigor didn't bother to respond. He shifted from the door to the peculiar black window. Without preamble, he hefted the staff and used it like a hammer.

Where glass should have easily shattered, the substance covering the window proved resilient. Grigor felt the force of the blow reverberate throughout his body, yet the window remained inviolate.

Grigor's frown deepened. He touched the window, which felt cool, but otherwise unremarkable. Squinting, he tried to see inside. There *was* something in there . . .

A dry, nearly fleshless face peered back at him.

Despite himself, Grigor gasped and stumbled back.

"What did you see?"

The witch scowled as he turned on Shiera.

"Nothing," he finally responded. "Nothing. A simple trick of the light."

In contrast to her earlier, somewhat flippant attitude, Shiera now eyed her captor with honest, almost urgent, curiosity.

Grigor considered for a moment longer, then said, "I saw my face, only as in death."

A slight tic briefly affected her mouth. Grigor glared, well aware of how he already looked.

To her credit, she let the slight tic be the only sign of her thoughts concerning Grigor's monstrous appearance. Peering at the window, Shiera muttered, "Not your face, I'd say. Something similar happened to me back at the fountain, only I could see my own face reflected next to the dead one. This place isn't as empty as it seems."

At this declaration, the two pitborn tightened their grips on their weapons. As for Grigor, he waited for something more from the woman. However, after several seconds of silence, he grew impatient. "So. Nothing else happened to you after that?"

"Nothing, but I—"

That was enough for Grigor. "Then we move on. I will not be kept from my destiny!"

He waved for the pitborn to push her on. Shiera easily dodged their touch before turning of her own accord and continuing the trek as if she were the one in command.

Grigor took one last look back at the sealed structure. No ghoulish face peered out through the black window, yet he couldn't help feeling that something watched him from within.

Grigor abruptly laughed at his own fears. *What does it matter who watches? Soon, very soon, I'll have so much power that I'll fear nothing! Nothing!*

With an arrogant wave of the staff, he turned and followed Shiera.

While it had been true that Shiera had initially wanted to slow her captor down in the hopes that Daryus might help her escape, she had also been curious as to what Grigor had seen. Having noticed nothing during her attempt at one of the windows, it intrigued her that Grigor had been confronted by something akin to what had looked over her shoulder when she had sought a drink of water.

What does it mean, though? Why these mummified faces? Are they meant as a sign?

Whatever the unsettling results of Grigor's inspection of the building, it had succeeded in causing a delay. She hoped that by slowing their journey she had given Daryus a chance to catch up to them again.

That Toy followed did not give her any comfort. Although she had only just learned of the weasel's ability to speak, Shiera had heard enough of the familiar's words and soothing tone to not trust the creature any more than she did his former master. Shiera had no doubt that Toy would sacrifice her life just as quickly if it meant achieving his goals.

The far edge of the temple-city beckoned. Shiera silently swore. She was taking a big risk. Grigor had been absolutely correct when he had come to the conclusion that the tomb would be found *behind* the great temple, not all the way across Uhl-Adanar, as she had sworn.

Shiera had led the witch on a wild goose chase . . . and she suspected it would not take him much longer to realize he had been tricked.

She surreptitiously eyed her surroundings. There were two smaller temple structures, one on each side of her, plus a taller, plainer building whose purpose she had yet to figure out, but that reminded her of part of an old roofed amphitheater she had helped excavate during her time with Amadan Gwinn.

Shiera fought back a smile. If it were anything akin to the ancient amphitheater from the previous expedition, it would offer her any number of passages and chambers she could use to trick the witch. That would in turn buy her time while she either puzzled out an escape on her own or managed to flee with Daryus's aid. The spell binding her throat concerned her, but there was nothing she could do about that. Obeying the witch would no doubt result in death anyway. If it came down to it, she'd rather go out on her own terms.

"There!" she called out, pointed with exaggerated determination at the edifice. "That should be the entrance."

"Plain but dominating," Grigor Dolch remarked. "Seems reasonable. We go through the main entrance?"

"Of course. Any hidden traps will only go off once we're well inside and can't escape. *Brilliant* strategy."

Grigor cocked his head, then said to the two pitborn, "You pair first."

She stared at him, wondering if her sarcasm had been lost. Had this been the actual tomb structure, going through the front entrance instead of searching for some hidden side door would have surely made sense only to someone planning suicide. Yet, Grigor intended to do just that. She had hoped to mislead him

with a long hunt for the presumed hidden door, but now she had
to think of other options, especially when her captor realized she
had been lying.

Daryus, if you're near, I hope you've got something in mind,
Shiera thought as the pitborn moved forward. Of course, she had
no intention of leaving things to him. If it came to the point where
she could rescue herself, she would do just that . . . or die trying.

The towering, rectangular entrance gave way to an equally
vast corridor inside. Once more, Shiera was reminded of the other
structure that had proven to be an amphitheater. If matters kept
on as they did, she would have to choose a chamber in which to
steer her captors before they understood that she had made fools
of them.

A slight hissing sound caught her attention.

Shiera froze. "No—"

The foremost of the two pitborn glanced at his feet, where the
floor beneath his right one had sunk in an inch.

A green cloud swept over the first pitborn. Only Shiera's expert
gaze enabled her to see that it erupted from underneath the stone
that had receded into the floor.

The pitborn engulfed by the cloud screamed. If he hoped that
help would come, he was sorely mistaken, for even his comrade
backed away rather than potentially suffer the same fate.

The stricken demonspawn tried to turn to them, but even as
he did, his armor began to melt.

No, not just his armor, Shiera saw. His flesh and even his bones
quickly sloughed off along with the melting metal. In seconds, the
pitborn became a horrific, dripping mound that managed one
more muffled cry before the body literally collapsed in on itself.
Even then, the melting continued, until quickly there was little left
but a grotesque puddle.

Shiera felt the tip of Grigor's staff at the back of her neck.
"Next time, I expect you to spot the trap first. Understand?"

She only nodded, eyes transfixed on what had once been a savage, armored warrior. The acidic cloud had done its work swiftly and thoroughly.

The acidic cloud that had been part of a trap that should not have existed in the first place.

Shiera realized she had outsmarted herself. She had not led her captor astray . . . instead she had led him directly to the tomb after all.

24

THE GUARDIANS

Daryus had abandoned the unconscious horse with regret, but knew he had to get back to Shiera as soon as possible. Despite both lingering stiffness and his own sturdy garments, he had managed to cover a fair distance in short order.

And then he had all but stumbled over Shiera . . . and her unsavory companions.

It had taken every effort to avoid being seen. Daryus had been forced to throw himself behind one of the ancient buildings, landing hard in the process.

Daryus had paid the two pitborn no mind, focusing instead on Shiera and the bearded figure with her. Here, at last, must be Grigor Dolch, the witch whom Toy had served. The witch looked like a strange cross between a young man of noble means and some macabre half-dead creature. Daryus also paid special attention to the staff, which Toy had mentioned was a source of great magic.

Shiera had not appeared bound, but Daryus knew that with witches and other wielders of magic, mundane things like ropes or chains were often unnecessary. He had watched the group vanish from view, his original intention to follow from a safe distance until he could calculate a plan. However, that had changed when he had realized they were already being followed.

Toy had trotted after Shiera and her captors, head high as he constantly sniffed the air. Daryus had kept himself planted against one wall, hoping Toy could neither see nor smell him.

The party had veered toward the entrance to a large edifice that, despite its rather plain exterior, Daryus would have preferred to remain far away from. First Shiera, Dolch, and the pitborn had entered, and Toy had trailed roughly a minute after. Only then had Daryus started out into the open.

Barely had he done so than the scream had arisen from within. It had taken all his will not to go rushing inside. Even though Daryus had immediately recognized the voice as male—and probably one of the pitborn—that had not meant that Shiera might not also be in danger. Yet, even now, even with what should have been a safe enough passage of time, Daryus did not enter. He knew he had to avoid confronting the witch directly. A sword was no match against the skilled use of magic—not directly at least. Daryus could name more than half a dozen old comrades who had learned that the hard way.

He started around the right side of the structure, seeking some secondary entrance. A building of this size had to have another way in, even if hidden. Shiera might be the expert, but Daryus had infiltrated his share of ruins and mysterious buildings himself and had picked up a few clues as to what to watch for.

Moving beside the structure, he looked for the minute but telltale signs of a hidden entrance, running his fingers along the wall, seeking even the slightest edge that should not have been there.

The hair on the back of his neck suddenly stiffened. He quickly looked behind him, certain that he was no longer alone.

There was nothing. Yet, Daryus did not consider himself someone to imagine things. He stepped away from the wall just long enough to reassure himself that there was no one else around, not even treacherous Toy, then returned to his efforts.

Only a few breaths later, he found what he was seeking. Daryus ran his fingernail along half the edge just to make certain he was correct. Sure enough, he had found another way inside.

Of course, he still had to figure out how to *open* it.

He had no sword, that having been taken by Raffan. Nor did he have the dagger he generally wore on his belt. What he did have, however, was a smaller, slimmer, still deadly blade he kept hidden at all times in the side of his left boot.

Drawing the stiletto, Daryus used the point to identify the sides of the hidden doorway. That done, he made an estimate of where the creators would have decided it most useful to place the opening mechanism. He knew that by now a Pathfinder like Shiera would probably not only have located it, but already entered, yet still he felt some satisfaction when he finally opened the way.

Slipping into the ancient edifice, Daryus moved through a darkened chamber. Despite his best efforts, he could make out nothing beyond arm's reach. He was forced to reach out with the dagger, using the tip to help him locate one wall and then use that wall to guide him to the end.

At first, he found only another wall, but fortunately after a short search, he located a long latch. With gratitude to the builder who had finally decided to give him a normal door, Daryus cautiously opened the way.

A soft, blue glow greeted him, originating from a series of small stones set into the walls every yard or so. Silently stepping out, Daryus found himself in a long corridor decorated by a series of macabre, full-length portraits of mummified people in dark robes. Some had improbable wings, but otherwise they were all of a similar kind.

Despite the unsettling nature of the paintings, even Daryus had to admit the artist had been highly skilled. He—or perhaps *they*, considering how many individual images there were—had added so much detail that Daryus could almost swear that if he touched the cheek of the nearest one, he would feel the dry flesh.

Returning his focus to Shiera and Grigor, Daryus tried to determine in which direction to proceed. After a short consideration, he chose the left, since it would lead him closer to the main entrance.

The figures continued to line the wall all the way, even when Daryus at last reached a new corridor. A few of the newer figures carried weapons, some of which made Daryus envious. His tiny dagger would not do against Grigor.

Voices echoed from ahead.

Planting himself against the wall, Daryus tried to peer beyond the limited illumination. He heard Shiera's voice, then that of a male who had to be the witch. The speakers were far enough away that Daryus dared to step away from the wall and head toward them.

A creak behind him made every muscle tense. Daryus whirled, ready to use the dagger to its best potential.

The corridor was empty.

Holding his breath, Daryus listened. The only thing he heard was the distant voices. He started to lower the blade—

Another creak echoed from somewhere close behind him.

Brandishing his weapon, Daryus took a few steps toward where he believed the creaking had arisen. Yet, the only thing he found was more of the painted images.

Daryus approached the nearest and tapped it twice with the dagger, reassuring himself that it was indeed merely paint on stone. Still ill at ease, he slowly turned back toward Shiera.

A scream erupted from that direction, so loud it shook Daryus's eardrums despite the distance.

Shiera.

He started running.

Despite the realization that she had led Grigor exactly where he wanted to go, Shiera hadn't given up just yet. If she could lead him around long enough for him to grow inattentive or call for a rest, then she stood a chance of finding a way to escape through one of the two secret passages she had already noted nearby.

"I think this corridor leads where we want to go," she had remarked.

"Get on with it," had been Grigor's only reply.

Shiera might have said more, but as she had entered that next corridor, she had paused in awe at what the builders of Uhl-Adanar had wrought. Lining both walls were intricate paintings of robed figures. She realized a moment later these were clearly all priests who had died at some point previous to these works. Every figure looked as if it had been mummified—

She halted, recalling what had happened at the fountain. Despite the briefness of that incident, Shiera could still very well picture the gaunt, almost fleshless face.

A face much akin to those she now saw.

"What is this?" Grigor muttered impatiently. "Some honoring of dead priests?"

"It . . . appears so." Shiera had some other ideas.

A creaking sound made her turn, only to find no source. Shiera frowned, hoping she had not just missed some slow-acting trap.

Grigor used his staff to shove her forward. "The tomb."

"Yes . . . this way."

"It had better be. And close at that."

Shiera said nothing as she strode farther down the corridor. As the stones in the walls lit, she found one more painting after another, each unique and yet disturbingly similar. They were all definitely of individual people. In addition, even though they clearly looked to be priests, many held weapons, including swords, lances, and maces.

More intriguing yet, some had *wings*. Shiera tried to understand what that meant. Perhaps these had been very senior or very respected priests. Perhaps they had been part demon, the taint of the Abyss seeping through as a precursor to the madness to come. Or—

There was another, much more audible creak. She paused again. Despite her circumstances, she dared ask, "Did you just hear something?"

"The settling of an ancient place." Grigor brought the point of the staff to her throat. "I'm growing impatient. If you—"

To their side, the pitborn let out a strange, grunting sound. As one, Shiera and the witch looked to see why.

Blood dripped out of the pitborn's mouth as he gaped at them. More spilled from the wound in the middle of his chest, the hole imperfectly sealed by a long lance ending in a barbed point.

Behind him, the mummified figure holding the lance stepped out of the wall and into the corridor behind his victim.

Shiera screamed and reached for her crossbow, only to recall that both it and her sword still lay on the other side of the temple-city.

The monstrous priest easily held up the impaled pitborn. Empty eye sockets turning Shiera's way, it twisted the lance slightly. There was a clicking sound and the barbs slipped inside the lance's head.

With ease, the undead shook the quivering form of the pitborn off the weapon. The dying demonspawn collapsed on the floor. He twitched once, then lay still.

Shiera's mind raced. The nearest weapon was the sword dropped by the dead pitborn . . . which unfortunately meant coming within range of the mummy's lance.

"I don't have time for you," Grigor Dolch commented bluntly. "Begone."

Grigor pointed the staff at the mummified priest. He twisted his wrist, turning the staff.

A fireball struck the undead in the midsection, blasting it to ashes.

"That's that, then." With some satisfaction, Grigor lowered the staff.

"I don't think so," muttered Shiera as she looked around.

Six *more* of the paintings had begun separating themselves from the walls, becoming desiccated priests wielding a variety of weapons.

Even as Grigor raised his staff again, Shiera lunged forward to retrieve the pitborn's sword. However, as she grabbed for the heavy blade, the clawed hand of a priest grabbed her arm. She kicked at its nearly fleshless knee, trying to knock it off balance, but the mummy was surprisingly solid.

Struggling, Shiera reached the sword. Despite the awkward angle, she managed to turn the blade around and cut the dry hand from the arm. To her relief, the hand ceased moving. Shiera knocked the appendage away, then rose up to her knees. With all the force she could muster, she jammed the point of the sword into the skull.

The priest stilled. Unfortunately, as she stood, she saw there were now as many as ten undead figures crawling out of the walls.

Grigor had not remained still while this happened. He used the spell that had destroyed the first undead on several more. However, this time, the fiery attack faltered abruptly, leaving the mummies virtually untouched.

Whatever spell animates them is also designed to adapt to magical attacks! Shiera realized. All Grigor did was waste precious time and energy that neither had.

"Don't use the same spell!" Shiera called to him.

"Yes, I'm quite aware of that now, thank you!" Grigor muttered something under his breath and twisted a ring.

A small bolt of lightning struck his target. The ghoulish figure attempted to continue toward the witch, but the magical current was so intense the dry flesh and bone of the priest burned to ash in seconds. The remaining fragments collapsed in a heap.

But in that short time, the other undead had nearly closed on the pair. Grigor used the staff as a physical weapon now, knocking off the head of one creature and then thrusting the staff through the chest of another.

Yet still that was not enough. Shiera brought the sword up in an attempt to fend off another undead, all too aware that she could not wield the heavy blade sufficiently to defend herself for very long—

"Best give me that one."

Shiera spun to find herself staring at Daryus.

"That one's more suited for me," he rumbled, extending a hand. "Let me try to get you something better."

Not knowing what else to do, Shiera handed over the sword. With that, Daryus charged into the fray. He brought the great sword around, cutting through a mummy's throat so deeply that the head fell backward. Not stopping there, Daryus grabbed the lance the creature held and pulled it forward, chopping both hands off the lance.

He shook the severed appendages off the weapon, then tossed it back to Shiera. "Try this!"

She seized up the lance and saw immediately that it was akin to the one that had slain the pitborn, albeit smaller. Another of the undead closed on her just as she gripped the weapon, and without hesitation, she thrust the head into the gaping mouth of the mummy, then manipulated the lance as she had seen the first fiend do.

The barbs burst out, ripping apart the face. Shiera tugged hard, pulling free the skull.

Meanwhile, Daryus lunged under one rusty but still deadly blade, then ripped through the dry flesh and moldering cloth. He seized the damaged undead and hurled it at one of its comrades.

As both mummies sought to untangle from one another, he speared both heads on the end of the sword.

Without warning, the rest of the mummies began retreating. Faces emotionless, they stepped backward without error to their original locations. Shiera spun in a circle, certain this was some trick.

Only then did she see Grigor uttering some incantation as he held the staff before him. The witch slowly walked toward the receding fiends, his muttering increasing in intensity with each passing second.

Yet, as Shiera watched, she wondered at this astounding power the witch suddenly wielded. She could not believe that after what had happened Grigor could so readily dismiss the threat . . . but here he was, doing just that.

One by one, the undead stepped up into their slots. As they did, their bodies reverted to flat designs of paint.

Grigor turned the staff toward the last. He now all but shouted the incantation.

Catching her breath, Shiera turned to Daryus.

Sword raised, Daryus charged the witch from his blind side.

But although Daryus moved in silence, somehow Grigor turned at just the right moment and gestured at his new attacker.

Daryus bounced back as if just having collided with a wall. The fighter landed in a heap, sword slipping from his hand. Despite the harshness of the strange collision, Daryus was back on his feet in the blink of an eye.

Yet not quickly enough. Looking more akin to one of the undead than anything living, the witch turned the staff vertical.

With a pained grunt, Daryus dropped down on one knee. A faint sphere formed around him. He tried to rise, but it was as if he were momentarily frozen in place.

Shiera did not wait. Bracing the lance, she went for the witch.

Grigor turned and expertly brushed aside her weapon, then brought up the staff and caught her in the throat.

Choking, Shiera dropped the lance.

Grigor returned his attention to Daryus. Striding over to the frozen crusader, the witch struck him hard on the jaw.

With a groan, Daryus fell to all fours. Grigor took the staff and touched it to Daryus's neck. There was a shimmer, followed by a groan from Daryus.

"I have placed a ward upon you. Do as I say and all will go well. Disobey, and your fate will be far worse than what you're both currently suffering." He looked to Shiera. "Stand up, Pathfinder."

She managed to obey.

"We are close," Grigor announced to both of them. "My congratulations on that, Pathfinder. You're earning your life." To Daryus, he added, "As for you, my friend, I venture to say that damnable Toy is nearby, isn't he?""

"I've . . . no idea where . . . he is," Daryus rasped. "Hopefully about to rip out your throat."

Grigor frowned. "You *are* strong. Small wonder Toy thought you might be sufficient. No matter. He can't stop me at this point, even if he had both of you at his command. We are within reach of the tomb. You can earn your life by helping with any more *physical* requirements that might arise. Do so, and I'll let you two go as soon as I've got what I want."

Grigor gestured, and Shiera watched as Daryus slowly rose to his feet.

"I'll need a sword at least," the mercenary said.

"Yes, that is fair. Take that one you wanted to cleave me with."

Doing as commanded, Daryus gripped the weapon and waited.

"Now, let us conclude this, Pathfinder."

Shiera had no choice but to take the lead again. However, as she passed Daryus, she managed a glance his way. Not at all to her surprise, he was already looking her direction. His gaze reassured her, even under the circumstances.

Then, once more in front of the witch, Shiera head down the corridor. In the process, she could not help eyeing the painted figures she passed, those of more and more cadaverous priests . . .

Could not help eyeing them and wondering if Grigor had actually so easily cast them back.

Daryus watched as Shiera and the witch moved past him. He had seen enough to know that Grigor did have significant power. However, much of his strength, including what he used to keep both of his companions captive, actually seemed to reside in the staff. Given the opportunity, Daryus swore he would rip it from Grigor's grip and snap it in two.

For the moment, however, he had to accede to Grigor's commands. That actually suited Daryus for the time being. Grigor needed both of them, and so long as that was the case, the pair would be all right. Daryus would use every second to analyze the witch's other weaknesses and how to exploit them.

He would also watch for Toy. The familiar had to be very near. Toy *and* Raffan. Somehow, he felt each and every one of them had a part to play in how this game finished out.

And most of all, Daryus could not help thinking there might still be one *more* player in this game. The most powerful player of all . . .

25

TOY

Although Grigor spoke often about the tomb itself, Shiera was well aware that what he truly wanted was a single item, something she no longer thought of as Tzadn's Eye, but rather its other name—Reaper's Eye. The events that had played out had made that second meaning of the ancient script seem more appropriate.

Grigor clearly expected the artifact would be found at the center of the tomb, a notion with which Shiera had to agree. Beyond that, she did not know what to expect, although clearly Grigor had more ideas concerning that than she did. She expected either a ceremonial tomb or, if a real one, the resting place of some ancient ruler or high priest of the same name, transformed by time and tradition into a supposed god.

Shiera almost smiled. Even though she and Daryus were prisoners of a mad spellcaster, she couldn't help thinking like a Pathfinder. Everything she did was in some manner bound to her chosen path in life.

And so, despite her predicament, Shiera had to admit she was growing more and more excited at the prospect of locating the tomb.

She paused. Instinct made her turn to one of the paintings to her right.

"What is it?" the witch demanded. "Another unwanted guest?"

"No . . . there's something different about this image." Shiera stepped up to the painting. On the surface, it looked like the rest.

A cadaverous priest clad much the same way as the rest. Like many, he held something in his hands.

Shiera fought back a smile. Unlike the others, what this priest wielded was not a weapon, but rather a *book*.

It could not be a mistake. She stepped up to the image. Behind her, she could hear Daryus shifting about, the fighter clearly not pleased she stood so near the painting.

Grigor, on the other hand, appeared to trust that Shiera would not get herself killed. Not certain if she appreciated his confidence in her, she nonetheless reached out and put her fingers on the book.

The area where she stood gave way.

She was sliding down a passage. She grabbed for support, but found none. For a terrifying instant, she considered that she might have misjudged and dropped herself into some abyss, and then she landed hard on her feet.

Shiera expected to find herself in some deep catacomb, but instead discovered she had ended up in some sort of large chamber open to the cavern air on her left. Beyond, another part of Uhl-Adanar beckoned, but she ignored the ancient glories calling to her and turned to face the wall behind. She could not believe she had simply been tossed out of the tomb. There was a purpose to this odd passage, one she felt certain she would be able to find.

She had by not forgotten Daryus, but Shiera had no means by which to rescue him, not yet. Only one possible hope occurred to her at this moment: if she did actually find the tomb, she could use the information to trade for both her life and that of the former crusader. Of course, not for a moment would Shiera trust any word the witch gave; not only would she have to find the Reaper's Eye, but she would also have to think of some way she could *force* Grigor to live up to any promises.

Thinking of the witch, she glanced again at the shut passage. Grigor hadn't immediately followed her, but that could change at any moment.

It occurred to her that perhaps the passage down which she had slid had been designed in case of a dire emergency. That emergency must also include reaching the tomb as quickly as possible, or else why go through all this trouble? The tomb would have been the builders' focus. Best to assume everything had been done with protecting it in mind.

She looked back over her shoulder, but saw no sign of him. Still, she was certain that Toy was nearby. The familiar was clearly a treacherous creature on par with the witch, but Shiera believed she was clever enough to make use of Toy in turn.

Feeling the wall, Shiera sought out another secret door. While certainly always happy to make use of her skills, she had to admit she was getting frustrated with the ancients' propensity for making any path to the tomb convoluted. Shiera could appreciate their attempt to protect it, but time was not on her side at the moment.

Once more, she abruptly looked over her shoulder.

This time, there *was* someone behind her.

Raffan.

"So. I thought that was you hunting me." The young man's stylish clothes were now unkempt and dusty, his well-groomed hair disheveled. There was a bruise on his chin. "But I'll be damned if I can figure out how you got in front of me. Good thing I heard your grunt. You were careless."

Shiera had no idea what Raffan was talking about, but what mattered was his immediate intent. In his left hand, he wielded a small, single-hand crossbow identical to the one Shiera had lost.

"Have to say, I did admire your choice in weapons," Raffan added. "Had to keep this hidden while I played the buffoon for you at the damned rat's request."

"It was a lie from the start, then?"

"Oh, my employer was real, the old fool. Would-be Pathfinder, you know. I was biding my time for when I could put him out of the way, but then Toy popped up and offered a proposition too enticing to wait for. Of course, he and I always knew that we'd never stay true to the bargain between us. It was just a matter of who betrayed who first."

Shiera tried to think about what to do against Raffan. In the meantime, she worked to keep him talking. "And who was first?"

He smiled. "Oh, I was."

Despite his confident answer, Shiera doubted the truth of it. Still, Shiera was not about to contradict a man holding a weapon on her.

"What does Toy want out of all this?" she asked. "Just vengeance against the witch?"

"You know, that's a good question, but one I don't need answered in order to get what I want." Raffan pointed the crossbow at her chest. "You were looking for a door or something, I believe. That would be of use right now. Get on with it."

"You don't want to go inside, Raffan. It's dangerous in there. There are traps, most of them magic—"

"Not afraid of that, Tristane." He held up what looked to her like an amulet or large coin. "Courtesy of the rat. Been very handy against monsters and magic, although its magic is about used up, I think."

For some reason, Shiera had no doubt the artifact would have the image of the wolf on it. She also believed it was every bit as powerful as he said it was. Still, as she turned back to the wall, Shiera wondered if the corridors might not hold a few more mundane traps against which Raffan's magic item would be no aid. She only needed the right one to help her remove the problem of Raffan.

A startled grunt from her companion made her spin around. To Shiera's astonishment, Raffan struggled with a muscular woman clad in a familiar uniform. She gripped the wrist of the hand wielding the crossbow while trying to cut off his air using her other forearm.

But Raffan turned out to be hardier than Shiera could have imagined. Slowly, he managed to turn the crossbow toward his assailant.

Shiera jumped at him. She grabbed the arm just below the other woman's hand, forcing Raffan to turn the crossbow away.

Eyes wide in a combination of anger and fear, he reached with his free hand into a pouch and quickly removed a small device. Shiera spotted a small needle sticking out of it. Suspecting what it might do, she abandoned her effort on the raised arm and grabbed Raffan's other wrist. Gritting her teeth, Shiera turned his hand toward his side.

She heard a slight click. Raffan grunted. As Shiera looked at him again, she saw that fear had entirely replaced anger.

He dropped the crossbow, then the dart device. Frowning, Shiera stepped back.

"No! Not that one—" Raffan began, his body shaking. "It was meant for—" His brow wrinkled as he clearly struggled to think. "Meant for him—"

His eyes rolled up, leaving only the whites showing. With a sigh, Raffan fell back into the armored woman.

"What happened to him?" the newcomer demanded as she let Raffan slide to the ground. "He's growing cold."

"He was trying to fire some dart! I turned it toward him just as he managed."

The brawny woman leaned over Raffan. "He's quite dead." She picked up the dart device and sniffed the area from which the tiny missile had come. "This is a poison I know. A very fast one."

As the other woman investigated, Shiera quietly plucked up Raffan's crossbow. It was a much sleeker, better crafted one than her own, but still capable of using the bolts she had.

The armored figure rose. She looked at Shiera, seeming not to care at all that Shiera had the crossbow.

"I am Captain Harricka Morn," the other woman finally announced to her. "You know Daryus Gaunt, don't you?"

It had taken but a single glance for Shiera to recognize just who and what the newcomer was. A crusader from the Order of the Flaming Lance. Despite being aware of Daryus's checkered past in that regard, Shiera nevertheless bluntly replied, "Yes, I know him. Have you come to help him?"

"I have come to help him face justice. Where is he?" The officer looked around. "And where is this? Some witchery seized me from the Worldwound and deposited me not far away from this building. I saw this one from a distance and recognized him from Kenabres. I followed him with the idea of seeing what he knew—and then found him assaulting you. I made a decision to interfere."

"How very noble of you." Shiera exhaled in exasperation. Her mind raced. She suspected she knew how Harricka had ended up here. Toy had been nearby when she had activated the mechanism that had first drawn Daryus and Raffan. The familiar had a strong mind. It might have been he who had brought her here, no doubt for another of his multitude of plans. The captain would be especially useful if Toy needed to do something about Daryus.

She kept her expression neutral as she added, "So you know, we're still in the Worldwound. This is a temple-city belonging to people who—"

Her new companion brusquely waved her to silence. "I am not a scholar, Pathfinder. Spare me your lectures. 'The Worldwound' is sufficient for my needs. Now, where is Daryus Gaunt?"

"Inside. He's a captive of a witch named Grigor Dolch."

"Grigor Dolch." The captain's eyes narrowed. For the first time, she reached down to touch the hilt of the sword sheathed at her side. She stared past Shiera, clearly thinking something over. "Grigor Dolch. That name has come up at least twice in the order, both times associated with heinous crimes and dark arts."

"He has Daryus under his power. I think there's a spell involved."

"Daryus can do nothing?"

"No."

Harricka Morn rubbed her chin. "If what you say is true, it might be possible to slay the witch while still keeping Daryus momentarily under the spell . . . at least long enough for me to bind him for the trip back to Kenabres."

Shiera couldn't believe what she was hearing. "He may not live that long!"

The crusader looked concerned. "He must! He has evaded justice too long!"

Shiera had thought she had found in this woman an ally, but now saw that Harricka Morn only represented yet another threat, at least to Daryus. That was something Shiera did not need. She backed away from the crusader as she tried to decide what to do—

But where Shiera expected to have a wall behind her, there was empty space.

Harricka Morn reached for her. "Look out!"

Too late. Shiera backed into a darkened space, then stumbled over something small. As she dropped, Shiera saw the wall shut before just before Harricka could reach her.

"Are you all right? Are you well?"

Toy. Of course. Shiera could not see the weasel, but knew he was near. She also knew that once more he had purposely gotten under her feet, the other time being at the dais in the temple. She was very tempted to use the crossbow on the familiar, but held off.

"Where are you?" she finally asked.

A brief, crimson glow about a foot off the ground and to her left caught her attention. That demon eye, winking open and shut.

Jumping up, she headed for where she had seen the glow. As she did, she heard the scampering of tiny feet.

"Where are you going?" Shiera quietly called.

"Keep moving! A door ahead!"

Keeping the crossbow ready, Shiera continued to follow. Then, just as she was about to say something again, a dim blue light stirred.

Stretching a hand before her, Shiera found the beginning of a corridor. She also found a straight panel on the side that she realized had to be the door to which Toy had referred.

As she stepped out, the corridor became more illuminated. Shiera took some comfort from her familiarity with the blue stones. She looked around, also pleased to discover there were no paintings of mummified priests.

That left only Toy.

She pointed the crossbow at him. He had the gall to look offended.

"You've tripped me twice," Shiera muttered. "Maybe I can appreciate this second time, but I never much cared for the first. You put me in Dolch's grip. For that alone, I should mount you on the nearest wall."

Toy's ears flattened. "So very sorry! It was necessary! Grigor Dolch would have killed you outright if I had not made you fall!"

Shiera had her doubts about that, and let the fact that she kept the crossbow aimed at Toy relay them. The weasel kept his ears flattened. He looked left and right, then suddenly his ears popped up.

"There is a clue, I think! A clue to the tomb!"

Despite her suspicions, Shiera lowered the weapon slightly. "Show me . . . and quick. I'm getting twitchy."

"This way! Not far! I swear!"

He trotted on ahead. Shiera rushed after, trying to keep her gaze simultaneously on her quarry and her surroundings. Toy turned a corner, then ran some distance down the new corridor. As he did, the blue stones flashed on, giving Shiera a fairly good glimpse of what lay ahead.

And so it did not entirely surprise her that she once more confronted a wall-sized carving of the wolf.

However, it *did* stun her to for once confront an image where the beast looked forward. Looked forward and verified that, like the wolf statues that had protected her, it did indeed have only one eye.

"I know this is of great import, but the key eludes me, Pathfinder," Toy all but purred.

"You found this, did you? While I was being attacked by guardians of this place? Thanks for your overriding concern for my safety."

"Oh, I am so sorry about that, Pathfinder! Had I known the danger you were in, I would have done what little I could!" The familiar made a circle in front of the image. "But surely this makes some amends for all that! Think of the glory, the honor! Think of all those who took what you deserved, how the accolades they gained are pale in comparison to those you will receive."

Crossbow still ready, Shiera stepped past the familiar and started work on the wall. "The key is in the eye, I think," she muttered. "Or do you have some other knowledge you've failed to impart? Anything at all?"

Toy said nothing. Shiera glanced back at the familiar . . . only to discover Toy nowhere to be found.

"Not again," she growled. "I should really know better by now."

She immediately returned all of her attention to the image. She suspected that Toy's abrupt departure meant she had very little time to do her work.

She slid her fingers around the eye, searching. With grim satisfaction, she located the hidden knob and pressed it.

The eye swung open . . . and then the wall itself began to do the same. Shiera had to jump back or risk getting trapped as the huge stone door swung enough to the side to admit entrance.

She stepped inside.

Instantly, blue stones on the opposing walls lit up. A chamber ending in a high dais akin to the one in the temple materialized from the dark.

And atop that dais, floating without support above a pedestal, was a glittering stone of smoky hue at least the size of Shiera's hand. Although rounded at the bottom, it rose at the top to a sharp point.

Deep in the center, a dark, crimson spot made it look as if the crystal stared back at her. There could be no mistaking what it was.

The Reaper's Eye beckoned.

Shiera took one very careful step closer.

There was a click.

Both walls began changing.

Grigor impatiently tapped the tip of the staff on the spot he had last seen the woman touch, yet the floor beneath him remained persistently solid.

"Not what you planned?" his prisoner asked nonchalantly.

Grigor spun on Daryus. "You live because the Pathfinder values your life, and I value her abilities. That does not mean my patience is infinite."

He intended to punctuate his words with a touch of pain, but before he could summon the spell, he saw Daryus's gaze shift past him. Grigor could think of only two things that should have been sufficient to steal his captive's attention from him. One was more of the mummified priests.

The other was Toy.

The witch turned and was rewarded with the fleeting glimpse of a tail just vanishing around a corner.

"Follow!" Grigor commanded, rushing after Toy. He had every confidence that Daryus would obey. The fighter had no choice unless he wanted to die for no good reason.

As Grigor rounded the corner, he caught sight of Toy disappearing into the wall on the left. A slight grating sound accompanied the familiar's departure.

However, this time Grigor could just see the edges of the hidden door as it shut. As Daryus joined him, he ordered, "Pull that open."

Daryus eyed the door. After a moment, he stuck his fingers on the edge and pulled.

The stone door opened with a deep groan.

Grigor pointed with the staff. "Inside."

With a shrug, Daryus turned and entered the darkened passage. The blue stones that Grigor had expected started to illuminate their path.

Far ahead, other stones were just fading into darkness again. Toy wasn't that far ahead.

Grigor followed, aware that Toy no doubt had some trick in mind. That was why the fighter went first. Grigor was happy to sacrifice Daryus if it meant catching the familiar.

From up ahead came a pained squeal. Grigor smiled at the thought of Toy either injured or dead. Still, as they neared the area where the noise had originated, the witch made Daryus slow. "The weasel is cunning," he warned. "Keep an eye out for hidden danger."

"I always do, especially with Toy."

Daryus slowly entered. Grigor stepped behind the larger man.

Something lay sprawled at the edge of the illumination. As they neared, the stones revealed Toy's body.

"Is he dead?" Grigor asked with mounting eagerness.

Leaning close, Daryus touched the weasel's throat. "No. Something struck him . . . I think." He looked past Toy. "There's another crack here, like a door, but it's hard to tell."

"Pick the damned thing up, but hold him tightly." While Grigor very much desired Toy's demise, this near to the Reaper's Eye, he wanted to make certain the weasel had not arranged any more surprises that might prevent the witch from seizing the artifact. Only with the Reaper's Eye could Grigor achieve his real goal: freeing the demon Tzadn from his tomb.

He will reward me with such power. I will be a hundred times stronger than I ever was . . .

Even when he had first sworn himself to his previous patron, Grigor had already been searching for a greater source of power. He had been forced to research the possibilities surreptitiously, but still he had at last stumbled across the lost legend of the demon god.

There had been little enough about how Uhl-Adanar had come to be built, only that those who had once worshiped Tzadn as a god had in the end sought to cast him into an eternal prison of darkness. Grigor had never been able to verify *everything*, but he had verified enough to believe the demon did exist and *was* a prisoner in the tomb.

As Daryus picked up the unconscious familiar, Grigor tested the other door.

"I wouldn't—" Daryus warned.

Toy's foul chuckle resounded in the witch's ears.

The door opened of its own accord . . . and the floor fell away just as the previous one had for the Pathfinder.

Both Grigor and Daryus slid forward, the latter losing his sword in the process. At the same time, Toy—treacherous, cunning Toy—wriggled free from Daryus's grip. The weasel leapt onto Grigor's back, then scurried down it.

Grigor righted himself as he slid. He tried to grab Toy, but first the familiar and then Daryus abruptly slid in a different direction.

Grigor landed hard in front of a huge stone door left ajar, one with a very different version of the wolf symbol. All thought of Toy and Daryus vanished as the witch plunged through it into the chamber beyond.

And finally, after so very long, Grigor stood within yards of the Reaper's Eye.

"If you'd like to live a little bit longer, I'd recommend you not take another step," Shiera murmured from elsewhere. "I'd *really* recommend it."

Grigor glanced around, only then seeing the opposing walls. Walls radiating the same blue energy usually stored inside the small stones. Walls in flux, shifting from plain stone to two great rows of paintings of mummified priests.

Mummified priests already trying to free themselves.

26

WITCH'S TRIUMPH

It was all Daryus could do to keep from landing headfirst. As he hit stone, out of the corner of his eye he saw Toy had landed ahead of him. The weasel let out a grunt, then rolled toward a dark form nearby.

Only when Daryus managed to come to a halt did he see that the dark form was a body. Raffan's body.

The former crusader tried to rise, but suddenly an ominous weariness seeming to originate from his right side overtook him. Daryus slipped a hand over to the spot and found a small dart there.

"Damn you, Toy!" How the familiar had managed to stick him with one of Raffan's needles, Daryus could not say. The needle hadn't gone deep, which gave him hope he could overcome its influence. Unfortunately, at the moment, all he could do was slowly crawl.

Toy lay as if frozen next to Raffan. It was clear from the expression and pallor that Raffan was dead, which made it all the more startling when the corpse's hands suddenly slid back and, with jerking motions, pushed itself to a kneeling position.

Mouth agape, the corpse stumbled to its feet. Once there, it reached into a pouch at its side and pulled out the artifact Raffan had used against the giant wasps. Replacing the item in the pouch, the corpse looked at Daryus.

"Not yet . . ." it croaked in what was not Raffan's voice, but a twisted version of Toy's. "Not yet . . . Daryus Gaunt."

The animated body twisted around to the familiar's body, picking it up. The corpse set Toy on its shoulder, whose paws and tail instinctively seized hold.

Again, the corpse's gaze shifted to the stricken fighter. "Always with more than one plan, the patron ordered! Always to keep the eye on the game."

"Damn you, Toy . . . just come close enough so . . . so I can wring your little neck . . ."

"Raffan" winked. As he did, the eye that winked briefly became Toy's demonic orb. "Rest now, Daryus Gaunt. I'll need your life later."

The mouth smiled, again somehow mirroring Toy. If Daryus had not already suspected the familiar somehow controlled the body—most likely through the artifact Raffan still had on him—then these brief expressions would have been enough to reveal the terrible truth.

The body moved on, stepping past the struggling fighter to the wall. Raffan's hand touched a spot and the wall opened.

Without another word, the familiar and the animated corpse vanished into the passage within.

Daryus continued to try to crawl, hoping that by exerting himself he would get his blood circulating and flush the drug from his system faster. He relied on the fact that Toy did not know much, if anything, about Daryus's mixed heritage. Elves were immune to magical sleep, and while he suspected these darts used a more mundane poison, he hoped that similarity—or his sheer body mass—would carry him through.

As he pushed himself on, he caught glimpses of the outside. At first, Daryus paid them no mind—the only part of the temple-city important to him being the part where Shiera was—but then, in the distance, he noticed a figure moving carefully around one of the buildings beyond.

Harricka Morn.

How she had gotten to Uhl-Adanar did not disturb Daryus half so much as the very fact that she *was* here. He knew Harricka well enough to assume that her primary concern would remain him, even despite Grigor Dolch's plot.

Harricka suddenly looked in his direction, as if noticing him. Daryus started to swear . . . only to see Harricka's gaze shift *above* him. She stood poised, then began climbing up a wall with the clear intention of getting to whatever she had just noticed.

While grateful she had not seen him after all, Daryus worried that Harricka had noticed some activity on Shiera's part. Yes, she would willingly face the witch if it meant helping Shiera escape, but for some reason Daryus feared his former comrade's intrusion would only cause further chaos—

Toy! While Daryus could not actually verify his suspicions, he knew in his gut that the weasel must be the reason for Harricka Morn's shocking arrival. Somehow, the familiar had utilized the same magic that had dragged Daryus and Raffan here to also bring along the captain.

But why?

Always with more than one plan, Toy had said through Raffan. The weasel knew he had to catch his former master off guard—no small task. Usurping parts of those plots already hatched by Dolch had enabled Toy to make use of Shiera and the pitborn assassins, while adding Daryus, Harricka, and Raffan had offered different paths.

Daryus pushed himself to a sitting position just as Harricka vanished from view. He accepted his minor victory as a good sign. The drug was fading from his system, surely at a faster rate than Toy would assume.

"Always with more than one plan," Daryus whispered, smiling grimly. "You're absolutely right, Toy."

Straining, he managed to get to his knees. Then, after taking a deep breath, Daryus shoved himself up on his feet. His attempt was only slightly less elegant than that of Raffan's corpse, but still he succeeded in remaining standing.

There was no weapon, of course, but Daryus still had the small blade in his boot, which he had put away when he had come across Shiera under attack. Daryus yearned for one of the sturdy old weapons wielded by the undead, yet was more than willing to do with what he had with him. He had not survived so long after escaping the order without being able to adjust to the lack of a sword or axe at the worst of times.

He dared a step. When that worked, he dared another. That second did not go as well, but at least Daryus was able to keep standing. Inhaling deeply, he forced his other foot forward again.

It worked . . . and with less stress than before. Daryus pressed, taking three more.

"Always with more than one plan," he repeated with more relish. "Let's see how your plans fare against mine, Toy."

With only one more stumble, he returned to the part of the wall where Raffan's corpse had stepped. Having watched, Daryus readily located the switch.

Keeping in mind that Harricka was also loose in the ancient structure, Daryus kept his eye out for something better than the dagger. If he ran across her first, he wanted to have the upper hand immediately. Then, he might have a chance to convince her there was something far more dangerous than him.

The blue stones kept his way lit, which at times frustrated him. Darkness would have served him better, but there seemed no way by which to douse the crystals. The only benefit was that he would be able to tell if someone else was—

Daryus froze. In the otherwise deep darkness ahead, a single blue stone lit, then faded away.

Keeping the dagger ready, Daryus pursued. He had no idea just how fast Raffan's corpse could move, but he would have assumed that it would be far beyond the spot ahead. Doubting that Shiera was the source, Daryus wondered if Harricka's path had somehow brought her to this corridor. That seemed unlikely considering where she would have entered, but the ancients had created what he considered a very strange labyrinth that made anything possible.

A short scraping sound echoed ahead. Daryus paused yet again. The scraping repeated, this time slightly closer.

Daryus had a very bad feeling. He took a step back, then eyed one of the stones.

Limbs still stiffer than he would have liked, he worked quickly to pry the stone from the wall. As he hoped, it continued to glow in his hand.

Daryus threw the stone as hard as he could into the darkness.

It started to fade as it flew from him, but, as he had hoped, enough of a glow remained through the flight that he was able to see a greater distance ahead.

And one of the undead priests.

Swearing, Daryus retreated farther. Prying off another stone, he tossed it after the first.

The priest was even closer. The empty eye sockets stared his way. One hand gripped a long sword.

With nothing else to do, Daryus started back. However, as he moved, he heard another scraping sound from the direction of the mummified figure. This time it reminded Daryus of metal rubbing against stone.

Aware that each hesitation increased the risk, he nonetheless removed one more stone. As soon as it was free, Daryus tossed it.

The stone clattered to the floor, the corridor empty.

No, not empty, Daryus saw. In the last glimmer of light, he made out the sword still there, only now propped against the wall to his left.

Suspecting a trap, Daryus broke off yet another stone, then threw it after the others. Nothing changed. The priest was gone, but the sword remained, propped against the left wall.

Cautiously—very cautiously—Daryus approached the weapon. Other stones lit up, enabling him to verify the absence of the ghoul and the curious presence of the weapon.

Seeing no visible threat, he reached for the hilt. As he took up the weapon, though, the wall upon which it had been set slid open.

Another, better-lit passage beckoned, with no sign of the priest.

Hefting the sword, Daryus noted the balance and weight. Had he not known better, he might have thought it had been chosen just for him. Not at all certain that he liked where that thought led, Daryus stepped into the new corridor, and saw immediately there only one direction to go.

With each passing second, his strength returned more and more. He put away the dagger. Having the sword helped much, but Daryus was still aware he would likely face magic in some form, especially from the witch and Toy. Daryus would have to strike as quickly and as accurately as he could.

If, he admitted, he even had a chance to strike at all.

Shiera wished she had been given at least a few more minutes before Grigor's intrusion. At least then, there might have been a chance to compensate for the trap she had half-sprung. The ancients had made a cunning, two-level trap. Despite her caution, she had set the first part in motion. Logic would have said that she should retreat, but logic often proved the death of the unwary. Shiera believed the ancients wanted any intruder to do just that. If she understood what they desired, a single step back would be all that was needed to unleash the tomb's protectors.

"Well?" rasped Grigor. "Do what needs to be done!"

Wishing she could trade places and let Grigor carve out his own destiny, Shiera put another foot forward.

"What are you—"

The walls shimmered brighter . . . and then not only did the priests return to being paintings, but the paintings themselves faded away to the empty walls Shiera had first come across.

The witch stepped up beside her. "Very clever, Pathfinder. Now how do we keep them from returning?"

"I think I have an idea, but it'll take me a moment."

"Take a moment. Take two. Just be certain they are very *short* moments."

Shiera kept her expression neutral. More than ever, she could hear Grigor's avarice. So close, it had to be difficult for him to remain still. She was tempted to tell him that the trap would not repeat, but doubted he would be so naive.

Besides, Shiera had to admit that she, too, was eager to see more.

Wishing that Daryus was here to add a more neutral perspective, Shiera studied the room. For the first time, she noted how there were slightly different shadings in the various tiles of marble making up the floor. It reminded her of what she had come across in not only her studies, but also Amadan Gwinn's expedition.

A swift analysis revealed no pattern of dark and light tiles, nor one involving shapes. Yet Shiera remained certain there was a pattern. There was always a pattern.

Then it occurred to her that she was still not thinking in terms of the ancient builders. Being careful not to step any closer, she adjusted her view so that she saw the floor at approximately the same angle as that in which the builders' script changed meaning.

And there she saw it. There *was* a slight difference in the spacing between the dark and light tiles. Shiera returned to her original location and checked again. Despite there being little difference in where she stood, the view altered significantly.

Grigor impatiently tapped the staff on the floor. "I hope you're on to something."

"We're about to find out." Shiera shifted to the second position, then noted how the tiles appeared arranged now. The builders of Uhl-Adanar had worked very precisely, but she thought she understood how she had to walk.

Without another word, Shiera took her first step. Behind her, the witch let out a slight gasp.

Nothing happened. The walls remained blank.

Feeling more confident, Shiera chose her second and more crucial step.

When again nothing happened, a sense of triumph filled her.

"You have it," remarked Grigor with a hint of admiration.

"It's all a matter of perspective." She chose her next mark. So long as she kept her view at the proper angle, the path continued to be perfectly obvious. A simple trail of identically shaded tiles leading to the dais. Shiera knew that if she had tried to follow these same tiles while staring at them head-on, she would have gone a different direction and finally stepped on the wrong one.

Step by step, Shiera neared the dais. Finally, with one last, confident movement, she reached the raised platform.

"You've done it!" Grigor started after.

She thrust a hand out. "Wait!"

He eyed her distrustfully. "Why?"

"I have to make certain the pattern didn't change after I completed it." That was partially true. What Shiera didn't say was that she was also still trying to buy time until she could think of something to prevent him from claiming the artifact and whatever else he thought the tomb could bring him.

"Rubbish! You're trying to delay." Grigor stepped onto the first tile.

Shiera stiffened. To her relief, nothing happened.

"You see?" Grigor prepared to take the next step.

"Not that one!" As her undesired companion eyed her, she pointed to his right. "That one there."

"You put your foot on the one here," he retorted, pointing with the staff at the tile nearest his foot.

"No. It only *looked* like that."

He studied the two tiles. The tip of the staff swung back and forth over the choices. Each swing back to the wrong one made Shiera flinch. Now was not the time for her to attempt any trick against Grigor. She and possibly even Daryus would suffer along with the avaricious witch.

Grigor stopped the tip over the tile to his right, the *wrong* one.

He stepped forward . . . to the tile Shiera had chosen.

Shiera exhaled. She looked up to the heavens—or in this case, the ceiling—in silent thanks for the damned spellcaster listening to her.

"Where next?" the witch asked.

"Over there," she replied, pointing again.

Brow arched, Grigor nevertheless obeyed. When all remained still, he smiled. "Very good, Pathfinder."

"One more thing."

Instantly, he brought the staff up to point at her.

She shook her head. "No. No betrayal. Just a warning. I never thought to look directly up until a second ago. Don't move from the spot when you do, though."

Shiera waited while Grigor looked up at the ceiling.

"I . . . see." He stared. "Were they there all this time, do you think?"

"I doubt that they were just painted while we were occupied with other things." She joined him in studying what lay above them. While the walls had returned to normal after briefly threatening to unleash more of the mummified priests, neither Shiera nor he had ever bothered to pay attention to the high ceiling.

A high ceiling covered in much-too-realistic images of more such guardians, these with webbed wings.

"Do you think—" Grigor began.

"I *know*. So try not to get us killed with your impatience."

"Show me the path, then. No tricks, and I will leave you unharmed."

Shiera doubted that, yet obeyed anyway. The guardians were unlikely to see any difference between her and her captor. Both were intruders.

Only when at last he joined her did Shiera breathe easier. Grigor had the gall to pat her on the shoulder.

"You did well, Pathfinder! Excellent, in fact."

"We still have to cross again. That may be more troublesome."

"Oh, I don't think that will be a problem." Grigor pushed past her. He headed up to where the Reaper's Eye stood waiting.

"Wait!" Shiera called. "You don't know what else might happen!"

"I would think the floor trap enough," he responded as he neared the artifact. "Besides, once I stir up the power within the Eye, he'll be only too grateful to let me—*us*—leave without hindrance."

"What are you talking about?"

He looked at her in some surprise. "Surely you of all people can see that this is not a tomb as we know it. Pathfinder, this temple-city, first built to honor what they believed was a god, was in the end turned into a *prison* for what they finally realized was actually a *demon* . . ."

"Tzadn the Reaper," she murmured.

"Yes, exactly. The Reaper has been sealed in here since centuries before the Worldwound. He will be very grateful to those who release him. You should remember that."

Her thoughts raced. What he said made sense in retrospect. Still . . . "If he's so powerful, how were they able to seal him in?"

"A detail of little interest to me. What is in the texts I have studied—and that you have not—is that his might is considerable. Far more considerable than that of the thing I once had to swear fealty to. He will not only restore me, but make me a thousand times more powerful!"

"And then you'll take over the world? Is that what all of this is about?"

He chuckled, a disturbing sight considering his deteriorating skin and surreal eyes. "Now what would I want with the world? I will have the power to do whatever I desire . . . and without the headaches of trying to rule over millions."

Shiera doubted it would all be as simple as he said. Even if Grigor had no dreams of conquest, at some point his continual lust for power would leave a trail of death. She suspected there already was such a trail, and that it would only widen terribly.

She knew her options at this point were few, but she could not let him achieve his goal. As Grigor turned from her, she used his fixation on the Reaper's Eye to act.

But the moment that she attempted to move against him, he flicked the staff in her direction. Her body locked, and she fell forward.

"Yes, I was expecting that about now," Grigor commented as he continued to where the Reaper's Eye floated. "I did offer you a chance to make things easier on yourself. I also promised you punishment if you tried to betray me."

She tried to speak, but could not. All she could do was watch as Grigor dismissed the staff and, with both hands, reached for the smoky stone.

Shiera tried to close her eyes, but even that reprieve was denied to her as Grigor gripped the Reaper's Eye. Shiera waited for the inevitable destruction.

And waited. The paintings on the ceiling continued to be paintings. The walls continued to be blank walls.

And Grigor . . .

Grigor held the Reaper's Eye high, and smiled.

27

THE REAPER

At long last, Grigor held the key to his glory . . . and his very life.

Beautiful . . . so very beautiful . . . He turned the Eye around, admiring its perfection, so simple and yet at the same time so obviously powerful.

"I will free you, Reaper, and all I ask in return is the power I deserve, the preservation I require, for the service I give you . . ."

Reaching out with his thoughts and power. *You can feel me. You can hear me. There is link enough. Give me the thing you see in my mind and I will be your servant forever.*

He waited. When nothing happened, he shook the artifact. When that proved just as ineffective, Grigor almost threw the thing at the floor, only at the last moment realizing what he was about to do.

With growing impatience, Grigor set the Eye back above the platform, where it again floated with no aid. Glaring at the artifact, he summoned his staff.

The "eye" in the center of the stone flickered.

Grigor hesitated, but when nothing more occurred, his anger and frustration returned tenfold stronger.

"I will not be ignored!" Yet, as he shouted, Grigor felt part of his left cheek tear apart. Pausing, he felt at the spot. Sure enough, there was a tremendous gap forming.

He could almost hear Toy's chuckle in his mind. *Running out of time, Grigor?*

Pain shot through him his bones began to crack. The exertion had proven far more stressful on his body than he had thought possible.

No longer able to control himself, Grigor spun and raised the staff with the clear intention of striking the stone.

The stone pulsed.

Lowering the staff, Grigor stared in anticipation. He was absolutely certain that the Reaper's Eye was a direct conduit to the trapped demon, which meant the creature should see that his full freedom depended on the witch's good graces. In Grigor's mind, his action with the staff had served to show Tzadn the determination the mortal had to see the demon fully free.

The stone pulsed again, and again. A humming sound now arose from the Eye. A dark aura formed around it.

Power flowed from the stone and filled Grigor.

Shiera felt the spell that Grigor had cast on her start to fade. She doubted that her captor had decided to be benevolent. Had the magic simply run out? Or had something else caused a disruption in it?

She had the horrible feeling that she knew just what that something else was. Shiera also doubted that Tzadn was rewarding Grigor for his efforts. No, something else was going on.

Grigor paid her no mind, instead spreading his arms and laughing as the stone's energies surrounded him. At the same time, Shiera noticed something subtle and unsettling happening above the stone.

Rising, the aura began taking shape. It was vaguely humanoid, with a head and a sweeping body like the ghosts of fanciful tales, only of the same smokiness as the Reaper's Eye. A vague spot opened in the "head," akin to the one that gave the stone the second part of its name.

And then, even as that happened, two lengthy appendages separated from the shadowy form, stretching to half again the body's length and sharpening into what resembled a pair of wicked scythes.

The Reaper . . . Shiera suddenly thought with growing fear.

That which might have been the god or demon spoken of in the fragments of text she had uncovered continued to grow and rise over both the stone and Grigor. Shiera couldn't believe he could not see what loomed above him, yet it was clear to her that he still only saw the stone.

The shadow moved over Grigor. The point of one scythe touched him on the shoulder.

The same smoky aura that surrounded the stone abruptly engulfed the witch. He let out a gasp.

The aura sank into Grigor, and as it did so, the shadowy form sank into the Eye again.

Grigor let out another gasp, and would have dropped to his knees if not for the staff supporting him.

Shiera felt her strength and mobility nearly fully restored. However, she remained still, certain that any movement would draw Grigor's undesired attention.

She need not have worried. He turned to her anyway.

Shiera gaped.

Gone was the dry, sallow flesh, the cracks and crevices where dead skin and sinew had broken away. Gone were the unreal eyes, the death's head grin . . . everything that hinted of Grigor's long overdue death.

Instead, the facade of youth that he had sought to maintain all this time was a facade no longer. Grigor stood before her in the bloom of life, his skin pale but pink. His hair was now lush jet-black, his eyes a brilliant gold.

"Yes! Yes!" He laughed with childlike glee. "You see?"

Shiera only nodded. Grigor hardly noticed, so caught up was he in what he had gained.

"Only the beginning!" Grigor cried. He took the staff and tapped the dais twice. Then, grinning wide, he returned his attention to the stone. "We are one!" he proclaimed to the stone.

"Grant me the rest of the power I desire and I will spread your influence beyond the Worldwound, beyond the known world . . ."

Grigor stretched out his arms in obvious expectation of something else happening. Yet after several seconds, Grigor continued to wait to no avail.

"Do you hear me? I will swear my allegiance to you, take your desires to the lands beyond! All I ask is the power to do all this! All I demand is my right as the one to find and free you!"

Shiera took a step back. Elements of the tableau unfolding before her began to take on a new meaning, one that contradicted everything she had assumed up to this point.

"It can't be," she murmured to herself.

Although she barely whispered, Grigor somehow heard her. "What? What sense does this make?"

"What does it matter, O dear master?" asked another, oddly familiar voice. "What does it matter, when you have so little time left to enjoy your regained youth?"

Shiera and Grigor turned as one. At first, she marveled at the sight of the newcomer, for of all of them, she would have doubted that Raffan could have found his way to this chamber without aid. Then she noticed his vacant stare and Toy clinging tightly to his back and neck. A chill ran through her.

"The patron is not done with you," Raffan's mouth started . . . but the familiar's finished. Toy straightened so that Grigor could see him clearly. "The patron is most certainly not finished with his most errant of servants."

The weasel opened his other eye.

The demon orb began to shine.

Grigor had known all along that at some point near his moment of victory Toy would attempt to destroy him. However, he had expected it to come sooner, not later. Now, even though for reasons he could not fathom he had yet to be granted the

Reaper's full favor, Grigor felt more than confident in his ability to rid himself of the accursed familiar.

The weasel's demon eye—the gift Grigor had himself granted the ungrateful wretch—burned with power that it should not have contained. Yet Grigor wasn't worried. Before Toy could do anything with the powers the witch's old patron had clearly granted him, Grigor began spinning the staff before him with one hand.

"Toy. My duplicitous little Toy. I've been wondering exactly when I would have the pleasure of your company." Grigor studied both the eye and Raffan. "But if this is your choice of weapons, you come poorly armed. *His* full power cannot reach this far. You may carry a glimmer of it, but not enough."

"You would be surprised what a glimmer of power can do, O Grigor . . . just see . . ."

Near the witch, Shiera shouted, "No!"

Too late, Grigor also saw what Toy intended. "Raffan" took a step onto the tiles.

The walls shimmered. Images formed on them—images of mummified priests who, weapons in hand, began stepping free.

Cursing, Grigor held the staff before him. The tip flared.

An explosion of fire struck just inches from Toy and his macabre mount. The familiar stared and stared at the flames, which died with unnatural quickness under his gaze.

Grigor attempted to crush the familiar and the corpse with the power stored in the staff, but again the demon eye worked against him. His spell easily dissipated.

He cannot have that much strength. The other's reach cannot stretch this far!

What sounded like the flapping of wings caught his attention. "Above!" Shiera called.

He knew she did not warn him out of loyalty, only survival. Still, Grigor understood that he could thus rely on the woman to guard his back, as her only true defense against the monstrous priests.

Grigor remained aware that none of this struggle would be necessary if only he could fathom why he had not been granted *all* the gifts the demon should have given him in gratitude. Without Grigor, Tzadn the Reaper would remain trapped in Uhl-Adanar. It might be a thousand years or more before anyone else cunning enough would locate the lost temple-city.

The flapping grew louder. Grigor thrust the staff point up over his head and felt it impact something that gave way.

He gave the staff a twist. Above him, a whooshing sound told that his spell had worked. Completely aflame, the winged undead that had been just about to pounce on him crashed into a wall.

"This isn't right!" Shiera insisted. "This is all wrong!"

Grigor didn't care what she meant. All that mattered was fending off the guardians, and he had a notion as to how to do just that.

Backing up to the Reaper's Eye, the witch seized the stone with his free hand. He held it high above him.

As he suspected, the guardians slowed.

"Don't do that, Dolch," Shiera muttered. "You have no idea what you'll unleash."

"Oh, I have every idea, Pathfinder! I've been remiss! So long as the Reaper's Eye exists, Tzadn cannot be wholly free. That is how they bound him to Uhl-Adanar—the Eye is the true key to his freedom . . . and my *triumph*!"

He threw the stone as hard as he could at the floor.

Time came to a halt.

The guardians froze where they were, even those flying through the air. There was no flapping of wings, no movement of cracking limbs and rattling metal. Grigor knew that he retained the ability to move, yet what happened next took place in such a short moment that he, Toy, and the woman barely had time to blink, much less act.

The Reaper's Eye ceased its plummet. Before Grigor's startled gaze, the smoky stone flew back up past him and onto its normal perch. However, once there, it did not simply come to rest. Instead, it began to shake violently . . . and as it did, the chamber followed suit.

A fearsome wind stirred from nowhere. It rose with such violence that it tore the drier and thus lighter undead from the floor and tossed them in the air. There, they collided with the already tangled winged figures, creating utter chaos above the witch and the others.

"You did the worst thing possible!" Shiera shouted.

"I nearly had him freed!" Grigor retorted.

"Yes . . . and *that* was the worst thing you could have done for him!"

Before Grigor could figure out just what the damned woman meant, he saw Toy, still astride the corpse, guiding his mount with ease across the tiled floor. With the mummified priests in chaos, nothing prevented the familiar from closing on his former master.

"*Our* master is not finished with you yet!" Toy repeated. "He—"

The weasel squealed as a small bolt struck him squarely, knocking him from his perch. The moment Toy's contact with Raffan's corpse broke, the body ceased moving.

A very startled Grigor looked over his shoulder, to where Shiera quickly worked to reload a handheld crossbow.

He gestured. The crossbow went flying.

"You are very skilled with that, but I suspect the second one would have been meant for me."

"I have a better chance of survival if you survive as well," she countered, pointing up. "Speaking of which . . ."

He did not have to ask at what she gestured. Grigor spun the staff up again, concentrating. A brief shot of blue flame engulfed the oncoming guardian. Sizzling fragments from Grigor's target went flying in several directions. Grigor used the staff to send some of those burning fragments at other mummified figures, setting a number on fire.

But as he finished, he sensed the magic stored in the staff fading to dangerously low levels. Grigor swore under his breath. While the demon had restored him to full life, none of his new power aided him against the guardians. Grigor could not yet understand why, since surely the undead represented Tzadn's jailers. If the demon hoped to be completely released from the stone and Uhl-Adanar, then surely he should have done more to help Grigor.

The answer came to him. Somehow, this must be *Toy's* doing. Furious, Grigor spun the staff in a swift circle. A strong wind stirred to life, sending the nearest guardians flailing back.

Grigor had no doubt that despite what he had seen, Toy not only lived, but still plotted. The corpse upon which the familiar had ridden continued to stand as if hung from the ceiling by some invisible thread, but Grigor knew that Toy would have other means at his command.

Where are you, you little vermin? The witch rapidly surveyed his surroundings. The guardians were already recovering from his last spell. Grigor calculated he had only a minute or two before they were again a danger to him. Yet no matter where he turned, there was no sign of the accursed creature—

Of course! Grigor turned to the stone. Staff before him, he moved behind the stand above which the Reaper's Eye floated.

Toy stared back at him from behind the display, both eyes wide open . . . but not in fear.

"Good Master Grigor," cooed the weasel. "So nice of you to join me finally."

In reply, Grigor lunged with the staff. Toy easily evaded the strike. Indeed, he used the staff to rush up toward the witch's face.

Only then did Grigor realize just what both the weasel and their former patron had in mind.

Grigor twisted the staff around, putting a halt to Toy's advance, but failing to shake the familiar free. Toy cackled as the witch tried in vain to toss him off.

"Be not so afraid, Master Grigor!" the weasel mocked. "Let us talk! Perhaps we will see eye to eye!"

"You'll not have your chance, you little vermin!" The witch looked around and found what he was looking for right beside him. He swung the staff—and Toy—as hard as he could at the stone's platform.

At the last second, the familiar released his hold and somehow landed on his feet. He scampered up the other side and popped up next to the Reaper's Eye.

Grigor nearly made the mistake of looking directly at the familiar. Fortunately, Shiera, perhaps actually believing Grigor would let her live once all this was settled, jumped forward and seized the weasel by the tail.

It was clearly one of the few things that Toy had not expected to happen. Hissing, he twisted like a snake as he sought to free himself from the woman's grasp.

She was smart enough, Grigor noted, not to hold on for very long. Shiera tossed the weasel in among the guardians, perhaps hoping they would fall upon him.

Indeed, one of them attempted to spear the familiar, but despite having been thrown, Toy yet again succeeded in shifting around to his feet and moving before the weapon could impale him.

It was enough, though, to buy Grigor the time he wanted. The witch's frustration had reached its boiling point. As far as he was concerned, the demons he served throughout his life had always owed him more than he owed them. Without him, none of them would have had nearly the influence in the mortal world that they had desired.

I will not be denied this time, Grigor determined. He concentrated hard, channeling all the power he could into the staff.

"Leave it be, Dolch!" Shiera cried, clearly aware of what he intended. "You'd be better off getting us out of here! You don't want to disturb him again! He—"

Grigor was grateful he had saved enough power to send the mouthy woman flying back. She had served every purpose he had needed her for and more, but absolutely no one would come between him and the stone.

Grigor had always preferred the use of magic over physical effort. Now, though, he had made an educated guess that the latter might prove more effective. Sometimes, the mundane triumphed over the magical.

With all his might and all his remaining power, Grigor swung at the Reaper's Eye. The mummified priests converged on him, but they were too far away.

The staff struck the Eye dead on. Grigor grinned with immense satisfaction as he heard the stone crack and watched its fragments fly everywhere. He had no idea why he had hesitated to do this earlier. It was almost as if something had purposely dulled such thoughts from his mind, but even Toy, with what link he maintained to their old patron, could not have managed such a feat.

Then none of that mattered anymore. The shards of the Reaper's Eye began to rain down on the floor and the guardians. In the midst of what had been the stone, the pupil still hovered, then started to swell. It swiftly became a huge shadow, a thing of inkiness with a pair of long, curved appendages ending in blades.

To Grigor, it was the most glorious of sights. "Tzadn! Reaper! I, Grigor, have freed you!"

The shadow tapped one point on the dais, then extended its appendages as if seeking to take hold of something.

The fragments rose from the chamber floor and began flying back to Grigor and the demon. The nearest ones instantly adhered to the shadow. As they did, they started to *compress* the demon into a smaller and smaller form once more.

"No!" Grigor could not believe what he was seeing. "No!" he shouted again, trying to deflect the pieces from the shadow. "Stop that!"

The fragments simply slipped around him. More and more of them gathered together. Already the shadow had been pressed into something half its size.

In desperation, the witch brought the staff up again. What he had destroyed once he would destroy again, this time making sure in the process that nothing remained of the shell.

He sent the pieces that had gathered together flying apart, but just as a smile started to spread across his face, one of the scythe-like appendages came down . . . and sliced off the staff's tip.

The spell Grigor had intended vanished. Confused, he peered up at the shadow. The Reaper extended both appendages again, taking in the fragments and remaining still as those pieces once more compressed Tzadn into the round shape of the Eye.

"I did warn you, Dolch!" Shiera called as she sought to fend off two of the priests. "This isn't a temple or a tomb! It's a *hiding place!*"

28

FEAR AND THE REAPER

Daryus was no witch or wizard, but he sometimes felt as if he had some sort of extra sense that stirred during danger. If so, then clearly whatever situation he neared was of catastrophic proportions, for that extra sense all but screamed at him to retreat.

But as was usual when that happened, Daryus went forward instead.

He tested the priest's sword one more time, assuring himself that it would not break from rust or age the first time he tried to use it. He still wondered why the sword had been left behind. Daryus did not believe it had happened by chance. The sword had been left for him. Why that was, he could not say. He only knew that, whatever the intent, he would do his best to use the weapon for one purpose only. He would not be the pawn of gods or demons.

A sound far ahead made him freeze. It was not the scraping he had heard earlier when the undead guardian had been nearby. Although brief, it had been a sound he associated with life, with someone like him trying to move through the corridors.

A blue stone far ahead lit up. A silhouette formed.

Daryus bit back an exclamation.

Harricka.

Barely had Daryus spotted her than she clearly noticed him. The crusader captain charged forward. Like Daryus, she wielded a hefty sword. Unlike Daryus, she looked ready to use it.

He looked behind him. There was nowhere but the corridor down which he had just come.

With no recourse, Daryus prepared to meet his former comrade in battle. He raised the sword with the point toward Harricka and braced one foot against the wall on his left in preparation to—

The wall opened up. Daryus stumbled back through the opening.

"Come back here!" Harricka shouted angrily.

Daryus was no coward, but neither did he want to face her. Despite everything, he did not consider her an enemy. She clearly felt differently.

Before he could try to shut the door, it slid closed of its own accord. Harricka pounded on the other side, using epithets that surprised Daryus.

Certain that she would soon locate the key to opening the door, he rushed off. Harricka would have been a useful ally at this juncture, but wishes and reality were two different things. Daryus could only concern himself with—

Another door slid open just ahead.

"I will not be your puppet," he muttered to whoever or whatever had opened the way. Still, Daryus paused only long enough to peer through before entering.

And found himself in the midst of a nightmare.

The mummified priests were everywhere . . . in some cases even hovering above, thanks to long leathery wings. They all sought to converge on a dais just a little ahead, a dais on which Grigor Dolch—no longer a walking corpse himself—stood surrounded by hovering fragments of what looked like smoke-colored glass or crystal. The witch held his staff—which looked oddly shorter than Daryus recalled—like a club and looked as if he was responsible for the flying fragments. Yet, clearly the destruction he had desired was not going as it should have. Even as Daryus watched, it was obvious that the pieces were attempting to recombine.

He squinted. There was something within the gathering fragments, something he could not quite focus on. He only knew that he had a tremendous desire to see to it that those pieces continued to regather, and the only way to accomplish that was to slay the witch.

Daryus stepped onto the tiled floor. As he did, he spotted Shiera. She was desperately attempting to ward off two of the undead, and it was immediately clear she would die if he did not intervene. Shiera was a competent fighter, but she had no weapon, relying solely on her agility to evade the weapons coming at her. While the mummified priests appeared slow and methodical when moving, once in combat, their reflexes clearly increased dramatically.

He knew that he should rush to her aid, but the urge to gut Grigor Dolch grew stronger with each passing moment.

No . . . this isn't right. As much as the witch was a danger to be dealt with, the unreasoning desire Daryus felt was not like him. Something was guiding his thoughts.

Something like Toy.

As if to confirm his suspicions, the familiar paused just long enough in dodging the weapon of an undead priest to wink at Daryus. Both eyes remained open now, the demonic one taking on a dangerous glow.

Daryus struggled against the urge. Shiera was his only concern. Toy, Grigor, and the entire temple-city could go to whatever hell they belonged to as far as he was concerned. Yet, his feet still moved him toward Grigor.

No! I will not bend to you! Baring his teeth, Daryus forced himself toward Shiera.

The urge faded.

Daryus lunged.

One of the two mummified figures started to turn as he neared. Daryus beheaded the creature before it could adjust to him.

The body immediately tumbled to the floor. Daryus dodged under the second priest's axe, then came under the mummy's guard to drive his blade up through the jaw and into the skull.

With all the force he could muster, Daryus ripped the skull free. As the body attempted a wild swing with the ax, Daryus smashed the skull against the wall.

The rest of the remains collapsed in a heap. Even as it did, he reached for Shiera. "Hurry! We can—"

"No! Above!"

He reacted as quickly as he could, but it was still a little too late. Daryus managed to dodge a fatal strike, but was bowled over by the winged form colliding with him.

The collision left him unable to use the sword properly against the undead. Hollow eye sockets stared down into his. The mouth hung open, and although there was no sensation of breath on him, the flow of decaying odors nearly overwhelmed him.

Then someone tugged the winged creature from him. The tip of a hefty sword shoved out of the front of the priest's forehead, and the next moment, the skull was ripped free.

Harricka brought the skull down hard on the floor, shattering it into tiny pieces. She tossed the stilling body directly at the foremost attackers, sending them sprawling, then glared at Daryus.

"Daryus Gaunt! You will be taken back to pay for your betrayal—"

Daryus scowled at her in frustration. "Gods, Harricka! This is not the—"

"—but that can wait while we deal with this demon-infested temple and protect this civilian!"

Shiera looked a bit annoyed at being labeled such, but was apparently prudent enough not to object. Instead, she slipped between the two crusaders and announced, "Listen to me! Things here are not as they appear! We don't want to interfere with what the ancients arranged here! If we can just keep Grigor from doing more damage, all will be well!"

Even Daryus looked at her with disbelief. Rising next to Shiera, he growled, "The witch's death I can understand, but you'd leave what's happening here be?"

"She's possessed," Harricka interjected. "We must bind her but keep her safe while we deal with the threats! I know you, Daryus Gaunt, and for all your sins, you would not let this witch and his demon master loose on the lands!"

Daryus wanted to argue about his supposed sins, but was grateful that Harricka saw the sense of dealing with Dolch and the demon. He was about to object to the idea that Shiera needed to be bound when suddenly the Pathfinder reacted as if Harricka's proposition had merit after all.

With an aggravated gasp and no warning, she shoved past the pair and in among the converging undead. Daryus made a grab for her, but Shiera proved quite lithe. She not only evaded him, but the nearest two mummified priests as well.

Yet as she ran, Shiera looked back directly at Daryus and called, "Look at the stone! It's sealing itself back up! Look at it!"

"She's gone mad!" Harricka roared. "Catch her!"

But as Shiera rushed deeper into danger, Daryus gazed at where she said he should and beheld something that made him seize his former comrade by the arm—a dangerous proposition at any time—then pull her back.

"Damn you, Daryus! I gave you one chance! What—"

"Let her go!" he shouted back in her face. "Let her go, but be ready to do whatever you can to help her!"

"Help her? You're as mad or possessed as she is!"

Taking a further risk, Daryus spun Harricka to face the tableau again. "Look at what's happening beyond the witch! Look at the stone!"

Harricka did . . . and her sudden silence was all Daryus needed to know she saw the truth.

I am mad, just as she says! Shiera threw herself into the fray. Insane or not, she knew she had the only chance to bring a safe conclusion to this madness. Grigor had no idea just how dangerous his continued efforts were. She calculated that if things went as she believed, the witch would release upon the Worldwound—and then very likely the realms beyond—a danger far greater than he could ever understand.

Not Tzadn, of course. Not the Reaper. As powerful and likely deadly the demon was, all it wanted to do was hide. It had somehow manipulated the people of Uhl-Adanar to serve it long enough to help build this sanctuary. It had even likely taught them the spellwork that they had eventually used to create what was not actually a prison, but a protective shield in which the demon had hidden all this time.

No, Tzadn was not the danger. The question was: what was so terrible that a great demon needed to hide from it?

Not for a moment did Shiera think she could possibly convince the witch of the horrific mistake he was making. For Grigor Dolch, there was only Grigor Dolch.

She slipped under another grasping priest, but then two more blocked her path. While she was able to evade the spear that sought her chest, it meant that she rolled into the second creature.

Dry but powerful hands grabbed her by the shoulders. The priest dragged her to her feet. The gaping mouth and staring eye sockets came within inches of her face.

A sword shot past her ear and expertly impaled the nearly fleshless head. The next second, the sword pulled back, dragging with it the skull.

"Go!" Daryus roared. "Do what you can! We'll fend them off!"

As he spoke, the crusader named Harricka disarmed the spear-wielding priest with one blow, then pierced it through the chest with the next. Tugging hard, Harricka pulled the mummi-fied guard to her. With her free hand, she crushed its throat so thoroughly that it took only a simple brush of her fingers to send the head falling.

"Go, Pathfinder!" Daryus's former comrade ordered. "May you be correct in this, or we will all suffer!"

With gratitude, Shiera continued on. The two warriors fended off the guardians nearby, giving her a cleaner path.

Atop the dais, Grigor thrust with the staff at the reassembling stone. Thus far, he had only managed a stalemate; while each strike sent pieces flying, they constantly turned back and tried to join together again.

He has no idea what he does! Or he doesn't care!

Indeed, it seemed the witch was also ignorant of the half-formed shadow above the stone. Now and then, Shiera caught glimpses of the scythe appendages reforming, yet each time they lasted only moments. It was not, she finally understood, because the shadowy creature could not maintain their definition, but because it *feared* to do so for very long.

This is a hiding place, she had shouted in vain to the witch. Everything she had feared appeared to be true. This was not a just a temple, not just a sanctuary. There was a very good reason why Uhl-Adanar had remained unknown so long. It had not merely been the efforts by the builders to hide the location, but the work of their supposed deity as well.

Most mortal creatures—humans, dwarves, elves—did not make much distinction between demons. Yes, there were a few demon lords so notorious, so feared, that even the crusaders knew their names. Yet, Shiera had learned enough about Tzadn to understand that the Reaper was no weak creature among his accursed kind. Despite that, the Pathfinder could now all but taste the shadow demon's tremendous *fear*. Indeed, if Shiera was correct, Tzadn even restrained from attacking the witch out of concern that every use of power would risk attracting the demon's true enemy to Uhl-Adanar.

The truth had been gradually dawning on Shiera for some time now, he realized. The absolute expunging of any mention, the ease with which the temple-city itself had been hidden physically from the world . . . Everything had been designed with Tzadn's *safety* in mind.

And what Grigor did not realize by continuing to insist that Tzadn accept his dubious "aid" was that he threatened to expose the demon. Indeed, Shiera suspected that the demon would have dealt much harsher with *all* of them save that using its power would increase the odds its foe would sense it. That was why it relied on the animated corpses of its followers to protect its "tomb," even though those servants were proving inadequate. Shiera feared that soon, instead of trying to simply make the mortals go away, it would at last do something more permanent . . . even if that meant further risking revealing itself.

Something struck her from behind. At first, Shiera feared that one of the guardians had caught her, but then she heard that familiar voice cooing in her ears. "Be not afraid, Mistress Shiera! Toy is only here to help you achieve what you hope!"

She tried to reach back and grab him, but the familiar avoided her fingers. Shiera knew she had no time to rid herself of Toy. She could only hope he was telling the truth.

Grigor stood just above her, attention still on the stone. Shiera continued to be amazed that he, with all his links to magic, evidently did not see the continually shifting shadow that was Tzadn attempting to gather its shielding stone together again. Shiera, unaware of any drop of magical ability in her family, could even sense the Reaper's growing anxiety and fury. Whatever hunted it, Shiera did not want to be nearby when it came.

As Grigor pulled back the shortened staff for another strike, Shiera seized hold of the back end. The witch pulled hard, but Shiera braced herself as best she could.

As he looked to see what prevented him from his task, *Toy* leapt over her shoulder, ran down her arm, and alighted on the staff. The act brought him to eye level with his former master.

"Our former patron would see you one last time," the weasel mocked.

To Shiera's surprise, the witch released his hold on the staff as he desperately sought to shield his gaze from Toy. Not expecting such a result, Shiera fell back.

Someone caught her before she could tumble off the dais. Daryus smiled grimly as he quickly set her down and shoved one of the guardians away. He then seized his sword, which Shiera saw he had dropped in order to save her.

Daryus deflected the sword of a new guardian. All the while, he kept glancing up, where three of the winged priests hovered as they awaited some opening. "You have that damned staff! Can you use it?"

Shiera had momentarily forgotten about the staff . . . and Toy, who no longer perched on it. He was on the dais, again seeking higher ground so that he could apparently stare the witch directly in the eye. What would happen then, Shiera could only guess, but she kept the information in mind even as she came to a decision. "Daryus! Can you remove Dolch from the dais?"

"How quickly?"

"Yesterday, if possible!"

He grunted.

Before she could say more, he leapt a couple of steps ahead, then abruptly spun in a circle. He cut a swathe with his sword not only around him, but above, then stormed the steps and tossed himself at Grigor, whose attention was still on Toy.

Daryus collided hard with the witch. Shiera only expected them to fall to the far side of the dais, but to her surprise they flew well beyond to another set of steps. It seemed to her that Grigor barely weighed anything, as dry and hollow as the priests.

Whatever the reason, it more than provided her with the gap she needed. Thrusting the staff under her arm, she leapt up the steps to where more and more of the Reaper's Eye reformed. The last of the stone sealed itself together just as she reached the artifact.

Deep within, the spot that gave the stone its name watched her.

"I don't know if you can hear or understand me," she murmured as she touched the stone, "but I've no desire for anything from you but my life and that of my companions. I'm more than happy to help you protect yourself, even go around and erase any traces left behind. Just—"

"Pathfinder!" Harricka called. "Beware!"

She had no idea what the captain was warning her about, with the guardian staying oddly distant and Grigor and Daryus momentarily out of view. Then, an incredible cold spread through her from her arm and her side, so quickly that she had no time to do anything.

The next instant, Grigor's staff shot from her, flying over to where she had last seen Daryus and the witch. Shiera tried to stop it, but her side and arm were frozen in position, which left her only one hand with which to grab.

The chill continued to spread, covering her leg on that side as well. Unable to stop herself, Shiera fell onto the Reaper's Eye.

The coldness faded as she draped over the artifact, yet Shiera experienced no relief. Through the Reaper's Eye, she suddenly found her vision altering, seeming to expand somehow, colors muting and everything growing wavery like a heat mirage. Above her, the shadow with the scythe appendages tried to cut away the very air around it, as if something in that air was a threat.

Without warning, a harsh beating of heavy wings resounded all around the shadow. Tzadn shriveled in fear as a shadow darker than himself draped over him. The shadows constricted around the demon, twisting him like a wet rag being wrung out. Shiera felt each twist as if she were the Reaper herself. The agony Tzadn suffered as he was reduced to a mangle of smoke and shadow shocked her, but not nearly as much as what she realized he was indicating.

The thing that even Tzadn the Reaper feared . . . had just sensed his presence in the mortal world.

29

DEMONS

Daryus noted with interest that Grigor was a much lighter man than he would have expected. Indeed, his lack of knowledge in that respect had caused both men to fly much farther than Daryus had intended, sending them tumbling down another set of steps on the far side of the dais.

Somehow they turned in mid-flight, which meant Daryus ended up being the one who first hit the steps. The collision jarred the two men apart, with Grigor landing slightly to the left and on top of Daryus's arm and leg. Thus it was that the witch was first to recover, a fact that a half-stunned Daryus knew would be to his detriment.

Sure enough, Grigor suddenly leaned over him, bringing forth from the air a curved dagger. Up close, Daryus saw that Grigor, who had looked younger and healthier before, now once again had peeling flesh.

The fact that Grigor was beginning to decay did little to comfort Daryus as he struggled to get a hand up to halt the dagger. Dolch might be lighter, but he still retained a wiry strength, especially when combined with the advantage of position. Daryus only managed to stop the dagger when the point was just an inch from his throat. He and Grigor fought for several precious seconds before once more Toy intruded on the situation.

The weasel came up out of nowhere and bit the hand wielding the dagger. Grigor shouted in pain and let the dagger drop onto

Daryus's throat. Fortunately, the loose dagger only skinned the fighter on the side of the neck.

If Daryus had any thought that Toy cared about his life, that notion was crushed as Toy also bit at *his* hand as he tried to grab the dagger. As Daryus pulled back the bitten appendage, the familiar spun to face the witch.

But in that short time, Daryus saw that somehow Grigor had regained his lost staff. Despite its ruined state, the short staff evidently still held some magic. Grigor quickly raised the staff, and with it swept the weasel from between them.

No sooner had the witch done so than he struck Daryus hard with the back of his hand. It was not the strongest of blows, but enough to keep Daryus distracted while the witch rose and fled from him back to the dais.

Rolling over, Daryus grabbed at Grigor's robes. Grigor stumbled forward, the staff keeping him from falling face-first.

As Grigor sought to regain his balance, he also reached into a pouch at his belt. He pulled out a small, roundish object, then looked around as if seeking something else nearby.

No, Daryus quickly understood. Not something, but someone. Where once he had flinched at the oncoming presence of Toy, now Grigor appeared more than eager to locate his former servant.

But as the witch turned one way to look for Toy, from the other came a figure Daryus had all but forgotten about. The corpse of Raffan strode up on Grigor's blind side and grabbed at the hand holding the roundish object.

"Thank you so much, Master Grigor!" Raffan said in Toy's voice. "It proved impossible to seize it in the corridor, but now we can be rid of that little hindrance!"

Raffan's hand squeezed Grigor Dolch's in what looked like a literal death grip to Daryus. Something slimy oozed out between their fingers.

Raffan laughed. The witch thrust the staff into the corpse's chest and twisted it.

The body shook violently, then collapsed in an ungainly pile.

"Oh, too late to do any good, Master Grigor!" Toy called from somewhere. "The link with good Raffan is no more . . . just as is Toy's old eye! There will be no threat to Toy from that."

Now Daryus understood why the weasel had played dead in the corridor. Toy had been attempting to seize his original eye, but had failed. Now, though, he had made up for that failure.

"I will flay you alive, you little rat!" Grigor shouted. Then, as if warned by something, his gaze suddenly fell upon Shiera.

Shiera, who Daryus now saw was frozen like a statue right before the Reaper's Eye. Harricka, who stood guard over her, shook her shoulder, to no effect.

More unsettling still, Daryus realized that every one of the mummified guardians had grown as still as Shiera. Once, Daryus might have thought that a good thing, but in this damnable place, he knew better.

"No," rasped Grigor. "She will not steal what is rightfully mine! She will not!"

With astonishing agility, he leapt up near Shiera. To Daryus's dismay, the priests abruptly regained their animation, converging on the dais.

The witch is the cause of this! The witch has stirred them up again! Why that was the case, Daryus did not care. He only knew that Grigor would be the end of all of them.

He lunged . . . only to have again that familiar sensation of something tangling his legs. As he dropped, he heard Toy laugh in his ear as the familiar ran past. The weasel headed toward the dais behind the unsuspecting witch. Daryus had a chance to reach for Toy, but paused at the last minute. Right now, he would take even the familiar's dubious aid.

Yet, as if sensing Toy's approach, Grigor swept the staff behind him. Toy stumbled back, falling off one of the steps and rolling back toward Daryus.

Daryus had had enough. As the familiar landed near him, Daryus returned Toy's earlier favor by seizing him by the tail and, with expert aim, throwing the swearing weasel at Grigor's back.

"Let's see you laugh at *that*," Daryus muttered.

Toy collided with his former master. Somehow, the familiar caught hold of Grigor's back and started climbing up over his shoulder.

Grigor could not help but turn his head toward where the weasel climbed. The two locked gazes.

Toy's demon eye glowed.

Grigor howled. His body began to shrivel.

Toy laughed. "The patron has offered me your power, your life, even your body! What I want most, though, is your pain, Master Grigor! I want your pain!"

"No—no!" Grigor's other hand rose. A dagger identical to the one he had dropped while atop Daryus formed.

For once, Toy was too slow. The dagger sank into the eager familiar's body just at the base of the neck.

Toy squealed. Rarely in his life had Daryus seen such a look of immense satisfaction as what crossed Grigor's face at that moment.

"At last! At last, I'm rid of you!" the decaying spellcaster roared madly. "Rid of you!"

With utter contempt, Grigor flung both dagger and body aside. He turned back to the stone and Shiera . . . Shiera who had not moved in the least during the entire struggle. Shiera who still stood unmoving even as Grigor plucked up the Reaper's Eye.

That finally brought Shiera back. With a look of horror, she fought to get the stone back.

"Grigor, you fool! You're about to not only destroy all of us, but countless others, too! Listen to me! The Reaper seeks to remain hidden! Tzadn is hiding from a demon far more powerful than him! That's what all this around us is about! That's why it was so hard to find! For all our sakes, we have to bury him and this place from the knowledge of all, and do it quickly!"

"He wants to hide? So much power, and he wants to *hide*?" Grigor laughed harshly as he shook the stone. "Very well! I will help him hide from *everything* so long as he first grants me what *I* want! If not, I am sure he who seeks the Reaper will be more than generous for such important knowledge!"

Shiera shook his arm, but could not free the stone from him. "The only thing the other demon will be generous with is death! Don't you understand—"

He shoved her back. As the guardians closed, Grigor held the stone toward them, shouting, "I think we know this part already! Take one step nearer and I *will* find a way to permanently destroy the precious stone! What will happen then, do you think?"

The guardians did not slow, but now they had only Dolch as their focus. Even those near Harricka ignored the captain in favor of seeking the witch.

Grigor growled at the open air. "Tzadn! Hear me! I will see all of this revealed to the world if I am not granted what I ask! There will be nowhere to hide! I will have my due, one way or another! I will have my power, patron or not!"

He waved the Reaper's Eye to emphasize his threat—

—and suddenly it crumbled in his hands.

At the same time, Daryus heard a voice he had not expected to hear anymore. Toy's voice.

"Daryus Gaunt . . . I have one last task for you . . ."

Shiera could not believe Grigor's obsession. He still thought he could gain the power he desired, if only by actually *blackmailing* a demon. If Shiera could credit Grigor with anything, it was an incredible confidence in himself.

Of course, that very confidence was about to get them all obliterated.

It did not surprise her at all when the Reaper's Eye crumbled. She understood exactly why, even if Grigor was too caught up in his threats to grasp just what he had set into motion. In fact, at the moment, Grigor smiled broadly—not a pretty sight considering his horrific state. He let the last of the stone spill to the dais.

"Finally . . ." the witch whispered. "Finally, no more fear of the wasting! No more rationing a dwindling amount of power! No more!"

And then the shadow with which Shiera was already too familiar coalesced above them. At the same time, the guardians ceased their advance and instead slowly began retreating, all the while watching what took place atop the dais.

Peering past her, Grigor Dolch noticed the retreat. His expression indicated that he took this as a sign of his victory.

The ominous shadow took on its vague form. The single eye, the long, sharp appendages . . .

Tzadn the Reaper hovered over them in all his demonic glory.

Only at that moment did Grigor notice that he and Shiera were not alone on the dais. As he looked up, she quickly stepped back.

The witch grinned at the demon. "Is it a deal, then?"

The Reaper raised one of its scythes.

The grin faded.

Shiera could not help shutting her eyes as the umbral blade descended. She heard a gasp from Grigor, but nothing more. Curiosity overwhelming her good sense, she dared open her eyes.

Grigor still stood next to her, eyes wide with fear, but still as alive as before.

"I don't—" he began.

The other scythe slashed through him, leaving no trace, not even a hint of blood.

Yet this time, Shiera beheld a change in Grigor. He shivered and his body seemed to shrink. His robes hung looser, as if underneath there were now only bones, not flesh or sinew. She could now see the shape of Grigor's skull underneath his hair and beard. Worse, his eyes had become deep, soulless pits.

Despite that, he somehow clung to a semblance of life. Weaving back and forth, Grigor managed to prop himself up with the staff.

"No, he cannot be yours," called the voice of Toy to the air. "His soul was long ago claimed by another."

"No . . ." the witch managed. He struggled to turn, to where both he and Shiera beheld Daryus holding up the limp body of Toy. Despite there clearly being no life left in the familiar, the weasel's voice rose again from the unmoving mouth.

"The soul of Grigor Dolch will and shall always belong to our shared patron . . . and he would claim it now . . ."

The familiar's demon eye flared once more.

Grigor struggled to raise the staff in order to defend himself. Yet, just as he brought it to eye level, the staff split apart like so much dry kindling.

"No, Master Grigor . . . it is time we both pay for your pact."

Grigor visibly struggled, jerking his head downward. As Shiera watched, it was slowly forced up again so that he met the demon eye.

He screamed the scream of the damned . . . and a turbulent, crimson force Shiera realized had to be the witch's soul poured from his mouth. In a single blink, it flowed to Toy's demon eye and sank within it.

And as the last of it vanished with a mournful howl, the mortal shell of Grigor Dolch fell to pieces. His body collapsed within itself. His legs tumbled over. Jaw slack, the head sank into the monstrous mound of bone and cloth.

The moment it was done, Daryus dropped the weasel's carcass as if it carried the plague, which to Shiera seemed not far from the truth. She exhaled in relief . . . and then realized that the Reaper still hovered over them.

"Shiera . . ." Daryus warned.

With the utmost caution, the utmost respect, Shiera attempted to back away.

The demon slashed at her.

But by then, she and Daryus were hitting the floor beyond the bottom of the dais. Daryus used the momentum of his flying tackle and twisted, making the pair roll even farther from the Reaper.

Daryus was also the reason they finally stopped. He shifted again, this time becoming as a wall. Shiera grunted as they slammed together.

"Find the exit! Harricka will guard you! It's her sworn duty to protect the innocent!"

Shiera wasn't certain how innocent she was, but what worried her more was the insinuation that Daryus was not coming with them. However, before she could say anything, he had separated from her and risen to face the Reaper.

Tzadn hovered over the remains of the stone, its shadow darkening ominously. Then, silently, it moved toward them.

"Get going, both of you!" Daryus called. "Take her out of here, Harricka! You know your oath!"

"Speak to me not of oaths, Daryus Gaunt! Get back here with us! You have crimes to pay for!"

"Are you both insane?" Shiera demanded. "He's planning to sacrifice himself for our sakes and all you can think about is that!"

"He—" Harricka gritted her teeth. "Is there a way out, Pathfinder?"

"Yes . . . and it's the two of you who are going to take it."

To the surprise of both—and to herself—Shiera started back toward the very demon from which she had just been rescued. A part of her—a very *big* part of her—screamed that this was not a wise thing to do. One ran *from* demons, and let those willing to stand against them do as they wished.

But at that moment, Shiera knew she had a far better chance against Tzadn than either warrior. It was not a realization that pleased her, and if there had been another choice, she would have taken it. But there wasn't.

Daryus noticed her too late. He grabbed for her, but she slipped past.

"Get back!" Daryus commanded. "You can do nothing!"

"No . . . it's you who can do nothing!"

Taking a deep breath, Shiera jumped back up onto the dais. For her reward, a shadowy scythe nearly cut through her. Shiera had no idea how it would affect her, only a certainty that it would be no less gruesome than what had happened to Grigor.

"Listen to me, Tzadn, O Reaper!" she shouted at the shadow. "I started to make an offer before! To help expunge all traces of you still left out there, to make certain the other will not find you! It can smell you even now! There is no time to waste! Let me and my friends help!"

The Reaper replied by slashing at her. Shiera knew there was no way she could leap aside this time.

But there was Daryus again, moving with that amazing swiftness his form belied. He stood in front of her and received the Reaper's slash instead.

Daryus grunted in obvious pain. He shivered, but did not fall.

"Go," he managed to mutter. "I'll try to distract him a little longer."

"Daryus! Run!"

"No. I stand . . . with you."

It was a gesture she could appreciate, but now they both faced certain doom. She couldn't understand why Tzadn didn't see the sense of her words. Instead, in trying to destroy them, the demon's actions would only make its presence even better known to that which hunted it. It was almost as if something else was agitating the Reaper—

She peered over to where Toy's corpse lay. Not at all to her surprise, the demon eye not only remained open . . . but active.

Without a word, she ran past a startled Daryus to the body. As she reached it, the mouth opened and hissed.

"The patron is not finished!" came Toy's voice. "The patron would have—"

"The patron can go to whatever hell it came from!" Shiera snapped, brought the heel of her boot down as hard as she could on the staring eye.

The orb splattered nicely. Toy's voice cut off.

Shiera looked at Tzadn.

The Reaper paused. Silence filled the chamber.

Aware of just how fragile the moment was, she took a deep breath and shouted, "Tzadn! Listen to me! We are your only hope!"

The shadow veered toward her, then paused again. Taking that as a good sign, Shiera continued, "The link to the other demon is gone! There's nothing else threatening your location, save your own fear! Return to your sanctuary! We'll obscure all knowledge of this place, make certain that no one will ever know of you! I meant what I said before! You know you can trust me! You've seen inside my mind, and I've seen in yours . . ."

As she spoke, Shiera did her best to instill in each word the utter honesty of her belief. It was not the way of demons, but perhaps it would make the difference.

"I understand the danger to you. I know all you want is your safety, and I can appreciate that! You gave the priests and their people much in return for protecting you, but some legends still spread! I am from a calling that does nothing else but ferret out secrets. I am what you need to guarantee that no one like me follows, that no other witch will ever seek you out to demand power! To the end of my days, I will see that there is no Tzadn, there is no Uhl-Adanar!"

The shadow hovered. As the seconds turned into a minute and the minute into two, Shiera began wondering if at least she could do something to get Daryus and the crusader to safety.

Then the remaining priests who had lingered at a distance continued their retreat into the walls and ceiling. Moving backward, they began climbing into their appointed spots, their bodies resuming their flat, painted forms.

Heart pounding, Shiera allowed herself a brief smile. The demon had accepted her words, her terms. She had meant everything, and that *had* made the difference. She was more than willing to keep any clues she uncovered concerning this place and its contents from ever being discovered again.

The last of the guardians reverted to paintings. The shadow shifted slightly, and one scythe slashed across the floor.

The ruined bodies of the other mummies faded into mist. The mist spread throughout the chamber, touching every area where the destruction of a guardian had left a space among the painted figures. As the trio watched, the missing images reappeared—which to Shiera said that, for all the three's efforts, Tzadn could have restored all his servants whenever desired. It was not a comforting thought.

With slow, deliberate steps, she returned to Daryus. As she neared, he whispered, "This is all good, isn't it?"

"I think so, but—"

The shadow swelled. It filled the view before them, rising so high that it finally touched the ceiling.

And then the Reaper lashed out at the roof of the chamber, sending tons of stone falling.

Daryus grabbed Shiera's wrist and started running.

At his side, she shouted, "I don't understand! It knew I was right! It knew I had the best plan for it!"

"It's a demon!" he shouted back. "It may follow an entirely different logic—like, if everyone's crushed under tons of stone, then no one can ever betray it! Seems quite reasonable to me!"

He peered over his shoulder just in time to see the demon spreading toward them, the two scythes slicing at the rest of the chamber as the demon grew. The Reaper was growing at an alarming rate, and Daryus doubted they could escape in time.

"Over here!" Shiera suddenly ordered. She tugged so hard that she actually managed to pull him in the direction she wanted. At the same time, she gestured for Harricka to hurry and join them.

Daryus still had his doubts they would escape the chamber, but as Shiera reached the wall, she ran her hand over the spot before her. Daryus saw nothing, but the wall opened.

"I thought it looked like . . . I don't know how I—" she blurted.

"Never mind! Go through!" Daryus all but shoved her ahead into the opening. Then, as Harricka approached, Daryus unceremoniously grabbed her arm and pushed her on, too.

Daryus turned to take one last glance at the demon, which now all but filled the room. Tzadn seemed unperturbed about the tons of stone coming down from the areas above. The eye continued to stare in the direction the trio had gone, and for a moment Daryus swore he heard a cold voice in his head. He couldn't understand what it said, only felt a compulsion to run as fast as he could.

He jumped after the others. To his surprise, he slid down. For a moment, there was only darkness . . .

"Here he is!" Harricka shouted, grabbing him.

"I see two horses!" Shiera responded in clear disbelief.

"One is mine," the captain answered. "I think the other belonged to that cur who tried to kill you. I'll get them. Take him!"

Shiera came to his side. Daryus regained his balance, then looked around. They were outside the tomb, out in the cavern city proper.

"I was hoping this was one of the ancients' emergency passages," Shiera explained. "I was lucky."

A rumble that reminded him of thunder made Daryus look up at the ancient building from which they had just escaped.

"We're not out of it yet, are we?"

"Regrettably, no." As she answered, the entire temple-city shook violently. Large portions of the rock ceiling broke off, some of them crushing in the roofs of the nearby buildings.

Harricka returned with the horses. "Do you know of an exit?"

Shiera grabbed one set of reins. "We have to make for the temple on the other end! It's the only way!"

At that moment, more of the ceiling collapsed, some of it directly over them.

"Move!" Daryus shouted.

Shiera leapt onto the one horse, Harricka on the other. Daryus rushed to joined Shiera, only to hear a grunt from the captain. As he looked, she slumped over in her saddle, the piece of rubble that had struck her head clattering away into the darkness.

"You go on! We'll follow!" Daryus ordered Shiera.

Nodding, she rode off even as more rubble fell. Daryus checked on Harricka, saw that she breathed well enough, then jumped up behind her and urged the horse on.

He raced after Shiera, at times losing sight of her but always aiming for where he remembered the temple had stood. Twice, they had to divert from the obvious route as collapses cut off those paths. It seemed to Daryus that the ride took forever, but then finally the entrance came into view.

Shiera did not pause. She rode right into the temple. The crusaders followed behind. Daryus believed he knew what Shiera intended and hoped it would work.

The horses' hooves echoed loudly as they entered. Shiera rode up to the dais, then jumped off her mount and peered down at the base. Daryus could not see what she was doing, but suddenly a small dust devil rose before her. Several small glowing spots appeared by her hands.

"Be ready! I'm going to try to send you to the border near Kenabres!"

"You can do that?"

"I think so."

It was not as confident a statement as he would have liked, but it was all they had. However, one thing disturbed him. "How will you follow?"

"There's a way to make it operate on its own for a brief time. Get ready to ride through!"

He held the reins tight. As he watched, the cloud swelled in size. An image formed—a landscape he thought he recognized.

"Ride now!" Shiera ordered.

Urging the horse on, Daryus rode up the dais, clutching Harricka tightly. The image swirled before him.

Daryus rode through, praying that he would not simply crash into the wall beyond.

A sense of displacement he had felt once before overtook him. Daryus sought to keep focused, but then the horse stumbled and it was all he could do just to keep both the captain and himself from falling off.

Finally, after several long moments of struggle, he brought the horse under control. Turning the animal about, Daryus looked for Shiera.

There was no sign. No cloud. No image. Nothing.

Shiera was still trapped in Uhl-Adanar.

30

ESCAPE

Shiera had known all along that she would not be able to manipulate the arcane device so that she, too, could escape the temple-city. What mattered was that she had saved both Daryus and Harricka.

Uhl-Adanar continued to shake violently, but for the moment, the temple remained intact. Shiera considered her options and found none.

An unsettling clattering sound, like the cracking of ice or the breaking of glass, echoed from beyond the temple. Despite herself, Shiera stepped from the dais and started for the entrance—

A smoke-colored, glassy substance burst through the doorway, crushing the entrance and everything else before it.

It took her only a moment to recognize it as the same substance as the Reaper's Eye.

In its midst appeared single burning orb.

Shiera backed up to the dais, where she fought to calm the remaining horse while awaiting certain death.

The oncoming stone paused. The point of light stared directly at her, and she finally dared to step forward. It struck her that the Reaper now appeared somewhat calmer.

Of course! That's what all this crystal is—he's shielded himself again. The Eye was now gigantic, feet thick. To him, the loss of Uhl-Adanar must be a small thing compared to his magical protections.

Something clinked by her feet. She looked down and saw a circular medallion akin to the one Raffan had carried. The side facing up bore the smoke-gray image of the wolf.

She picked it up. As she did, Shiera felt a compulsion to look at the other side.

The rune emblazoned there was a simple arrangement of curved lines, yet somehow managed to seem sinister. Several clearly suggested a wing, and a hook to the right seemed almost like a raptor's beak . . .

The sense of dread she felt upon gazing at the image made her understand immediately what this other side represented. "This is . . . the other, isn't it?" As usual, Shiera received no answer, but somehow knew that she was correct. "I'm supposed to take this and do as I said I would, but also watch out for signs of this one?"

Without warning, the medallion shimmered. Shiera gasped as images flooded her mind. After an endless moment, she managed to choke out, "I don't understand. Could—?"

But Shiera got no farther, as from the great stone, one scythe extended . . .

Daryus circled the area in vain. He could find no way to return to Uhl-Adanar. Shiera was trapped with the demon—

The air just ahead shimmered.

Shiera rode through at a breakneck pace. As she neared, Daryus noticed that she almost looked as if she were not even conscious. She would have ridden past him if not for his quick reflexes. He pulled up beside her and seized the reins, managing to bring her horse to a halt only a few yards after.

For a moment, she simply stared ahead. Then, as if awakening, Shiera blinked and looked at him.

"Let's get as far away from here as we can, as quickly as we can," she suggested breathlessly.

He did not argue. Checking Harricka again, he rode along with her at as safe but as fast a pace as they could manage. They would not make it out of the Worldwound that day, but at least they could put some distance between themselves and the spot upon which they had been deposited.

Hours later, as they made camp, Shiera took over where the captain was concerned. She studied Harricka's wound. "A strong blow. She may not wake up for some time. I think we need to bring her to a healer."

"We'll need another day at least to reach the edge of the Worldwound from here." Still, Daryus knew he would see to it that his former comrade was brought to someone she could trust.

Shiera nodded. "If we could only—"

Too late, Daryus sensed the slight movement.

Harricka suddenly stood straight. Although he had removed her sword earlier, she now had in her hand a dagger he had seen on Shiera. Daryus knew the captain well enough not to try drawing his own sword. The dagger would be in his throat before he moved a muscle.

"Your sword, Daryus Gaunt. Drop it gently to the dirt, then kick it away."

"You are *mad*," Shiera started. "He saved—"

Dropping his weapon as ordered, Daryus cut Shiera off. "Your words will not change her mind. Save your breath. Harricka, she is not part of this."

"I have no quarrel with the Pathfinder, only gratitude. She is welcome to leave whenever she likes, if that is her choice."

"I'm staying with Daryus."

Harricka cocked her head. "You always had a way of drawing those who would stand beside you, Daryus Gaunt. I know. I was one of them."

"Harricka, just leave her be and I'll go with—"

"No!" Shiera paid no heed to the dagger. "This has gone on far enough! What was so vile about his crime?"

"He broke his oath to the order. He protected the lives of renegade demonspawn—"

"They were farmers," Daryus interjected. "They couldn't help their births. There was nothing demonic about their nature, only their blood, and they overcame that."

"They broke the law—"

"A law that treated them like enemies! They weren't saboteurs, Harricka. They just wanted to live free."

Harricka kept the dagger steady. "So, you would do it again?"

"I would do it every time."

To Daryus's surprise, Harricka tossed the dagger at Shiera's feet. She deliberately turned her back to them as she located her sword on the other side of the horse that had carried the two.

Shiera quickly scooped up the dagger, but Daryus left the sword where it lay.

Hooking the sheath at her side, Harricka mounted. Once atop the horse, she rubbed her head near the wound. "Kept me unconscious until shortly before we stopped. It still throbs. Old Machiah should be able to treat it. You remember him, Daryus?"

"Of course. He saved many of us with his battlefield dressings."

"I think he'll outlive us all." The captain adjusted her place in the saddle. "He'll be sorry to hear that you died."

Daryus stiffened. "Harricka—"

She shook her head. "I owe both of you my life, but you know that's not why I'm doing this. I saw you long enough, Daryus Gaunt, to see the man I fought beside. You are neither devil nor coward. You betrayed the order, but only because you would not betray your code. When you said you would do it again, even facing trial and death, that put a finish to the matter." The captain turned the horse. "One animal will do good enough for the pair of you. My only requirement is that you steer clear of Kenabres. There are a few who still know you by sight, and most are there."

Daryus reached a hand to her, but Harricka looked away. Without another word, the crusader rode off.

"What does this mean?" Shiera asked him.

"It appears I've just been pardoned . . . so long as I stay clear of Kenabres."

"Some pardon. You deserved better. You deserved a *lot* better."

Daryus didn't answer. He only stared into the darkness after Harricka. Stared . . . and marveled.

Shiera didn't say much more to Daryus that night. Not only was it clear that he still had much to mull over after the captain's astonishing departure, but she herself had much, much to think about. Only when morning came and the decision about what to do next was upon them did she finally say something.

"You never asked about what happened at the end in Uhl-Adanar."

"You lived. You escaped. That was all that mattered. The rest is your choice to tell."

Shiera appreciated his honesty and directness. "Then let me tell you."

He worked on readying the horse as she revealed what had taken place after he had ridden through. Daryus listened silently, only speaking when it was clear that his companion was finished.

"So the demon just cast you out of the temple-city?"

"Yes. Right after it gave me the medallion."

Daryus frowned. "You made a pact with it? With a demon?"

"Well, not in blood or anything like that, if that makes a difference. I just made a promise that made sense to keep, anyway. I did what I had to for all of us to survive." Shiera cocked her head. "Am I worse than a pitborn now?"

"Probably only as a farmer."

326 RICHARD A. KNAAK

It took her a moment to recognize the joke. She smiled. "There's one more thing to consider."

"Only one? Out of all this?"

"I was dealing with a creature who thinks in terms of eternities. Tzadn has been hiding for centuries. Millennia even. It's quite possible—very likely even—that nothing will happen during my lifetime . . . or that of any children or grandchildren I might have. Even longer."

"Or it could happen tomorrow," he bluntly reminded her. "Even tonight."

"Hmmph. I prefer my way of thinking."

"As you like." He finished with the animal. "I've made some adjustments with the balance. We should be able to ride together for quite some time, at least until we can buy another horse. Then I can return you to Nerosyan and fulfill my contract."

Shiera said nothing as he first mounted, then offered her a hand up. She slid in behind him. "What will you do now that you don't have to fear being hunted?"

"It'll take time for word from Harricka to reach Nerosyan. I'll still need to be careful. And even so, the best thing would be to leave the city again as soon as possible and stay away."

"Hmmph." She reached into her pouch, where she felt the medallion the Reaper had given her. Memories of the entire expedition flashed through her mind. As breathtaking as it had been at times, the medallion was all she had to show for it. "Would you consider extending your contract?"

He had just been about to encourage the horse on. Instead, without looking back, he asked, "What do you mean?"

She fingered the medallion. "I think I'd like to look into this other demon . . . just to be safe, you understand? It might have sensed something about me when it sought Tzadn. It would be better not to take a chance."

"And in the process, you might also happen to find something that could help build your reputation further?"

Her tone was all innocence. "That could happen, too, I suppose. I think I can get sufficient funding for at least the two of us to go searching."

Daryus finally looked over his shoulder at her. "It would take us far from Mendev?"

"Very far."

He smiled and gently kicked the horse in the sides. The animal started on, slowly at first.

"There will be no need for a contract," Daryus said.

"You'll do it, then?"

"Someone needs to be there, just in case you *do* run into the demon in the process."

Shiera exhaled, feeling relieved in more ways than one as Daryus urged their horse to a faster pace.

However, as the animal obeyed, Shiera felt some guilt. Daryus was more now than just a hired hand. He was a friend. She supposed that meant she should have told him about what Tzadn had shown her at the end, the tantalizing images of places and objects, and what they might mean for them both.

But then, there was still plenty of time.

About the Author

Richard A. Knaak is the *New York Times* and *USA Today* best-selling author of *The Legend of Huma*, *WoW: Wolfheart*, and nearly fifty other novels and numerous short stories, including works in such series as Warcraft, Diablo, Dragonlance, Age of Conan, the Iron Kingdoms, and his creator-owned Dragonrealm. He has scripted comics and manga, such as the top-selling Sunwell trilogy, and has also written background material for games. His works have been published worldwide in many languages.

In addition to *Reaper's Eye*, his most recent releases include *Black City Saint*, the first in a new urban fantasy series from Pyr Books; "Wyrmbane" for the Iron Kingdoms; and *The Horned Blade*, the final novel in the Turning War trilogy for the Dragonrealm.

Currently splitting his time between Chicago and Arkansas, he can be reached through his website at **richardaknaak.com**. While he is unable to respond to every email, he does read them. Join his mailing list for e-announcements of upcoming releases and appearances, or join him on Facebook and Twitter.

ACKNOWLEDGMENTS

I'd like to thank everyone at Paizo who enabled me to play in their world, and especially Executive Editor James L. Sutter and Senior Editor Christopher Paul Carey for their work on this book.

GLOSSARY

All Pathfinder Tales novels are set in the rich and vibrant world of the Pathfinder campaign setting. Below are explanations of several key terms used in this book. For more information on the world of Golarion and the strange monsters, people, and deities that make it their home, see *The Inner Sea World Guide,* or dive into the game and begin playing your own adventures with the *Pathfinder Roleplaying Game Core Rulebook* or the *Pathfinder Roleplaying Game Beginner Box,* all available at **paizo.com.** Readers interested in the Worldwound specifically should check out *Pathfinder Campaign Setting: The Worldwound.*

Abadar: Master of the First Vault and the god of cities, wealth, merchants, and law.

Absalom: Largest city in the Inner Sea region, located on an island far to the south of Mendev.

Abyss: Plane of evil and chaos ruled by demons, where many evil souls go after they die.

Abyssal: Of or pertaining to the Abyss.

Aroden: The god of humanity, who died mysteriously a century ago.

Brevoy: Frigid northern nation famous for its swordlords.

Crusaders: Soldiers, often organized into military orders by ideology, religion, or governmental allegiance, who fight against the invading demons coming through the Worldwound. While many crusaders are high-minded zealots bent on protecting civilization from destruction, the crusade's forces also include mercenaries, criminals, and other undesirables.

Demonic: Of or related to demons.

Demons: Evil denizens of the plane of the afterlife called the Abyss, who seek only to maim, ruin, and feed on mortal souls.

Elven: Of or pertaining to elves; the language of elves.

Elves: Long-lived, beautiful humanoids identifiable by their pointed ears, lithe bodies, and single-colored eyes.

Familiars: Small creatures that assist certain types of spellcasters, often developing greater powers and intelligence than normal members of their kind.

Five Kings Mountains: A large and ancient mountain range inhabited by the dwarven nation of the same name.

Golarion: The planet on which the Pathfinder campaign setting focuses.

Grand Lodge: The headquarters of the Pathfinder Society, located in Absalom.

Grimslakes: Armored, maggotlike creatures that devour nearly any living creature they come across, or else use the corpses as incubators for their young.

Hallit: Primary language of Sarkoris before its fall, as well as many modern northern peoples.

Inner Sea: The vast inland sea whose northern continent, Avistan, and southern continent, Garund, as well as the seas and nearby lands, are the primary focus of the Pathfinder campaign setting.

Kenabres: Fortified crusader city along Mendev's border with the Worldwound, somewhat infamous for its hunting and persecution of perceived demonic sympathizers.

Mendev: Cold, northern crusader nation that provides the primary force defending the rest of the Inner Sea region from the demonic infestation of the Worldwound.

Mendevian: Of or pertaining to Mendev.

Nerosyan: Fortress city and capital of Mendev, situated along the nation's southwestern border. Also called the Diamond of the North, after its shining towers and diamond-shaped layout.

Order of the Flaming Lance: Crusader order based out of Kenabres, known for its fervor and hardline approach.

Pathfinder Society: Organization of traveling scholars and adventurers who seek to document the world's wonders.

Pathfinders: Members of the Pathfinder Society.

Pitborn: One of many names for mortals with a demon somewhere in their ancestry.

Plane: One of the realms of existence, such as the mortal world, Heaven, Hell, the Abyss, and many others.

Planar: Of or pertaining to the planes that compose the realms of existence.

Queen Galfrey: The current monarch of the crusader-state of Mendev, and leader of the Mendevian Crusades. She rules from the capital city of Nerosyan.

River Kingdoms: A region of small, feuding fiefdoms and bandit strongholds, where borders change frequently.

Sarkoris: Northern nation destroyed and overrun in the opening of the Worldwound.

Torag: Stoic and serious dwarven god of the forge, protection, and strategy. Viewed by dwarves as the Father of Creation.

Venture-Captain: A rank in the Pathfinder Society above that of a standard field agent, in charge of organizing expeditions and directing and assisting lesser agents.

Vescavors: Toothy insectile creatures from the Abyss that are ruled by queens and possess an insatiable hunger. Known to travel and attack in swarms.

Vescavor Queens: These enormous insectile beings control swarms of their lesser kin via pheromones and mental commands.

Warmonger Wasps: Native to the Abyss, these wasplike metallic constructs are now found throughout the Worldwound.

Witches: Spellcasters who draw magic from pacts made with otherworldly powers, using familiars as conduits.

Wizards: Those who cast spells through careful study and rigorous scientific methods rather than faith or innate talent, recording the necessary incantations in spellbooks.

Worldwound: Constantly expanding region overrun by demons a century ago. Held at bay by the efforts of the Mendevian crusaders.

Turn the page for a sneak peek at

THROUGH THE GATE IN THE SEA

by Howard Andrew Jones

Available February 2017

2

THE BLACK SHIP

MIRIAN

As she played the glowstone over the hull, Mirian imagined the vessel surging along the waves in its glory days, full canvas spread from the trio of towering masts, the dragon-shaped prow rising and falling with the ocean current.

And then she was once more staring at a sunken hulk.

She was swimming slowly toward the bow, wand at the ready, when Jekka joined her. She gave him the hand sign for caution. There was no telling what might be using the wreck as its home.

The figurehead was even more lovely than she'd supposed, carved with that minute detail she'd seen on many lizardfolk objects. Upon closer inspection, Mirian recognized it as a stylized rendition of one of her least favorite creatures: a sea drake. She scowled at the thing. One of the monsters had stalked her when she was a child, and another had chased her expedition through the tunnels of a lizardfolk city before killing Ivrian's mother.

Her hand tightened around the wand and she came perilously close to blasting the serpentine image into floating chunks.

But she had better sense. Provided they could get the figurehead free, they'd probably get a tidy sum for it from some collector. Being a Pathfinder, she knew not to let personal feeling interfere with a historical find.

Mirian drifted away from the figurehead and back along the narrow bow, light from her glowstone glinting off something half hidden in scum. She swam closer to investigate.

A lumpy object was set into the planks six feet below the rail and about the same distance from the bowsprit, in the approximate place that Osirian mariners painted eyes on their ships.

Often she wore gloves on salvage runs, but having anticipated recovering nothing more than a ring down here, she'd dived without them. She reached to touch the object gingerly with her left hand, wiping fingers through grime to reveal a large violet jewel.

At that her eyebrows rose. If this were a real gem, it could easily be worth thousands of gold pieces.

Realizing she'd been focused single-mindedly upon her discovery, she checked behind, above, and around her. Her father had taught her not to be so intent you forgot your surroundings. *Nearly everything under the water is a predator*, he'd told her, *and some of them are larger than you.*

She saw Jekka's light still playing farther back. Time to confer. She swam over to him and the lizard man's slit pupils contracted in her light beam. She shined the light at her hand so he could see her signal to surface.

His tongue extended, as it sometimes did when he was thoughtful or uncertain, but he followed as she kicked up, and in a few moments they were drifting in the darkness under the stars. Mirian's instinctive sense of direction told her the *Daughter of the Mist* lay to her left, but she couldn't see it, or even hear the lap of the ocean against its side.

"Isn't it amazing, my sister?" Jekka asked. "A ship of my people!"

"It *is* amazing. I'd give a lot to know what they painted on the hull to preserve it so well. But there are two things, my brother. Listen well."

Sometimes, when she spoke with the lizard man, Mirian found herself unintentionally adopting his formal diction. She supposed she was learning some of his habits, just as he learned some of hers.

"You have my attention," he answered.

"You must *always* signal me. And be watching for me, under-water. Don't dart off like that."

He nodded, an exaggerated bob on that long neck.

"We have to watch for each other," she went on, "because there may be something watching us ."

"So you have said. Forgive me, Sister."

"No harm done, yet. Don't forget, you need to swim back to the ship and report in. Tell Rendak what we've found and borrow his air bottle."

"I don't need it."

"You damned well do. You can't keep popping up and down the whole time. I want to go inside the hull and look around, and I want someone to back me up. You could get trapped in the hull and drown."

"I don't need it," he repeated stubbornly.

"You promised to defer to me in salvaging. Are you going back on your word?"

He hissed. "You shame me, Sister. Very well. But how am I to watch you if you're going alone to the wreck?"

"You're going to come back quickly. And I'm going to continue my inspection on the outside." Not the safest option, admittedly, but Mirian was an old hand at this, and the seas seemed pretty calm at this drop.

"I will do these things."

"Thank the oracle while you're there," she continued, "and apologize to her for the delay. Tell Rendak to turn four points to starboard and come a half mile before dropping anchor. And when he asks if he or Gombe should drop, tell him I'll let them know when we're done scouting."

"I will remember," Jekka assured her.

She was fairly certain he would. The lizard man had an amazing ability to retain oral information and repeat it word for word. Habits, like those of salvaging routines, however, were different from rote memorization.

"Get it done and come find me. I'm as eager as you to see what lies aboard."

Then she waved and dove below.

On her return trip to the wreck, she wondered what would have happened if she'd descended for the ring alone, or with Rendak or Gombe. Nothing, probably. She'd chosen Jekka in part because he needed to get used to what a salvaging run was like, but also because he'd been so excited to become a salvager. She guessed that was because he now saw the crew as part of his extended clan and wished to contribute to its well-being.

While she waited for Jekka, she carefully surveyed the ship's perimeter, familiarizing herself with the length and breadth of the vessel and searching for telltale warning signs that something large and unpleasant lurked within. Ocean predators weren't especially noted for their intellects. If there were anything nasty living here, there'd likely be discarded carcasses crawling with bottom-feeders nearby.

She saw no such indications. That didn't rule out the possibility of more intelligent creatures, like aquatic ogres or sea devils, lairing there, but she saw no sign of tracks or prints along the rail or upon any of the closed cabin doors leading into the bowels of the ship.

Mirian almost missed the large gash at the vessel's stern, in the shadow of the hull. She studied the damaged wood and realized she was probably looking at the ship's death wound. Most likely she'd struck a reef.

After a very careful examination, Mirian had a pretty clear picture of the ship. It was half again as long as a typical three-master, but perhaps a third shallower across the beam. The decks were high and rose steeply at the prow. Probably there were a good three decks below, and back of the quarter deck were two more above. Two masts were forward and a mizzenmast stood broken off almost to the deck, right through the wheelhouse itself.

Mirian was looking at the wheel when Jekka finally rejoined her. He took hold of the wheel with one hand to steady himself. Straps of a haversack crossed his chest.

Jekka had slid an object used by the other salvagers in her crew into a side pocket of his haversack, an item colloquially known as an air bottle. Once someone learned the trick of using one, it was possible to spend long hours below the water with them. It was her grandfather who'd invested in two for the family's help, and hit upon the idea of a tube to affix to the bottle so the fragile object could be kept in a padded back satchel.

The tube worked much better if you had lips to close around it—something Jekka lacked. When he'd first attempted to use it, he couldn't pull air without water coming in as well, unless he jammed the tube so far down his throat he nearly gagged. She understood why he didn't want to repeat the experience, but he'd have to adapt if he was going to become a salvager.

A cool current buffeted Mirian as she examined a peculiar column rising beside the wheel. At first glance, it looked like another mast had been sheared off, but that made no sense. That would have placed it off-center from the rest of the vessel.

She scraped at a layer of blue algae. Instead of a broken mast, she uncovered a diagonal plate resembling a display in an expensive jewelry shop. An array of gems was set into its black metal. She scrubbed harder, exposing tiny symbols incised beside each jewel.

Jekka leaned close, running his scaly fingers over the letters.

The writing certainly resembled the same language Mirian had seen on the lizardfolk book cones, but she knew many languages looked similar to the uninitiated. She pointed to the symbols and then back at Jekka.

The lizard man nodded vigorously, touched a set of characters. "No wind!" he shouted, air bubbling out of his mouth.

He put his fingers beside a flat, violet stone, and it took him three attempts before she could understand him through the water: "Opener of the way."

Jekka paused to suck in the tube, then pulled it out, coughing more air bubbles.

There were four more gems with inscriptions. Mirian spread her hands apart in a silent question.

Clearly perplexed, the lizard man shook his head.

She traced the multifaceted ruby he'd told her meant "no wind." It looked like it might turn in its pitted housing.

Interesting. Slowly, carefully, she set her fingers on the gem and tried moving it clockwise. It didn't budge. When she twisted in the other direction, the gem lit from within.

Mirian looked to Jekka for explanation, but he merely shrugged.

She made a second twist and the deck shook beneath them. Clouds of silt billowed up, and from somewhere below came a loud scraping noise. It wasn't until she looked to port and turned her beam there that she noticed the landscape moving...

No, the ship was! Mirian let out a colorful oath and quickly twisted the jewel all the way to the right so that it returned to its original setting. It ceased glowing and the ship slowed.

She looked at Jekka as if to say, *What the hell was that?*

The lizard man stared back at her, reptilian eyes blinking.

This was a major find, but there was no way they'd pry any of the gems out of here. "No wind" apparently meant the ship could be set in motion magically when there was no breeze. She marveled at that, wondering whether a skilled enough magic-worker could remove it from the ship and install it on another. Like, say, the *Daughter of the Mist*, or that behemoth Ivrian was so set on building.

She pointed to an opening into darkness and directed her glowstone onto a barnacle-encrusted ladder. Apparently only the hull had the special protective coating.

Jekka tapped his chest and pointed into the hold, letting her know he intended to lead, then brandished his own glowstone.

She almost objected, then decided he was at least communicating this time, and remembered he was both an experienced warrior and excited to be searching a ship made by his own people. She allowed him to swim in the lead, staying a few feet back from the swish of his whiplike tale.

Most of the hold's contents had shifted to starboard. Her light played over brown and green weeds dusted by occasional splotches of red and blue. They obscured the hold's contents in a soft, furry blanket.

Jekka floated above it all, shining his own light on something to the right, then pointed at a long segmented worm with pincers. Mirian's father had always called them rot worms, though to Mirian they looked more like oversized centipedes. Their bite was deadly poisonous and they tended to be aggressive when disturbed, so she moved quickly.

The arm-length creature shifted away at Jekka's spear thrust, rearing up and stirring the water with its legs. Mirian cut it in half with her cutlass. It floated apart, wriggling in its death throes.

Jekka brushed it out of the way and shined her light on the patch of growth where the rot worm had been hidden. It didn't seem to have any nest mates.

She floated on with Jekka, imagining the hold moving with robed lizardfolk, perhaps lashing down that stack of crates over there, or walking on through the narrow archway into the next chamber.

Jekka stopped beside three large chests resting against the hull, each rotten with age. As Mirian played her light over the area, tiny crustaceans swam frantically for darkness. Little silver fish flashed away in alarm.

Mirian signaled Jekka to keep watch and he turned from her to survey their surroundings.

She had never seen a lizardfolk chest before, but this one proved little different from those built by humans, save that the lock mechanism was inset along the top right. That in itself was of interest. She made a mental note to record the information in her Pathfinder journal.

Normally, she would have simply smashed open a chest this old and rotten, but it was such an odd, rare find she wanted to handle it with care.

The bronze lock was green with corrosion and looked as though it had been designed to accommodate a cylindrical mechanism rather than a key. It couldn't possibly be picked, but there were other ways. She removed a small pry bar from her pack and set to work on the hinges.

The tool's teeth sank easily into the rotten wood, and in moments both hinges were floating free. After that, the lid came up easily. Mirian drifted back as she lifted it. There was no telling what might come crawling out.

Nothing did.

She again swam closer, her light settling on a rotted wooden frame inside the chest that kept a dozen blue cylindrical bottles upright and separate. Five were broken along their necks, but the others, though empty, looked intact—more tube than jar, with a peculiar fluted opening at the top.

Mirian played the light over the inside, then carefully lifted one of the vessels free and drew it closer it for examination.

Jekka drifted beside her. His long, forked tongue flickered with excitement.

She looked at him questioningly.

"Drinking glass! My people!" His head cocked in interest.

Mirian handed it to him to examine, then signed for him to put it in his pack. They could spend months clearing this wreck. It was probably time to fetch Rendak and Gombe.

Desna had truly blessed them. The wreck was a fantastic find. There was no telling what sort of oddities might be left aboard, let alone their value and historical significance. As a salvager, her livelihood depended upon scavenging sites like this. But as a Pathfinder, she was dedicated to uncovering the secrets of Golarion's past to preserve and disseminate knowledge. If the magical wind mechanism built into this ship could be understood and replicated, it might very well change the future of sea travel.

Jekka pointed to the chest next to the one they'd opened. He clearly wanted to see what was inside.

She decided to humor him and signaled for him to guard once more.

The hinges on the second chest were even more worn, and yielded with no resistance.

Within stood twelve rows of sculpted lizardfolk heads fashioned from a thin metal alloy and inlaid with jewels. Each eye socket was set with amber stones, the figures themselves rich with the minute symbols of Jekka's people.

The sight so thrilled her blood brother that his frill rose, and Mirian had to remind him to keep watch, though she did acquiesce to setting all two dozen of the sculptures within her pack.

The haversacks they wore had been gifts from Ivrian's mother, and were ensorcelled to contain more space on the inside than was apparent without. All of the sculptures fit easily without altering the haversack's weight in the slightest, another wonderful feature.

Jekka signed to indicate they should open the third chest, but she shook her head and pointed to the surface. Then she looked back to the chests and smiled, trying to reassure him they'd come back for all of it.

Mirian led the way out. Jekka trailed some length after, seemingly reluctant to leave.

Sooner than expected she found the anchor line and, looming above, the dark bowline of the *Daughter of the Mist*.

Her hands closed on the familiar rungs of the ladder built into the vessel's side. She felt the magical gills fade the moment she thrust her head above the water and breathed deeply of the crisp salty air.

All was silhouettes and shadows against the lesser darkness of the sky, but she thought she made out Gombe's lean outline near the ladder. She grinned at him as she stepped forward, slinging her bag off her shoulder.

"You won't believe what we've found," she told him.

A man with a sword stepped around Gombe, the point of the weapon at his throat. "I'm all ears."

Shaia "Shy" Ratani used to be a member of the most powerful thieves' guild in Taldor—right up until she cheated her colleagues by taking the money and running. The frontier city of Yanmass seems like a perfect place to lie low, until a job solving a noble's murder reveals an invading centaur army ready to burn the place to the ground. Of course, Shy could stop that from happening, but doing so would reveal her presence to the former friends who now want her dead. Add in a holier-than-thou patron with the literal blood of angels in her veins, and Shy quickly remembers why she swore off doing good deeds in the first place . . .

From critically acclaimed fantasy author Sam Sykes comes a darkly comic tale of intrigue, assassination, and the perils of friendship, all set in the award-winning world of the Pathfinder Roleplaying Game.

Shy Knives print edition: $14.99
ISBN: 978-0-7653-8435-5

Shy Knives ebook edition:
ISBN: 978-0-7653-8434-8

Shy Knives

A NOVEL BY Sam Sykes

Once a notorious pirate, Jendara has at last returned to the
cold northern isles of her birth, ready to settle down and
raise her young son. Yet when a mysterious tsunami wracks her
island's shore, she and her fearless crew must sail out to explore
the strange island that's risen from the sea floor. No sooner have
they delved into the lost island's alien structures than they find
themselves competing with a monstrous cult eager to complete
a dark ritual in those dripping halls. For something beyond all
mortal comprehension has been dreaming on the sea floor. And
it's begun to wake up . . .

From Hugo Award winner Wendy N. Wagner comes a sword-
swinging adventure in the tradition of H. P. Lovecraft, set in the
award-winning world of the Pathfinder Roleplaying Game.

***Starspawn* print edition: $14.99**
ISBN: 978-0-7653-8433-1

***Starspawn* ebook edition:**
ISBN: 978-0-7653-8432-4

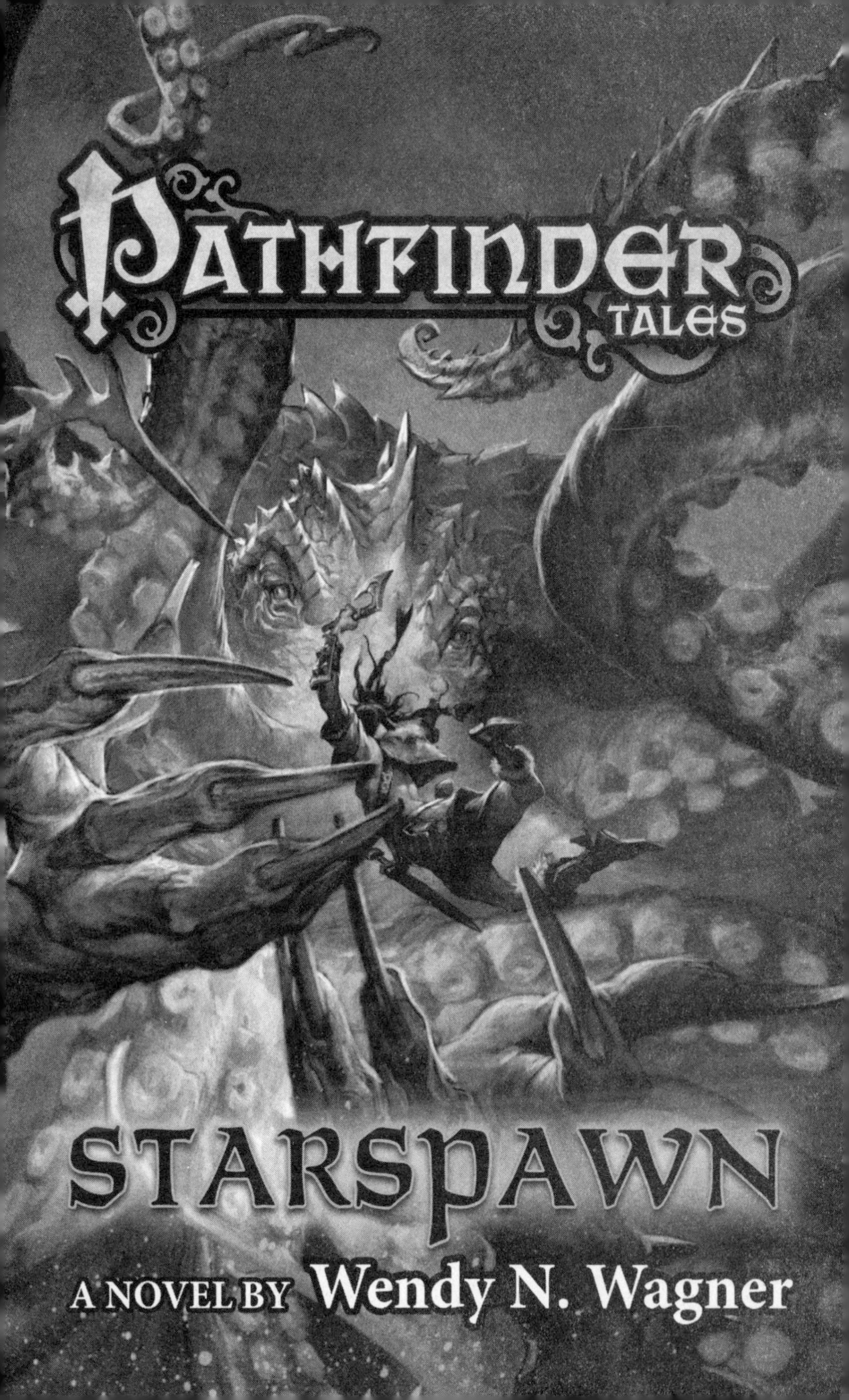
PATHFINDER
TALES
STARSPAWN
A NOVEL BY Wendy N. Wagner

When caught stealing in the crusader nation of Lastwall, veteran con man Rodrick and his talking sword Hrym expect to weasel or fight their way out of punishment. Instead, they find themselves ensnared by powerful magic, and given a choice: serve the cause of justice as part of a covert team of similarly bound villains—or die horribly. Together with their criminal cohorts, Rodrick and Hrym settle in to their new job of defending the innocent, only to discover that being a secret government operative is even more dangerous than a life of crime.

From Hugo Award winner Tim Pratt comes a tale of reluctant heroes and plausible deniability, set in the award-winning world of the Pathfinder Roleplaying Game.

Liar's Bargain print edition: $14.99
ISBN: 978-0-7653-8431-7

Liar's Bargain ebook edition:
ISBN: 978-0-7653-8430-0

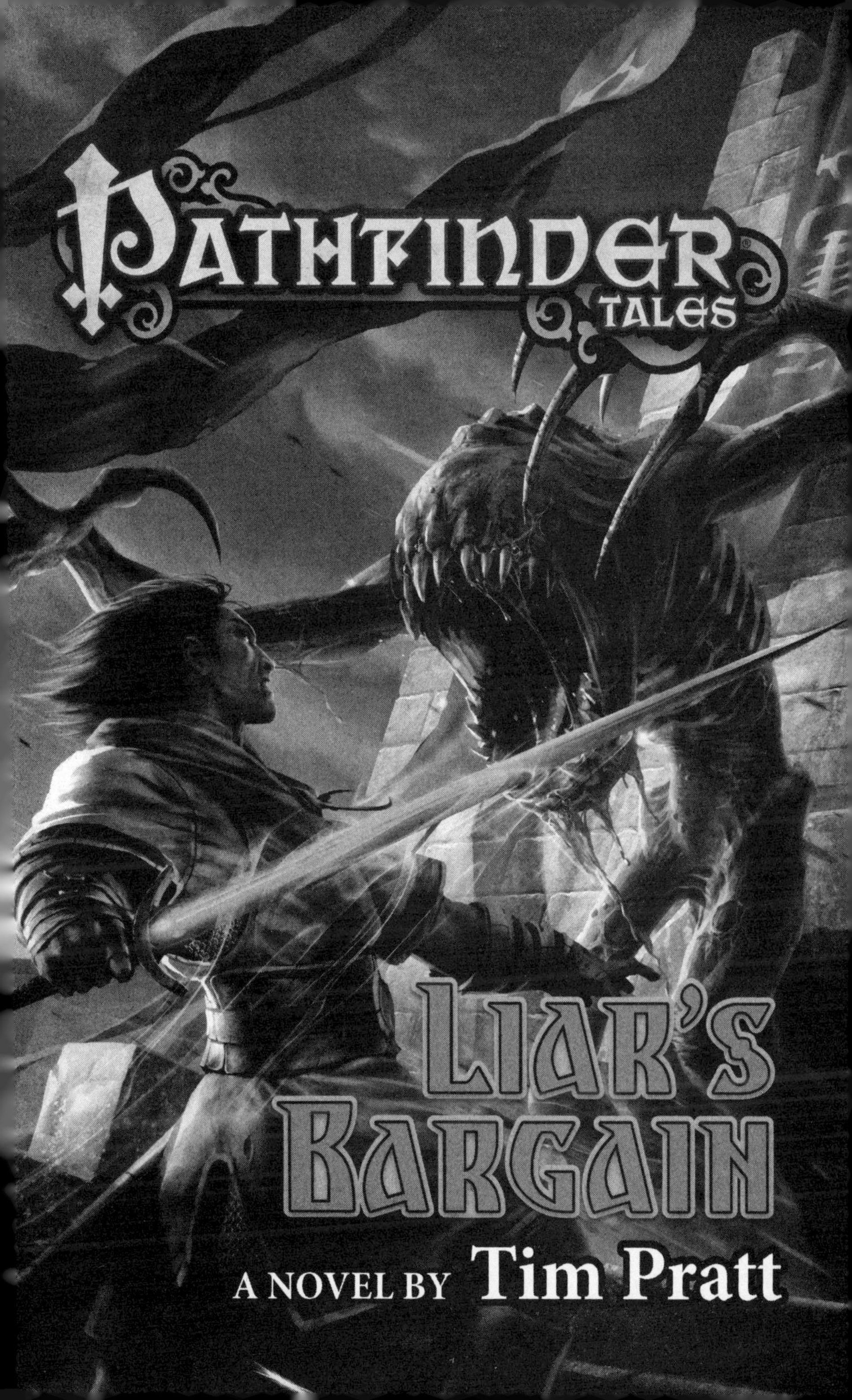

Pathfinder
Tales
Liar's Bargain
A NOVEL BY Tim Pratt

The Hellknights are a brutal organization of warriors and spellcasters dedicated to maintaining law and order at any cost. For devil-blooded Jheraal, a veteran Hellknight investigator, even the harshest methods are justified if it means building a better world for her daughter. Yet things get personal when a serial killer starts targeting hellspawn like Jheraal and her child, somehow magically removing their hearts and trapping the victims in a state halfway between life and death. With other Hellknights implicated in the crime, Jheraal has no choice but to join forces with a noble paladin and a dangerously cunning diabolist to defeat an ancient enemy for whom even death is no deterrent.

From celebrated dark fantasy author Liane Merciel comes an adventure of love, murder, and grudges from beyond the grave, set in the award-winning world of the Pathfinder Roleplaying Game.

Hellknight print edition: $14.99
ISBN: 978-0-7653-7548-3

Hellknight ebook edition:
ISBN: 978-1-4668-4735-4

PATHFINDER
TALES

HELLKNIGHT

A NOVEL BY
Liane Merciel

Captain Torius Vin has given up the pirate life in order to bring freedom to others. Along with his loyal crew and Celeste, the ship's snake-bodied navigator and Torius's one true love, the captain of the *Stargazer* uses a lifetime of piratical tricks to capture slave galleys and set the prisoners free. But when the crew's old friend and secret agent Vreva Jhafae uncovers rumors of a terrifying new magical weapon in devil-ruled Cheliax—one capable of wiping the abolitionist nation of Andoran off the map—will even their combined forces be enough to stop a navy backed by Hell itself?

From award-winning novelist Chris A. Jackson comes a tale of magic, mayhem, and nautical adventure, set in the vibrant world of the Pathfinder Roleplaying Game.

Pirate's Prophecy **print edition: $14.99**
ISBN: 978-0-7653-7547-6

Pirate's Prophecy **ebook edition:**
ISBN: 978-1-4668-4734-7

PATHFINDER
TALES

Pirate's
Prophecy

A NOVEL BY
Chris A. Jackson

Larsa is a dhampir—half vampire, half human. In the gritty streets and haunted peaks of Ustalav, she's an agent for the royal spymaster, keeping peace between the capital's secret vampire population and its huddled human masses. Meanwhile, in the cathedral of Maiden's Choir, Jadain is a young priestess of the death goddess, in trouble with her superiors for being too soft on the living. When a noblewoman's entire house is massacred by vampiric invaders, the unlikely pair is drawn into a deadly mystery that will reveal far more about both of them than they ever wanted to know.

From Pathfinder cocreator and award-winning game designer F. Wesley Schneider comes a new adventure of revenge, faith, and gothic horror, set in the world of the Pathfinder Roleplaying Game.

Bloodbound **print edition: $14.99**
ISBN: 978-0-7653-7546-9

Bloodbound **ebook edition:**
ISBN: 978-1-4668-4733-0

PATHFINDER TALES

Bloodbound

A NOVEL BY
F. Wesley Schneider

Mirian Raas comes from a long line of salvagers—adventurers who use magic to dive for sunken ships off the coast of tropical Sargava. With her father dead and her family in debt, Mirian has no choice but to take over his last job: a dangerous expedition into deep jungle pools, helping a tribe of lizardfolk reclaim the lost treasures of their people. Yet this isn't any ordinary dive, as the same colonial government that looks down on Mirian for her half-native heritage has an interest in the treasure, and the survival of the entire nation may depend on the outcome.

From critically acclaimed author Howard Andrew Jones comes an adventure of sunken cities and jungle exploration, set in the award-winning world of the Pathfinder Roleplaying Game.

***Beyond the Pool of Stars* print edition: $14.99**
ISBN: 978-0-7653-7453-0

***Beyond the Pool of Stars* ebook edition:**
ISBN: 978-1-4668-4265-6

Beyond the Pool of Stars

A NOVEL BY Howard Andrew Jones

Rodrick is con man as charming as he is cunning. Hrym is a talking sword of magical ice, with the soul and spells of an ancient dragon. Together, the two travel the world, parting the gullible from their gold and freezing their enemies in their tracks. But when the two get summoned to the mysterious island of Jalmeray by a king with genies and elementals at his command, they'll need all their wits and charm if they're going to escape with the greatest prize of all—their lives.

From Hugo Award winner Tim Pratt comes a tale of magic, assassination, and cheerful larceny, set in the award-winning world of the Pathfinder Roleplaying Game.

Liar's Island print edition: $14.99
ISBN: 978-0-7653-7452-3

Liar's Island ebook edition:
ISBN: 978-1-4668-4264-9

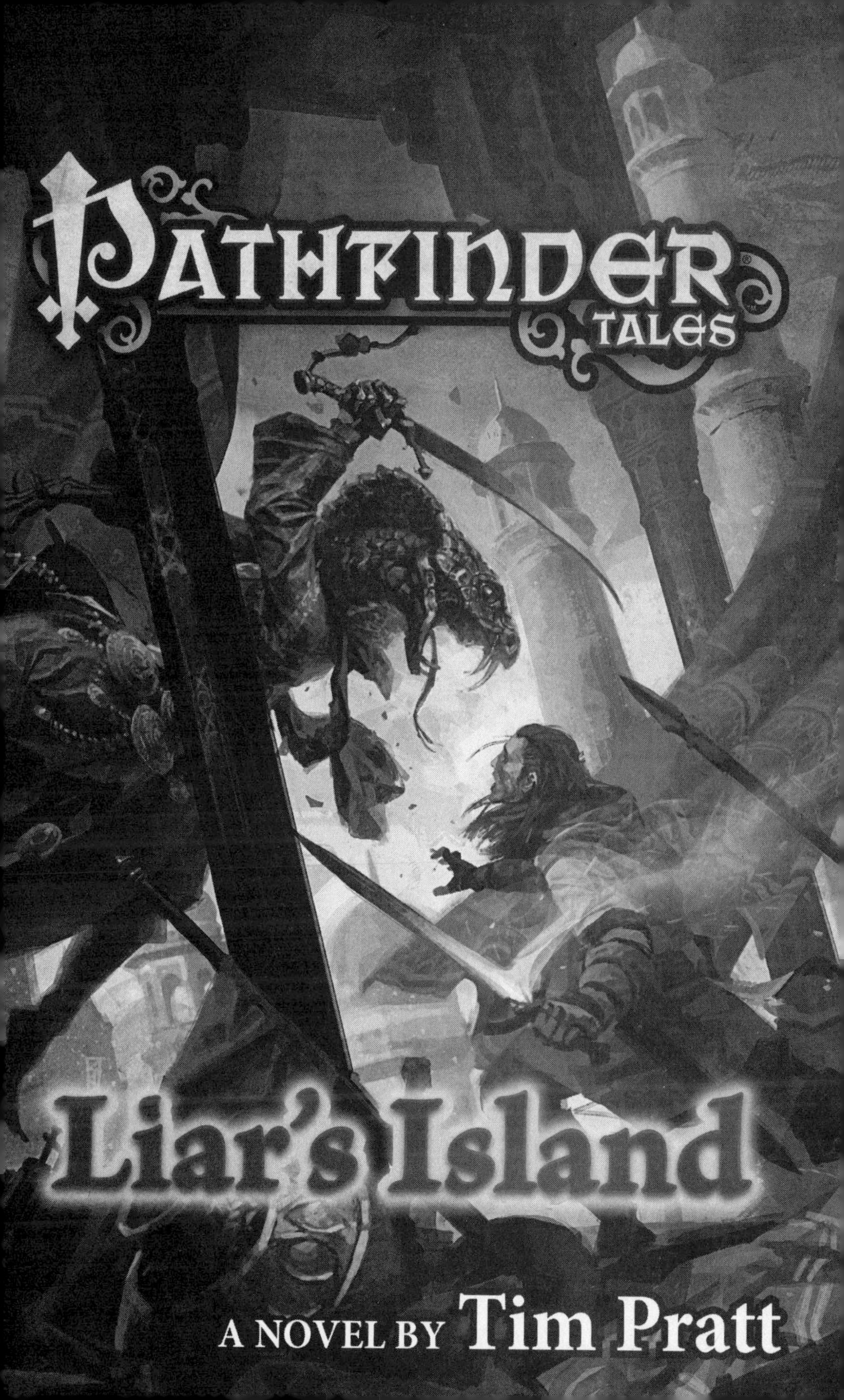
Pathfinder® Tales
Liar's Island
A NOVEL BY Tim Pratt

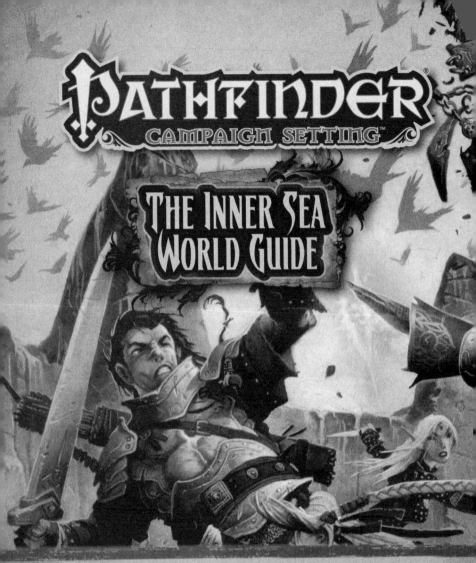

PATHFINDER

CAMPAIGN SETTING

THE INNER SEA WORLD GUIDE

You've delved into the Pathfinder campaign setting with Pathfinder Tales novels—now take your adventures even further! *The Inner Sea World Guide* is a full-color, 320-page hardcover guide featuring everything you need to know about the exciting world of Pathfinder: overviews of every major nation, religion, race, and adventure location around the Inner Sea, plus a giant poster map! Read it as a travelogue, or use it to flesh out your roleplaying game—it's your world now!

EXPLORE YOUR WORLD!

paizo.com